Operation Te

By

Robert Cubitt

Carter's Commandos – Book 6

Having purchased this eBook from Amazon, it is for your personal use only. It may not be copied, reproduced, printed or used in any way, other than in its intended Kindle format.

Published by Selfishgenie Publishing of, Northamptonshire, England.

This novel is entirely a work of fiction. All the names characters, incidents, dialogue, events portrayed and opinions expressed in it are either purely the product of the author's imagination or they are used entirely fictitiously and not to be construed as real. Any resemblance to actual persons, living or dead, events or localities is entirely coincidental. Nothing is intended or should be interpreted as representing or expressing the views and policies of any department or agency of any government or other body.

All trademarks used are the property of their respective owners. All trademarks are recognised.

The right of Robert Cubitt to be identified as the author of this work has been asserted in accordance with sections 77 and 78 of the Copyright Designs and Patents Act 1988.

In memory of all the Commandos of World War II and in memory of one commando in particular.

The truth of what they did is often stranger than any fiction that can be written.

Other titles by Robert Cubitt

Fiction

The Deputy Prime Minister
The Inconvenience Store
The Charity Thieves

Warriors Series

The Warriors: The Girl I Left Behind Me
The Warriors: Mirror Man

The Magi Series

The Magi (The Magi Book 1)
Genghis Kant (The Magi Book 2)
New Earth (The Magi Book 3)
Cloning Around (The Magi Book 4)
Timeslip (The Magi Book 5)
The Return Of Su Mali (The Magi Book 6)
Robinson Kohli (The Magi Book 7)
Parallel Lines (The Magi Book 8)
Restoration (The Magi Book 9)

Carter's Commandos Series

Operation Absalom (Carter's Commandos Book 1)
Operation Tightrope (Carter's Commandos Book 2)
Operation Dagger (Carter's Commandos Book 3)
Operation Carthage (Carter's Commandos Book 4)
Operation Leonardo (Carter's Commandos (Book 5)

Non-Fiction

A Commando's Story
I'm So Glad You Asked Me That
I'm So Glad You Asked Me That Again
I'm So Glad You Asked Me That the 3rd
I Want That Job

CONTENTS

Author's Note On The Language Used In This Book	7
1. Lo Bello	9
2. Operation Manchester	33
3. Bova Marina	67
4. Manfredonia	119
5. Termoli	135
6. The Guglionesi Road	149
7. 5th October	175
8. Dawn Attack	205
9. Homeward Bound	241
Historical Notes	247
Preview	259
And Now	299

Author's Note On The Language Used In This Book

This is a story about soldiers and to maintain authenticity the language used reflects that. There is a use of swear words of the strongest kind. It is not my intention to cause offence, but only to reflect the language that was and still is used by soldiers. Apart from the swearing there is other language used that may cause offence. I don't condone the use of that language, but it reflects the period in which the story is set. While we may live in more enlightened times and would never consider using such words, the 1940s were different and the language used is contemporary for the period. We cannot change the past, we can only change the present and the future and I'm glad that our language has changed and become more sensitive to the feelings of others but we must never forget our past. We should, however, seek not to repeat it.

Abbreviations of rank used in this book (in descending order of seniority):

Army Ranks

Lt Col – Lieutenant Colonel (often referred to simply as Colonel by their own subordinates)
Maj – Major
Capt – Captain
Lt – Lieutenant
2Lt – Second Lieutenant
RSM – Regimental Sergeant Major (Warrant Office Class 1)
CSM – Company Sergeant major (Warrant Officer Class 2)
TSM – Troop Sergeant Major (Warrant Officer Class 2) as used by the commandos.
SMjr – Sergeant Major (generic)
CSgt – Colour Sergeant

SSgt – Staff Sergeant
Sgt - Sergeant
LSgt – Lance Sergeant; a Brigade of Guards rank, but sometimes used by the commandos instead of Corporal.
Cpl – Corporal
LCpl – Lance Corporal
Pvt – Private
Tpr – Trooper, a cavalry rank equivalent to Private but used by the commandos.

Cdo – the abbreviation used when naming a specific commando, eg 15 Cdo.

Royal Navy ranks

Lt Cdr – Lieutenant Commander, equivalent to a Major.
Lt – Lieutenant, equivalent to its Army counterpart
SLt – Sub Lieutenant – equivalent to a Second Lieutenant in the Army.
CPO – Chief Petty Officer – equivalent to Warrant Officer Second Class in the Army.

RAF Ranks

Sqn Ldr – Squadron leader, equivalent to a Major.

Other military terminology is explained within the text where the narrative allows, or is explained in footnotes.

1 – Lo Bello

July drifted into a hot Sicilian August and 15 Cdo settled into a training routine, attempting to get the few available replacements properly bedded into the commando and up to the high standard expected of the men.

Without any idea of what the next operation might bring, the training concentrated on the generics of all operations: map reading and navigation, radio procedures, cross country marches and sea landings. Catania eventually fell, followed quickly by Messina as the enemy evacuated the last of their troops from the island. The roads became clogged with long crocodiles of German and Italian prisoners who had been cut off or failed to make it onto the last Axis boats off the island. They were marched south, away from where the Allies were massing their forces ready to make the jump across the sea to Italy.

News of Mussolini's resignation[1] came through, which cheered everyone up, then Catania fell. Everyone knew that the Germans would have to evacuate the island through Messina. It was the shortest crossing to the mainland; only five miles wide in parts. The opposite coast could be seen clearly. The Allies concentrated their efforts on making their departure as difficult as possible.

The commando was told it would move north to Messina to prepare for the invasion of the mainland, just as soon as the Germans were gone. But for the time being they remained in Lo Bello, just outside Syracuse, which might have been a Butlins holiday camp as far as the commando was concerned.

Carter stopped outside the HQ tent and wiped his face with his neck cloth. It was still hot even in the late afternoon and the route march that he had led his troop on had drained him of all his energy. But the CO's clerk, Ecclestone, had told him that the CO wanted him as a matter of urgency and he shouldn't even stop to take a shower.

Pulling back the tent flap, Carter stepped inside. "CO's with the 2IC, Sir." Ecclestone informed him. "Won't be more than a minute or so, I 'spect."

The tent was dark, but not any cooler than the outside. In fact the lack of air made the interior feel more oppressive. Carter could hear the voices of the 2IC and the CO, screened behind a wall of canvass, but he couldn't make out what they were saying. Probably plotting the next operation, which suggested a reason for Carter having been summoned. Perhaps he was to lead it, or maybe go along with the 2IC, as his second in command. The lack of any other officers assembling suggested that whatever it was, it wouldn't involve the whole commando.

There was a rustle of canvass and the 2IC appeared from the back of the tent. Even in the gloom Carter could see that he had a broad grin on his face. "Afternoon, Steven." He said as he passed him. Carter could have been mistaken, but he was sure the 2IC had winked at him. Surely not. The 2IC had many quirks in his personality but winking at a subordinate was a new one on Carter.

"Is Captain Carter here yet, Ecclestone?" The CO's voice called from behind the canvas.

"I'm right here, Sir." Carter replied.

"Come on through." Doing as he was bid, he pushed the canvass screen to one side then let it drop behind him again.

"Take a pew, old chap." Vernon acknowledged Carter's salute with a nod. That eased Carter's mind a little. If he was here for a rollocking he wouldn't be invited to take a seat. Not that he had done anything wrong, at least, not for a while.

Carter sat himself on the camp stool that was the only furniture available other than the trestle table that served as a desk and the camp chair on which the CO himself was sitting. The only adornment to the trestle table was a field telephone sitting in its canvas carrying case. Its cable trailed off the table and disappeared under the side of the tent. Part of the new organisation for the commando was a signals section, made up of commandos who had attended special training while they had still been in Egypt. Their pride and joy was a tiny telephone exchange which had four extensions, one of which sat on the CO's desk. A single telephone line connected it to 8th Army HQ, which was now located in Catania. For the first time in its three year history, the commando was no longer dependent on radios or dispatch riders for its communications with higher authority.

"I've some good news and some bad news, Steven. Which would you like first?"

Whatever the bad news is, get it out of the way first, Carter thought. "The bad news, I think, Sir."

"I thought you might say that. The bad news is that I'm to leave the commando, effective from this evening."

Vernon was right, that was bad news. To most of the men, the CO was the commando, its beating heart and intelligent brain. "I'm sorry to hear that, Sir. Where are you going?"

"Monty wants me to take command of both 15 and 49 commandos. I'll also take an outfit called the Special Raiding Squadron^2 under my wing. It's effectively a Brigade, but it can't be called that, because I'm not a Brigadier. Even Monty hasn't the authority to promote me to that level. He's made me acting Colonel though, which is nice."

"We'll miss you, Sir."

"Don't worry, you can't get rid of me that easily. Wherever you are, you can be sure I won't be far away."

"I take it that the reason that the 2IC was grinning like a Cheshire cat is that he is to replace you."

"Yes, he is. Which brings me to the good news. You are to take over as 2IC, with the acting rank of Major."

"Me ... but ... surely the QM ..." As a substantive major the Quarter Master would be the natural choice to take over as 2IC.

"The QM is coming with me as my Chief of Staff. My only staff in fact, for the moment. So I've had to go looking for the new 2IC amongst the Troop Commanders. You are the natural choice. You have an established reputation and the men think highly of you. I can think of no one better for the job."

"But Angus Fraser, Sir. He has more seniority than …"

The CO cut him off. "Promotion in the commandos isn't about seniority, it's about suitability and I think you are more suitable. Besides, I want Angus to take over as QM. He seems to have a natural talent as a scrounger."

That was true. Fraser seemed to be able to get his hands on many scarce items and when asked where they came from the answer was always "A bloke I know over in …" and then some other unit would be named. Scrounging was an essential skill for a commando quarter master. The commandos had always been at the tail end of any queue for equipment and sometimes it was only the QM's skills that allowed the men to get anything at all, including essential items of uniform.

"Well, in that case, Sir, all I can say is thank you for your faith in me. After that incident at Ponte Bridge I thought …"

Vernon waved away Carters reminder about him falling asleep and allowing himself and his men to be captured by a German patrol. "The man who never made a mistake never made anything, Steven.[3] I'm sure it won't happen again. Now, go and find Angus and tell him I want to see him. But don't spoil my fun by telling him why. Oh, and the three of you are buying the drinks tonight."

[1] 25th July 1943. He was replaced by King Emmanuel III, making Marshall Pietro Badoglio his Prime Minister. He was a senior member of the Fascist Party and the Army who had been out of favour since the failed Italian invasion of Greece in 1940. When Italy surrendered in September 1943, it would be Badoglio who would travel to Cassibile in Sicily to sign the Armistice agreement and declare war on Germany. When the Germans disarmed the Italian military, the King, Badoglio and some other senior Party figures escaped from Rome to Brindisi to form a government in exile.

[2] We now know this unit by the much more famous name of the Special Air Service (SAS) but as both Brigadier John Durnford-

Slater and Brigadier Peter Young (see *Further Reading*) use this name in their books, we must assume that they were known as the Special Raiding Squadron in Sicily in 1943.

[3] A common misquote of a phrase attributed to Albert Einstein. The correct quote is "A person who never made a mistake never tried anything new." However, the attribution to Einstein is very weak and there are a number of variations on the theme going back as far as 1832, with an anonymous attribution. The earliest version that fits with Vernon's usage is Josh Billings in 1874. Josh Billings was the pen name of American humourist Henry Wheeler Shaw.

* * *

"Back here in an hour." Carter instructed the men in his work party when they reached the dockyard gates. Safely parked up inside was the truck they had arrived in, with its cargo of two long packing cases and another half dozen cube like ones. Carter knew what they contained, which was why Andrew Fraser had asked him to collect them. But he wasn't letting on just yet. The surprise could wait.

"And don't get into any mischief!" he called at their retreating backs as they headed for the Salvation Army canteen. It would do no good. He would no sooner be out of sight and they'd change direction and go looking for something more appealing than tea and sticky buns.

He headed towards the Officer's Club that had been established in one of Catania's better restaurants. With so little food available the place would struggle to survive if the military hadn't commandeered it and kept the staff on, paying them to serve Italian wine and beer, which is all that was available locally.

He had just reached the door when he heard a voice call his name.

"It is you, Steven. I thought it was." Carter looked around to see a tall, elegantly uniformed figure striding across the square towards him.

"Ewan Flamming, as I live and breathe." Carter said, before he spied the three wavy[1] gold rings on the cuffs of the man's uniform. "I'm sorry, Commander Flamming that should be."

The man laughed. "Don't stand on ceremony, old chap. After all, it was my little jaunt with you that helped get me the extra thick ring." He tapped the centre ring of the three, which had previously been thinner, denoting the more junior rank of Lieutenant Commander. "And you've gone up in the world as well; a Major now. Last time I saw you, you were still just a Lieutenant. Come, on, let me buy you a drink and you can tell me all about it." he pushed the door of the club open, then stood to one side to allow Carter to enter first.

"Not much to tell, really. I got my third pip through dead men's shoes, quite literally. But my crown[2] came about because my CO was promoted and everyone moved up one rank to fill the gap."

"Honfleur or Tunisia; for the dead men's shoes I mean."

"Have you been keeping tabs on me?" Carter laughed. "Honfleur actually. We lost a lot of good men there. Tunisia was a walk in the park by comparison." They had reached the bar and looked around to find a table. Spotting one at the back of the room, away from the few other customers, they made their way across to it. The club was quiet at that time of the day; most officers had duties to attend to. Carter had only agreed to take a break before returning to Messina because it was so hot and his men were thirsty after the journey and loading the vehicle.

"I have to admit, I do take an interest in what your unit has been up to. You're quite famous these days. You're attracting a lot of attention in London. I hear you added to your lustre by capturing a bridge a few miles from here." Flamming raised his finger to attract the eye of a waiter and one appeared at their table as though summoned by magic. Some people had a knack for that, Carter noted and Flamming was one of them. His easy manner spoke of jazz clubs, expensive cocktails and women who were generous with their favours. Those sorts of people weren't usually Carter's type, but he knew that under Flamming's louche exterior there was a core of steel.

"*Vino rosso, per favore.*" Flamming said to the waiter. "What about you, Steven?"

"Just a beer for me."

Flamming placed the order and the waiter scurried away.

"The wine isn't up to much." Carter advised him.

"I know, but until we get the French vineyards back from the Germans it will have to do. And I doubt that chap would know how to make a decent vodka martini." Carter had to acknowledge that the unshaven and rather scruffy Italian hadn't looked like a cocktail barman. But then, with soap and razor blades in short supply for the civilian population, looks could be deceiving. He might have been the Maître D' at the restaurant before it became the Officer's Club, for all either of them knew.

"So, where are you based these days?" Carter asked. He had a tingling in the nape of his neck that told him that his meeting with Flamming hadn't come about by chance.

"Still in London. I'm out here trying to put together an operation. I was in Malta for the invasion and I've only just arrived here this week. But it is fortunate that I've bumped into you."

Bingo! Carter thought. He is after something. Flamming had previously tried to recruit him into a new unit he was forming and Carter wondered if this was just another attempt to do the same.

"Look, I'm 2IC of the commando now. I have responsibilities. I can't just swan off ..."

"Nothing could be further from my mind, old chap." Flamming hurried to reassure him. "I just need a bit of advice."

Carter doubted that, but it would be churlish to refuse to offer advice if it was sought. "Well, just to be clear, that's all. Now, what can I advise you on?"

Flamming leant in closer to Carter and lowered his voice. "You mustn't breath a word of this to anyone. Is that understood?"

"I think you can rely on my discretion." Carter was a little bit miffed that Flamming should need to remind him about the need for secrecy.

"Sorry, but lives are at stake here. OK. My operation is to bring somebody out of Italy. They have vital information that will be of use to the Allies. But I haven't been allocated any resources for the job. Let's just say that if it goes wrong, people don't want their names associated with it, so they've dropped it on my shoulders and told me to get on with it as best I can. No doubt if the operation is a success then my part will be forgotten as the big-wigs in Whitehall all scrap over whose idea it was, but that's for later."

"Why not use 30 Commando[2]?" Carter asked. "After all, you set them up."

"Partly true. I was involved with them being established, but only as part of a bigger team. But they're massively overworked right now. As well as hunting for intelligence here on Sicily, they're still sifting through the mountain of stuff they've already gathered. And as soon as we cross the Straits, they'll be tied up in Italy doing the same. Besides, they're not parachute trained."

"Is that an essential?" Carter asked.

"The target is too far inland for a seaborne operation alone. There's almost no chance of a ground force getting all the way to the target without being discovered and the target can't get closer to the sea; at least, not without arousing suspicion. So, the force would have to drop by parachute, grab the target and then hope to escape across country to be picked up on the coast. So we need a second force to take and hold the beach where they'll be evacuated from."

"You aren't asking for much then." Irony was heavy in Carter's tone. "Paratroops, aircraft, commandos and ships to extract them."

"I know I'm asking a lot. Which is why I thought you might be able to suggest a unit I might be able to use."

"The parachute insertion might be a job for the Special Raiding Squadron. They were set up in North Africa by a former commando by the name of David Stirling. He's still their CO. They're currently under the command of our former CO, Col Vernon. They're all parachute trained. In fact it sounds like it might be right up their street, so to speak. The extraction could be done by any commando unit, I suppose."

"How many commandos would it need?"

"That depends. If the beach is undefended, a troop could probably do it, though if it was me I'd want a floating reserve out at sea to come to my rescue if things got sticky. If it's a heavily defended beach, then it might need a whole commando."

"Could you do the job?"

"I told you, I'm too busy right now."

"But what about your unit, 15 Commando?"

"That's our bread and butter work, so we could certainly do it but getting us released to do the job wouldn't be easy. We're no longer in the free and easy days just after we were set up and anyone could suggest a raid and Combined Ops might rubber stamp it.

Everything's much more structured now, with a full chain of command going all the way to the very top. Officially we're part of XIII Corps, but our tasking comes direct from 8th Army HQ. Brigadier Laycock is the man to speak to."

"Isn't he the chap that tried to kidnap Rommel[4]?"

"Yes. In fact, this sort of operation might appeal to him. But he'd still have to convince Monty. Given his focus on conventional soldiering, he might take some persuading. He's only just started to appreciate what we have to offer, so madcap schemes involving parachuting behind enemy lines might not appeal to him, unless it can be linked directly to the needs of his strategy."

"That would be a tough idea to sell him. Our target is high value, but more in political terms than military."

"In that case you would need someone in the War Office, or even in the Government, to influence him. Out here, Monty is Lord of all he surveys. Nobody can give him orders. Even Eisenhower[5] has to ask nicely." Carter swallowed the last of his beer and stood to leave. "Now, if you'll excuse me, I have some rather important equipment to get back to camp."

"Of course. Well, it was nice seeing you again, Steven." Flamming extended his hand to be shaken. "Perhaps we'll run into each other again."

Carter hoped not. Anything that Flamming was involved in was likely to be dangerous. Not that it bothered Carter; he was a commando after all. But he didn't fancy getting involved in any harebrained schemes either. But he didn't say that. Instead he shook Flamming's hand, thanked him for the drink and said some polite words of farewell.

[1] Wavy golf braid rings on the sleeves or epaulettes of the of Royal Navy officers indicates that the holder of the rank is a reservist, rather than a regular. Of the three armed services in the UK, the Royal Navy is the only one to make that distinction between the badges of rank of regular and reserve officers.

[2] The badge of rank for a Major is a crown.

[3] 30 Cdo were established in 1942 as an intelligence gathering unit capable of going ahead of an assault to try to capture documents and other intelligence assets before the enemy had time to destroy them.

[4] This was Operation Flipper, carried out in Libya between 10th and 18th November 1941. It failed because Rommel wasn't at the location where he was expected to be. He had actually left there several weeks earlier. Soldiers from 11 Commando, part of Layforce, carried out the raid and it was led by Colonel (as he was at the time) Laycock in person.

[5] General Dwight D Eisenhower was the Supreme Allied Commander in the Mediterranean theatre and commanded the Allied armies for the invasion of Sicily and Italy. He would later take command of the Allied forces for the invasion of France. After the

war he went into politics as a Republican and became the 34th President of the USA.

* * *

The following morning saw Carter standing in front of a group of a dozen members of 2 Troop, the designated heavy weapons troop. Beside him stood Giles Gulliver, their OC. To his other side stood a sergeant with the maple leaf badge of the Canadian army on the sleeve of his shirt.

At Carter's feet lay the two long packing cases that had been unloaded from the truck on its return to the camp the previous evening. Behind him were the dozen cube like boxes that had accompanied them. It was time to open his surprise.

"Good morning gentlemen. I am pleased to inform you that you have two new additions to the heavy weapons inventory." He stretched out his hand, which contained two screwdrivers. "Collins, MacIntyre, if you would do the honours."

The two named troopers took the screwdrivers and set to work on the top case, It was the work of several minutes to remove the screws and lift the lid off the box. Nestled into cradles of horsehair padding were two long, tube like weapons. Each had a wooden butt like that of a rifle, but the working parts and barrel looked more like lengths of drainpipe, with a cavity cut into each at the end nearest the trigger.

"May I introduce you to the projectile, infantry, anti-tank, otherwise known as the PIAT[1]." This produced a buzz of conversation through the dozen men, pleasing Carter that he had managed to surprise men who thought that little could surprise them after all they had experienced. They had heard of this new wonder-weapon, but none of them had so far seen one, let alone used it.

"Sgt McLean here," Carter indicated the Canadian soldier, "Is on loan to us for a couple of days to teach you how to use these weapons. He has real combat experience using them, so he knows what he is talking about. How many tanks did you say you had stopped using these weapons?"

McLean seemed to swell with pride. "Three, Sir. Two Mk III *Panzers* and one Tiger."

"Thank you. Now, you will be taken a few miles north to where there are some German and Italian tanks that have already been introduced to these, to their cost." There was a ripple of laughter. "And there you will be trained in their use. You will be trained in teams of two, an operator and a loader. Sadly, we have a limited amount of ammunition available, so most of the training will be dry runs using dummy projectiles. But each team will be allowed to fire one live projectile each at one of the dead tanks. You will be taught the best firing positions for each tank, with emphasis on the Tiger, as they are the hardest to disable. Any questions?"

The men muttered some comments to each other, but no one had any questions to ask at that point. "Very well. I'll leave you with Capt Gulliver and Sgt McLean."

As he marched away, Carter heard the men push forward to examine their new acquisitions. He smiled again. Soldiers loved new hardware, especially something that gave them an advantage over a weapon as fearsome as a Tiger tank. After their experiences at Ponte Bridge, they were itching to get their revenge on the German behemoths.

But Carter had other concerns to occupy his mind. The 2IC held the additional role of training officer. His main responsibility while in camp was to improve the skills of the commando and make sure they were prepared for whatever operation they were next engaged on. The problem was that no one had any idea what that operation might be. The crossing of the Straits of Messina was the next obvious move for the Allies, but no one knew what part the commando might take in that. A sea landing was pretty obvious, but against what sort of terrain with what sort of defences? And what would the commando's objective be?

Another artillery battery perhaps? Or perhaps the clearing of beach defences. They had done both in Sicily. Or maybe it would be another bridge.

Reaching the HQ tent, Carter sat down behind the trestle table that he used as a desk, He drew a sheet of paper from the stack that sat on one corner of the table and started to write a list of possible targets. He then numbered them in order of likelihood, in terms of the commando being used to attack them. To the three he had already considered, he added a fourth, triggered by his conversation with Flamming the previous day: relief of parachute forces. But he made it the lowest priority.

Examining each item on the list, he then considered the unique skills the commando would need to have to attack each type of target. The list was similar for each, but each also had its differences. From that he was able to draw up a prioritised list of training activity, supplemented by the normal routine of physical fitness training and small arms skills.

That gave him the 'what' of his training plan, but not the how. For that he would need resources. He started work on a list of equipment that he would need Angus Fraser to provide and thought of the amused laughter he would get at some of his requests. But none of them would be dismissed. If Fraser could get his hands on the stuff, it would appear.

Top of his list of other resources was sea transport. He would need one of the commando carrying ships, because each training task started much the same way: a run into shore in landing craft, under the cover of darkness. Unless they sprouted wings and flew, there was no way of getting to Italy without crossing the short expanse of water that separated Sicily from Italy.

The other unknown was how much time they might have. It was already early August and it was certain that Monty would want to establish himself in Italy before the autumn rains started and clogged the roads with mud. He had to assume that their next operation was imminent. He studied his list of training tasks again and wondered how many the whole commando would manage to complete. He started cutting out those which he knew added the least value, or which the commandos were already proficient at. More training in them would be beneficial; no training was ever wasted; but some skills were more important than others.

[1] The PIAT was originally developed by the Special Operations Executive (SOE) for use by agents and resistance fighters operating behind enemy lines. However, the Army heard of its effectiveness and introduced it into their inventory. Its first major operational outing was in Sicily, where several were issued to the Canadian infantry and it proved to be a great success, especially against older marks of tanks, up to the Mk III Panzer. It was usable against the Tiger, but only at very short range and from an angle that could get at either the drive wheels and tracks, or the thinner belly armour of the tank. By the time of the Normandy landings much of the impact of the PIAT had been countered by the introduction of "skirts" around the tank which exploded the warhead before it could strike the armour. In France and Germany they only accounted for about 7% of all enemy tanks destroyed, about the same as for airborne rocket attacks.

* * *

"Good morning, Colonel Vernon." Ecclestone, the guardian of the tent flap, said loudly to alert the rest of the tent's occupants to the fact that they had a senior ranking visitor. Carter and Fraser, the other two occupants, sprang to their feet and stood to attention.

"As you were, chaps. Carry on." Vernon grinned at them.

"Welcome back, Sir." Fraser said. "We weren't expecting you."

"I told you I would never be far away." Vernon smiled. "Is Col Cousins in?"

"I'm right here." The CO appeared from behind the canvas screen that offered him a modicum of privacy in the corner of the tent.

"Ah, Charlie. Settled into your new role, eh?"

"Getting used to it, Sir."

"Good, good. I need a word with you. Steven, Angus, you may as well hear this as well. Your input would be valuable."

"Bring your chairs through, please." Charlie instructed. "Ecclestone, a pot of tea if you will."

Everyone had been surprised when Vernon had elected to leave his trusted clerk behind when he took up his new job, but Ecclestone didn't seem to mind. "It's not like I'll get to do any proper soldiering if I go with the Colonel." Ecclestone had confided to Carter after his old boss had departed. It was typical of a commando not to seek out a 'cushy billet'.

The two majors carried their camp chairs through to what Charlie Cousins called his cubbyhole and they settled down, an air of anticipation present as they waited for Vernon to explain the purpose of his visit. Was this when they would find out about their next operation? It was certain that Vernon hadn't arrived just to inquire about their wellbeing.

Vernon didn't keep them waiting. "I've had a request from 8th Army HQ to examine a proposal for a small operation." He explained. "It isn't related to our impending invasion of the mainland, but apparently it's quite important."

A little bell started to jingle in Carter's mind. It might be a coincidence, but it was only a few days since he had run into Ewan Flamming. That would have allowed him time to exchange communications with London and make a few requests for assistance and the exerting of influence.

"There's a plan to drop some parachutists into Italy to bring out some big-wig who wants to change sides. I don't have the details yet. But it's been suggested that the SRS do the drop and either yourselves or 49 cover the extraction from a beach. What do you think?"

"Does the name Flamming have anything to do with this?" Carter asked. "He's a Navy chap, a Commander."

Vernon gave Carter a look of curiosity. "What do you know of Cdr Flamming, Steven?"

"We met on one of those secret jobs I did when we were based in Troon. I bumped into him last week in Catania and we discussed something just like this. He asked for my advice. There didn't seem to be any harm in helping the chap."

"You may not feel that way if you get tasked with doing the job, but that is hypothetical for the moment. At the end of the day, we do as we're ordered and it does sound like a job for commandos. And yes, Flamming's name did crop up during the conversation. So, what did you advise him?"

Carter told them of the content of his conversation. "And that's just about it. He didn't share any details with me about location or the target. It was just the practicalities of getting in and out of Italy with him."

"I must say I haven't been told a great deal more." Vernon replied. "I can tell you that the intended location isn't anywhere near our planned landing beaches for the invasion, so there would be a bit of a sea voyage involved. Monty wouldn't tolerate any action on the other side of the Strait that might raise the enemy's level of preparedness any higher than it already is. I've already spoken to David Stirling about how his men would reach the target. How would you do the extraction, if 15 Cdo were given the job?"

"Steven, you seem to have given this some thought. Would you like to answer?" The CO deferred.

"I'd set up two teams, each made up of half a troop. One team would stay on the beach, or very close to it, just to defend it in case any Italian patrol turned up unannounced. The other team I'd take about half a mile to a mile inland to wait for the paratroops. If they're being chased they can offer fire support and then close up behind them and act as a rear guard until they reach the beach. I'd also want some naval gunfire available. There's nothing like a bombardment to slow the gallop of a pursuing enemy. With our own mortars and Vickers guns in reserve, I think we could hold off anything less than a battalion strength."

"Andrew, what would you need in terms of additional supplies?"

"We're short on Bangalore torpedoes[1], for a start. They're essential for a beach landing. I'd also want more three-oh-three ammunition and mortar bombs and more PIAT rounds."

"I don't think the enemy would have time to mobilise armour ..." Carter started to say, before falling silent as Fraser gave him a warning look. Col Vernon spotted it and gave a laugh.

"Well done Angus. I can see where you're coming from."

"I'm sorry, have I missed something?" Carter's voice told of his puzzlement.

Vernon was the one to reply. "Angus has spotted that this would be an opportunity to ask for materials that are in short supply in the commando, even if you aren't going to need them for the op. It's a chance to fill up his stores with scare items. The ability to spot opportunities such as this is one of the reasons I appointed him QM. And I'll pretend I didn't hear your objection, Steven"

Carter felt himself blushing. He should have spotted the opportunity as well.

"I've been told that the nearest troops are about five kilometres away in a fishing village. They're a platoon strength of Italian garrison troops who spend most of their days drinking wine and most of their nights fornicating with the wives of the fishermen who are at sea or in the army. If the alarm is raised, they'll be ordered out to intercept. The next nearest enemy force is a company strength of Italians about ten kilometres further north. You could expect them to be mobilised as well. Could you deal with them?"

"It depends on whether they head inland to try to intercept the intruder force before they reach the coast, or if they decided to get between the intruders and the sea and lie in wait for them. The first case we couldn't do anything about because we wouldn't know where to look for them, but in the second case we could probably ambush them before they could set up any defensive positions. If we can drive them off, the Navy could keep their heads down with gunfire. The main problem would be to stop the two forces from joining up. But even then, with the SRS on one side and us on the other, they'd be in a far worse fix than we would be."

"OK., Final question. If you were offered this operation to undertake, would you accept it willingly or would you be reluctant to risk your command?"

"From the commando's perspective, I'd rate it as reasonably low risk. We would hold the beach and the means of escape, so I'd accept it willingly. It's the SRS that would have the hard work."

"And they've said they'd love to take it on." Vernon stood up and pushed his hat onto his head. "OK, gentlemen, thank you for your input. I've got to go up to Catania to discuss this with the Brigadier but be on standby to come up for a planning session. If you are happy for Steven to take the lead on this, Charlie," Vernon addressed the CO, "Then there's no need for you to come, but Angus will need to be there, so he can add his two-penn'orth."

[1] A Bangalore torpedo is a hollow tube filled with explosives which can be slid underneath barbed wire entanglements to blow a hole in them. The tubes are about 5 ft in length and can be extended by joining them to empty tubes to provide additional reach. They are also a quick way of clearing mines, by producing sympathetic explosions in the buried weapons. Modern versions are still in use with the British army.

* * *

The summons came the following morning, creating a rush to get to Catania over the damaged roads and through the choking transport. Fraser and Carter shared a Jeep borrowed from a neighbouring infantry unit because, despite pleas to XIII Corps, they still couldn't get transport allocated to them. It was a perennial complaint from the commandos, having to go cap in hand to beg for something so basic.

The roads were choked with lines of prisoners snaking along them under the guard of infantrymen using bayonet tipped rifles. Most of them seemed to be Italian, from what Carter could see. The Germans were mainly fighting the Americans. It was a fluke of how the Axis had organised the defence of the island. But the Germans had put up a stout defence of Catania, delaying the capture of the port and airfield and delaying the British advance.

They were the last to arrive. Brigadier Laycock was chairing the meeting as he would be the one to go to the Commander in Chief to get the go-ahead for any operation. His advice would be crucial to getting the mission agreed. Carter recognised Flamming, of course and introduced him to Fraser. There was a good looking Major that Carter had recognised from the Officer's Club in Syracuse. The man introduced himself as David Stirling[1] of the Special Raiding Squadron. Also present was a Commander by the name of Hanning, representing the Navy, who would have to provide the ships and an RAF Squadron Leader.

"Gilchrist," the RAF man introduced himself. "7 MORU[2]." He saw the puzzlement on Carter's face. "We're the chaps who support the air force in the field."

Carter really was none the wiser but decided that life was too short to ask questions. All he had to worry about was whether he got the fighter cover he needed for the withdrawal phase of the operation and he assumed that the RAF man was the right person to make that happen for him. Besides, Laycock was tapping his fingernails on the table, impatient to get started.

"OK, chaps. Some of you may be wondering why you have been invited here today, others will already know what this is all about. We're calling this Operation Manchester. That name is Restricted, but all the detail behind it is classified Top Secret and mustn't be discussed outside this room until the operation is mounted and you can brief your personnel in a secure environment. Is that understood?"

There were mutterings of agreement. "OK, we'll go around the room and introduce ourselves and then Cdr Flamming will tell you what this is about."

As the introductions were made, Flamming got to his feet and turned over a chalk board to reveal a sketch map of a stretch of coast. It could have been in any country in the world. "I'm sorry to be so secretive about this, but a man's life and that of his family depends on no one knowing this operation has even been discussed. If we don't get the go-ahead for the operation, then his identity has to be protected and even a tiny detail such as the town in which he lives cannot slip out. Which is why this map uses only code names. I can tell you that the map is a stretch of coastline and is on the west coast, somewhere between here and Rome."

He paused and started to point out the features on the map. "The objective for the airborne element, that's David Stirling and his men, is a town approximately 10 kilometres inland from the coast. Is everyone happy with me talking in kilometres?" There were nods of assent. "Thank you, it's just that the maps we're using are all metric, so for consistency I'd like to keep it that way for the entire operation. Now, the town is codenamed Albert. Once the target is located, the airborne element will take him and his family to the beach, to be met by Major Carter and his commandos who will secure the beach."

"I didn't realise that the target would have his family with him." Stirling interjected. "How many people are we talking about?"

"There's the target, his wife and two children, aged nine and ten. Is that a problem?"

"Not the children. If the worst comes to the worst we can carry them, piggy-back style. No, it's the woman. She'll have to be properly dressed. I've seen these Italian fashions. She wouldn't make it across the fields in the sort of shoes they wear."

"OK, we can talk about that later." Flamming was anxious not to get side-tracked into detail at this stage of the briefing. There would be time for that later. "What about reaching the target after you've made the drop?"

"We need to be able to move through the streets without being spotted; That's for sure. Could we mount a bombing raid to coincide with the drop?"

"Won't that put your men at risk?" the RAF man asked.

"You don't have to bomb the town itself, just close enough to the town for the population to stay in their shelters. But it would need to be sustained over a period of time; say thirty to forty minutes. If the all-clear is sounded while we're still in the town we're likely to be spotted and we'll be no better off."

The Sqn Ldr looked dubious. "Keeping aircraft loitering over a target for that length of time is dangerous. It would give the Jerries time to direct night fighters into the area."

"Could you send them in singly over the time period?" Andrew Fraser suggested.

"It won't stop the night fighters, but it will reduce the target size, so it might work." The airman conceded.

"OK, that's settled." Flamming closed down the discussion before it could get bogged down. The Sqn Ldr made some notes on a pad but didn't make any further objections.

"Now, in terms of getting onto the beach, the Italians haven't considered it important enough to defend. It is formed by a dip in the cliffs on either side, about a hundred metres long. Inland there's sand dunes for about five hundred metres, then the coast road. On the other side, which the SRS will approach from, is open farmland criss-crossed by cart tracks. The beach is nicknamed Victoria. Aerial reconnaissance shows no habitation, and no defences other than barbed wire."

He pointed to the southern side of the map, where a dot had been marked on the coast, with the letter B next to it. "Here we have the nearest town, well it's no more than a village. It has a small garrison, no more than a platoon strength. They have trucks though, so if the alarm is raised they can be expected to respond. That village is nicknamed Bertie. To the north," he moved his pointer, "About ten kilometres from the beach and two kilometres inland, is a small town, which I've nicknamed Consort. There's a company of Italian troops there.

Now, there's no direct road from Bertie to Albert, which means that any attempt to intercept from there would have to go via Consort, so they don't represent a risk for you, David. However, they could stumble across your commandos, Steven. The garrison at Consort, however, is connected to Albert by road and could move inland to intercept the SRS or along the coast to meet up with the troops from Bertie."

"They could also split their force and do both." Stirling interjected.

"They could, but there's no way of knowing which they will do until they do it, so you'll have to be prepared for all eventualities."

"We always are, old chap." Stirling drawled.

"What I'd like to do now, is go through each of the four phases of the operation with David and Steven taking the lead as appropriate and explaining how you plan to go about each phase, what you need in terms of support, etc. The phases I see are the insertion followed by the extraction, which are both a matter for the SRS; then the securing of the beach and the evacuation, which is where Steven comes in."

"There's also the withdrawal." Carter said. "Once we're off the beach and in the landing craft, we're in the hands of the Navy and, as we discovered the last time we mounted an operation that involved a return sea journey, the operation isn't complete until we all get safely back home."

"OK, Steven; point taken. That makes it five phases then. The way we'll tackle this is for each of you to say how you want to complete each phase and what resources you will need to make that happen. Aircraft, landing craft, ships etc. Then our colleagues from the RAF and the Navy can tell us what they can do to meet your needs. Don't worry about whether or not your lords and masters are willing to provide those resources …" that brought a chuckle, "… it will be Monty who is asking for the whatever is needed, so the arguments can take place at his level, not ours." That brought more laughter, though Carter knew that if either the RAF or Navy officers suggested that something couldn't be done, their 'lords and masters' would probably also take that view.

"So, David, tell us how you intend getting your men to the target." Flamming sat down, raised his pen above his note pad and prepared to write.

[1] For those of you who are military historians and know that Stirling couldn't have been present at this meeting, please see the explanation in the Historical Notes at the end of the book.

[2] MORU – Mobile Operations Room Unit. A mobile RAF organisation that liaises with army commanders in the field to ensure that air support is provided as required. They provide the same functions as a Group Headquarters would have done in Bomber Command or Fighter Command. A MORU operated out of 3 Ton lorries that had been converted into mobile offices and communications centres. General Montgomery was so impressed by what they achieved in North Africa that he insisted on their presence for all his future campaigns.

2 – Operation Manchester

The falls were released and the landing craft dropped the final couple of inches into the sea, sending a wave coursing outwards from the side of the mother ship. At once the power was applied and the craft surged forward, further destabilising the commandos who were already off balance after the short drop. Curses were muttered and the NCOs had to hiss words of warning to maintain silence.

Things had happened fast once the briefing had finished. The outline plan for the operation had been taken to Montgomery's HQ and the official sanction for Operation Manchester had come back within hours. Once Monty's blessing had been given, doors that had previously been shut were magically opened.

So, it was only two days later that the Prince Leopold had slipped its moorings off the small port of Syracuse and started the long journey around the western coast of Sicily and northwards towards the Italian coast. It would have been much quicker to pass through the Straits of Messina, but the Axis forces still controlled that narrow waterway and were busily evacuating their troops across it. They kept the Allied Navies at bay with shore batteries and any attempt at daylight bombing was met with ferocious anti-aircraft fire from both shores. The only attacks the Allies could make on the retreating Axis armies were from their own pursuing ground forces and night time bombing raids, which were still fraught with danger from the intense ground fire.

Passing along the southern coastline the Lucky Leopold, as she was now known after narrowly missing being torpedoed by an Italian submarine, rendezvoused with the Corvette which would act as her escort and provide artillery cover for the commandos should they need it once they were ashore. The corvette also used its onboard electronics to sweep the sea in search of submarines. While the Italian Army hadn't performed well, their submarines were a different matter and had accounted for a lot of Allied shipping around the coast of Sicily during the preceding weeks.

There were a lot of things that Carter would have liked to have changed about the operation, but time had been against them. He would have liked to have identified a beach on Sicily similar to the one where they would land, so that he could rehearse the landings, the defence and the withdrawal, but that luxury had been denied him. Montgomery had set strict time limits on the operation so that it wouldn't interfere with his greater goal of invading Italy. The German withdrawal may be delaying that, but everyone knew that once the Straits were clear, the Allied armies would be unleashed across the five mile stretch of water. Even now a vast fleet of landing craft was being assembled along the coast from Catania to Syracuse, ready to embark the troops that would storm ashore when the time came.

But that was for later. Right now, Carter had to get his men ashore and keep the beach open for the arrival of David Stirling's Special Raiding Squadron. The sixty men, in three Dakota aircraft, would already have dropped close to the small town of Priverno, about halfway between Naples and Rome and the home of their target, who still remained anonymous, known by the codename Cassius[1]. The choice of codename was significant, Carter thought, if his knowledge of Shakespeare was anything to go by.

Carter had refined his thinking on his tactics since his initial discussion with Col Vernon.

Four landing craft would now go into shore. Two would carry the landing force, made up from 4 Troop, his old troop who would have been highly offended not to have been chosen for the operation. The other two landing craft would carry the two 3 inch mortars and two Vickers guns from the heavy weapons troop..

The mortars themselves would stay on board the landing craft, which would act as a firebase for them, steadied by the beach on which the crafts' bows would be resting. The Vickers gun crews would take their weapons forward to provide a wall of covering fire in the event that the Italians turned up uninvited. The remainder of 2 Troop, the heavy weapons troop, would be Carter's floating reserve and would stay a hundred yards offshore until called for. That would be just before the SRS arrived on the beach where they, Cassius and his family would be spread around the craft to make best use of the available capacity. A final, seventh craft would remain in reserve in case there were any mechanical problems.

Clear of the ship, the landing craft turned into line abreast for the run in to shore. This was always the worst part of any raid. Nobody could do anything except wonder what the future held. Would the enemy be waiting for them? Would their machine guns already be lining their sights up on the bows of the flimsy craft, about to unleash a hail of bullets at them, which would chew into the defenceless flesh of the commandos as they huddled within? But worse might follow, because the beaches provided no cover for the raiders as they dashed ashore, trying to get at the enemy and stop the machine guns before too many of them died. The intelligence might say that the beaches were undefended, but the intelligence had been wrong before, as many of the commandos on board the landing craft had reason to remember.

In the darkness Carter could make out the cliffs on either side of the beach, that spread away along the coast. Five kilometres to the south was the fishing village which had been codenamed Bertie, nestled in a similar cleft in the cliffs. To the north they went as far as a place called Anzio, where they dipped down to form a much longer beach. That beach was defended, as it offered the possibility of being used in a major assault. Between the beach and Anzio, slightly inland, was the small town of Latino, code named Consort, where the threatening garrison was based. Carter hoped they were all asleep that night, but knew it was unlikely. Even the Italians would have a platoon of men on standby, ready to react to any threat.

The pitch of the engine changed and Carter could feel the landing craft start to slow. They must be getting close.

"Stand by!" a warning was whispered, being relayed forward from the Cox'n to Carter's ears at the front of the craft, where he stood ready to lead his men ashore. The weight of his responsibilities lay heavily on Carter's shoulders. He'd commanded his own operation before, but never one on which so many lives had depended. More than a hundred and eighty men and at least one woman were relying on him to make the right decisions that night. And that didn't include the sailors on the landing craft, the Prince Leopold and the corvette.

The power to the engines was cut and the craft coasted in to drive its bows onto the sandy beach. With a clatter of chains the ramps dropped and the first men rushed ashore, spreading left and right along the beach before advancing. The sand was soft, dragging at Carter's boots as he ran directly up the beach, waiting for the hammer of machine guns to hunt him down. But the sand dunes in front of him remained silent.

The first men reached the tangles of barbed wire that coiled along the sand dunes, setting to work with wire cutters to create gaps through which the men behind would move forward. Still no sound of alarm was raised. Carter flinched at the sound of the wire rattling and clattering, but there seemed to be no one to hear it other than his men. It would have been worse if they'd had to use the Bangalore Torpedoes, of course.

Able, Baker, Charlie and Dog sections would form the beach party. They were the ones working on the wire. Easy, Fox, George and How sections would advance with him across the dunes, along with the Vickers guns crews, to take up positions along the coastal road.

Road was too grand a name for the track that the fishermen used to pass to and fro to Latina with their cargos of fish. In England Carter would have called it a farm track. But it was wide enough to take lorries and lorries could carry troops.

Ernie Barraclough arrived at Carter's shoulder. "It's going well so far, Lucky." He observed. Barraclough had taken over command of 4 Troop following Carter's promotion, supported by two section commanders who had arrived straight from training at Achnacarry.

"Don't get overconfident, Ernie. The night is still young."

A Sergeant arrived. "Wire's cut, boss." He announced to Barraclough.

"OK. get the men through. How section to scout ahead and stop when they reach the road. Make sure Lt Villiers doesn't do anything stupid." Villiers had replaced Barraclough as section commander and had earned a reputation of being a bit rash. As Carter's second in command for the operation, Barraclough himself would be remaining on the beach with the other new section commander, Tony Askew. A third officer would also be present, Giles Gulliver, 2 Troop's CO. He would command the mortars and the reserve if they came ashore.

In the darkness the sergeant's teeth flashed a grin. "No problems, boss."

The Sergeant trotted off to convey the order. Already Carter could see the men filing through the gaps that had been cut in the wire in several places.

To the left and right of the new section commander, Tony Askew, Able, Baker and Charlie sections were clambering up the shifting sands to dig in on top and provide a defensive screen for the beach. Only Dog section would remain at the bottom, to act as a reserve and fill in any gaps that became apparent.

"Come on then, James." Carter said to his radio operator. "Time for us to go." They headed for the nearest gap in the wire, where Lt Villiers was waiting for the last of his sections to pass through.

"You've got a sergeant for that job. Jeremy." Carter admonished. "You should be up front, right behind your scouts. The men expect to see you in the lead."

"Sorry, Major."

"And don't use my rank in the field." Carter snapped, more severely than he had intended. "It's Lucky or nothing at all. I don't want some sniper picking me out because you think you're on a parade ground."

"S ... sorry Maj ... I mean Lucky."

"OK. Look, we all get a bit disoriented on our first operation. Keep calm and think things through before you act. Now, how are you feeling?"

"Like you said, a bit disoriented. No, worse. Nervous. This is my first time in combat."

"We're not in combat yet. This is just a night training exercise at the moment. Think of it that way. It will help you feel less nervous. You aren't doing anything you haven't done before, either out here in Sicily or back home in Scotland."

"Of course. Sorry."

"And stop apologising. Now, get up with your men before they start wandering off in the dark."

Villiers turned away and hurried off. Carter waited a moment to allow him to get clear, then followed. *Was I ever that green?* He asked himself. He probably had been. In fact, he had been so green that on his first operation he had managed to get himself left behind when the commando had withdrawn.

"And wipe that grin off your face." Carter said to his radio operator as he stepped off into the darkness, knowing the man had heard every word of the exchange. He turned to look at him, noting that he wasn't wearing a steel helmet. Instead he wore his commando beret with the radio set's headphones clamped over the top. One earpiece was slid back so that he could hear Carter's orders while he monitored the radio with his other ear. Most of the men didn't like wearing their helmets and Carter had laid down the law for this operation, but had granted an exemption for the radio operators. The headphones didn't fit well under the tight fitting liners.

The radios were a weak point in his plan. Because of their fragile valves they were a weak point in any plan. It only needed one of them to be dropped or shaken by a shell blast and they were likely to stop working. The commandos also had too few of them. Carter had commandeered several from sections that weren't on the operation just to make sure he had communications all the way from the forward positions back to the landing craft. From there the Navy would relay his communications to the Prince Leopold and HMS Violet, the corvette that was their escort. David Stirling had taken three radios with him in the hope that one of them might survive the parachute drop and be able to communicate to Carter when they got in range.

The sand shifted under Carter's feet as he walked, making for heavy going. They would struggle to make a quick retreat if the enemy were close behind them. But, then again, if they struggled, so would the enemy, so it probably all evened itself out. They kept to the valleys between the dunes, though, anxious that their shapes shouldn't appear on the skyline and give their presence away. There was little light, the moon having already set, but Carter knew not to take anything for granted.

As they meandered their way inland the dunes started to get smaller, until about a hundred yards from the track, where they flattened out into a series of ripples, as though the sea itself had been frozen in mid flow. Already he could hear the thud and ring of trenching tools from the left and right as the Vickers gunners prepared defensive positions. The four sections lay along the edge of the road waiting for him to give the next order. Although he had briefed them, he wanted to make a physical check of the ground to make sure it matched up with what they had seen in the photographs and on the maps.

Across the road lay an empty field, bounded by a wall on the far side. Carter found Villiers by identifying the bulk of his radio operator's set.

"OK, Jeremy. Take one section to set up behind the wall over there. Two other sections to dig in on either flank, with their Bren guns aimed along the side of the road. The fourth section will stay with me to act as a reserve, here in the middle." It was very much as he had briefed it.

"No problem, Lucky." As he rose from where he had been lying, he tapped his radio operator on the shoulder and the two of them crossed the track as he signalled to his three sections to follow him.

"How section. Dig in here." Carter ordered. He split them into two groups, one which would face left and the other facing right. They dropped their packs and started digging. Tpr James lowered his radio to the ground and unstrapped his trenching tool from its rear.

Carter did the same with his pack and they started to dig themselves a slit trench.

The soft ground yielded easily enough and they were able to pile the spoil up on three sides to act as a wall, but a lot of it slid back in, to fall to the bottom of the shallow pit. It was a problem soldiers always had when digging in sand. Old hands from the desert war swore it doubled the time it took to dig a trench. At last Carter announced that he was happy with what they had done. The combined wall and trench was just about deep enough to provide cover for a kneeling man, which was as good as time allowed them.

James placed his radio on the front lip of the trench and started heaping sand around it to prevent it from being damaged by stray bullets. It would have made more sense to place it in the bottom of the trench, but they had found that the set's whip antenna wasn't long enough to pick up a signal when it was down that low.

Carter checked his watch, finding it was just after two a.m. Dawn was around 6.20 and the plan was for them to be off the beach an hour before that, so they would be over the horizon before the daylight revealed their presence. So, three hours to wait.

Carter reached for the radio's headset and microphone, which James handed to him.

He pressed the button on top of the microphone. "All stations, this is Eagle, radio check, over."

"Hello Eagle, this is Albatross" Came the reply from Villiers' operator, a hundred yards away across the field. "Reading you loud and clear. Over."

"Roger Albatross, loud and clear also. Out to you." He dismissed the section commander, which allowed the next operator to respond. One by one the sections confirmed that they could hear him: Bullfinch, that was Ernie Barraclough, back on the beach; Chaffinch, who was Giles Gulliver with the mortars: Dove, who was Gulliver's section commander, bobbing around on the waves still out at sea; Falcon, who was the Cox'n on the spare landing craft and who was providing the relay back to the Prince Leopold and the Violet. The only radio not to respond was Gannet. That was David Stirling, somewhere out in the Italian countryside ahead of them. They should be within range, but as the Signals Officer in Catania had explained, if they were in a valley, or behind a large building, or in thick woodland, their ability to pick up radio signals would be affected.

So, Carter had anticipated that and agreed to try to make contact every fifteen minutes. Stirling, on the other hand, could call him at any time and Carter didn't doubt that he would do that if he needed to.

All Carter could now do was wait.

Commandos got used to waiting. They waited for their next operation, they waited for their ship to reach its destination, they waited for the enemy and they waited for their relief forces. They waited in the dark, in the light, in the sun, the wind and the rain. Here in Italy it was still late summer and the night was warm, but comfortable. Carter's mind took him back to his first combat action and having to hide in the freezing waters of a Norwegian fjord in December. A smile played around his lips as he remembered gritting his teeth so hard that he feared they might break, but it was the only way he could stop the chattering from being heard by the German patrol that was only a few feet from him.

There would be no chattering teeth that night.

But there was the chattering of a machine gun.

As Carter had been immersed in his memories, his senses had picked up the sound of an engine approaching. It was high-pitched, like the buzzing of an insect. Some sort of motor-cycle, his mind prompted him, but not one with a powerful engine. More likely one of the smaller bikes that some of the Italian boys rode, when they could get fuel. Sometimes they had a girl perched on the back.

Was that what the sound signified? Some amorous Italian youth returning home after spending the evening with his beloved? Carter's brain snapped him back to the present and he turned his head to peer into the darkness. That was when the machine gun opened fire.

Carter was out of the trench in an instant, sprinting towards the gun, intent on preventing the gunner from giving them away. It was too late of course; his mind told him that. The gun fell silent and Carter heard the barking voice of a corporal berating the gunner.

"You dozy fucker! What did you want to do that for, you dozy …"

"OK, Corporal. That will do." Carter said as he slid to halt in the sand behind the machine gun nest. "Where is he?" he asked, meaning the motorcyclist.

"About fifty yards along the track, Sir." The corporal pointed.

Carter could just about hear the burbling sound of the motorcycle engine. Visible in the darkness was a thin sliver of light from a masked headlamp. The bike was stationary, but there was no sign that its rider had suffered any injury.

So, the cyclist had probably seen the muzzle flashes of the machine gun. He might have heard the hammer of the weapon's firing, but that was less likely given the sound emitted by his own transport and the rushing of the wind. But he knew something was in front of him, even if he didn't know what.

The next question was whether or not the rider was military or civilian. If he was military then he would probably be able to recognise the flashes for what they were. If he were civilian, he might not know. Which would account for why he hadn't already turned the bike around and fled. Curiosity was keeping him there.

But had he heard the corporal's shouted insults to the gunner? Probably. In which case …

In which case the rider had made a decision. The sound of the bike's engine increased as he applied the throttle and turned the bike around to return the way he had come. The noise diminished as the bike disappeared along the track, just a tiny red dot of the bike's rear light visible until that too, disappeared.

There was nothing more Carter could do for the moment. Their presence had been discovered, so all he could now do was wait to find out how the Italians would react. For all he knew, the cyclist might not even report the incident. But that seemed unlikely. If the gunner hadn't fired, there would have been the chance that the cyclist might pass them by in the darkness without ever knowing they were there. But there was no point in crying over spilt milk.

"I'll deal with you later!" Carter snarled at the machine gunner. He was one of the new intake, wet behind the ears in real terms. Many of them went straight to Achnacarry after serving with the Young Soldiers' battalions[2]. They hadn't seen combat before. But that was no excuse. They were still trained commandos and one with an itchy trigger finger was a liability. If they had been lying in ambush waiting for an enemy force, they might now be under attack and fighting for their lives. That might even be the case before the end of the night.

"S ... sorry, Sir." The soldier stuttered.

"Too late for that, lad." The corporal interjected.

"And you should know better than to start shouting, Corporal." Carter reminded him sternly. Carter couldn't see the man's face, but he hoped he was blushing. He certainly didn't feel the need to answer. "Well, the damage is done now. Keep a sharp eye out. I have a feeling we'll have company before too long."

Carter trudged away through the sand, back to his slit trench. Tpr James offered him the microphone and slipped the headset off, passing that across as well. "It's Gannet, Lucky." He reported the call sign of the SRS.

Gannet, at last. "Hello Gannet, this is Eagle, go ahead, over."

"Hello Eagle. Good to hear you. We're on our way."

"How far away are you?" Carter asked.

"About 8 kilometres."

Checking his watch, Carter swore, but his finger wasn't on the 'press to talk' button so Stirling wouldn't have heard him. They should have been much closer. They had allowed an hour's lee-way before dawn, but every metre that Stirling had to cover now was another few seconds of their safety margin eaten into. Eight kilometres meant they could still be two hours away. If it had just been them, they could have force marched the distance in ninety minutes or less, but with civilians, including children, that wasn't an option.

"Roger Gannet. Have you had any trouble?"
"Not the sort you mean, Eagle. Long story. I'll save it for later."
"Roger, Gannet. Report progress every half hour, over."
"Roger Eagle. Out."

Carter handed the microphone and headset back to his radio operator. The waiting had to go on.

[1] Gaius CASSIUS Longinus was the instigator of the plot to assassinate Julius Caesar along with Brutus (Marcus Junius BRUTUS) a former friend and ally of Caesar. His name and role is prominent in the Shakespeare play named after the Roman dictator.

[2] Young Soldiers' battalions were what they sound like they might be. Volunteers for the army who were found to be under eighteen were assigned to them and given basic military training, before being posted to undemanding, non-combat duties, such as guarding barracks and stores depots. When they reached the age of eighteen, they were transferred to a regular battalion where they were given additional training and took on normal military duties, which could include combat operations. By 1942 the commanding officers of other army units were fed up with having their best soldiers recruited by the commandos and the Parachute Regiment, so they were barred from making direct appeals for recruits other than from the Young Soldiers' battalions. The commandos and paratroops got plenty of volunteers from the bored young soldiers, but this reduced the average age and experience of the commandos who came out to Italy as reinforcements and also to Burma and, later, to North West Europe.

* * *

Another hour ticked by. Gannet's progress improved and they covered the anticipated four kilometres during that period. But the clock was still ticking.

The first sign of trouble came with the sound of another engine. This one had a deeper rumble to it, a truck or some other sort of heavy vehicle. Carter hoped it wasn't a tank.

The engine sound grew louder, then stopped abruptly as the vehicle came to a halt. A trooper slid into Carter's trench. "Cpl Moody's complements Lucky. One truck, approaching from the south. Seems to have stopped about a hundred yards away. Can't see whether or not anyone is getting out."

That question was answered soon enough. A narrow beam of light sprung out from the south, too bright to have been from a torch. Carter guessed at a spotlight mounted on the side or top of the vehicle's cab. It tracked from side to side, seeking out any sign of intruders.

"Shall I tell the Corp to put the light out?" It was well within the capability of any rifleman in the commando to get a first time hit at that range.

"No. It shows us where they are. Just tell him to make sure that the men take precautions to protect their night vision. But if you see any sign of troops approaching, you have permission to open fire with the Vickers." It wouldn't do to let the enemy get close. Their one hope of completing the operation successfully was to maintain a corridor for the SRS to pass through. One truck wouldn't even hold a complete platoon, so Carter wasn't worried about numbers.

The trooper scurried off into the darkness, narrowly missing being picked out by the spotlight as it swept back across the road. But it did come to rest on the trench that had been dug a few yards along from Carter's, where half of How section lay.

The ragged slope of the front of the trench looked unnatural and it wasn't surprising that the heap of sand that formed the parapet should come under scrutiny. The four men in the trench kept their heads down, as the shapes of their helmets couldn't be disguised.

After a few seconds of scrutiny, the beam swept onwards, traversing towards the sea and lighting up the higher dunes. There was nothing to see in that direction, unless the beach party had moved forward. It was possible that Ernie Barraclough might send out a patrol, just to keep the men occupied, but he would have warned Carter over the radio in order to prevent friends opening fire on friends. The Americans euphemistically called it 'friendly fire' but there was nothing friendly about such carelessness, in Carter's opinion.

But the thought of friendly fire reminded Carter that he needed to warn the rest of his force of what was happening The light scattered from the beam would be visible from the beach and the commandos there would be wondering at its source. He sent an "all stations" radio message, then waited for the Italians next move.

It wasn't long in coming.

Even in the darkness Carter could make out the shapes of men moving out into the fields on the other side of the road. They formed a skirmish line before moving northwards towards Carter's positions. On that course they would pass into the gap between himself and Carter's forward positions, threatening Villiers' right flank.

A parachute flare fizzed into the sky from the truck. Foolish, Carter thought. It was more of a danger to the Italians than to the British, as it illuminated the whole of their force. The Vickers at once started to hammer out a welcome tattoo, as did the Bren gun of How section just to Carter's right. Two men dropped, injured or dead Carter didn't know, while the others dived for cover. A second Bren opened up from the forward area, along with the crack of rifle fire as Villiers' men joined in.

The flare fizzled out and darkness fell again. "Cease fire" Carter called to his men. There was no point in wasting ammunition by shooting at shadows. "Tell Albatross to cease fire." Carter ordered his radio operator. Total silence fell a few seconds later as the forward troops reacted to the relayed order. Then an eerie moan echoed across the fields as a wounded solider cried out. The Italians hadn't fired a single shot in retaliation.

Carter raised his binoculars to his eyes, but they only served to bring the darkness closer. He checked his map by the light of a shaded torch and estimated the truck's position. It was well within range of the 3 inch mortars. Perhaps he could encourage the Italians to withdraw with a salvo of bombs. It would all have to be guesswork: the bearing from the beach and the distance. But the enemy wasn't close enough to risk the bombs falling on his men if he got it wrong. Worth a try.

He gave the orders for Tpr James to relay to the mortar teams on the beach, waited for a few long seconds before he saw the flash of the first bomb to fall, followed at once by the crump of the detonation. Long, definitely. The flash had illuminated the truck in front of it. He relayed the range correction and watched as the second bomb fell much closer.

"Tell them 'two star shells.'" Carter instructed James. There was another lengthy delay and two bright lights lit up the whole area as the illuminating ordnance burst into bright, phosphorous light. At once the automatic weapons sought out the Italians, cowering in the field behind whatever cover they could find. The slower, more measured crack of rifles followed.

The first Italian, furthest from safety, broke and ran back towards the truck, the bullets of the Vickers gun stitching a line through the dirt behind him as they chased him and caught him, bowling him over to lie still. But it was the crack in the dam. Others rose and sprinted to try to take advantage of the bulk of the vehicle, the Bren guns and the Vickers sending them on their way.

As the star shells dimmed and then fell dark, Carter heard the splintering of glass, a higher counterpoint to the hammering of the Vickers as it attempted to batter the vehicle into scrap.

"Cease firing!" Carter called again. He requested another salvo of high explosive bombs from the mortar team. Huddled in the lee of the truck the Italians would make a big target and the flying shrapnel was bound to inflict further casualties.

"Cpl Hemmings!" Carter summoned How sections leader. They were his reserve and he had a job for them.

The Corporal arrived in the slit trench from Carter's left. "I want you to take your section and work your way round behind the Vickers on the coast side; say about two hundred yards to their right." Carter indicated the line. "Try to get around behind the Italians and close to a range of about one hundred yards, then open up on them when you see the next star shell from the mortars. I'll get the Vickers to open up at the same time. It should be enough to force them to withdraw to get away from you. If they attempt a counter-attack, retreat into the dunes and hold them off and I'll call up reinforcements from the beach. If they don't counter, then return here with your men when the Italians retreat."

Hemmings repeated the orders back, to show he had understood them, then returned to his position to gather that half of his section, before passing behind Carter to collect his other four men from the right. He withdrew them towards the sea and Carter saw them go into a huddle while the section commander briefed his men.

Carter checked his watch. It should take them no more than five minutes to get into position, but he would allow them ten, just in case.

"Gannet calling, Lucky." Tpr James told him. "Reporting two kilometres out. They've heard gunfire and want to know what's happening."

"Tell them we've got company, but not to worry. Tell them the way to the beach is still clear."

Carter could hear James repeating his words faithfully. The second hand on Carter's watch swept towards the nine minute mark. "OK, James. Tell Chaffinch 'one round illuminating', same range and bearing.'"

The star shell lit up seconds later and the Vickers at once barked into action. Carter could see holes appearing in the metal work of the truck. In the distance the steady beat of How section's Ben gun added to the noise, then the rattle of musketry from the rifles. A Bren from Villers' positions in front of him also added its weight. The realisation that they had been outflanked sent the Italians into a full-scale retreat, sprinting back along the track into the darkness to escape the onslaught. Carter saw at least one man fall and was sure there were other bodies lying around the truck.

But they wouldn't go far. If their officer was still alive he would eventually get them to stop, or maybe the NCOs. After giving them time to catch their breath he would bring them back, probably trying to get through the dunes behind them, where there was more cover.

* * *

The respite didn't last as long as Carter had hoped. The sound of engines growled through the night once again, this time coming from the left, the direction of the town code named Consort. The force there was larger; company strength and Carter knew from the overlapping sounds of more than one engine that several trucks were approaching. He daren't give them time to stop and deploy. He tapped James on the shoulder and told him to pick up his radio, then scrambled across the open ground to the left hand Vickers gun. The corporal in charge was ready for him.

"Still some distance off, Lucky." He pointed. "You can just about make out headlights." Sure enough, Carter picked out the twin slits of the leading vehicle. Distance was hard to gauge at night. They could be bright lights far away or dim lights much closer. But by allying sound and vision, Carter guessed they were still probably half a mile distant. He looked at his map, calculating angles. He wrote the order on his pad and passed it to James, who read it out over the radio, repeating it to prevent any miss-hearing.

"Wait my order." were the last words he said before ending the transmission.

Aiming mortars was like trying to throw a ball over a high wall and expecting it to land in a bucket. It was far from being an exact science. Carter's orders would get the mortar bombs into the garden behind the wall, but it would be a very lucky shot indeed to find the bucket first time. The first bomb would just tell Carter how much adjustment he had to make. Unfortunately, it would also alert the enemy to their presence. The sound of the enemy's own engines would have covered up the sound of the short period of combat that had erupted a few minutes earlier and they would have seen the lights of the flares, but no one could ignore the explosion of a mortar bomb just a few yards away.

The sound of the engines diminished as the small convoy slowed down. Whoever was in command was suspicious, it seemed. Of course, they would be expecting to meet the platoon from the fishing village about here. The sound reduced to a barely audible murmur. This was an opportunity Carter couldn't afford to miss. With the trucks standing still, they were a much easier target. "James, tell Chaffinch, new bearing." It wouldn't be more than a few degrees difference, but how many? He had to guess. "New bearing three one three magnetic. Three bomb salvo, fire when ready."

It was unlikely that the trucks would move forward again once they were under mortar attack. That would enable Carter to make fine adjustments to range and bearing to 'bracket' the target.

Well trained mortar operators could easily keep three bombs in the air at any time, so the armaments would land in quick succession. Vibration would induce small shifts in the mortar's base plate, so it was unlikely they would all land in the same small area of ground. A fraction of an inch of deviation back on the beach would be magnified into several yards where the trucks stood.

The first bomb hit, quickly followed by the second and third. They were all too long and all south of the trucks by at least fifty yards. He'd misjudged the distance quite considerably. He did a hurried recalculation and sent fresh fire orders. The three fresh bombs seemed to form a triangle around the second truck in the line, one short, one long and one in front of it. There was no point in doing any further fine tuning. They were close enough to the bucket to keep lobbing balls at it until one went in.

"Three more" Carter instructed.

The requested bombs landed soon after. Lights appeared behind the targeted truck as the rear vehicle sought to escape from the area. But the lead truck could only go forwards. Which is what it did. With the flashes of the mortar bombs to aid him, the Vickers machine gunner started firing. The truck slewed to one side and came to a stop. Carter didn't need to imagine the panicked soldiers spilling over the sides and the tailgate in their effort to escape.

"Aim to the left!" Carter shouted into the gunner's ear to make himself heard. The left-hand side of the truck was the closest to the sea. If the enemy got behind them it would make life much more difficult. It was better to force the enemy into the fields where he had an effective crossfire laid out between himself and Villiers' forward positions.

With a heavy frump the truck that had been bracketed by the mortars caught fire, probably caused by petrol leaking from a shrapnel damaged fuel tank. Carter shouted orders into James's ear to re-target the mortars onto the far side of the leading truck. It was only a minor adjustment. A degree or so on the compass bearing and a fraction lower on the angle of the barrel to project the missiles a few yards longer.

The Bren gunner on Villiers' left flank must have seen a target because Carter heard it staring to fire. A flare soared skywards from the Italian positions as the Italian commander sought to make sense out if what would seem like confusion to him. All it did was illuminate his own men. Rifles cracked out from in front of Carter as the whole of Villiers' left flank joined in the sport.

But it would only take the Italian officer a few moments to work out that if his enemy was in the fields, the weak point would be the dunes behind them. If Carter could see that, then the enemy must too.

"James, tell Bullfinch to send a section forward to the top of the dunes to the left hand side of the beach. Keep a lookout for any infiltration by the enemy."

While James was sending the radio message, the Vickers gun behind Carter, the one on the southern side of the position, started firing again. The enemy commander on that side must have felt emboldened by the sound of his comrades approaching from the north and decided that they were creating enough of a distraction for him to try another attack.

But Carter could direct fire on two positions at the same time. Satisfied that the enemy to his north wasn't going to be in position to attack for some time, Carter tapped James on the shoulder and the two of them sprinted the hundred yards back to the other Vickers position. Sprint might have been an exaggeration for the heavily loaded radio operator, which meant that Carter arrived at the Vickers gun by himself.

"Where are the enemy?" Carter demanded from Cpl Moody as he slid into the back of their trench.

"Advancing in single file along this side of the track." The reply came back. "They're just about to pass the truck again."

"Is How section still out there?"

"As far as I know, they are Lucky."

"OK, they'll know what to do."

Tpr James interrupted, breathing heavily. "Gannet calling, Lucky. They're about a kilometre out and want to know if it's safe for them continue."

"Tell them I'm going to send up an illuminating shell from the beach. They should advance directly towards it." Strictly speaking, if Stirling's navigation had been good, they shouldn't need it. All they should have to do is continue on the bearing they had been following all night. But Carter knew how small errors could occur by having to go around obstructions or difficult ground. A signpost to follow would do no harm. "Then warn Albatross he has friendly troops in front of him. He must stop the enemy from getting between him and them and also between him and us."

"OK, Lucky." Carter waited until the orders had been sent, then led James back to their position in the centre. The NCOs would keep the enemy under harassing fire and could be relied on to send runners to ask him for assistance if they thought it was necessary. He had to avoid getting bogged down in the combat. It was easy to lose sight of the bigger picture if you got too involved in the fine detail.

The illuminating flare soared up from the beach behind them from a mortar firing directly upwards. It hung there for over a minute. Plenty of time for Stirling to take a compass bearing.

* * *

A machine gun opened up from the Italian positions on Carter's left. Almost at once the sound of a Bren gun sounded from the dunes towards the sea. So, that was the enemy's plan. Keep the forward troops occupied while he sent the rest of his force behind them. He couldn't have known that Carter had already anticipated the move.

"James, I want you to go to the Vickers," Carter pointed to his left, "Tell the gunner to locate the Bren gun that's firing from the dunes on the left and then sweep back and forth between the Bren and the trucks. That's where the Italians will be." Firing blindly into the darkness the gunner probably wouldn't be able to hit anyone, but it would force the Italians to take cover and slow down their advance.

Timing would be the important thing now. Once the SRS arrived, which could only be minutes away, they would have to collapse the perimeter with a fighting withdrawal. They weren't even close to being outnumbered, but at the same time Carter didn't want to lose any of his men. He had no idea who 'Cassius' might be, but as far as Carter was concerned, he wasn't worth any of the men Carter had brought with him.

At once he saw the irony of that thought. If Cassius was of no value, why had Montgomery agreed to this operation? But as far as Carter was concerned, his men came first. But again, he immediately saw the flaw in his thinking. The operation came first. For the commandos it always did. Otherwise there would be no point in the commandos. They did the things no one else had the nerve to do. If St Nazaire[1] had taught the world anything, it had taught it that.

OK, the operation came first, but that didn't mean Carter had to be profligate with the lives of his men. As the northern Vickers gun began to sweep the ground in front of the sand dunes, Carter reviewed the plan for his withdrawal. Things had changed since the plan had been made, so the plan itself might need amending.

The problem with mounting operations at short notice was that there was no time for rehearsals, or training as the commandos preferred to think of it. A complex withdrawal under fire with non-military personnel involved was something that should have been practiced and more than once.

Plan A had been simple enough. It depended on their not having been discovered by the enemy, Gannet arriving on time and passing through the commando positions, the commandos forming a protective screen behind them and all of them making their way back to the beach in an orderly military fashion.

Carter didn't like having a Plan B, because that meant that Plan A hadn't been good enough, but he had remembered the old adage about no plan surviving first contact with the enemy[1] so, with that risk in mind, he had devised his Plan B, which was essentially the same as Plan A but with a lot of shooting going on.

He started to give his instructions. "Eagle calling Dove, bring all the nesting boxes in."

"Dove calling Eagle, roger."

"Eagle calling Chaffinch, maintain fire with tube two on current range and bearing. Conserve ammunition."

"Chaffinch calling Eagle, roger."

That was all he could do on the radio, for the moment. "James, I'm going forward. You stay here and if I need you, I'll call using the Albatross callsign."

"And if you don't get as far as Albatross, Lucky?"

"Call Bullfinch and tell him he's in command." Carter gave a grim smile. Ernie Barraclough would be up to the task, Carter was sure. He had proved himself to be a steady officer.

---

[1] Operation Chariot (28th March 1942), a daring raid to destroy a dry dock in the port of St Nazaire. It had a particularly high casualty rate, well above that which a regular military commander would find acceptable. Most of those that weren't killed were taken prisoner.

Carter slid over the front edge of the slit trench and made a crouching run forward towards Villiers' positions. He found Villiers central section of men sitting on the ground behind the wall, their weapons across their laps. Considering how much shooting was now going on to either side of them, they looked pretty relaxed. One man stood sentry, keeping a lookout forward.

"Villiers." Carter hissed, though he hardly needed to; habitual behaviour.

"Over here." Carter saw an arm raised. Beside Villiers sat his radio operator. "What brings you out here?" The voice was light, cheery not challenging.

"Easier than trying to relay orders over the radio. So, here's what I want you to do. Once Gannet gets here, you'll need to tell them what I want from him." The SRS had sixty men and they would add a lot of weight to Carter's defensive plan. "First of all, radio to tell me that they're here. That will be when I tell the two Vickers guns to cease fire and get ready to withdraw." A well drilled machine gun crew could dismantle their weapon in less than a minute and be ready to move, but they needed a warning to stop firing and they needed cover while they withdrew. Carrying their heavy burdens of the gun. tripod, ammunition and its cooling water, they would be defenceless against enemy fire.

"Once the guns stop firing, I want Gannet to put one third of his men on the left flank and another third on the right flank, between the ends of your two flanking sections and the track. The final third will remain with Cassius to provide close protection. Once they're through, radio back to me to tell me, then start to withdraw behind them. It's a fighting withdrawal, so expect to maintain contact with the enemy, but don't hang around waiting for them. If you can put distance between you and them, so much the better. Try and keep about a hundred yards between you and Cassius, so they can still get away even if the Ities manage to break through your line."

"They won't do that; not while I draw breath, Lucky."

"Good man." It was a bold statement to make, but the sort of determination he needed to hear from Villiers right now.

"I'll be moving out as soon as Gannet reaches me, so don't look for me when you cross the road. Maintain that arc around Cassius all the way back to the beach, then pass through the wire where you came through after we landed. This time it will be OK for you to be the last man through." He patted Villiers on the shoulder to reassure him.

"Bullfinch will provide the final cover after you pass through his positions, so keep going, straight into the landing craft. Chaffinch will be directing traffic, so send your men wherever he tells you. Once you're onboard, wait for the signal to leave the beach, which will be two red Very flares. Got all that?"

"Radio to tell you that Gannet has arrived. Gannet to deploy men onto my flanks; I withdraw behind Gannet; keep going to the beach and onto the landing craft, withdraw when I see two red flares."

"Good man. If anything untoward happens, act on your own initiative, but make sure you protect Cassius at all costs. If we lose him the whole night has been a waste of time!"

Carter didn't waste any more time but scurried off back to re-join Tpr James. "When we get the message from Albatross, to tell us Gannet has arrived, I want you to go and tell that northern gun to cease fire and withdraw to the beach. I'll be doing the same on the southern side. We meet back here and wait for Gannet to reach us, then we go with them."

"What about How section? They're out on the southern side still."

Carter hadn't fogtotten them. "I'll send the corporal in charge of the gun crew to get them. He'll know where they are."

That was it. Plan B was now in force. Carter hoped that there would be no need for a Plan C, because he didn't have one.

[1] Various people have been attributed with this quote, probably because it is something so well understood by military commanders that it has been said many times by many of them. However, the first written citation is from Field Marshall Helmuth von Moltke (1800-1891), Chief of Staff of the Prussian General Staff (1864-1871). His exact words were "One cannot be at all sure that any operational

plan will survive first contact with the main body of the enemy." While this is the earliest quote in this precise form, others have voiced similar sentiments, including Carl von Clausewitz (1780-1831), Napoleon Bonaparte (1769-1821) and Sun Tzu (544BC-496BC). In civilian terms it has been reinterpreted as "Shit happens" or, in boxer Mike Tyson's words, "Everyone has a plan until they get punched in the mouth!"

* * *

Back to the waiting again. The combined effects of machine gun fire, Bren guns and mortar bombs were making the Italians cautious. They had no idea about the strength of the incursion. They might assume that this was the long awaited invasion of the mainland. Or they may guess correctly that it was a raid and the enemy strength was not as large as the darkness made it seem.

Carter decided to keep them guessing a bit more. He held his hand out for the radio's headset and microphone.

"Hello Dove, this is Eagle, over."

"Hello Eagle, this is Dove, go ahead."

"Hello Dove. Request Heron to provide support. Fire on grid square …." Carter consulted his map, checking the co-ordinates again to make sure he hadn't got them wrong, before sending the eight digit grid reference. "Three rounds rapid fire."

"Roger Eagle." Dove read the numbers back so that there could be no doubt, before Carter terminated the conversation.

"All stations, this is Eagle, standby for incoming artillery." Carter returned the headset to James, then shrunk himself into the smallest target possible at the bottom of the slit trench. While the Royal Navy thought themselves the finest gunners in the world, as a soldier Carter was taking no chances.

The whistling sound grew to a shriek and the first shell from the corvette's four inch gun landed with a mighty blast just beyond the Italian trucks. Carter felt as though the air was being physically pumped out of his lungs as the shock wave swept over the trench. What it would do to the Italians, he had no idea.

A second shell landed only seconds later, sending one of the trucks spinning through the air to add to the mayhem. The final shell completed the job, exploding on the same truck and sending fragments of metal flying in a lethal rain around the Italian positions. By the light of bits of burning wood and canvass, Carter could see Italian soldiers sprinting away from the area. But there would still be some on the nearer side of the track, though they would now be hunkering down in order to try to gain what little protection the ground might have to offer. Carter daren't target them, however. They were too close to his own men. The mortars wouldn't be effective either. The bombs would land in the soft sand of the dunes and the detonators in their noses probably wouldn't go off.

But without their friends to provide covering fire, the flanking force would have little choice but to withdraw as well.

* * *

"Go ahead Albatross." Carter heard James murmur.

This must be the SRS arriving, Carter felt sure. His nerve strings were twanging with the tension of the night's action. The enemy had been quiet for several minutes, but Carter was pretty sure they hadn't gone away completely. Somewhere out there, on either side, the enemy commanders were working out their next move.

"Roger Albatross, Understood. Gannet is here." James turned towards Carter. "Lt Villiers' reports that the SRS have arrived in his positions, Lucky."

"OK, let's get this show on the road." Carter ducked to the right as James did the same to the left. The radio had to be left where it was if they were to move quickly enough. Carter arrived back first, but James wasn't far behind him. Carter lifted the radio from its sandy nest and held it high enough for James to slip his arms through the harness. It seemed to weigh more now than it had earlier, but that must be fatigue setting in, Carter assumed.

He sensed movement in the darkness in front of him, seeing shapes moving under the thin light of the stars.

"Christmas." Carter snapped out the challenge word for the night.

"Hogmanay." Came the reply.

"Come through." Carter commanded, lowering the barrel of his Tommy gun. He hadn't even realised he had raised it; a reflex action. "Keep going, straight back to the beach. Mind you don't fall into the trench." He warned, as the soldier's booted foot slid dangerously close to the side of the hole as the sand shifted under it. The Trooper passed a warning back and the following file of men moved to one side to give the obstruction a wider berth.

"Where's your CO?" Carter asked as a man brushed past him.

"Middle of the file." Came the reply. "You can't miss him, he's got the Itie and his wife with him."

The man was right. The sound of querulous voices reached him before he picked out the shape of a woman and the man she was arguing with. Behind them walked the tall figure of David Stirling. But the next two troopers to pass him each bore a heavy burden. Carter was surprised that they needed so much equipment, then one of the bundles moved to reveal the nodding head of a child.

Allowing the two Italians to pass him, Carter stepped into the path of the SRS's CO. "David, good to see you."

"Lucky! You too!" Stirling replied. "Sounds like you had some trouble."

"Nothing we couldn't handle. Are your men out on the flanks?"

"As requested, old chap. Sorry we were late, by the way."

"I was starting to get worried." Carter moved them forward, following the escort and their Italian charges. Tpr James fell in behind. "Anything serious?"

"Yes and no. It appears that Cassius neglected to tell his wife what he was planning until about ten minutes before we arrived at his house. They were having a furious barney when we got there. She was still in her night clothes and was refusing to get dressed. Cassius's English isn't great, but I managed to gather that much. Anyway, it wasn't until he started dragging the children out of the house that she gave in. Then she wanted to pack everything including the kitchen sink and they had another row about that. Finally, we had left the house before I spotted the shoes she was wearing. Very stylish I have to say, but she wouldn't have got to the end of the street before she started to hobble, so we had to go back and get a change of footwear. We did get going eventually, but we lost at least half an hour."

"The children were OK?"

"They seem to be a bit dazed, not sure what was going on. My men have been taking turns to carry them. It was the only way to maintain the pace. Will we get off the beach before daylight?"

Carter checked his watch then glanced towards the eastern sky. "Should do, dawn isn't for another half hour yet, sunrise will be thirty minutes after that. So long as our friends out in the fields don't decide to contest the issue, we should make it far enough out to sea to avoid detection."

"They'll have aircraft up at first light looking for us." Stirling observed.

"By that time the RAF should have arrived. They'll chase them off."

"I hope you're right. We wouldn't want all this to be a waste of time."

They had arrived at the barbed wire and Carter came to a halt. "I'll stay here and see my men through, if you don't mind. Chaffinch is acting as beach master and he'll direct you to your landing craft. Don't hang around waiting for the rest of us, get straight back to the ship. If all else fails, you'll get away."

"Expecting more trouble?"

"Always!" Carter's teeth gleamed as he grinned into the darkness. There was a low chuckle from Stirling as he followed his men through the wire and down to the beach. Carter breathed a sigh of relief. Even if his men had to fight again, the main part of the mission had been accomplished.

"Morning, Lucky." Carter almost jumped as Ernie Barraclough gave him a cheery greeting. "I trust all is well."

"It is, Cassius is on the beach and the cover force is starting to arrive." Carter could hear the occasional grunt and swearword as the soldiers struggled across the soft sand of the dunes.

They arrived from two directions, left and right, as the two flanks closed on the gaps in the wire that had been cut so many hours earlier. The SRS with their domed parachute helmets and camouflaged smocks could have passed for Italians if Carter hadn't already identified them as friendly. His own men wore lightweight desert uniforms. Carter noticed that most of the troopers had shed their steel helmets in favour of their green berets, probably as soon as they were out of his sight. He shook his head in wonderment, fascinated that the men would rather risk a head injury than relinquish their beloved symbol.

The commandos streamed past Carter, heading back towards the landing craft. But one was moving more slowly and Carter was about to berate him for taking his time when he saw that it wasn't one man, it was two. The second man was being half carried and half dragged along towards the gap in the fence. Behind him came Villiers, recognisable mainly because of the close proximity of his radio operator, wearing his bulky backpack. Carter stood aside to allow the wounded man to be carried through.

"Who's that?" Carter asked, when the man had passed.

"Townsend. George section. Caught a stray bullet. Damned bad luck, actually." Villiers replied.

"Was he dug in?"

"No, sheltering behind the wall."

"In that case it wasn't bad luck. You knew that the troop was more vulnerable to a flanking attack than an approach from the front. The men should have been dug in."

"S ... sorry, Lucky. Never thought. The sections on the flanks were dug in ..."

"They should all have been dug in. Bullets ricochet in all directions." Carter took pity on him a little. He would learn. Unfortunately, the lesson had cost one of his men dearly. "How bad is it?"

"Just a flesh wound; clean entry and exit as far as I can see. He'll be back in …"

"He'll be shipped out to Oran or Malta." Carter interjected. "I doubt he'll be back with the commando for months. Is that all your men through?"

"Yes, Lucky."

"Good. Go with your men." Carter let the man pass him.

"Bit hard on the lad." Barraclough said quietly.

"He's got a man injured because he didn't follow the basics. When we get back, put him through some question and answer sessions on immediate actions in combat. Make sure he gets the idea that the enemy can come from any direction if you're a commando, not just in front. Now, it's time we were gone. Are you ready?"

Carter pulled a Very pistol from his belt and broke it open, sliding a flare into the chamber.

"Ready!" Barraclough confirmed.

They both cocked their Very pistols and raised them skywards. Carter fired his first, closely followed by his deputy. There was a fizzing sound as the flares shot into the night sky, before bursting into twin green balls of light. The commandos still out in the sand dunes, forming the final line of defence, knew what that meant: Two minutes to get back to the beach.

They must have been waiting for the signal, because the first of them arrived only seconds later.

The only sound was the thud of their boots on the now packed sand, then gunfire blotted that out. The men dived for cover and Carter followed them. He spat sand from his mouth.

"Easy men." Barraclough's laconic voice cut through the swearing. "They aren't firing at us."

Now able to stop and listen properly, Carter realised the troop commander was right. The sound was some distance off, back on the far side of the dunes, much closer to the track where they had come from.

"That's one lot of Ities running into the other lot in the darkness." Carter said, clambering back to his feet. "That will keep them confused for a while."

But the firing had dwindled to a few random shots, which meant that someone had managed to regain control of the situation. But the firing meant that the Italians hadn't realised that the commandos had withdrawn. Now that they had discovered it, they would send soldiers towards the beach in pursuit. The flares would point the direction.

With the panic over, the men continued their evacuation.

Carter reloaded his Very pistol and raised it once again, while he followed the path of second hand of his watch as it counted down the remainder of the first sixty seconds of the two minutes that had been set aside for the final evacuation. As the thin sliver of metal passed the twelve mark, he fired the pistol again, as did Barraclough. One red flare, one green. One minute remaining.

"Let's go, Ernie." Carter patted his subordinate on the shoulder and set off down the beach, the faithful Tpr James following in his wake.

Carter headed for the centre landing craft in the line that still sat on the beach. The ramps were being raised on two that were already full and ready to go and there was a gap between two craft further along where Stirling had already set off to take Cassius to safety. Barraclough went to the next craft in the line and stood on the ramp, ready to board.

"Ok, Ernie." Carter shouted across to him, before firing the final signal. Two red flares signified that the landing craft were leaving in thirty seconds and if anyone was left on the beach, they better shout out now or they'd be left behind.

As the second hand of Carter's watch swept towards the twelve again, he strode up the ramp. Chains rattled and the thick metal plate started to rise at the same time as the sound of the engines roared and the craft backed away from the beach.

In the darkness of the dunes, they would leave a puzzled Italian officer, wondering what could possibly have brought a reading party to his quiet section of the coast.

* * *

Carter pulled the door of his cabin shut and turned along the narrow gangway towards the stairs to the lower deck, where his men were relaxing after their night's exertions. A few doors down Cdr Flamming was also pulling a door shut. Carter walked along to meet him, Flamming extending his hand for a welcoming shake.

"Well done Lucky. A good night's work."

"We hardly did anything, Sir. It was David Stirling's boys that did all the hard work. In fact, if we hadn't been there they probably would have got out without the alarm being raised. I fear we were more of a hindrance than a help."

"I'll put it down as a team effort. Someone had to take those landing craft in and that's your speciality."

Carter could hear the sound of raised voices emanating from the other side of the door. "Mr and Mrs Cassius don't seem to have patched up their differences yet."

"No, and I doubt they will. Mrs Cassius, as you call them, is the daughter of another member of the Italian government. Her loyalties are very much split."

"Another member?" Carter noted the slip.

Flamming laughed. "Caught out, eh? Yes, you have just smuggled a senior member of the Italian government out of his country. The first rat to leave the sinking ship, but I doubt he'll be the last. But already he has been of use. He told me that it's likely that Italy will surrender within days of an invasion of the Italian mainland. That bit of news must be relayed to London, Cairo and Oran as quickly as possible. This could be the turning point of the war."

"It will certainly save a lot of lives if we're only fighting the Germans. Will they withdraw?"

"I think they'll have to. They can hardly continue to occupy the territory of a friendly nation without its agreement."

"That has never bothered the Nazis up to now, but we could be in Rome within days, then."

"You might be, but I have to babysit Cassius. We're stopping off at Palermo and I'll take him ashore and fly him to Malta. An interrogation team will come out from London to meet us there. Cassius is going to be doing a lot of talking over the next few days, but that was the deal. Everything he says will have to be gone over with a fine-tooth comb to make sure he isn't a double agent sent to confuse us."

They had reached the stairs that led both upwards and downwards. "Will you be joining us for a drink?" Carter asked.

"Later. Got to get this signal off before I can think about relaxing. Make sure they don't drink all the gin."

"Not really the drink of choice for my men." Carter laughed. "They prefer beer."

The celebrations were cut short an hour later with the arrival of a squadron of Italian SM.79 bombers, but they turned away as a pair of Mosquito fighter bombers swept down from above. One Italian aircraft trailed smoke as it dipped back over the horizon, before the sky cleared and the small flotilla made its way south to Palermo and safety.

3 – Bova Marina

The camp at Lo Bello was quiet as the two troops marched back through its gate, having been left on the harbour side at Syracuse by the landing craft from the Prince Leopold. The men were tired but they had all had time to shower while aboard the ship. Carter tried to recall what training tasks he had detailed for the day, but it eluded him, pushed out by his need to recall the details of the operation for his after-action report, or AAR as they called it. Whatever it was, it had taken the majority of the remaining troops away from the camp.

After dropping his kit onto his camp bed, he headed for the HQ tent.

"Colonel's up at Catania." Ecclestone reported.

"Major Fraser?" Carter asked.

"Out with the men, umpiring a defensive exercise."

That was it, a two-day defensive exercise. With the Prince Leopold up north with him, landing exercises hadn't been possible, so he had paired the four troops off and set them against each other, one to dig defensive positions and the other to attack them.

"Do we know why the CO is in Catania?"

"No. The call came this morning, requesting him to attend this afternoon. I heard General Dempsey's[1] name being mentioned, though. Could be another operation."

"We'll find out soon enough. No warning order issued?" A warning order was normally given in advance of an operation, telling the commando how long they had to prepare. It wouldn't contain the details, only the highlights; the number of men required, the anticipated duration and the method of transport. At least, that was the theory, but in Sicily the commando had found that the system didn't seem to apply to them. 'Go now' had been the only warning they had been given for Operation Leonardo.

"Not yet." Ecclestone rooted around in a bag on the floor. "Mail arrived while you were away, Sir." He sorted through a bundle of letters, handing five over to Carter.

The top one he recognised from its handwriting as being from his father and the second was in the feminine script of his sister. The other three were all from Fiona. The envelopes were all typed using the farm's ancient typewriter, though the letters themselves would be handwritten. Mail was something to treasured, not to be read hastily between other tasks. With the two troops he had brought back now cleaning their kit or queuing for a meal at the mess tent and the other four troops occupied in a training task, it gave him time to read the letters.

"I'll be in my tent if I'm needed." He told Ecclestone, before ducking out through the flap.

He was only halfway through his father's letter when he was summoned back to HQ. He was glad he had elected to read that one first. He would have hated to have been dragged away from reading his wife's letters.

He found the CO waiting for him, pinning a map to the chalk board. It was a large scale one featuring an area of the south coast of the toe of Italy.

"Is this it, Sir? Are we invading?" It was all the commando had talked about since the fighting had moved north to concentrate on the area around Messina, where the Axis armies were fighting a desperate rear-guard action as they tried to evacuate across the straits.

"No, a much smaller operation, for which I am going to pull rank and lead myself. You will take over command while I'm away."

Carter felt himself deflating as the disappointment hit him. While on the return from Operation Manchester he had wished for nothing but a few days of rest and relaxation while he wound down but now, after being back in camp for less than an hour, he found he was already itching to get back in action once again. He tried to disguise his feelings.

"Anything interesting?"

"Sort of. Something we've not been asked to do before. I'm to take a small team ashore at a place called Bova Marina, scout around a bit and then come back and report. We're going in tomorrow morning just before dawn, spend the day ashore and then we'll be picked up tomorrow night."

"Looking for anything specific?"

"Not really. Priority objective is Italian or German prisoners, preferably officers. Secondary is to scout the coastal area and identify any strong points that might not show up on aerial reconnaissance."

"Could they be planning a landing there as part of the invasion?"

"That was what crossed my mind. But they didn't say as much." He pointed at the map, picking out the dot that marked the objective. "It would be a good place to land and then march north to attack Reggio Calabria from the rear. Or perhaps make a diversionary landing to draw troops way from Calabria."

The town of Reggio Calabria was the well defended port on the eastern side of the Straits of Messina; the water that would have to be crossed in order to invade the Italian mainland. The well sited shore artillery was already keeping the Royal Navy at arm's length and preventing the RAF from operating over the Straits in daylight. A flanking attack would relieve a lot of pressure from a more direct assault.

"How many of you are going?"

"Just me and ten men. I'll take a section from 1 Troop and Ronnie Pickering can be my 2IC." With 1 troop being the specialist reconnaissance trained commandos, it made sense to select them for the task, though the men of the other troops would be unlikely to agree. Rivalries were just as strong within the commando as they were with other units.

"What are my orders while you're away?"

"Keep the men occupied, but don't tire them out. The invasion can't be too far away now and I don't want the men to lose their edge. I don't know what Monty has planned for us yet, but I'm sure we won't be left out."

[1] General Sir Miles Christopher Dempsey GBE KCB DSO MC, Commander in Chief, XIII Corps 1942-44.

* * *

Being left in command of the commando wasn't as demanding as it had sounded when Carter was told about it. For a start he was under no illusion that he was anything other than a caretaker. That meant that he wasn't able to implement any new initiatives. Not that he had any planned, but it would have been nice to think about what changes he might make.

But his idea of not tiring the men out was probably not what Charlie Cousens had in mind. Carter organised a series of sporting challenges that varied from football and rugby in the morning to a cross country run in the afternoon, followed by swimming races as the sun went down. By commando standards it wasn't exhausting, but it wasn't exactly restful either.

Points were recorded for wins in each event and the victorious troop was allowed into Syracuse for the evening to celebrate in the bars and cafes. Angus Fraser had ribbed him about the success of his former troop before accompanying his men into the town for the evening.

Carter settled himself into the HQ tent and focused on his latest letter to his wife. The strict censorship rules didn't allow him to report on anything related to the war. He couldn't even mention his involvement in their recent operation, so he had to restrict himself to descriptions of the landscape, the people and the culture. Though he did manage to slip in a reference to the effect that the landscape further north on the Italian mainland seemed very similar to that around Syracuse. Fiona would be able to read between the lines, providing the censors at Brigade HQ didn't spot the remark. To keep things less personal, officers' letters weren't read by anyone from within the unit. It was a lesson learned from the previous war.

* * *

The patrol arrived back in the mid-morning, but Cousens had gone straight to Catania to report after disembarking from the landing craft. He was back by mid-afternoon, riding a lorry, in the back of which sat six rather bemused looking soldiers wearing the cap badges of the Royal Artillery. They clambered down from the rear, pulling with them radio sets, batteries and other paraphernalia.

"Ecclestone! Troop commanders to me, ASAP." Cousens returned Carter's salute as he strode past him and into the HQ tent. "You too, Steven."

"Gunners?" Carter queried as he followed him in.

"Radio operators. Our sets don't have the range for what we've been asked to do, so they've been leant to us by 156th Field Regiment."

"And what have we been asked to do?"

"All in good time, Steven." Cousens set about pinning the map of the toe of Italy back onto the chalk board.

"How was your trip?"

"Uneventful. Bova Marina isn't much of a place. It's a small fishing harbour with a few houses and what looks like it might once have been a canning factory. There's a tall chimney that isn't marked on the maps which serves as a useful landmark. We landed on a beach just outside the village. No defences worthy of the name. We managed to grab an Italian prisoner. To be honest, I think he came looking for us with the intention of handing himself over. We laid a couple of the land mines I took with us. We heard one go off just after we boarded the landing craft to come back, so that will have been a nice surprise for someone."

"Could we make a major landing there?"

"Not really. The beaches are too small and the terrain isn't well suited for armour. I guess it would serve for a diversionary operation, but that's all."

The troop commanders started to arrive from wherever they had been occupying themselves. The men had been engaged in various training tasks all day, moving from one station to another to do first aid, target location, camouflage, air raid drills and so on. For the veterans it was 'make-work' but it had shown up some weaknesses in the newer arrivals, which the NCOs set about correcting.

The CO brought them up to date with what he had been doing. "Now we've been asked to do the same again, but this time with more patrols and for a longer duration." He studied their faces, trying to gauge their reactions, but most of them were focused on writing in their notebooks. This operation is called 'Tablet'

I need each of you to select a patrol of one officer and four ORs and before you get any ideas, none of you Troop commanders are going." That brought a groan of disappointment. "I'm afraid 2 Troop are excluded, Giles" Gulliver, the troop commander, let out a grunt of acknowledgement. "We won't need heavy weapons and we can't risk your trained men on an operation like this." Cousens focused his attention on the other five troop commanders.

"What your men are going to do is set up observation posts for a couple of days and report on troop movements along the coast road. When you withdraw, you're to try and take prisoners, Germans for preference but anyone who crosses your path will do. The patrols can attack targets of opportunity, but they mustn't jeopardise the main mission, which is observation first. The patrols go in tomorrow morning and Steven here," He waved in Carter's general direction, "will bring the landing craft back in to pick you up at midnight on the second day. Steven, you'll take four men with you, as well as a radio operator to call the patrols back in. If there's no response, you'll go ashore anyway and wait for them. If they aren't all back you withdraw at dawn and repeat for the next two nights. Gentlemen, if your men don't appear by then, they'll be assumed to be lost."

* * *

It was an LC(I), not the sort of craft that the commandos liked to use. While it was big enough to hold a hundred and eighty men and their equipment, it didn't have a drop-down ramp at the front, like the smaller craft. Instead it had walkways that dropped down on either side of the high bow. It meant that men could only descend in single file on either side and while the rest were waiting to get onto the ramp, the soldiers were horribly exposed to machine gun fire and snipers.

But it was the craft that the Royal Navy preferred, so the Army had no say in the matter. Carter could see the advantage for them, of course. One of these used fewer crew than the six LC(A)s[1] that they replaced and they were also better for long journeys, meaning they didn't need a mothership to stand off of an invasion beach and make itself a target for air attacks.

But that didn't mean that the commandos were any better disposed towards them. Their one advantage was that the passenger deck was covered in, meaning the soldiers were better protected from the weather. Not that the weather was really much of a consideration in September in the Mediterranean Sea.

This particular LC(I) was bucking around like a bronco at a rodeo in the heavy swell that was being pushed up by a southerly wind. The Mediterranean was usually a placid sea, but even a placid sea can be whipped up by strong enough winds. This Sirocco wind was coming straight off the Sahara Desert, warm and dry but none the less forceful for that.

Carter felt a tap on his shoulder. It was Gunner Merrell, the radio operator from the Royal Artillery who had been assigned to the operation.

"No reply from any of the shore units, Sir."

"Thanks Merrell. But please don't call me Sir while we're on this operation. Ranks and titles make people into targets. Call me nothing or call me Lucky, like the rest of my lads. Until we get back to Sicily, anyway."

"Sorry, S… Yes, I'll try to remember."

"Keep trying on the radio."

Carter made his way back to the bridge section at the rear of the craft. Compared to what he was used to it appeared to be enormous. A head appeared through a side window. "We're going to have to go in, I'm afraid" he called up to the young Lieutenant who was skippering the landing craft.

"Where do you want me to go?"

73

"If you can pick out the chimney, try to steer towards the eastern end of the beach from it. That way we'll be the furthest from the village and least likely to attract attention."

"Will do." The head disappeared and Carter felt a slight alteration to the landing craft's course.

Carter returned to the front of the craft and climbed over the beam that jutted out to either side of the bow to suspend the landing walkways. With the wind behind them, he hardly felt its affects even though he was no longer shielded by the bridge structure. But the lack of passengers meant that the craft was riding high in the water, making it more vulnerable to the wind.

He could just about make out the mass of the land in the thin starlight, darker than the sky above it. The bow lurched upwards as a larger sea washed beneath it, causing Carter to lose his balance and step backwards. The knee-high beam caught him high on his calves and he almost toppled over it.

He pushed himself upright again and then sat on the beam to avoid a repeat. It wouldn't do for him to be injured before they got ashore.

They must be about a mile offshore, Carter thought. It wouldn't take long for them to reach the beach and disembark.

He had brought four men with him, the same size of team as the patrols that he was trying to recover. Beneath the craft's decks were Sgt Prof Green, Cpl Danny Glass and LCpl Paddy O'Driscoll, his companions from previous adventures. It was unthinkable, at least to those three, that he should take anyone else with him on this jaunt. He didn't need three NCOs, but that is what he had ended up with. The fourth member of his team was Tpr Henry James, released from the burden of his radio by the presence of the Royal Artillery gunner and anxious to do some 'honest soldiering', as he had called it when he had pleaded his case to be allowed to come.

"Merrell!" Carter called back along the length of the deck, raising his voice to be heard above the sound of the wind and the rumble of the engines. "Any response from shore?"

"Nothing!" There was no title used. Good, the young man was a quick learner. Carter was unsure about the wisdom of using non-commandos on a commando operation. Artillery radio operators had to move in and out of forward observation posts in the dark, so he wasn't too concerned about their ability to creep around. But he expected a commando to be able to march all day and still be fit enough to fight at the end of it. That wasn't something that the Royal Artillery trained for. Their guns had wheels and were pulled by trucks, in which the crews also rode. It didn't make for high levels of physical fitness; at least, not as high as that demanded of the commandos.

Letting out a sigh, Carter resigned himself to the inevitable; having to move at the pace of the slowest man. Of course, it shouldn't come to that. They were simply going to land on the beach, set up a basic defence and wait for the patrols to arrive back. Once they had collected them up, they could signal the landing craft to return. Repeat for two more nights if necessary and after that any patrols that hadn't been recovered would have to fend for themselves. If they were still alive and at liberty.

Carter made his way back to where Merrell was sitting in the middle of the deck, his radio in front of him.

"Any reason why they aren't able to hear us? Or we them?"

"Could be any number of reasons. If they've used their radios a lot it could be they have flat batteries. Or they may be on the wrong side of a hill, so we can't pick up their ground wave." Carter was tempted to ask what that was but decided he didn't need to know. "Or a set might have been damaged."

Five patrols, five radio sets; was it feasible that something had happened to all of them?

"What about our set. Is it sending OK?"

"Everything looks OK to me. I did a radio check with HQ before we left and it was fine then and it hasn't had any rough treatment. All the indications are that it's working."

"Can you do a radio check with the Navy? You know, the radio on the bridge of this LC?"

"No. We're on HF, they're on VHF. Different frequencies. Even if we were both on HF they would still need the right crystals to be able to tune to the same frequency." It was another technicality that Carter decided he didn't need to know about. The Gunner knew what he was talking about. Asking him for an explanation wouldn't make the radio work if it didn't want to.

There was a groan of metal and a snick as something locked into place. Carter looked up to see a hatch open in the deck, a head appearing through it as someone climbed up the hidden ladder. It wore the flat topped hat of a naval rating. Seeing Carter, the man headed straight for him.

"Just letting your men know, we're five minutes from shore, Sir. They're on their way up."

Carter could see that for himself as the stocky figure of Danny Glass emerged from below decks, his rifle held in front him to prevent it from snagging on the hatch's coaming. They hadn't brought any automatic weapons other than Carter Tommy gun. They consumed too much ammunition and the landing craft had Lewis guns mounted either side of the bridge and if they got into a fight where they couldn't use their protection, there was little point in such a small group trying to fight its way out anyway.

The rating made his way forward to the controls that operated the winches that lowered the ramps while Danny Glass made his way to the point in the boat's rail that allowed access to the disembarkation platform. The platform ran halfway along the side of the craft, allowing the men to queue at the top of the ramp, ready to run down along it the moment the end touch the ground or, more usually, two or three feet of cold seawater.

He was joined there by the other three men who had been waiting below.

"OK, Merrell. Pick up your set and let's join them. Do you want a hand?"

"A lift up would help."

Carter heaved on one shoulder strap, easing the radio set to waist height, while the gunner bent and slid his arm through the other. He straightened, Carter lifted and the gunner shrugged his way completely in. He flexed his knees a couple of times, allowing gravity to balance the load and settle it comfortably in place. He bent at the knees, lowering himself until he could reach his rifle with one hand and the carrying straps for the spare battery with the other. It was big, at least the size of a car battery and weighed as much.

But Merrell swung it as though it was half its weight and made his way across to the boat's side.

Carter slid back the bolt that held the boarding gate in place, then slid the gate open. Turning, he used the rungs set in the boat's side to climb down the few feet to the platform, then headed off to wait at the top of the ramp, which still projected forward horizontally. The ramp would drop suddenly, as soon as the naval rating released the brake that held it up. The winch was only used to raise it once again. Standing on the ramp before it was lowered was a quick way for a commando to get an early bath.

The engine noise slackened a little as the skipper reduced the power in readiness for landing. Carter could feel that the craft was still moving at speed, propelled forward by its own weight and the thrust of the waves. He turned to look back towards the bridge, thinking to shout a warning but held his tongue. The Lieutenant knew what he was doing.

Silence fell as the power was cut completely. Well, silence but for the sound of the wind and the crash of the waves on the beach. The landing craft struck much harder than Carter was used to. He was almost thrown over the side, only saving himself by hanging onto the cable barriers that ran the length of the platform and the ramp. There was the grating of the handbrake as it was released and the ramp dropped, creating a big splash of water as it hit the sea's surface. Having regained his balance, Crater grabbed the stock of his Tommy gun, slung across his chest and ran the length of the ramp, anxious to get onto the beach before an enemy could open fire.

Once on the beach he could see that every time the sea withdrew after depositing a wave on the beach, the landing craft's bow stood well out of the water. Not only that, but there was quite a lot of sand and shingle heaped about it.

Timing his jump for when the sea withdrew from the beach once again, Carter landed dry shod and hurried a few yards up the coarse sand. His men followed, spreading out to either side. He didn't need to tell these men what to do. They headed straight for the highwater mark and the higher ground beyond, looking for positions from where they could fire on the enemy, if he was present.

But the night stayed quiet. Merrell hurried past and Carter followed him as he struggled through the sand under his burden. Behind him Carter could hear the clank of gears as the ramp was raised again, then the increasing roar of the landing craft's powerful engine as its 1600 bhp diesels dragged it back out to sea.

Carter was therefore surprised, when he turned around to look, that the landing craft was still there. Looking along the side Carter could see white foam at its transom as the propellers churned up the water, but the craft itself wasn't moving.

A head appeared over the bow. "Lieutenant Keith's compliments, Sir, but we appear to be stuck aground."

Letting out a muffled curse, Carter tried to think what to do, but came up blank. Boats weren't his thing. "Can you float it off at high tide?" he seemed to remember reading something in the newspapers when a ship had run aground off the coast.

"The Med isn't tidal, Sir[2]." If the sailor thought his lack of knowledge worthy of mockery, he managed to keep it out of his voice. Sailors were always ready mock landlubbers like Carter.

"Holy sh…." From his position Carter was able to see something that the rating couldn't. Even in the darkness he could make out the swell of an extra large wave bearing down on the shore. He turned and ran up the beach, not stopping until he was past the highwater mark.

The wave slammed into the back of the LC, lifting its stern. With the bows firmly dug into the beach they acted as a pivot and the whole landing craft was turned sideways on and driven hard against the beach. The sea withdrew after completing its victory, leaving only a small amount of the LC's stern quarter still in the water.

A landlubber Carter might be, but you didn't have to be Long John Silver to know that the landing craft would never float again; at least, not without a lot of assistance, which Carter was unable to provide.

Carter returned to the side of the now beached craft. He could see the silhouette of its commander standing next to the wheelhouse.

"Better get your men ashore." Carter shouted up to him. "If you stay there, you're bound to be taken prisoner."

Normally an LC(I) had a crew of three officers and twenty one men, but for this operation it had been reduced to just one officer and 4 men; just enough to get it in and out of port and on and off the beach. Though in this case it had failed to get off the beach. He heard splashes from the seaward side and assumed that the crew were getting rid of anything that might be of use to the enemy. Too late he realised that this would include the Lewis guns. One of those guns and a drum of ammunition for each man to carry would have been a useful asset. No point in crying over spilt milk, he thought. But the skipper could have asked him if he wanted anything salvaging.

Carter made his way back up the beach to where his men were strung out in a short defensive line.

"Bad news chaps." He whispered, his voice barely audible, "Looks like we're going to be here for some time."

[1] Landing Craft (Assault). The type of landing craft familiar to viewers of the film "Saving Private Ryan" and others. It carried 30 men and had a drop-down bow ramp that allowed the soldiers to run straight ashore from within its protective sides.

[2] The rating was wrong, all seas are tidal to some degree, but the tidal range (the difference between low and high tides) was so small that it wouldn't have provided sufficient additional depth the float the LC(I) off. The Royal Yachting Association, which issues

certificates for sailing competence in the UK, regards tidal ranges of a foot (0.3m) or less as being 'non-tidal'.

*　*　*

After an hour, Carter let them all rest. Straggling up the hill was the naval contingent. The landing craft's skipper, Henry Keith, had tried to apologise for the loss of his boat.

"I don't understand how it happened, Lucky. They teach us to approach the shore at half speed, before cutting the power. That's exactly what I did."

If he couldn't understand what had happened, then Carter wasn't going to explain it to him. If they ever got back to Sicily, Carter felt sure Keith's flotilla commander would explain it in detail and in language the sailor would understand. He had neglected to factor in the additional speed provided by the following sea. It was probably several knots. Enough to drive the landing craft hard aground. The rogue wave coming in behind completed the job. There was no point in adding tension to their situation by having a discussion about it. They would probably be here for several days before a rescue boat could be sent.

"I've made contact with Catania." Gnr Merrell offered Carter the microphone and headphones.

"Hello Daffodil, this is Peony, over." Carter said, feeling slightly silly using the callsign. It hadn't been his choice. They were just a series of words selected off a pre-prepared list somewhere in HQ.

"Hello Peony, go ahead, over."

"Daffodil, the wheels have come off our chariot. Request a new one be sent. Over"

There was a long pause and Carter wondered if the radio link had been broken.

"Negative Peony. All our chariots are busy right now. Unlikely we can reach you for a while." Carter had half expected the reply. It wasn't as if they could go to the local shop to buy a new landing craft when they needed one. "Have you located the other travellers? Over."

To avoid having to encrypt every message, they used what was known as 'veiled speech', essentially euphemisms for what was really meant. Carter assumed that the 'other travellers' referred to patrols he had been sent to recover.

"Not yet, Daffodil. No radio contact. They could be anywhere."

"Roger Peony. Keep looking and gather together if it is possible. Safety in numbers. We'll send a new chariot as soon as one becomes available. Daffodil out."

All Carter could hear in the headset was the hiss of electrons through the radio set's valves. HQ had just confirmed that they had to fend for themselves.

"How long will the batteries last?" Carter asked the radio operator.

"The one that's on the set is about half discharged. Just listening we'll probably get about five hours out of it. But every time we send, we knock at least ten minutes off that. The spare battery will last ten hours under the same restrictions."

Carter checked his watch; oh one thirty. So, if he kept the radio switched on, they'd run out of power by sixteen thirty, four thirty in the afternoon. If they actually used the radio to try to make contact with the missing patrols, that time would be reduced dramatically. He reached a decision. "We'll stay here for the time being and try to make contact in the morning. Oh eight hundred seems as good a time as any. We'll send out one transmission then wait ten minutes for a reply. We'll do the same again in the afternoon and keep that schedule going until the batteries are both flat."

"Sorry, but I think we need to move." Merrell seemed nervous about contradicting his officer. "If the Ities or the Jerries have got RDF[1] units in the area, they can locate us from our transmissions. Not precisely, it isn't that accurate, but good enough to flood the area with troops and search for us."

"Hmm. Yes, you're right." Carter acknowledged. "In that case we'll move to the next peak and set up there. Rather than keep moving the men around, we'll find a new location for the radio every time we want to use it."

Carter called the group together and gave them a hurried briefing. There were audible groans from a couple of the sailors, but Carter tried to ignore them. They weren't trained for this sort of operation and it wasn't their fault their skipper wasn't much of a sailor.

As they hiked towards the next peak in the chain of low hills that ran inland along the coast, Carter's mind turned to food. In their small packs, he and his men carried rations for twenty four hours, but the sailors had nothing but what was in their pockets, which Carter suspected wasn't much. They would share the food around, of course, but it meant that finding a food source was a matter of urgency.

Carter caught up with Merrell. "Is it possible that the reason we can't raise anyone on the radio is because they've been located by RDF?"

The gunner shrugged. "Possible, but my money would be on flat batteries. They've been here for two days. Depending on how much they used the radios, that's plenty of time for them to go flat."

Carter realised he hadn't asked Catania what contact they'd had with the patrols and when they'd last heard anything from them. That wouldn't tell him much but at least it might tell him if he was hunting for ghosts.

[1] Radio direction finding (RDF) works by using highly directional antennae to locate a radio signal. The direction the antenna is pointing when the signal is at its strongest provides a compass bearing to the signal's source, A second unit does the same, working from another location, which gives a second compass bearing. Where the two bearings cross is where the signal's source is located. This method was used by the Nazis to locate resistance groups throughout Europe. The only counters to it are to keep transmissions as short as possible to prevent the direction finders fixing the bearing and to change locations as soon as the message has been sent.

* * *

At the top of the hill stood a ring of jagged rocks, like broken teeth. It was ideal for their purposes, giving them a clear view out over the surrounding terrain. To the south the sea glinted in the sunlight, while below them were rugged fields interspersed with the odd stands of pine trees and citrus groves. The coastal highway snaked along the bottom of the valley on the north side of the hills and Carter could make out the junction where a smaller road branched off to go to Bova Marina. Beyond it was a bridge that spanned a narrow gorge, probably enclosing a dried out riverbed at this time of year.

Yes, Carter thought. It was as good a location as any. Provided the men stayed low they could only be seen from the air and if anyone tried to reach them they would be visible in plenty of time to allow an escape down the opposite side of the hill. Carter posted Paddy O'Driscoll as sentry on the inland side, where the road represented the greater danger and placed one of the naval ratings on the southern side. The ratings all had rifles and twenty rounds of ammunition, but Carter hoped they wouldn't have to use them. Lt Keith had a revolver holstered at his waist and Carter thought it about as useful as a potato masher in the present circumstances.

Once the sentries had been posted, Carter started sharing out hard tack biscuits and slices of bully beef. He had pooled their meagre supplies, taking them into his own care. He trusted his commandos not to keep the rations for themselves, but the sailors had brought nothing and he wanted to make it clear to them that they wouldn't be left out. There were tins of stew which would do for their lunch and more hard tack and bully for their supper. After that they would go hungry if they couldn't find any food. Carter wrapped a portion of the food in paper and held it back for Merrell, the radio operator. He was away finding another location from which to try to make contact with the missing patrols.

It was around seven thirty that O'Driscoll gave a hiss and waved Carter over to him. Carter crawled into the gap between two of the rocks that were providing the Irishman with a view down to the road below.

"Looks like some of the lads are still around." He pointed and Carter followed the line of his arm towards the bridge that spanned the gorge. Sure enough, there were five tiny figures working their way along the side of the road, moving in short sprints. From this distance it wasn't possible to identify to which army they belonged, but Carter thought it unlikely that either the Germans or the Italians would be sneaking around like that. It had to be one of the commando patrols. They were coming from the west, the far side of Bova Marina. That probably meant they were the patrol from either 1 or 3 troops.

When the patrols had gone ashore, they were instructed to head in set directions. 1 and 3 troops were to go west, 4 troop straight inland and 5 and 6 troops went east. That way the patrols could cover more ground and not risk running into each other in the dark.

"No sign of the radio operator." Carter noted.

"I'm not surprised. Not much point lugging something like that around if it isn't working, Sorr. It would only slow them down."

"I wonder what they're up to?"

He wasn't left waiting long for an answer. The sound of an engine could be heard and Carter looked east to see what its source was. A Fiat truck was lumbering along the road. Was it a regular run? Carter wondered. Had the patrol spotted it on the previous days and were now deciding to target it? Their orders allowed them to do so if it wasn't too high risk. He looked back towards the patrol and couldn't spot them. "Where are they?" he wasn't really expecting an answer. Good commandos had an ability to disappear into thin air when it suited them.

"Either side of the road at the far end of the bridge." O'Driscoll provided.

Straining his eyes, Carter thought he might just be able to make out the barrel of a rifle extending from behind one of the concrete posts that marked the start of the bridge. But he might be wrong.

The truck rumbled on, the driver oblivious to the danger he was in. "Wait for it! Wait for it!" Carter muttered under his breath, willing the commandos to hold their fire until the optimum moment, which would be when the truck was in the middle of the bridge and not able to turn around. Ideally, they would have had commandos positioned at both ends of the bridge, to seal the trap, but there was only so much they could do with five men.

He saw the truck skid diagonally across the road to block the bridge before he heard the distant pop of the rifle shots that caused the crash. Then came the sound of tearing metal as the truck slid along the crash barrier before coming to a halt.

Four of the distant figures moved, two running straight to the truck and wrenching the cab doors opened while the remaining two aimed their rifles at the cab windows. Two more shots were heard as the occupants were dealt a coup de grace. The group moved on towards the rear, one breaking off to sprint to the end of the bridge and cover the approaches.

The three still at the lorry unhooked the tail gate and let it drop. Two clambered in while one, probably the officer, remained on the ground. Carter strained his eyes to try to identify him. By his size and build it could be Ben Flanders, the leader of the patrol that had been drawn from 1 Troop. The fifth man stayed in cover at the other end of the bridge.

A packing case was heaved over the rear of the truck and allowed to drop to the ground. It splintered, scattering the contents across the road. The man on the ground gave it a cursory examination, then stood back. Clearly there was nothing in it of interest to the commandos. They were almost certainly looking for food.

A second packing case dropped to land on the wreckage of the first. It too splintered and was subjected to scrutiny. Still nothing. A third was ejected from the truck and the two men inside followed it to the ground. Obviously the last bit of the truck's cargo. This case hadn't broken, so the two men set about it with rifle butts, splintering the lid.

Still nothing.

The leader waved an arm, recalling his sentry and the four men trotted off in the direction they had arrived from. The whole operation had been concluded in under five minutes.

Passing the truck's fuel tank, one of the commandos bent over and stabbed at it with his bayonet. Satisfied with the result, he stood back, struck a match and dropped it into the spreading pool of fuel before sprinting after the others. It took a second or so for the dull whump of the erupting fire to reach Carter's ears, but he could see the effects before he heard the sound. A pall of oily smoke climbed into the air above the truck. At about a hundred feet the plume flattened and started to drift northwards on the gentle breeze, which was all that could be felt on that side of the hill.

"I think we can expect company" Carter muttered to O'Driscoll. "Keep your eyes peeled and let me know when it arrives."

O'Driscoll gave a resentful grunt of acknowledgement, as though he needed reminding of his duties as a sentry.

He told the remaining commandos and the sailors what he had seen. "So, there's at least one patrol still in action around here. The trouble is, we don't know where they're going and by the time we get down to the road they'll be long gone. I think we'll stay here, where we can see any movement on the road and the next time we see them I'll send a pair of you down to try to make contact. In the short term, whoever comes to investigate that smoke may well carry out a search, so we'll have to be ready to move at a moment's notice."

He split the men into two groups, one of which was allowed to sleep while the other stayed awake, ready to move straight into the cover of the rocks to provide a defence if necessary.

At around nine o'clock Merrell returned, lowering his heavy radio to the ground and stretching to ease the strain in his back that his burden had inflicted.

"Nothing, Lucky." He reported. "I picked up some crackling which might have been someone keying a microphone switch, but nothing audible. I finished by broadcasting that we'd try again at twenty hundred hours, just as you said. I'll have to leave earlier, because I'm going to have to go further afield to find a suitable location. It isn't safe to use that one again for a couple of days.

An Italian patrol arrived two hours later, travelling from the west, which suggested it was looking for an overdue vehicle rather than having had the incident reported to it. Carter was aware that there were no telephone wires in the local area, suggesting that communications were poor in this part of Italy. The patrol was travelling in two Fiat trucks, not dissimilar to the one that had been attacked, though these weren't enclosed by canvass awnings.

Spotting the truck on the bridge the commander brought the vehicles to a halt a good hundred yards short. Men spilled over the sides and rear of the vehicle and went into defensive crouches around the small convoy. The commander climbed out of the cab and took a few steps long the road towards the bridge before coming to a standstill. He raised his binoculars and surveyed the scene, satisfying himself that he wasn't leading his men into a trap.

He waved two men forward and they jogged along the road, one on either side of it, until they reached the start of the bridge. From there they slowed to a walk and approached the truck with some caution. The fire had burnt itself out through lack of fuel, but wisps of smoke still drifted upwards from the smouldering remains.

Satisfying themselves that there were no survivors, they continued to the far end of the bridge before returning to report.

The officer split them into sections and dispatched them to the four corners of the compass, but their search was only cursory. Having seen the wreck of the truck, no one was keen to become the next victim of whoever had done that. After a short while the platoon reunited and the officer set them to the task of recovering the bodies of the crew before hooking the wreck up to one of the other trucks. With s screech of tearing metal, the truck was hauled off the bridge and tipped off the side of the road where it wouldn't cause an obstruction. No doubt a recovery vehicle would be sent out in due course. The patrol then set about salvaging the scattered cargo.

Carter's men watched out of curiosity, from their perch high on the top of the hill. From what Carter could see the Italian officer never even glanced in their direction.

With the road re-opened, the soldiers re-mounted their vehicle and returned the way they had come.

For the rest of the day the traffic was light. There was the occasional car or motorcycle, a small convoy of military vehicles led by an armoured car headed west but for most the time nothing moved east or west. It was as though the whole of Italy was holding its breath, waiting for the other shoe to drop. The shoe that was the Allied invasion.

* * *

The going was difficult once darkness had fallen, but Carter and Merrell picked their way carefully across the hillside, heading back to hilltop where the rest of Carter's men still lay concealed. Once again, they had failed to make contact with any of the other patrols, though they had made contact with Catania to let them know they were still at liberty.

He would have to send a man back to the beach to see if anyone turned up that night. It would be a lonely job as he wasn't going to risk losing more than a single man if the enemy were waiting there. The landing craft was bound to have been discovered, so their presence would be no secret, even without the attack on the truck by the other patrol.

He would give the Naval officer that job. He'd got them into this fix, he could now make himself useful. He could build a bonfire from driftwood to attract attention but stay hidden in case anyone other than commandos turned up to see what it meant.

A cough came from behind Carter and he froze. He could have sworn there was no one there as he walked along the path.

"Don't panic, old chap." The voice was pure English Home Counties, but not one he recognised.

"Who's there?" He challenged, not turning around in case whoever it was saw the movement as a threat. Just because he spoke flawless English it didn't mean the unidentified man was a friend.

"Very much a friend, old boy." There was a chuckle. "I thought you commandos were supposed to be good at moving around undetected."

"I'll need more than just your assurances that you're friendly." Carter wasn't about to drop his guard.

"You can call me Walter, if you like." The voice said. "It isn't my name, but I suppose you have to call me something."

"Are you British?"

"As British as you, old chap. And, as I said, I'm a friend."

"Can I turn around?"

"Be my guest."

Carter turned slowly, not wishing to alarm the man. What seemed like a giant stood behind him. All he could make out in the darkness was a shape, but it was a big shape.

"So, Walter, what are you doing skulking around in Italy."

"Much the same as you, I would guess. I've seen your chaps wandering around for the last few days. Dammed good ambush they set up this morning. Textbook stuff. Was that you?"

"I'm glad you approve. No, not me." Carter peered into the darkness, trying to pick out more detail, such as whether the man was carrying a weapon. "Look, if you aren't one of my men, which I'm now sure you aren't, just who the hell are you."

"Can't answer that, I'm afraid. But I can tell you that I'm working with local partisan groups. We have very much the same interests as you. Inflicting damage on the Ities and the Jerries and making life difficult for them."

That rang a bell with Carter. There had been rumours of a secret organisation[1] based in London who dispatched agents across occupied Europe to work with resistance groups. No one would admit they existed, but every commando seemed to know someone from their unit who had headed off to a meeting in London, never to return. What they had in common was a knowledge of European languages and a thirst for adventure, which was what had enticed them into the commandos in the first place.

"What made you introduce yourself tonight?"

"I've had my men shadowing your patrols, keeping an eye on them as best we can, watching what they were doing. I was just waiting for the right opportunity to make contact. That opportunity came this evening when one of my men saw you heading down this hill. You seem to be new to the area, not one of the patrols we've seen before. Anyway, I guessed what you were doing when my man said you had a radio with you. Wise precaution by the way. The Jerries have had RDF teams in the area, though we haven't seen any recently. I just sat playing doggo till you came back past me again."

"It gave me a bit of a start."

"Sorry old man. But if you'd seen me you might have taken a shot at me. It's risky enough out here without my fellow countrymen shooting at me."

"So, what can I do for you?"

"I've got a bit of a joint venture that might be of interest to you. Should be right up your street. There's an Italian military vehicle workshop and warehousing site a few kilometres north of here. I've been thinking of hitting it for months now, but I don't have enough men for the job. But with your assistance, we'd be able to pull it off. What we're really interested in is the warehouses. I'm pretty sure one of them is storing food. We rely heavily on friendly locals not giving us away to the authorities, so to be able to play Lady Bountiful with some food supplies would go down well."

"You know that the invasion is being mounted any day now, don't you? You only have to hold out for a little bit longer and there will be British or American troops all over this area."

"I know. I have a network of contacts telling me what's happening on the west coast. But we won't be staying in the area once the invasion starts. Our job is to stay behind the Axis lines and disrupt their operations. We'll be moving north as soon as the landings start. We'll go all the way to the Alps if need be. So having food for ourselves and food we can hand out to pay our way is essential. The Italians are pretty hungry these days, so a little bit of food goes a long way when it comes to establishing good will."

"I'll need to check you out, you know. You could be a Jerry for all I know. Or a traitor who's gone over to their side."

The man let out another good natured chuckle. "Of course. Tell you what, when you make your next radio contact with your HQ, tell them that Pietro sends his regards to Andrea. It may take a while, but someone will get a message back to you confirm my identity."

"And how do I contact you again?"

"Be here tomorrow evening. I'll be on my own and if you're happy, I'll take you to see the target and you can decide how you want to attack it."

"You're pretty sure I want to be involved."

"If I know anything about your lot, you're probably itching to have a go at something. You're stuck here just like me, so you want to make yourself feel useful."

"How do you know we're stuck."

"That bloody great boat of yours stranded on the beach at Bova Marina wasn't left there by the Tooth Fairy. Clumsy that."

It was Carter's turn to chuckle. "Yes. Well, you're right. We are stuck here until they send another boat for us, or until the Army gets here after the invasion."

"There you are then. May as well make a nuisance of yourselves in a good cause then."

"I don't suppose you have any food to spare, do you?" Carter asked hopefully.

"No, I'm afraid not. But you know where the ambush happened this morning. If you go north along this side of the gorge for about two kilometres, you'll come to a farm. The old couple that live there are anti-fascist. If you've got something to trade, they'll probably give you some bread, eggs and maybe some sausage. Signore Manfreddi his name is. Doesn't speak a word of English, but you can probably get by with a bit of mime. You can trust him."

"Thanks, well, I guess I'll see you tomorrow evening. Are you on your own, by the way."

Walter gave another of his wry chuckles. "You've had four rifles aimed at the pair of you since the moment you got here. But you won't see the men holding them. Not unless they want you to."

A shiver ran along Carter's spine. If he had been German he might well have been lying dead by now.

"Oh, one final thing. Don't mention this to the rest of your men. If they get caught I can't have them telling the Ities about us, so keep it under your hat for the moment."

"Of course. I understand. Goodnight then."

But the man was gone. Carter hadn't heard him move.

"Come on, Merrell. Let's get out of here before we meet anymore ghosts."

[1] This was the Special Operations Executive (SOE). They were so secret that their name was completely unknown to all but Churchill and few senior government officials until after the war. Their American counterpart, set up after they entered the war and using the British model, was the Office of Strategic Services (OSS) who transformed to become the Central Intelligence Agency after the war. For a very good (and readable) account of the work of the SOE, read "Churchill's Ministry of Ungentlemanly Warfare" by Giles Milton

* * *

Carter sent Merrell off by himself to carry out the radio check and took Prof Green with him to the meeting with Walter. The man had said he would be alone, but he hadn't said that Carter couldn't' have a bodyguard with him.

They didn't have long to wait before a low whistle came out of the darkness to let them know someone was close by. Again, Carter had heard nothing. He wondered if Walter had been waiting in the darkness to make sure they hadn't been followed by an enemy patrol.

Walter, as he chose to call himself, appeared from the darkness. "Follow me. We've about seven kilometres to cover." He set off at a brisk pace. Carter and Green had to stride out to prevent themselves losing him in the darkness again.

"You seem confident we won't run into an enemy patrol." Carter whispered when he had caught up with him.

"We're well off the beaten track, miles from anywhere. The Germans and Italians have no cause to bring them out this way. My men went ahead of us about an hour ago, so if there had been any activity along the route, they'd have warned me. Not much happens in these hills without us knowing about it."

Carter wasn't sure whether to feel re-assured but reasoned that Walter wouldn't have been alive still if he had taken any unnecessary risks.

At the pace Walter set, they covered the distance quickly. He didn't even slow down on the hills and two commandos found they were beathing heavily trying to keep up with the man.

"Are you part mountain goat?" Carter puffed as they crested a ridge. Walter laughed.

"These mountains keep you fit. But surely you commandos aren't struggling, are you?" It was banter, Carter felt sure, rather than mockery. He decided to retaliate in kind.

"Don't you worry about us. We'll still be marching when you're on your knees. We go for distance, not speed."

"Fair enough." They fell silent as they slid and skidded their way down the other side of the hill and into a valley. "Last one." Walter said, leaning forward to address the slope on the other side. "I'll stop just before the summit and we'll crawl forward. F there are nay keen eyed sentries, they'll be able to see us as we go over the top, so we will have to start being more careful."

"Won't they have screening patrols out?"

"No. They feel pretty secure. Besides, they don't have enough men for that sort of thing."

Ten minutes later, Walter dropped to his knees and they started a slow crawl forwards for the last hundred yards of their journey. At the top of the hill stood a cluster of stunted pine trees, bent to one side by the wind. Walter steered them into their shadow.

Carter saw their objective for the first time. It was a large, fenced compound, lit up along its perimeter but dark in the middle.

"No blackout." Carter observed.

"No. If the air raid sirens sound, they shut off the lighting, but I think they feel more secure with their fence lit up like that."

"Helpful for us though." Carter pulled his binoculars out of his pack and raised them to his eyes.

The compound was about two hundred yards along its near side and perhaps half that across. The end closest to them, which Carter thought was probably the eastern end, had two warehouses filling up most of the area. He could see the pale line of a road along the front of them, used for deliveries and collections, he assumed. The road separated the warehouses from the fence, with a little bit of ground left over, forming a verge on both sides.

To the west of that another long building stood at right angles to the first two. Its sides were open, like a Dutch barn. Along the fence on both sides stood a mixture of vehicles.

"The two big buildings are the warehouses," Walter explained "and the other building is a workshop. The vehicles on this side are the ones that have been repaired and are awaiting collection and the ones on the far side are the ones still waiting to be dealt with. Our thinking was to use a couple of the trucks that have been repaired to load the food supplies into. The rest we'll set fire to."

"Are you sure about what's in the warehouses?"

"Reasonably so. We've been watching this place off-and-on for weeks. The mechanics from the workshop are in and out of the left-hand warehouse all day, and we're pretty sure they're collecting spares for the vehicles. The big doors on the other warehouse are kept shut and the storemen use a Judas gate to go in and out. They only open the big doors if there's a delivery or collection. We've seen sacks of various sizes being loaded onto the lorries, which we think may be rice or flour, or both. They also load cardboard cartons of various sizes, which we think probably contain tinned goods.

They definitely have cans of olive oil in there because they're big enough to read the labels on them through binoculars.

"How many men?"

"As close as we can tell, the total strength is about thirty. They mount their own guards, presumably on some sort of rota basis. They seem to split into three shifts. One lot in the workshop and the warehouses, one lot on guard and the last lot off duty. They're billeted in a village about two kilometres down the road, so once they've finished work for the day there's only the guard force on duty. Eight to ten men, presumably under an NCO. Three on duty at a time; two on the gate and one on mobile patrol around the fence. They change over at the end of each circuit."

Carter panned the binoculars westward and made out the glow of cigarettes at the far end of the compound, next to a large hut that must be the guardhouse. He also noticed that there were watch towers at each corner and about halfway along two long sides of the compound. "Nobody in the watchtowers?"

"Never seen anyone in them. They just don't have enough men. The Ities lost so many in North Africa and their coastal defences are taking priority these days. Every man who can hold a rifle seems to be in a pillbox. There's been a lot of desertions too. We've even picked up a few recruits that way, not that we trust them as far as we can throw them. I think the only reason this place is still operating is because the Italians are so short of transport that they need to keep on fixing everything they can. The minute our lads hit the beach, this lot will head for the hills."

"So you could just wait for them to leave."

"Yes, but they might take the food with them or, worse, set fire to it all so the Allies don't get their hands on it. So we need to make sure they don't get the chance to do that. Besides, as I told you, we'll be withdrawing at the same time and we may not have time to hit this place before we find ourselves on the wrong side of the lines and having to play catch-up. We'd rather be on the other side, blowing up bridges to slow down the retreat."

"OK. What's your plan?"

"I've got eight men available in the area right now. Four of them would go down the road towards the village and cut the electricity supply, so we can operate in darkness. Power-cuts aren't unusual these days so the guards won't think too much of it. They'd then set up an ambush to stop the soldiers in the town from coming to the rescue. Not that I think they would, but you can never be sure.

The other four will do a recce of the area and then withdraw to wait for us. How many men can you bring?"

That morning Carter had managed to intercept one of their patrols, moving along the road to try and lay another ambush. Instead he ordered them up the hill to join his men. Thanks to Walter's tip-off about Snr Manfreddi, they had been able to buy food from the old man and the patrol didn't need to risk their lives trying to ambush a vehicle that might be carrying nothing worth having in the first place but might equally be full of armed soldiers.

"I've got ten commandos, including myself. I want to put a party on the beach to try and attract the attention of any ships at sea that might be able to lift us off, so I'd probably only bring six with me. How does that sound?"

"Your six, plus my four plus me. Yes, I think that should do it. What would be your plan of attack?"

"Wait for the patrolling sentry to pass, then cut our way in. make our way along the opposite sides of warehouse. Then we sneak up on the guards. Finally, we throw grenades into the guard house to take care of the ones that are asleep."

"You're sure you can do that without raising the alarm? If the other guards are roused, we'll end up in a firefight, which may mean not getting what we came for. And neither of us want to lose any men without achieving a result."

"Nothing can be certain, but I'd bet my pension on us getting to that gate without being detected."

"Well, if we don't, you may never live to draw your pension. OK. While your men are going down one side of the warehouses, I'll send my four down the other to take care of the mobile guard. They can cut their way in further along the fence line and lie in wait for him. Then they'll go straight to the food warehouse and wait for me to bring the first truck up."

"I haven't asked this up until now. It seemed a bit rude, but what's in this for us?"

"You mean apart from the glory?" Walter gave a low chuckle. "We'll drop as much food as six men can carry at the hole you make in the back fence. I assume you'll be going out that way?"

"Unless there's a quicker way to where we started."

"No, that's your quickest way back."

"What do you think, Prof?" He had brought his sergeant along to provide his opinion on the operation, so it seemed silly not to get it.

"Doesn't seem too demanding. Like you said, I back our boys against a bunch of Itie mechanics any day of the week; even ones with rifles. And we may need that food if we can't get a boat to pick us up and we have to wait for 8th Army to arrive."

"Any changes to the plan you can think of?"

"Only to leave a couple of men at the back fence, just in case. I know there aren't any other enemy troops in the area, but we've been caught napping before."

Quite literally, Carter knew, but he didn't think Green was referring to his lapse in Sicily. "So, four men to tackle two sentries who probably won't be that alert in the first place, then deal with the guardhouse. Yes, I think we can do that."

"OK. Looks like we have a plan then. Meet me with your men at the same place tomorrow night, an hour after sunset."

"That's very early."

"We won't be going in at that time. We'll rest up when we arrive and go in about two in the morning. Now, I've got go and find my men."

"And how do we get back tonight, without a guide?"

"Compass bearing one six five magnetic[1] will take you straight to the base of the hill you're sitting on and there shouldn't be anything in your path except trees, bushes, walls and the odd stray goat."

[1] Compass bearings used in land navigation come in two sorts: grid and magnetic. The grid bearing will be the one taken by plotting the bearing on a map. Magnetic bearings compensate for the variation caused by the continual drift of the magnetic North Pole. Grid north on maps produced by the Ordnance Survey is updated at regular intervals to account for the shift in magnetic north, the latest update being applied in 2014. Depending on the direction of drift, sometimes it is necessary to add the margin of error to correct the grid bearing and sometime to subtract it. It is also subject to continental, national and regional variations. Currently in the UK, east of a line that stretches from Anglesey to Plymouth, it is necessary to deduct a small fraction of 1 degree from the grid bearing. This has been the first time the adjustment has been deducted, rather being added, since 1690 and is contrary to the old navigator's mnemonic of "Mag to grid, get rid; grid to mag, add". Over the next 12 years this variation will shift to include the whole of the UK mainland.

* * *

The men were allowed to rest up the next day to prepare them for the night attack on the Italian compound. He didn't even send anyone to see if Snr Manfreddi had any more food he would be willing to sell. What they had they shared out during the day, with the promise of fresh supplies the next day if the operation went according to plan.

The naval personnel were sent down to the beach, tasked with keeping a watch on the coast for any passing ships and to keep a bonfire burning at night. They took 1 Troop's radio and their operator, with the spare battery from Merrell's set, but with strict instructions to conserve power by only transmitting if help was in sight.

There had been no sign of any other patrols, either on the road or on the beach and Carter assumed that they were in the hills doing much as he was about to do, harassing the enemy by night and resting up during the day. That was if they hadn't been killed or captured. Though Walter had assured him that if they had been captured, he would have heard about it, so that seemed an unlikely possibility.

As the sun started to set, he led his raiding party down the side of the hill, across the road and through the deserted countryside to his rendezvous with Walter. Carter had checked him out with Catania, using the code words that Walter provided. After a considerable delay, presumably while London was consulted, he was told that he was legitimate and could be trusted. More than that, he was instructed to offer Walter what assistance he could while he was in the area.

At the same time, Catania had told him that they still didn't have a ship or a landing craft that could pick them up.

They crossed the road in a rush of bodies, sliding down the embankment on the far side, then made their way across the hills. By the time they arrived at the rendezvous, dark had fallen but they were early. Walter, on the other hand, appeared exactly on time and once again Carter wondered if he had been observing them from a safe distance.

They didn't exchange any conversation on this occasion. Walter just beckoned and they rose from their meagre cover and followed. There was no need for conversation. Carter had briefed his men, sketching a map of the objective into the dust of the hilltop with a bayonet tip to illustrate the plan. They each knew their role, right down to deciding who would throw the grenades into the Italian guardhouse.

Their pace wasn't quite as brisk as it had been the previous night, but they still arrived at the objective with more time to spare than Carter felt was necessary. But at least it gave him time to observe the compound from the top of the hill and for his men to convert their mental image of the place into a real one.

Nothing had changed, so far as Carter could see. The sentries still made their rounds at regular intervals and the shift changed every two hours. Carter wondered if there was an army anywhere in the world that didn't use a two hours on, four hours off rotation for their guards.

Shortly after midnight they left the hilltop to follow a circuitous route down the side to bring them close to the rear fence of the compound.

Whoever had first established the site, had created a two hundred metre clear zone, giving sentries an unobstructed field of fire across which to see anybody approaching the wire. But that was in daylight. At night it just seemed to deepen the darkness outside of the pools of light illuminating the ground for about thirty yards outside the wire. The same lighting robbed the sentries of their night vision, which meant that they would be virtually blind when the lights went off. It would be a short-term blindness of course, their eyes would adjust, but it would give the commandos time to get to the fence and cut their way through it.

To protect their own night vision, the commandos used a trick developed by sailors during the days of sail, when they had to go from bright sunlight into the darkness of the lower gun decks. They kept one eye covered. It was the origins of the stereotype of the pirate wearing a patch over one eye.

Carter's watch ticked slowly round to oh one hundred hours, the agreed time for the electricity to be cut. The second hand swept past the hour mark and nothing happened. Carter wondered if the partisans had been discovered or prevented from carrying out their task, then remembered that there had been no opportunity to synchronise watches. They weren't late, they were just working to a slightly different time.

The fence was plunged into darkness so suddenly that Carter was taken by surprise, despite the fact that he had been expecting it. Beside him Prof Green rose to his feet and dashed towards the fence, followed closely by Paddy O'Driscoll. The rest of the party waited in cover, just in case the lights came back on as suddenly as they had gone out. No point in risking more men than necessary and a precaution against there being a back-up electricity supply.

But the lights stayed out. After five minutes Carter led his men forwards. There had been no sound from the fence, but he could see that a hole had been cut, large enough for them to crawl through. Prof Green was just strapping the wire cutters back onto the side of O'Driscoll's pack.

Two men held the wire apart while two others made their way through, then they held the wire in turn to allow the rest through. Equipment snagged, causing the fence to rattle, but it couldn't be helped. They had to carry all their equipment with them because they could never know what might be needed and what they wouldn't. They also couldn't guarantee being able to return to the top of the hill to collect any equipment left behind.

Carter took an angled route towards the corner of the nearest warehouse, then waited for his men to catch him up. They used their 'ghost walk', placing their weight carefully onto the outside edge of their boot, so that they could pause if they felt a stone or twig might move to give them away, then rolling the foot flat to take their full weight once they were sure they wouldn't make any noise. It was slow, but it was a tried and tested method of moving silently.

Their patience paid off and they made it to the final corner of the open sided workshop without making any sound that was loud enough to attract the attention of the sentries on the main gate. At this end, however, the workshop did have sides, enclosing what was probably office space.

They stopped to catch their breath, then Carter heard a voice calling out. He couldn't make out the words, but it sounded like a question being asked.

The absence of the third sentry, the one patrolling the wire, must be starting to cause concern, Carter thought.

Which was good in one way, thought Carter, because it meant that the partisans that had entered the compound from the northern side must have done their job and silenced the man. But it was also bad, because it was raising the suspicions of the two men on the gate and making them more alert.

What would they do? Would they wait to see if the man arrived? Would they wake the guard commander and report the man missing? Would one of them go and look for the man?

Carter could just make out a shadow moving close to the gate. Barely more than a slightly blacker shape against the darkness. So, there was one man still there. He saw Walter detach himself from the side of the workshop and head straight towards the fence line. The man would be looking to Carter's right, so Walter was going to approach along the fence from the left, coming up behind the sentry. But what about the second sentry?

Carter beckoned behind him, summoning the commando closest to him. In the darkness he couldn't even tell who it was.

He pulled the man close, his lips almost touching the man's ear.

"Go around the back of the workshop. Wait at the far corner. If you can see the guard, make some noise to attract him towards you". He breathed.

He felt the man nod, then move away into the darkness.

He beckoned another man forward. "Go through the workshop to the far side and wait. When the guard passes you, get behind him and deal with him." Carter didn't have to explain what he meant by that euphemism.

The fact that the workshop had open sides to allow vehicles in and out, turned out to be useful. The bulk of a truck parked inside even provided shadowy cover.

Carter felt the tension building inside him as he waited. There was nothing he could do and that was frustrating. His men would either succeed in dealing with the guard or the guard would raise the alarm when he heard the noise.

A clattering split the night air as Carter's man took his instruction to make a sound a bit more literally than Carter had intended. Or perhaps he had tripped over something in the darkness. Either way, it resulted in a frightened sounding shout on the far side of the workshop. A few seconds later, there was the sound of scuffling from Carter's front. Almost certainly Walter attacking the sentry at the gate while he was distracted by what was going on elsewhere.

A beam of light appeared, a torch lighting up the ground in front of the guardhouse. "*Cosa sta succedendo là fuori?*" a voice called out. The torch started scanning the area, lighting up features at random.

"*Scusa, sono un po 'goffo stasera*" Walter replied from the gate.

The torch shone on the figure stading there, but the light was weak at that distance. All it showed was a figure sitting bheind the sandbags of a gun pit, holding his hand in front of his face tom protect his eyes from the light.

"*Justy tieni basso il rumore.*" came a reply, before the door was shut, extinguisihing the light at the same time.

Of course, Carter had no idea what the words had meant, but Walter seemed to have satisfied whoever had come to the door that everything was OK.

"The guard commander's awake." A voice whispered from the darkness, followed by Walter's large body alsmost tipping Carter off balance as he arrived back at the workshop.

"There's been no sound from the other sentry." He replied. "I think he must have been dealt with."

"Only one way to find out." Walter replied. "Are you ready?"

"As I'll ever be."

Before they could move, a rising blare of noise assaulted their ears and a siren started up. It was far enough away to be in the village, but loud enough to wake the guard force, if they weren't already awake. Carter cursed. An air-raid. No sooner had the thought crossed his mind than the door of the guardhouse opened and Carter could hear the crash of boots on the ground as figures tumbled out, heading for the slit trenches that served as air-raid shelters. Voices gabbled and there was laughter. Presumably this was a regular enough occurrence for it not to be taken too seriously.

Ahead of them, along the valley towards the west, Carter could make out bright fingers probing the sky as searchlights sought out the bombers. Flashes reflected off the base of the clouds as anti-aircraft guns started firing.

"This could be an opportunity for us." Walter said in his ear, not loud enough to be heard above the muttering of the distant guns. "If we attack the air-raid trenches, it will be like shooting fish in a barrel."

"But where are the trenches?" Carter asked. In answer to the question, a match flared in the darkness. A stream of angry Italian resulted in it being extinguished before it could be used to light a cigarette.

The drone of approaching aircraft could now be heard, but Carter paid them no heed. Wherever their target was, it didn't concern him.

"OK. I need to brief the men, though." It wasn't what had been planned, so the men needed to know what was going to happen.

He beckoned the small group towards him, though they were already within touching distance of each other. The two he had dispatched to take care of the sentry had returned, he saw. "The guards are in the air-raid trenches." He breathed. "Walter and I will go forward, with two more of you," he tapped the two closest men on the shoulders. He thought they might be Green and O'Driscoll. Danny Glass, he knew, was one of the two men watching the rear fence. "We rush them and start firing into the trench. Walter's got a Sten gun and I've got my Tommy gun. We'll rake the length of it. If anyone tries to get out, use your rifles on them."

"What if they have their hands up?" Green asked.

"No prisoners." Walter hissed.

"Yes!" Carter almost shouted to over-rule him. "If they want to surrender, we let them."

"In that case, you can take care of the fuckers." Walter grumped. "I didn't know the commandos were bloody choir boys." He muttered, just loud enough for Carter to hear. Carter decided to ignore the jibe. He had never allowed a surrendering soldier to be shot and he wasn't about to start now. Most of the Italians in the compound would be prisoners within days anyway. It would hardly make any difference to them if they saw sense and surrendered now. They wouldn't take the men with them, it would just slow them down, but he wasn't going to waste time explaining that to Walter.

Disarmed and without boots, the Italians wouldn't be able to cause any trouble for them as they withdrew.

"You two," he tapped the remaining two men on the shoulder, "Cut through to other side of the workshop and watch our backs. OK. Follow me." Carter said, rising to his feet and edging towards the corner of the workshop, ready to make the diagonal run across the open ground towards the guardhouse and the slit trenches alongside it.

"You go left," he instructed Walter, as he turned right.

Walter ran out with his long, loping stride. Carter had just stepped into the open when the ground in front of him erupted and threw him bodily into the end wall of the building.

* * *

The only thing that Carter could sense was pain. It felt like his body was just one massive ball of agony. But worst of all was his head, which felt like someone was on the inside trying to hammer their way out. That must have been one hell of a party, he thought.

No, that wasn't right. His memory rushed back, like the sea filling a hole in the sand. He was in Italy, on an operation. Or at least, he thought he was.

And why couldn't he hear anything? It was like his ears had been filled with cheese. And why cheese? Why not wax, which is what you normally found in your ears.

And why was someone slapping his face? Maybe he *was* at a party and this was some girl he had got a bit fresh with, like Gladys, the barmaid in the student's union. She'd slapped his face when he'd tried to … what had he been trying to do?

His head was reeling from one idea to another, confused and unable to join two coherent thoughts together.

"Lucky!". His face was slapped again and a muffled voice managed to break past the cheese barrier. "Lucky! Can you hear me?" Another slap.

"For fuck's sake stop slapping me." Carter attempted to fend the hand off, but he could barely raise his own hand from the ground.

He tried force his eyes open. It felt like they were gummed up. He flinched as cold water was splashed on his face and some of the gum came loose, enough for him to sense some flickering lights, but not enough to make out what they were. Bad fieldcraft. They shouldn't be showing any lights. He'd have someone on a charge for that.

Arms lifted him so that he was sitting upright. When they let him go again, he felt himself falling backwards until he was grabbed once more.

"You've had a bang on your head." The voice continued. "Try to stay awake." More water splashing on his head and face while one hand continued to support him. "You've got a headwound. Superficial, I think, but it's bleeding a lot." The voice was getting clearer now. The water must be washing the cheese out of his ears. Why did he think he had cheese in his ears? Oh yes, he was in Italy and they had nice cheese. That was why.

Pull yourself together! Carter's inner commanding officer berated him. You do not have cheese in your ears. You were hit by a blast of some sort and that's affected your hearing.

Of course. that makes far more sense than the cheese, he thought.

A cloth wiped his face, starting at his eyebrows before moving more gently across his eyelids and then roughly across the rest of his face.

"What happened?" He managed to force some words between his lips.

"Fucking RAF dropped a stick[1] of bombs on us. Well, maybe it was the Yanks. It's dark, so who knows."

It was Danny Glass's voice. But Glass was supposed to be two hundred yards away at the far end of the compound.

What compound? Oh, that's right, we were attacking an Italian compound, Carter reminded himself.

"Prof? Paddy?" Carter knew his speech was slurred but hoped that Danny Glass could make out what he was saying.

"Don't try to talk. Prof's got a gashed arm and Paddy's dealing with it."

"Lights. Get the lights out."

"Not lights. Flames. There's several buildings on fire."

"What about Garrard and Linton?" They were the other two men, he recalled; the two he had sent through the workshop to cover their approach from the other side.

"No sign of them, but I haven't been looking. Ingram is looking for survivors."

Ingram. Who was Ingram? Oh yes, the man that had been at the back fence with Glass. One of the men from the other patrol they had linked up with.

Carter continued through his mental roll call. "Walter was with me. Is he OK, or has he got a sore head as well?"

Glass said nothing.

"Walter's dead, isn't he?"

Still Glass said nothing, but his eyes flicked to the side. Carter turned his head to follow the man's gaze. About thirty feet away was a mangled heap that might once have been a man. Or it might have been something painted by Picasso. No two body parts seemed to be in the right place, that was for sure.

That was right, Carter recalled. Walter had been a few feet closer to the guardhouse when the blast happened, heading to the left. He must have shielded me from the worst of it.

"What about the Italians? They were in the slit trenches next to the guardhouse."

"Do you mean where that crater is?" Glass asked, jerking his head sharply to the right.

Carter strained to see around him. Where the guardhouse had stood was, just as Glass had described it, a large crater. That was where the flames were still flickering, where bits of the wooden building still burnt. They provided enough light to show that the slit trenches had been subsumed into the crater. Anyone in them wouldn't even have known they had died.

Who else was still not accounted for? Carter racked his brains. Oh yes. "The other Italians? Walter's men?"

"No idea. Depends where they were. The bombs hit right along the line of the compound. As well as the guard house, one hit the far side of the workshop, then the bit of open ground between that and the first warehouse, then the second warehouse. That's on fire from end to end. Most of the trucks are on fire as well, from burning debris. Just the canvass at the moment, but without anyone putting them out they'll probably burn to the ground."

The food warehouse; that was where the four Italian partisans were supposed to go when they had dealt with the patrolling sentry. The warehouse that was now on fire. Carter didn't hold out much hope for them if a bomb had scored a direct hit there. "The final bomb missed the compound and exploded about fifty yards past me and Ingram. Fortunately nothing hit us."

Glass tied a neat knot in the bandage he had been applying to Carter's head as he had been talking. "Do you fancy trying to stand up?

"We can't stay here all night." Carter tried to lever himself upright, helped by Glass lifting him under the arms. His body screamed in agonised protest, but he was able to gain his feet and put his weight on them. No bones broken as far as he could tell but he knew he would be sporting some gigantic bruises before long.

Glass spotted something on the ground and went to retrieve it, offering it to Carter. It was his Tommy gun.

Perhaps Glass's hearing was generally more sensitive, or perhaps Carter was still suffering some deafness, but the commando heard something. He dropped to one knee and took up a firing position with his rifle aimed along the road that led to the compound from the west.

"Don't shoot." Carter warned. "There's friends out there as well." He was thinking of the four partisans who had been responsible for cutting the power. After the bombing raid, their instinct would have been to find out what had happened to their comrades.

"Amigo!" Carter shouted into the darkness, unsure of whether or not it was the right word. He only knew that much from the westerns he'd watched in the cinema.

It must have been good enough, because the partisans moved forward into the flickering light cast by the flames. Their weapons, Sten guns, were held at the ready, but they lowered them when they saw the commandos' uniforms.

"Walter?" One of them queried.

Carter indicated the mass of blood-soaked rags in front of them. One of the men stepped forwards and examined the mangled form, turning to his friends, nodding his head and, presumably, confirming Walter's identity.

"*Gli altri?*" The man asked.

Carter shrugged his shoulders, not knowing what he had asked.

"Giovanni? Stefano?" The man persisted.

Carter recognised names, at least.

"*Mort.*" He replied, hoping again that it was the right word or, at least, a reasonable approximation. "*Tutti mort.*"

The man nodded his head in understanding. "*Dove?*"

Carter shrugged his shoulders again, not understanding the question.

But one of his companions must have remembered the plan and there was an exchange of Italian. The four men headed off along the internal road, making their way between the burning trucks and the wreckage of the workshop towards the warehouses beyond.

"We're not serving any purpose here now." Carter said to Glass. "We may as well head back."

"Are you up to it, Lucky?"

"I won't know until I try. But if we stay here, the rest of a garrison are bound to turn up to see what the fire is about. They'll have heard the bombs going off and will suspect there are casualties."

Green and O'Driscoll joined them, the Sergeant's arm wrapped in bandages from shoulder to wrist. "Are you OK, Prof?"

"He needs stitches." O'Driscoll answered for him. "But I think I've stopped the bleeding for now. He'll have a lovely scar to show his grandchilder."

"I don't think grandchildren are in my future. But yes, I'm OK otherwise, Lucky."

Carter wondered what he meant by the remark about grandchildren, but let it slide. He had other things to think about for the moment.

"We'll need to do a search for Garrard and Linton. They might just be wounded."

"Danny and I can do that, Lucky." O'Driscoll said. "You two stay here."

They headed around the front of the workshop, as the wreckage of the building prevented any passage through it.

"That was a close one." Prof Green said.

"Too close. When I heard the aircraft, it never occurred to me that we might be the target."

"They'd have had no idea we were here. This place is just a cross on the bomb aimer's map as far as anyone else is concerned."

"I always thought the RAF couldn't hit a barn from the inside, but they certainly got this place spot on."

"A bit of luck, maybe. Just the one stick of bombs though."

"It's all a place this size needed." Carter forced himself to move towards Walter's body and take a look at him. "If I'd have been first out of cover, that would probably have been me."

"Or me, or Danny. Luck of the draw, Boss."

They fell silent, contemplating their own mortality and the fickleness of fate that marked Walter for death and themselves for life.

"Fiona' going to be livid when I tell her about this." Carter knew how much his wife worried about him.

"So don't tell her. If she doesn't know, she can't fret over it. You can always tell her about it when the war's over."

"That assumes I make it to the end of the war."

"If you don't, then it won't matter anyway. Fiona will have other things to worry about by then."

Like how to bring up twins without a father at the same time as running a farm. But he didn't say that out loud. Fiona's would be just one of thousands of similar stories, some of which were already being acted out after four years of war. All over the Empire there were widows grieving and worrying about their futures without their husbands. All over Germany and Italy too, come to think of it, though Carter had less sympathy for those widows.

Glass and O'Driscoll returned after about ten minutes. O'Driscoll held his hand out, the palm facing upwards. In it lay two identity tags.

"Was it quick?" Carter asked, anxious that his men might have been lying wounded and suffering while Glass and O'Driscoll had been dealing with himself and Green.

"I doubt they'd have even heard the bombs go off." Glass reassured him. "If the blast didn't kill them, the building collapsing on them will have done the job. We only found Garrard because Paddy spotted his boot sticking out from under the debris."

They were interrupted by the partisans returning. Only the four of them, as before. They didn't stop. They just waved a goodbye as they passed, the leader saying *"Addio. In bocca al lupo."*

Addio was sufficiently like adios for Carter to assume it meant goodbye, but he wasn't sure about the rest.

"Addio." He said, returning the wave as the men disappeared into the darkness.

"OK, let's go. Paddy, can you take the lead and Danny, bring up the rear."

Painfully, Carter took the first step of the return journey.

[1] The bomb load of an aircraft was referred to as a "stick" for some reason. The expression is unique to the British and dates to World War II. When the aircraft's bomb aimer pulled the bomb release lever or pressed the release button (depending on aircraft type), the bombs would drop from their racks one at a time in a pre-

ordained sequence, to prevent them colliding as they left the aircraft. Because of the fractional time delay between each bomb, they landed in a line that followed the course of the aircraft that dropped them. Air Raid wardens could work out if there were any unexploded bombs from a load, by counting the number of craters, providing they knew the type of aircraft that dropped them, because each aircraft type carried a different sized bomb load. It is, perhaps, the straightness of the line that resulted in the comparison to a stick, as in a length of wood.

* * *

With Carter injured it took them far longer to make their way back to the top of the hill and the sun was quite high. They found the hilltop deserted but for Merrell, their radio operator and Ben Flanders, the officer who had commanded the only patrol they had managed to link up with.

"You look worse for wear." A concerned look crossed Flanders' on his face.

"You should see the other guy." Carter responded, lowering his webbing harness to the ground to give some relief to his aching back. "Where is everyone?"

"I sent them down to the beach. They've managed to attract the attention of a ship that was heading west along the coast. It's sending a boat in to shore."

"How did they manage that? They operate on different radio frequencies."

"Old fashioned methods sometimes still work." Flanders chuckled. "They used semaphore, apparently. The Captain of the ship sent a message ashore with the boat's crew. He can stay for an hour, but no longer."

"Starting from when?"

"How long since we received the radio message, Merrell?"

"Ten minutes. No more than that."

"We'd better get going then. Carter said, straightening up and reaching for his webbing and Tommy gun.

"We'll move faster if I take that." Flanders reached for the webbing. Carter was about to resist, then realised that his pride might result in them getting left behind. He handed his burden over but kept a hold of his weapon. He would feel naked without that.

What sounded like a peel of thunder reached them and Carter glanced west, searching the sky for cloud, but there was none.

As they hurried down the south slope of the hill towards the beach, he heard another rumble.

"We've been hearing that since before dawn." Flanders commented. "I think the invasion must have started."

Down in the valleys they navigated, trying to avoid Carter having to climb too many hills, they had been screened from the coast, where the artillery was firing.

"We've waited long enough for it. I wonder if our boys are going ashore."

"I'm sure they must be." Flanders said, putting out a hand to steady Carter as he stumbled over a bit of rough ground. "I can't see Monty invading without trying to silence the shore batteries first.

"And here we are, stuck behind the lines, no use to man nor beast."

"We've been doing our job, Lucky. It might feel like we haven't achieved much, but I've seen plenty of Italian patrols out searching for us. They'd be manning coastal defences if we weren't here. More men for the first wave to have to deal with."

Carter gave a non-committal grunt. Perhaps Flanders was right, but he knew he was only here because a clumsy sailor had left them stranded high and dry. He'd be glad to get back to the Commando.

It took them all of forty-five minutes to reach the beach, to be greeted by a ship's life boat already filled with the sailors who had been ashore with them. Carter was pleased to see that the commandos were less complacent and were lying in defensive positions, just in case. A Sub Lieutenant was pacing up and down the shoreline, looking at his watch. He hurried across to greet Carter.

"Are you the last of them, Sir?"

"As far as I know, we are."

"What do we do about them?" The Subby pointed to the west, where a group of Italian soldiers were clustered around the ruins of the old cannery. Carter was just about to order his men to open fire on them when he realised that the Italians were unarmed. "Apparently they want to surrender."

There must have been about thirty of them and even Carter could tell that there wouldn't be enough room in the boat.

"We'll take any officers, and whatever ORs we can fit in, but the rest will have to stay behind." He saw that an officer was making his way across. "Better do your sums quickly, or they'll swamp the boat trying to get in."

"Ten! Only ten." The Subby said, raising his hands, fingers extended. The Italian officer seemed to understand and shouted some orders. There was some heated exchanges, but eventually nine men followed the officer to the water's edge and waited for Carter's men to finish boarding before they, too, climbed over the thwarts.

Carter called in the last defenders and they pushed the boat out far enough for it to float, then pulled themselves aboard. The sailors backed the oars to turn the lifeboat around and started to pull towards the corvette that was standing about a mile off shore. Carter could see a small bow wave rising at it started t head eastwards and the Subby changed course, estimating the angle he would need to take for the boat to intercept the corvette.

"You're lucky we spotted you." The Subby said, by way of conversation. "We should have gone past this stretch of coast while it was still dark, but someone reported seeing a periscope and we had to stop and carry out an anti-submarine sweep."

"Did you find it?"

"No, false alarm. At least, that was what the Skipper thought when we couldn't get any trace on asdic".[1] He made a slight course adjustment, keeping the bow of the lifeboat aiming well ahead of the corvette. "We'll get plenty of practice at that. We're heading for

Messina to help with the anti-submarine patrols to keep the enemy out of the straits."

[1] Asdic – an early form of sonar used for detecting submarines. There were two types, passive and active. Passive sonar listens for the sound of enemy submarines while active sonar sends out pulses of sound (called "pings") which reflect back off the hull of submarines. The disadvantage of active sonar is that it can give false returns off the bed of the sea, rocks or other submerge objects. Anti-submarine ships will often use passive sonar to detect the submarine from the sound of its engines and propellor, then "ping" it to measure the range, so the crew knows the best time to launch the depth charges.

* * *

Carter had to suffer the indignity of being winched aboard the corvette in a bosun's chair while everyone else used the scramble net that had been draped over the boat's side. He had tried to climb the net, but his aching muscles let him down and he almost fell into the sea to be crushed between the lifeboat and the pitching hull of the corvette.

The Captain of the corvette introduced himself as Carter saluted. "I'll get our sick bay attendant to take a look at your injuries, and those of your other wounded man." He shook Carter's hand. "What were you doing there anyway?"

Carter gave him a brief run down on the operation and the beaching of the landing craft as the skipper escorted him below decks and along the narrow companion way to the sick bay.

"Can you drop us at Syracuse?" Carter finished up.

"Sorry, old chap. Our orders are to make best speed into the entrance of the strait. Now the invasion has started, everyone is scared stiff the Italians or the Jerries will get a submarine in there and start sinking the shipping. It would be a happy hunting ground for an intrepid submariner."

"Can you get us ashore anywhere?"

"I'll tell you what. I'll radio ahead and see if we can get something to meet up with us at sea. There may be a launch or something available."

Carter thanked him and the skipper left to return to his bridge.

* * *

It was almost dark when Carter and his men clambered ashore from the Italian fishing boat that had been sent out to collect them. Carter shook the hand of the Petty Officer that was commanding it and the man wasted no time in turning its nose back out to sea to continue whatever vital war work Carter had interrupted. The quayside of Syracuse was deserted, not even an old man repairing fishing nets to be seen. All the action had shifted northwards and the ancient port had been left to return to its more peaceful preoccupations.

Carter had just resigned himself to walking back to the camp outside the town when he heard the sound of approaching engines. Two three ton trucks pulled to a halt at the landward end of the pier and Carter could make out the familiar form of the CO clambering out of the leading vehicle.

Carter hurried to greet him as best he could. "I thought you'd be over on the mainland by now." He said, extending his hand to shake that of Cousens.

"I'm afraid we're the bridesmaids for this one. Monty couldn't think of anything for us to do so we've been sat here twiddling our thumbs while the rest of 8th Army are pouring ashore in Calabria. Well, I have to say, you're a sight for sore yes." he cast his eyes over the other commandos, who were now making their way towards the rucks. "Not many with you."

"No, we only managed to link up with Ben Flanders. I have no idea what has happened to the rest of the patrols."

"They'll turn up. In fact, we may get a chance to go looking for them. We haven't been totally side-lined. We're to cross the straits the day after tomorrow and head east along the coast road. Maybe we'll see a bit of action then."

"Unlikely, I'd say Sir. We've been sat overlooking that road for the last couple of days and hardly a thing is moving along it."

"We know the Jerries are moving north, but we expected the Ities to put up a bit of a fight for their own country." Carter could see that his CO was disappointed by the news. Carter indicated the group of prisoners who were still stood along the quayside.

"Not if they're anything like this lot, they won't Sir. These and another twenty or so came to find us and give themselves up. There doesn't seem to be any fight left in them."

"I have to say that's what the rumours have been saying as well. The grapevine is saying that the Ities have already surrendered."[1]

"So what's our job going to be in Italy?" Carter asked.

"Our job is going to be dealing with any opposition there may be on the southern coast. But you, Steven, will not be joining us."

"But …"

"But nothing. Just look at the state of you. I'm not risking you, or Green, in combat. I'm sending you up to the field hospital in Catania for treatment. You're not coming back on duty until a doctor has said you are fit."

[1] For once the grapevine was correct. The Italians signed a surrender agreement in Cassibile, Sicily, the same day as the Allies started landing on the Italian mainland. However, it didn't come into effect for two days to allow the Italian army to save some face by mounting a token opposition. Unfortunately, the Germans found out about the deal and disarmed all the Italians, who were supposed to come over to the Allies and help to defeat the Germans but were then unable to until they had been re-equipped.

4 - Manfredonia

Standing out on the harbour wall, Carter could just make out the dots of three LC(I)s as they headed northwest towards the entrance to the Port. It had taken them three days to reach Bari from the southern port of Taranto. It would have been hot below decks, even in October, and Carter wondered if the men had been allowed to sit up on top. The risk of an attack by the Luftwaffe was low, so there was no need to keep the men confined.

It would be at least an hour before the landing craft arrived and the men could be allowed to disembark. He wondered if they would be sent to the same area on the outskirts of the town that 49 (RM) Cdo had already occupied. It was rarely a good idea to put marines and soldiers so close together. The rivalry between the two commando forces had been known to tip over into fights, especially when alcohol had been consumed.

Officially alcohol wasn't allowed in camp, but they commandos always seemed to manage to lay hands on illicit supplies. Carter wondered how they did it but dare not ask. If he knew the answer, he'd have to put a stop to it and that would be bad for morale. Providing things didn't get out of hand he was prepared to turn a blind eye.

It was almost a month since he'd last seen his men, having been confined in the field hospital until the medics were satisfied he wasn't suffering any long term effects from his injuries. It had been frustrating, sitting around all day, with news of the fighting arriving with every ambulance carrying casualties from the front line, on the other side of the Strait of Messina.

But, at last, he had been pronounced fit enough to return to active service. It had then taken him several more days to scrounge lifts along the southern coast road as far as Taranto, only to find he had missed the commando by minutes as they had been dispatched on an operation to land ahead of 78th Division's advance and cut off the

German garrison at Manfredonia. But the operation had been cancelled and now the commando was being diverted to Bari.

From Taranto, Carter had managed to get a lift in a lorry with a draft of fresh troops, heading up to Bari to join their unit. The detachment's commander had dropped him at the gate to the port, it being the most likely place for the commando to arrive. That had been two days ago and Carter had been cooling his heels ever since, waiting for his unit to arrive.

But he had managed to locate Colonel Vernon, their brigade commander, who was trying to establish a base from which the commandos could operate.

To their north, 78th Division sat astride the road to Termoli, which would be a tough nut to crack. The port city, also a strategic railhead, was on the north side of Biferno river, the eastern end of the German defensive line that ran from the west coast, at Naples, across the Apennine mountains to the Adriatic Sea. It was a defensive line the enemy must hold if they wanted to keep control of the country of their former allies.

Only days after the Allies invaded the Italian mainland the Italian dictator, Benito Mussolini had been freed from his prison in Grand Sasso, high in the mountains, in a daring raid by the *Waffen SS* and elite paratroops. He was once again in control of Italy, at least the part of Italy which was still occupied by the Germans. Carter wondered how much he was actually in control and how much he was a puppet of the German High Command.

Progress northwards by the Allies was much slower than anticipated. Restricted to the coastal strips along both sides of the mountainous Italian interior, the Allies couldn't bring their massive firepower to bear on the enemy. The enemy, on the other hand, had their flanks protected by the mountains on one side and the sea on the other. The irresistible force had met the immovable object.

The whine of an engine in low gear caught Carter's attention and he looked behind him to see a Jeep making its way along the harbour wall towards him. He recognised the figure of Col Vernon sat beside his driver. It came to a stop and the Colonel unfolded his lanky frame from the passenger seat.

"Bloody Navy!" Vernon cursed, as he walked from the vehicle to join Carter on the seaward side of the wall.

"Problems, Sir?"

"The bloody Port Officer is being totally unreasonable. After three days at sea he wants the men to march ten miles south to set up camp in some village or other. There won't be any tents available for them for days, because 78th Division are using all available transport right now. In the meantime, I know there are spare tents lying in a field on the north side of town, just waiting for someone to erect them. But that bloody sailor-boy won't let me use them because they're earmarked for a reserve unit that's on its way up from Taranto, he thinks but he isn't sure because no one really knows."

Carter had never seen Vernon's feathers so ruffled. The Colonel was usually so calm and laid back. The Port Officer must heave really got under his skin. Or maybe it was just an accumulation of frustrations.

"So, what will we do?"

"I've already done it. I'm sending four-nine up to Manfredonia to set up camp. Fifteen can join them there."

"Isn't Manfredonia still under German control?"

"Technically yes, but the latest reports from 78th Div say their reconnaissance units are reporting only a company strength of Jerries still in the area. Four-nine won't have any trouble clearing them out. I'll send fifteen up in the LC(Is). Technically they should disembark here and I'll have to bluff the skippers into thinking that they have orders to continue the journey."

"It won't be the first time we've had to pull the wool over someone's eyes." Since their inception, the commandos had often had to beg, borrow and steal resources in order to do the job they were supposed to do. "Would you like me to take care of that?" It might be important for Vernon to be able to claim innocence if his actions were later questioned.

"No, I'll do it. I quite fancy causing the Navy a bit of grief tight now."

"The men won't be happy about staying on the landing craft."

"They'll be even less happy with a ten-mile hike. I'll let them ashore for a brew and a sandwich. Fortunately, the Service Corps are being more co-operative and I've got some water and rations on the way."

There was the sound of the jeep's horn, attracting their attention. They both turned to see the driver holding up the headset of the jeep's radio.

"Excuse me a moment, Steven."

Returning his gaze out to sea, Carter could see the landing craft more clearly now. Three of the large vessels in line astern, heading arrow straight for the port entrance, flanked by the wall on which he was standing and its twin, projecting eastwards from the other side of the harbour.

"It seems you will have to take care of the Navy for me after all, Steven." Vernon announced as he returned to Carter's side. "I've been summoned to 78th Div HQ for a briefing."

"Another operation?" Carter couldn't keep the hopeful note out of his voice.

"Maybe, but it could just be a routine intelligence briefing. Anyway, I'll meet up with you in Manfredonia in a few hours. Make sure you keep your hand on your wallet when you join up with four-nine."

Vernon seemed to be in a cheerier mood as he walked back to his jeep, which the driver had turned around while he was waiting for his passenger to return.

* * *

As the LC(I) nudged its way into the quayside, Carter could see marines patrolling along the top, Bren guns were set in key positions to give interlocking covering fire. 49 Cdo weren't taking anything for granted now that they had control of the small port. It had been home to generations of fishermen since the days of the Romans and was little bigger than it had been back then.

The lack of fishing boats suggested that the population had moved them to a safer place, or perhaps they had been commandeered by the Germans to compensate for their lack of shipping in the Mediterranean Sea.

Carter lept nimbly up onto the quayside, partly to prove that he was no longer suffering from any injuries. A fresh-faced Lieutenant hurried along the harbourside. "Are you the CO?" he asked.

"No, He's in that boat." Carter pointed to the LC(I) that was tying up behind the one he had just vacated.

"Can you pass a message, Sir. He, yourself and your QM are to report to the harbourmaster's office." He pointed to where a solid stone-built structure sat at the landward end of the quay. "Col Vernon's orders."

"What about the men?"

"I'll take care of them, Sir. We're billeting people on the local population for now, but I suspect they won't be getting much sleep tonight."

"Oh, is there something going on?"

The young man gave a toothy smile. "Not for me to say, Sir, but they're pinning maps on the walls in there."

Carter cursed under his breath. After three days at sea his men needed to rest. If an operation was in the air, then it would probably be happening soon, maybe even as soon as that night.

"OK, but can you make sure that the men get fed and watered as a matter of urgency."

"Not a problem, Sir. When we arrived the Jerries beat a hasty retreat and left their rations behind. It's not to everyone's taste, but it will be filling." The man turned and hurried away, while Carter went to locate his CO, who had just climbed up to the quayside. He was stretching his back, having spent the last three days sitting around. Carter had reported back at Bari, the CO welcoming him with open arms after his enforced absence. His face had fallen when he was told about the order to move on, but he realised it was preferable to a long march just to sleep in a field.

"Col Vernon's orders, can we join him in the harbourmaster's office." Carter greeted him.

"Don't tell me; we're not stopping."

"Looks like it, Sir. I haven't any details, but the marine officer I just met seems to think there's an operation being planned."

Cousens bit back the curse he was about to let rip with. No point in railing at the Gods, because they never listen. If a decision had been made, it wouldn't be unmade just because the men were tired.

He stalked along the quayside, acknowledging the nods of the marine sentries. Like the army commandos, they had been trained not to salute when they were in the front line. Another sentry stepped aside from the door of the harbourmaster's office to allow them to enter, then pulled the door closed behind them.

The room was lit by Tilley lamps, their harsh glow casting black shadows on the wall. As the marine Lieutenant had described, maps festooned the walls.

"Welcome to Manfredonia, Charlie, Steven." Vernon beamed. "I'm sure you were hoping for a couple of days rest, so my personal apologies for what I'm about to tell you, but 78 Div has requested our services. Well, to be accurate, 8th Army HQ has requested our services, but Major General Evelegh[1] is the man in charge here. What I am about to brief you on is called Operation Terminus and is aimed at being a farewell present for General Montgomery. For those of you that didn't already know, he has been ordered to return to England[2] and this operation is likely to be his last significant engagement on the east coast before the weather makes operations more difficult."

Vernon's batman handed Carter and Cousens mugs of steaming tea and laid a plate of sandwiches on the table in front of them, behind which Vernon was standing. He crossed to one of the maps pinned to the wall, a small-scale map showing the southern half of Italy. He pointed to a spot on the map. "We're here, Manfredonia, which gives its name to the gulf formed by Italy's eastern spur. At eleven thirty hours tomorrow morning, both Fifteen and Four-Nine commandos, with the Special Raiding Squadron, are to set sail." Carter breathed a sigh of relief. At least the men would get a night's sleep ashore. "The destination is on the north side of the spur, at the town of Termoli. As you know, Termoli is a large seaport and a major rail terminus that makes up the eastern end of the defensive line that runs across Italy from Naples on the other side of the mountains. 78 Div's advance is blocked by the Biferno river, which is to the south of the town and the road to it has a single bridge. Your mission, indeed our mission, because I'm going with you, is to seize the town, take the bridge and open the road for 78 Div."

A shiver of recollection ran down Carter's spine. The last bridge they had been tasked to capture had nearly led to the destruction of the whole commando. Had they been regular troops, rather than the highly motivated raiders they were, they would probably all be dead or prisoners of war by now. As it was it had been a close-run thing, for Carter in particular.

"Now, Charlie," Vernon addressed Cousens directly, "I understand that your men have had a rough time of it for the last few days …" Cousens was about to protest and insist that his men were up to whatever task they would be given. Vernon waved away the protest before it could be made. "… I know, Fifteen are up for it. I would expect nothing less. But I'm giving you the easier job. You are to land first to take and hold the beach. From the aerial reconnaissance photos, the defences appear to be minimal. I don't think anyone ever envisaged the Allies ever getting this far north, let alone landing from the sea. Once your men have done that, Four-Nine and the SRS will come ashore and head inland. Four-Nine will go around the south of the town and the SRS will head straight for the bridge to seize the northern end. Once the beach is clear, Fifteen will then move around the northern side of the town to complete the encirclement.

Now, I'm sure that Fifteen will remember Operation Leonardo and the fact that the relief force got stuck in a dog fight at the town of Lentini. That will not happen this time. There are no significant

German forces between their front line and the river. Their advance units will cross the bridge shortly after dawn and they will advance through the town to take up positions to the north, to prevent any Jerry counterattack."

Why don't I believe that? Carter wondered.

[1] Maj Gen Vyvyan Evelegh commanded 78th Infantry Division from May 1942 until December 1943.

[2] Montgomery returned to England on 29th December 1943, to be replaced by Lt Gen Oliver Leese, commander of XXX Corps.

* * *

Looking along the deck towards the bows, Carter could see the sky being lit up by flashes. He thought for a moment that it was an artillery barrage, but it was much too far away. Each flash lit up the peaks of the mountains momentarily. There was some sort of storm in progress up there. He hoped it didn't move eastwards. All the commandos were still in lightweight desert clothing, their heavier northern European uniforms having not yet caught up with them. All they had were their ponchos to keep them dry. This early in October, no one in authority had considered that the weather might get cold, but he could feel a chill edge to the wind. He put that down to the temperature of the sea, but the nights in general weren't as warm as they had been.

A naval rating appeared and opened the door in the superstructure that led below decks, where the men were crowded in for the journey. They must be getting close. The lights below deck must already have been switched off, because the door was no more than a black rectangle. They only used red lighting while at sea, preventing a stray light from giving away their position, at the same time as helping to preserve night vision.

The rating shouted down the ladder and Carter heard the voices of men as they started to move. The rating crossed the deck to an identical hatch on the other side and repeated the process. A louder voice called for silence.

4, 5 and 6 Troops were onboard this LC(I), with Carter in command. One hundred and eighty men, cammed in like sardines. That was why he had pulled rank and travelled on the deck, along with Tpr James, his radio operator.

4 Troop came up on his side of the deck and made their way to the gangway that ran along the side of the boat and led the way to the ramp at the side of the bow. They would queue up there, waiting for the ramp to drop. The dim shape of another naval rating stood beside the winch, waiting to release the brake that would release the cable drum. On the far side of the deck, 5 Troop were also emerging. 6 Troop would come up last, split between the two doors.

As the men raced down the ramps, the troop on the port side would fan out to the left of the beach, the troop on the starboard side would head to the right and 6 Troop would join up from both ramps to form a line across the front of the bow. It was a well-rehearsed manoeuvre, but Carter knew that, in the dark, men were likely to lose their bearings and end up with the wrong troop. They would be sorted out later.

There was no sign that the enemy were waiting for them. No machineguns had opened up, nor artillery. Not even a flare had gone up. All that Carter could see ahead of them was the darker blackness that differentiated land from sea and the line of foam that showed where the two met. To their right was the other LC(I), carrying the CO and 1, 2 and 3 Troops. Behind them in the darkness were the craft carrying Four-Nine Cdo and the SRS. They wouldn't come ashore until the 'success' signal had been fired, a single green flare.

The tannoy crackled into life. "Stand-bye"" came the word of command. In other words, brace yourself, because this boat is about to be deliberately run aground!

The vibration beneath Carter's feet died as the power was reduced to the propellers. Carter hoped that there was no repeat of Bova Marina, where the landing craft had become stuck fast. But this time the sea was treating them far more gently, with barely a ripple breaking the surface.

There was a grinding sound and Carter felt himself being thrown forward. He put out his leg to brace himself and stopped his momentum before he lost his balance. There was a whirring sound then a splash as the LC(I)'s ramps were released, followed by the yelling of the commandos as they stormed ashore. Someone fired a round, but no answering shot came back. It had been Carter's intention to lead the men ashore but Ernie Barraclough claimed the honour. "My troop, so I should go first, if you don't mind, Sir." Carter had yet to get used to being called 'sir' by Captains.

As Carter was no longer going to be the first ashore, he decided he would adopt an air of dignified confidence. He stood to one side as the designated four sections of 6 Troop passed him by to take their places on the gangway and he strolled over, his Tommy gun hanging by his side, to stand on the bows, in full view of any sniper that might decide he made a juicy target. It was foolish, he knew, but he knew the men would be looking in his direction, admiring his confidence or, more likely, commenting on his stupidity.

But no sniper took aim on him and 6 Troop trotted down the ramps to take up their positions beneath him and then advance into the low dunes to their front. Not a single shot had been fired, except for the one fired by the commando, which had probably been an accident.

Carter strolled down the port side ramp and angled left to Ernie Barraclough's Troop. Although no longer his responsibility, he always felt more at home with the men he used to command and sought out their company whenever he could. He found his men lying along the top of the dunes.

"Wiring parties cutting a way through now, Lucky." Ernie informed him in a whisper. "No sign of any opposition, so we'll be off the beach in a few minutes."

He was right and they were soon beyond the beach and into the scrubby farmland beyond. Carter called them to a halt so that they didn't become separated from the rest of the Commando. There was the crack of a pistol firing, the fizzing sound of a flare ascending into the night sky and the familiar muffled pop as it burst into a bright green light. Success! Four-Nine and the SRS would start their run to shore immediately.

"Send out scouts to the front." Carter instructed Barraclough. "No more than three hundred yards. If there are any enemy in the area, they may be lying in wait."

But it was unlikely. The way to prevent a landing was to stop it before it happened; while it was still at sea. Once ashore the dynamic shifted, especially if the raiders were commandos who were prepared to give their lives to see their mission succeed.

"And send guides back to direct Four-Nine through the gaps in the wire. There's no point in them wasting time cutting new paths."

Satisfied that all was well on the left-hand end of the beachhead, Carter moved to his right to pass on the same instructions to 6 and 5 Troops, in that order. It was unnecessary; their commanders having acted on their own initiative.

Carter continued towards 1 Troop's stretch of the line and found Charlie Cousens sitting with his radio operator in a shallow hole they had dug. He had the radio's headset on and was just concluding a message.

"Damn!" Cousens said, to no one in particular.

"Trouble?"

"Yes. A recce unit from 78 Div have just reached the bridge. Only there isn't one. The Germans seemed to have destroyed it already. They must have spotted our troops assembling for the advance and decided not to wait until the last minute."

It was a setback, but Carter new that the Royal Engineers[1] would be with the division and would have the capability to replace the bridge. If the banks were shallow enough they would use pontoons, if not they would span it with a Bailey bridge. It would delay 78th Div's advance, but not halt it. Experienced engineers could bridge a river in a few hours, he knew.

49 (RM) Commando passed silently through the ranks of their 15 Cdo colleagues and headed inland, with the SRS sticking to the left

flank so as to head for the bridge. It made no difference that it had been destroyed; they would now need to keep the northern bank free of Germans so that the engineers weren't hindered in their task.

Behind Four-Nine came Colonel Vernon and his small Brigade HQ. He gave the order for 15 Cdo to advance and they angled northwards to enter the town through the port. The aerial photographs had shown that it wasn't a large town or a significant port. Larger than Manfredonia but nowhere near the size of Bari to the southeast. But even a small town has an extensive circumference, and it would take most of the rest of the night for 15 Cdo to make their way around the northern side to link up with Four-Nine on the western side.

And by now the Germans would be awake.

There would be a garrison in the town, providing support for the troops tasked with defending the Biferno. The garrison troops would post sentries to guard the key points within the town, not least the garrison HQ and probably also the telephone exchange, police station and a few other buildings. They may also be guarding the port, which the lead elements of the commando were now approaching. One of those sentries must have seen the green flare soar into the night sky. At the very least he would have reported it to the Guard Commander.

As the commando advanced around the town, troops were detached to clear the local area of any enemy troops, but none seemed to be found as occasional sounds of combat drifted from the south, where Four-Nine were engaged in similar activities. Once their areas were cleared, the troops would leave the town's environs to find high ground where they could set up a defence against sniper attack.

Tpr James tapped Carter on the shoulder and handed him the radio headset, which Carter clamped to one ear. "The CO, Lucky." James informed him.

"Red One to Red Leader." Carter used the call-signs for the operation. 15 Cdo were using the names of chess pieces, from king to pawn with himself and the CO designated as just red and red one.

Four-Nine were using "white" as their designation, with the SRS using call-signs based on a deck of cards. Carter frequently wondered whose job it was to come up with these ideas.

Cousens' voice crackled back at him "Our scouts report a train just north of the railway station, raising steam ready to depart. Take Red Pawn and stop it. When you've done that, take the shortest route to the western side of the town to link up with White."

"Roger Red." Carter replied, before handing the headset back to Tpr James. Red Pawn was 6 Troop, who were still behind him. He made his way past the column of advancing troop to find their commander, 'Molly' Brown. He found him consulting his map, though Carter couldn't understand why. For the present it was a game of follow-my-leader. Crater quickly briefed him, consulting his own map as he did so.

Leaving the rest of the commando to continue their circuitous route, Carter cut through some back streets, heading due west. They were bound to cut the railway line at some point. Experience showed that the Italians didn't put up any sort of barrier to stop people trespassing on the railway lines. They found their way blocked by a large warehouse , which Carter guessed ran along one side of the tracks, possibly with its own siding to enable the transfer of freight onto trains. The maps they were using were copies of street guides produced before the war, which Carter suspected had probably been found in local petrol stations, so the building wasn't marked.

North or south? He considered. North was more likely to provide an access he decided. The closer they got to the railway station, the more likely they were to encounter similar obstructions. Sure enough, the warehouse wall gave way to some open ground before a row of terraced houses began. Railway worker's homes, Carter thought. He ordered Molly to send a section to check them out to make sure there were no troops hiding inside and led the rest across the waste ground to locate the railway lines. As he passed the end of the warehouse wall he heard the sound of escaping steam. Sure enough, there was a locomotive with … he counted … three carriages behind it.

He briefly wondered why Cousens wanted the train stopping. Letting it go would do no harm. But then again, it might be used to transport reinforcements or ammunition into the area. No point in letting the enemy retain the use of a valuable asset.

Without waiting for orders, Molly Brown sent half his men across the railway line to the far side of the train, then led the other half down the nearer side. Carter didn't intervene. They were' Molly's men. All he had to do was go along for the ride and intervene if Molly did something stupid, which was about as likely as Winston Churchill joining the Nazi party. Molly Brown had been with the commando since before Carter had joined, so he knew what he was doing.

It occurred to Carter that he didn't know how he was going to disable the train. He didn't think blowing it up would be a good idea. He could unhook the carriages and cut their steam lines so the brakes would lock, but the locomotive was different matter.

Think, he ordered himself. What do you know about trains?

They run on steam. He answered. How is the steam produced? By the fire in the engine's furnace. So how do you stop the steam being produced? You put the fire out.

That was the answer then. They could either turn a hose on the fire, or they could rake the coals out, whichever was easiest. Well, when he said 'they' he meant the crew, who were now looking down the business end of Lee Enfield rifles tipped with wicked spike bayonets.

But if the train was leaving, what was it carrying? The carriages, he realised, weren't actually passenger coaches, they were freight cars. Their sliding side doors stood open.

He sent men along to check inside. The troopers he reached the first one stood back and raised their rifles, aiming inside.

Carter ran along to see what they had found. Stretched out on the floor of the waggon were a dozen men in German uniforms, their helmets and rifles lying alongside them. The sound of snoring could be heard. A dozen Jerry prisoners taken without a shot being fired.

He spotted something. Oh, this was too good to be true. The nearest helmet was the unmistakeable shape of those issued to the Fallschirmjäger, Germany's elite parachute troops. The same troops that had captured him in Sicily. Well, probably not the exact same men, but from the same division, at least.

"Wake up, sleepy heads!" Carter shouted. They wouldn't understand the words, but they would understand the noise.

One, perhaps more alert than his companions, leapt to his feet reaching for his rifle, but stopped, crouched over, as he spotted the British soldiers. His eyes opened wide with surprise.

He said something in German, but Carter couldn't guess from his tone whether he was cursing or telling his comrades to be careful because they were in danger of being shot. He thought it might be the latter, because as the soldiers emerged from their sleep they raised their arms in surrender.

The men clambered down from the train and a delighted 6 Troop searched them for weapons and documents that might provide intelligence. The most senior man was an *Obergefreiter*, barely the equivalent of a Lance Corporal. It accounted for all the men being asleep, rather than one remaining awake on watch. The man probably hadn't tried to exert any authority.

But what to do with them now? There was no choice, they would have to take them with them. All dozen men had been armed with rifles, which were easy to disable by removing the bolts, extracting the firing pins and then hitting them with a rifle butt to bend them. That done, Carter left a section to make sure the locomotive engineer and his fireman completed the job of putting out the train's fire and led the rest along the railway lines in the direction of the station. It was possible that there were more soldiers there.

As they continued the advance, Carter realised the significance of the sleeping soldiers. They were elite troops and so must have been sent to bolster the defence of the town. But they wouldn't have been alone. Like the commandos, the Fallschirmjäger were lightly armed and unable to contend with armoured units. While 78 Div were an infantry division, the 1st Canadian Division had armour with it and would be crossing the Biferno further upstream, as

They were tasked with keeping contact with the American units advancing through the mountains.

Which meant, Carter concluded, that the Germans would have armour in the area somewhere. In Sicily the German paratroops had been attached to the Herman Goering Panzer Division. Were they attached to them here as well? It had to be a possibility. He wasted no time in reporting his suspicions to his CO. What Cousens did with the information was up to him, but no one would relish the idea of a German counterattack by tanks.

What had the men been doing on the train though? Just a dozen men suggested that they weren't withdrawing. Perhaps men sent to load ammunition from a supply dump further north. Col Vernon had a German speaker attached to his staff, a trooper from 10 (Inter Allied) Commando[2]. He would ask the questions that Vernon wanted answering and it was unlikely that the prisoners would refuse to answer.

The railway station proved to be deserted and bomb craters on the tracks, the platforms and the concourse suggested that it had been targeted by Allied bombers at some time, which would account for the lack of people. No one would want to risk being in the area if the bombers returned.

Daylight was starting to make objects visible as Carter led the troop westwards towards the edge of the town. Early risers opened their doors to start their daily routine, only to slam them shut again on seeing the strange uniforms and pale faces of the commandos as they hurried through the dawn.

---

[1] The 214th Field Company, RE, were the unit tasked with bridging the Biferno river. They still exist, in the form of their descendants, 125 (Staffordshire) Field Squadron, RE who are part of Britain's Reserve Army. They were formed in 1967 by the merger of 213 and 214 Field Squadrons, as they had been renamed in 1947. They are based in Stoke-on-Trent.

[2] 10 (Inter Allied) Commando were made up of volunteers from the 'free' armed forces of the occupied countries of Europe. There were two French troops and one troop each from Belgium, Holland, Norway, Poland and Yugoslavia. X Troop were all German speakers, many of them Jewish refugees who had fled Germany before the start of the war.

5 – Termoli

Carter found 4 Troop digging in on the side of a hill on the north western side of the town, not far from the edge of the suburbs. It was typical Italian countryside in front; small fields dotted with olive, orange and lemon groves. There was good visibility over quite a wide area.

News didn't seem to have reach the Germans who were responsible for resupplying the Termoli garrison, because a Bren gun started firing from further north, where the main road entered the town, targeting an enemy truck as it ambled southwards. As he watched, Carter saw it veer off the road and cant over to one side.

Locating Ernie Barraclough, Carter asked him what orders he'd been given.

"Dig in, sit tight and wait and see." Barraclough summarised the orders for him. "1 Troop are out doing a recce along the road to the north and there are patrols out to the west. But there's been no reports of any contact with the enemy yet. They don't seem to know we're here."

Carter caught sight of a couple of German paratroops working in what appeared to be a field kitchen, located on the edge of the town.. "What are they doing here?" he demanded to know.

"They're cooks from the Jerry parachute regiment that were in the town. They've volunteered to cook breakfast for the lads. Hoskins in 2 Troop says he recognised them from Malati Bridge and they recognised him. They'd held him prisoner for a couple of hours before they let him go when they were ordered to withdraw. They seem pretty pally."

Carter shook his head. This war sometimes made no sense at all to him. "Well, keep an eye on them, just in case."

He stood up and started to move towards 5 Troop, who were a little further north.

"Would yez like a cuppa tea., Lucky" A familiar voice called to him. He spotted O'Driscoll squatting on the edge of a slit trench with a mess tin held over a Tommy cooker.

"Actually, I would Paddy. But shouldn't you be finishing that trench?"

"Ach, it's terrible hard digging here. It's all stones and rocks beneath the surface. How the Ities get anything to grow is a miracle. Give me a nice Irish meadow any day. So, with me back breaking I ordered meself to take a break and brew up."

O'Driscoll decanted some of the tea into Carter's proffered mess tin and added some powdered milk. "If yez want sugar you'll have to provide your own." He said. Sugar was a commodity always in short supply, as the commandos believed it gave them energy and consumed as much of it as they could. Carter had asked the medical officer about it and he had given a rueful smile. "No, that isn't true." He had said. "The body converts carbohydrates into a particular type of sugar, which then provides muscles with energy. But the only thing you'll get from the stuff that comes out of a packet is bad teeth." But the commandos ate sugar by the bucketload anyway. After all, what do doctors know?

"Where's Danny Glass?" Carter asked. The two were normally inseparable.

"Captain Barraclough sent a couple of Bren guns out onto the left flank and he put Danny in charge, leaving me on me tod to dig this trench."

"And the Prof?"

"Babysitting some of the new boys further along the line."

More replacements had arrived just before they had left Sicily and this would be their first action. Green was proving to be a good Sergeant, making sure that the men knew what was expected of them and checking that they were doing things right. But even with replacements, the commando was desperately understrength; no more than two hundred men out of a full compliment of four hundred and fifty.

O'Driscoll nodded towards the distant mountains. "Looks like bad weather is on the way."

Carter glanced in the direction he had indicated. There were certainly plenty of black clouds over the tops of the distant mountains, but above their heads the sky was blue and bright. "Looks fine to me." He replied.

"I'm a country boy and we know about the weather, Sorr. We have mountains like those back home; maybe not so high, but when they get covered in cloud like that it will move eventually. It's the weight of the water in them. It can't defy the laws of gravity forever, so they slide down the mountains. After that it just depends on which way the wind is blowing, which happens to be towards us"

Carter wasn't convinced but he didn't feel confident in arguing about it. In the countryside where he grew up, a mole hill was about the nearest thing they got to a mountain.

One of the cooks arrived, carrying a big cooking pan in each hand. In one there floated boiled sausages of some sort and in the other was scrambled eggs. O'Driscoll stabbed a sausage with his knife and scooped some egg into his remaining clean mess tin with the ladle that was in the pot. As the cook straightened up again he gave O'Driscoll's trench a disgusted look. "Zat would never do in the German Army." He said.

"*Suas do thóin.*" O'Driscoll replied.

"What did he say?" The cook gave Carter a mystified look.

"Tpr O'Driscoll here is Irish." Carter explained. "He said the sausages are good."

Carter took hold of O'Driscoll's knife and stabbed one, lifting it from the pot and taking a bite out of one end. It had a smoky smell and a flavour of garlic. But he nodded his head in approval. Satisfied, the German moved on.

"What did you actually say?" Carter asked after the German had moved out of earshot.

"Up y'r arse." O'Driscoll chuckled.

"Well, he does have a point about your trench, Paddy." Carter climbed to his feet, tipping the remnants of his tea from his mess tin and finishing off his sausage.

As he ambled away, Carter could have sworn he heard O'Driscoll repeat his phrase in Gaelic.

Behind 3 Troop's position he found a German burial party. He stood in respectful silence as the soldiers filled the grave of their fallen comrade, took a step back and saluted, before moving to the next. It was a solemn moment and Carter wondered if he would have to do the same before the relief force arrived.

The morning passed quietly and drifted into the afternoon. Apart from the sound of artillery from the south, where it appeared that the Biferno river crossing was still being contested, it would have been difficult to imagine that they were behind the enemy lines. In fact, the Germans seemed to be still unaware that they had lost the town, as lorries continued to be ambushed as they sped southwards on re-supply duties. 1 Troop's commander, positioned astride the road, told Carter that his men had accounted for eleven so far.

On his way back from one of his tours of inspection, Carter bumped into his CO. "Briefing at sixteen hundred hours. Colonel Vernon wants to update us on progress."

"What do we know, if anything?"

"The SRS have patrolled to the west and have sighted German SP[1] guns. They're moving forward, dropping shells onto the river crossing then withdrawing as soon as 78 Div starts counter-battery fire. They've got infantry with them, more than the patrols could handle, so they withdrew. Stirling thinks it's more of the Jerry paratroops.

"There only seemed to be about a company strength in the town" Carter observed.

"There were more, but they withdrew when Four-Nine arrived. The town seems to be expendable. It's the river they're defending."

"Will they try to re-take the crossing?"

"When they're strong enough. Their SP guns are just trying to slow us down until reinforcements arrive.

"How are they doing constructing their pontoon bridge?"

"No idea. The Colonel will tell us that at the briefing, I assume. Now, it doesn't need both of us here, so I suggest you get back into the town after the briefing and grab some rest. Let Ecclestone know where you are and I'll call you later and you can take the night shift. There's even a couple of cafes open, if you want to buy yourself something to eat that doesn't come out of a tin. How does that sound?"

"Pretty damned civilised."

"If the Jerries counterattack, you'll hear the noise so you can come back and join in."

Together they headed for Col Vernon's brigade HQ, which he had established in a small hotel on the edge of the town. Next door a house had been converted into a dressing station. Carter was surprised; A brigade HQ would be bound to be targeted by artillery if it was identified, putting the wounded in more danger.

Vernon had managed to persuade the Royal Army Medical Corps to attach a surgical team to the brigade. It had seemed like a wise precaution the day before, but now it looked as though it was something of a luxury. The medical team were sat in front of the house, sunning themselves when Carter and Cousens arrived.

The senior officers of the brigade assembled ready for their briefing. Carter spotted a face that didn't look familiar, a young Captain. On his sleeve he wore the battle axe emblem of 78 Div. It seemed that some of them, at least, had made it this far.

"Welcome gentlemen." Vernon called the meeting to order. "This is Capt McInnes of the Argyle and Southerland Highlanders. His reconnaissance company has just made it into the town and on their way is a machine gun platoon of the Kensington Regiment and behind them is a battery of six-pounder anti-tank guns. So we are no longer alone. I understand that 36 Brigade HQ will be joining us here this evening. So, gentlemen, I think we can say that this operation has been a success."

There were mutterings of agreement around the room.

"This morning we took ninety prisoners and captured about fifty jerry vehicles, suffering only minor casualties ourselves, which was a damned fine show. Now, I've had the chance to interrogate some of the prisoners. They've been quite chatty, I'm pleased to say. As you are aware, the town was occupied by FALLSCHIRMJÄGER AND WE NARROWLY MISSED CAPTURING GENERAL RICHARD HEIDRICH[2]."

THAT REVELATION LEFT EVERYONE SILENT. IF THE DIVISIONAL COMMANDER HAD BEEN STAYING IN THE TOWN IT MEANT THAT THE REST OF HIS DIVISION OF ELITE TROOPS WERE STILL IN THE AREA. THE BATTALION THEY HAD ENCOUNTERED IN THE TOWN WAS ONLY A FRACTION OF WHAT THE GERMANS HAD AVAILABLE IN THE AREA. IT MEANT THAT A COUNTERATTACK COULD NOT ONLY BE EXPECTED, IT WOULD BE OF CONSIDERABLE STRENGTH.

"THE GOOD NEWS IS THAT HEIDRICH LEFT HIS PERSONAL CAR BEHIND, SO IF ANYONE WANTS TO HAVE A GO AT DRIVING A PORSCHE, PLEASE DO FEEL FREE." THAT AT LEAST BROUGHT AN APPRECIATIVE LAUGH.

THE BRIEFING CONTINUED WITH AN INTELLIGENCE REPORT WHICH TOLD THEM NOTHING THEY DIDN'T ALREADY KNOW AND A WEATHER FORECAST, WHICH WAS FOR HEAVY RAIN.

"THE STORMS THAT HAVE BEEN UP IN THE MOUNTAINS FOR THE LAST FEW DAYS ARE HEADING TOWARDS US THIS EVENING." IT SEEMED THAT O'DRISCOLL HAD BEEN RIGHT.

"THE MEN HAVEN'T GOT ANY WEATHERPROOF CLOTHING, SIR." SOMEONE POINTED OUT.

"THEY'LL HAVE TO MAKE DO WITH THEIR PONCHOS BUT ROTATE THEM INTO BUILDINGS AS OFTEN AS YOU CAN. WITH BAD WEATHER I CAN'T SEE JERRY BEING TOO KEEN ON ATTACKING ANYWAY."

THE MEETING STARTED TO DRIFT TOWARDS THE DOORS.

"OH, BY THE WAY." THE COLONEL BROUGHT THEIR ATTENTION BACK INTO THE ROOM. "TELL YOUR MEN TO BE CAREFUL OF CIVILIAN SNIPERS. WE SEEM TO BE IN A TOWN THAT HAS A LOT OF SYMPATHY WITH MUSSOLINI AND THE LOCALS HAVE GOT WEAPONS. I'VE ROUNDED A FEW OF THEM UP AND THREATENED TO EXECUTE THEM IF THE SNIPING DOESN'T STOP."

HE SMILED AT THE EXPRESSIONS OF HORROR THAT HE MANAGED TO CREATE ON HIS AUDIENCE'S FACES. "DON'T WORRY, I WON'T CARRY OUT THE THREAT. BUT I'M BANKING ON THE GERMAN PROPAGANDA ABOUT US WORKING IN OUR FAVOUR FOR A CHANGE. HITLER DESCRIBED US AS THUGS AND GANGSTERS, SO I'M HOPING THAT THE ITALIANS WILL BELIEVE HIM AND NOT RISK US CARRYING OUT THE THREAT. OK, THAT WILL BE ALL FOR NOW. NEXT BRIEFING DIRECTLY AFTER MORNING STAND-TO."

THIS TIME THE BRIEFING DID END AND CARTER AND COUSENS MADE THEIR WAY OUTSIDE.

"A FULL DIVISION OF PARATROOPS. I DON'T LIKE THE SOUND OF THAT, SIR."

"THEY WON'T BE AT FULL STRENGTH, I'M SURE. THEY'VE BEEN IN ALMOST CONTINUOUS ACTION SINCE LENTINI AND THE GERMANS DON'T HAVE THE RESERVES THAT WE HAVE."

AND NEITHER DO WE, CARTER THOUGHT, REMEMBERING HOW UNDERMANNED THE COMMANDO WAS. "BUT EVEN A WEAKENED DIVISION IS STILL A DIVISION, SIR."

"TRUE, BUT WE'RE WELL DUG IN AND THEY HAVEN'T GOT ANY ARMOUR. THEY HAVE TO COME TO US AND I'D BACK OUR COMMANDOS AGAINST ANY TEN OF THEM. NOW, YOU GO AND GRAB SOME SHUT EYE. I'LL HAVE YOU CALLED AT ABOUT TWENTY-THREE HUNDRED."

[1] SP = Self-propelled. A 105 mm or 150 mm calibre gun mounted on a *Panzer* chassis and protected by armour. They were more mobile than field artillery and their tracked wheels gave them good cross-country manoeuvring ability. Up until they encountered German SP artillery in North Africa in 1941, the British army had none of their own and hastily improvised some using the 25 pounder (approx 105 mm) field gun mounted on a Valentine tank body. For reasons unknown it was given the name of "Bishop". The new version that came into service in 1965 maintained this clerical theme and is called the "Abbot". American SP guns, mounted on Sherman tank chassis, were called "Priest".

[2] Not to be confused with *SS-Obergruppenführer* Reinhard Heydrich, Protector of Bohemia and Moravia, who was assassinated in Prague by Czech SOE agents on 4th June 1942. Richard Heidrich was commander of the 1st FALLSCHIRMJÄGER Division from 1st May 1943 to 16th November 1944, when he took command of the 1st Parachute Corps. He was taken prisoner in Italy on 3rd May 1945. As a prominent Nazi, he was held at the Island Farm PoW camp, Bridgend, South Wales, until July 1947 when he was released because his health was deteriorating. He died in December 1947.

* * *

"Hands off cocks, on with socks!" a voice bellowed. "Begging your pardon Sir." Carter opened his eyes to make out the dim but clearly smiling face of a commando standing at the foot of his bed. "CO's compliments, but it's almost twenty three hundred hours."

"Thank you, Salmond." Carter swung his feet over the side of the bed and sat upright. "Please tell the CO I'm on my way."

The trooper vanished into the darkness and Carter took a moment to gather his thoughts. After he had eaten a dish of pasta with a vegetable sauce in one of the cafes that the CO had mentioned, the café's owner, a surly middle-aged woman, had directed him across the road to what she referred to as an *Aberge.* Carter assumed the word had the same meaning as a similar sounding French word and that it would provide him with a bed. He was right and the male owner, equally as surly as the female across the road, relieved him of a wad of *Lire* and directed him to the room.

Carter lay down without undressing, only taking off his webbing and wrapping the sling of his Tommy gun around his wrist to prevent it falling on the floor – or being stolen.

As he rose to leave the room, Carter noticed a pool of water where the commando had been standing a few moments earlier. So, the rain had arrived and it must be heavy to be dripping off the clothing like that. He unbuckled his poncho from its position under his small pack and wrapped it around his shoulders until he could do up the buttons that held it closed along one side. He decided his helmet would offer more protection from the rain than his beret and crammed it onto his head.

He had been right; a steady downpour was washing the streets as he left the guest house. Hurrying along the street he made good time to the perimeter of the town where the commando was still dug in. Cousens had made his HQ in a small house at the very edge of the town, the rear windows offering an uninterrupted view of the surrounding countryside. Not that anything could be seen in the darkness and with the rain decreasing the visibility even further.

Making his way through the house to the rear, Carter shed his dripping poncho and slipped off his webbing. "I found a hostel for the night." Carter told Cousens as he rose from the table where he had been studying a map. He probably knew it off by heart already,

Carter thought, but it was what officers tended to do when they had nothing else to think about. 'Know the ground' was something they had all been taught at Officer Training School.

"Bad news, I'm afraid." Cousens reported, a gloomy expression on his face. "The pontoon bridge has been washed away. The river level rose rapidly, apparently, and the stakes holding the ends ripped free. The pontoons crashed against the piers of the old bridge and the deck was smashed to matchwood."

"So what happens now?"

"They're going to build a Bailey Bridge, but can't really start work on it until morning. First it has to be brought up from the engineer park and then they've got to make sure the piers don't collapse under it when they put it in position. I don't think we'll see any more troops across it before tomorrow night at the earliest. More realistic would be Tuesday morning[1]."

Nearly three days away, Carter thought. That was a long time for them to hold out. They had some anti-tank artillery now, thanks to the units that had managed to get across the river, but it wouldn't stop a full scale counterattack. What they really needed were tanks, but 78 Div were an infantry outfit. Even their recce unit, the 56th Reconnaissance Regiment, only had lightly armoured Humbrettes[2]. They were fast but didn't stand a chance against even the oldest marks of Panzers.

"Is it possible they'll send the Canadians this way?" It was a faint hope. The 1st Canadian Armoured Division was at least fifty miles away at Lucera and were heading in the wrong direction, towards the mountains.

"We can only hope, but this rain is going to be churning up those mountain roads. Even if they're ordered to come to our aid, they'll be slowed down. But we don't have to worry about German armour. According to Colonel Vernon there isn't a *Panzer* formation this side of the mountains." They both knew that it wasn't the tanks that would be the problem, but the fuel bowsers needed to keep their engines running. They needed roads under their tyres, preferably mud free roads.

Cousens focused on the minutiae of handing over command to Carter, showing him on the map where the commando was positioned, their fields of fire and details of the units on their flanks. In reality it was only 49 Cdo to their south; their northern flank was wide open because they had nothing to anchor it on except open countryside; which troops had patrols out (all of them) and in which directions.

The trooper that had woken him, Salmond, brought him a tin mug filled with tea and Carter took an experimental sip. As usual it was far too sweet, but it was an act of kindness, so he said nothing except 'Thank you."

He'd finish his tea and then carry out a circuit of the defences. The commandos would be awake, he knew, but they had to see that he was also awake.

The night passed quickly. There were occasional bursts of fire from in front of their positions as a German patrol encountered a British one. The Germans were probing the defences, looking for weaknesses and the commandos were there to prevent them from achieving their aim.

Reports came in: one prisoner taken, sent to the rear under guard; one trooper slightly injured by stone chips when a bullet hit a wall that he was taking cover behind; bandaged and fit for duty.

A patrol from 4 Troop, under the command of Sgt Prof Green, had seen a German patrol returning to their positions, followed them and attacked them just as they crossed through their own lines, killing or injuring several of the patrol and also the sentries in the forward listening post. No British casualties.

Dawn broke with the fury of artillery rounds falling as the Germans sought to start the day with a bang. The British had expected it and were hunkered down in their slit trenches to ride out the onslaught. The Germans were nothing if not predicable. The 'dawn chorus', or 'daily hste' had been a regular feature of life in the trenches of the last war and it seemed to have continued to be their preferred morning routine in this war.

But there were German aircraft in the air as well. Two flights of six Ju88 light bombers flew over the town and dropped their bombs. The commandos weren't affected as the bombs all fell in the area where Carter estimated the railway station to be. Their own divisional HQ had been in that area when the Germans still held Termoli and no doubt they thought that the British would set up their command in the same building, which was common practice. But the commandos never did what was common practice. Unless 36 Bde had set up their HQ in the town centre when they had arrived, just before the bridge had been swept away, it would have been Italian civilians who suffered at the hands of their so-called German allies.

As the hour allotted for dawn stand-to drew to a close, Carter sent a runner to wake the CO and radioed the Quartermaster, Andrew Fraser, to tell him he had command until either he or the CO returned, then made his way to Col Vernon's HQ for the morning briefing.

[1] That would be 5th October. The commando had boarded their landing craft on 1st October and landed at about two in the morning on the 2nd.

[2] The Humber Light Reconnaissance Car was nicknamed the Humbrette or Ironside. It was built on a Humber Super Snipe motorcar chassis.

* * *

"You know those tanks that the Colonel said didn't exist?" Charlie Cousens said as he returned to the house being used as their HQ, having been summoned with some urgency to speak to the Colonel.

Carter felt his heart skipped a beat, knowing that bad news was about to be delivered.

"Yes, what of them?"

"Well, half a dozen have been spotted five miles north of the town and they're heading our way."

All day the Argyll and Sutherland Highlanders had been sending out patrols along the roads radiating from the twon, using captured German vehicles, trying to find any trace of the enemy. It seems they had finally found them.

That morning's briefing had ended with Vernon reporting that the telephone lines to Guglionesi, a town ten miles inland, were still intact. He had spoken, through an interpreter, to the town's Mayor, who reported that the area was filling up with Germans tanks. Vernon had laughed at the idea. "Bloody Ities jumping at shadows! If there are any tanks nearer than Rome, I'll eat my hat." He declared. Carter hoped he had a good appetite.

"What are our orders?" This new threat would mean some re-deployment of the commando.

"Guglionesi is to the west of us; almost directly in front as we're sitting here right now. The Colonel wants three troops to advance about two miles down the road and set up a position on the top of a hill that dominates the area. You can just about make it out from here." Cousens walked to the window and pointed. "The Jerries will have to stay to the north of the road to prevent themselves being observed by 78 Div's artillery spotters, so we have to defilade[1] their advance and force them to turn and face us."

"What about our flanks?"

"We'll have to protect them as best we can. The SRS are being told to send a troop to the rear of the hill to cover our backs."

"Are we getting artillery support?"

"Yes, we're getting a couple of 6 pounder guns. Plus we have our own heavy weapons. We've also been given two machine gun teams from the Kensingtons to add to our own. They'll keep the Jerries heads down if they get within a thousand yards."

"Who's going to command this suicide mission, Sir?" But Carter already knew the answer.

"We've been given this job because we're more experienced then Four-Nine and you're getting it because you're my most experienced officer. Take 4, 5 and 6 troops."

"Will we get any support from Four-Nine?"

"Not directly. They and the rest of the SRS are being pulled in to provide close defence of the town, along with the troops that made it across the river before the bridge was lost. The three troops staying with me will provide a buffer here on the west of the town that you can fall back on."

"At what point do I do that, Sir?"

Cousens gave a grim smile. "When you think you can no longer hold the position. It will be down to your judgement. But if the tanks get into the town, it's unlikely we'll be able to hold it."

In other words, if the town falls, it will be your fault, Carter interpreted. No, that wasn't fair. He wasn't expected to sacrifice his men in that way. There were many options still available to them, including withdrawing by sea. Vernon had left that option open by ordering the landing craft to stand offshore out of range of German artillery. They could be in the harbour within an hour of being summoned.

"If it's any consolation, the Colonel has requested that we're reinforced by sea. Div HQ have agreed and its being organised."

"When can we expect relief?"

"That they haven't told us. But moving regular infantry isn't as easy as moving commandos. They'll want to make sure that the Mess silver[2] is properly packed."

Carter chuckled. The commandos made plenty of jokes, mainly unjustified, about the luxurious conditions enjoyed by regular troops compared to their own rough and ready existence.

"How long do you think I've got?" Carter asked. Almost on cue an artillery barrage started up, peppering the front line.

"I think that's your answer." They both knew that a barrage of that intensity was intended to keep defenders' heads below the parapets of their trenches while infantry moved into position to mount an attack.

"I better get going then." Carter rammed his helmet onto his head, picked up his Tommy gun and headed for the door.

As a shell blast deafened everyone within range, he didn't hear Cousens shout 'Good luck!'

[1] To defilade is to attack an enemy from the side, rather than head on, which is known as enfilading.

[2] Units in the British army own a considerable amount of silverware which is used to decorate the dining tables of the Officers' and Sergeants' messes on formal occasions. While it is now normal for that to be left behind in the regimental depot, up until late Victorian times units used to take their silverware on campaign with them and it was used to serve dinner in the field.

6 - The Guglionesi Road

Hurriedly briefing his Troop Commanders, Carter dispatched them along the Guglionesi road, ordering them to make the best possible speed. For a commando, the idea of running two miles in full kit wasn't one they would argue about.

On the edge of the town he found the crews of the 6 Pounder guns and the machine gun teams of the Kensington Regiment sitting in their carriers[1] drinking tea and smoking. He went to look for the battery commander, a Lieutenant.

"Why aren't your men on the move?" he demanded when he found them.

"We're waiting for orders, Sir" The Lieutenant snapped to attention.

"Have you been told where you are going?"

"Oh yes, we've got a map reference and everything." The Lieutenant seemed especially pleased that he knew where he was going.

"In that case, you have your orders. Now get a move on."

The young officer's mouth dropped open, about to protest, when he saw Carter's grim expression and thought better of it. Instead, he began shouting orders, engines were started and the short column became a hive of activity as the gunners climbed aboard their transport. Carter hauled himself into the rear of the lead vehicle so he could hitch a lift to catch up with his men. It was crowded, the gun's full crew already being on-board. The carrier gave a lurch and was steered off the verge and onto the road.

By the time they caught up with the rearmost sections of commandos, they were almost half way to their destination. Carter was pleased to see how far they had come and the NCOs were hurrying the men along.

Instructing the driver to slow down, Carter jumped over the side and went to march with his men. As he passed the driver, he told him to stay behind the rearmost units. He didn't want to lose his artillery support by them blundering into advancing Germans before his own men arrived to occupy the hill.

Breaking into a run, Carter passed along the column and caught up with the Ernie Barraclough, who was at the head of 4 Troop; the lead troop of the column. They jogged along side by side, the gradient becoming noticeably steeper as the hill rose in front of them. The crown of the low hill was about five hundred yards long and covered in olive trees. That helped in one way, because the trees provided some cover, but on the other hand, branches hit by heavy fire would drop down to risk injuring anyone beneath. But they should be in trenches anyway, so the risk was reduced.

Carter found a Sergeant from the Argylls waiting for him, along with a Private.

"Is this all of you?" Carter asked, surprised. He had expected to patrol to be larger.

"Ach nay, Sir. They're deployed along yon road there." he pointed northwest, where a narrow road ran. "I've been told to brief you on the ground."

"Thanks. So, what can you tell us?"

The sergeant briefed him on the terrain around the hill. Behind them the Guglionesi road continued westward to pass by a factory about four hundred yards away at the bottom of the hill. Before that, the road formed a Y junction with the minor road, more of a track really, heading more northerly. "Y'll find a wee bridge over a stream about three quarters of a mile along there. He pointed west again. "Y'can see another hill there, to the north of the road, so with you holding this yin, my OC[2] thinks the Jerries'll try to get between the factory and the bridge and move along the valley, so they don't have to climb this wee hill. That's why he's deployed the company there."

The valley wasn't deep, but it would screen the Germans from observers in the town until they were much closer to 15 Cdo's positions on the outskirts. "And we'll have to stop them from doing that."

"Aye, well, we'll do our best." The sergeant replied fatalistically. He was wearing the ribbon for the Africa Star, so this wasn't his first encounter with German armour, Carter guessed.

"I'm sure you will. Where were the tanks when you saw them?

"Aboot two mile doon the road there." The Sergeant pointed. "Three o' them with a couple of Hanomags. Sat there bold as brass, ha'ing lunch by the look o' them."

"Did they see you?"

"If they did, they didnae stand-to. But we were in a truck, so it would be hard to miss us."

"But it was a German truck, so that might have confused them. I'll assume they saw you though. Where are your trucks now?"

"The OC sent them back to Termoli when we got the order to dig in. No point in making them a target and if we have to pull out, they'll be more of a liability if we're being chased by tanks."

It was a mistake that other troops had made, thinking that a vehicle was a good way of evading the enemy. But a lorry made a better target for a tank gunner than individual soldiers spread out over several yards.

Carter became aware that there were men behind him now and he turned to find the three troop commanders waiting patiently for their orders. He picked out the man he wanted. "Jeremy, I'd like you to take 5 Troop and go with Sgt …sorry, what's your name?"

"McCallister, Sir."

"Sgt McCallister and reinforce the company of Argyles that are positioned along that track you can see down there. Take the right flank and cover the bridge across the stream."

Jeremey Groves didn't stop to ask questions. He knew what was required of him.

"Ernie, I want 4 Troop to dig in astride the road to prevent any encroachment from the west. Jerry will at least try it before he changes direction. 6 Troop I want to dig in along the northern side of the hill, just on the edge of the olive grove."

"What about my guns?" The artillery Lieutenant had arrived as Carter was talking.

"One gun with 4 Troop covering the road and the other two facing north to cover the valley. I'll leave it up to you where you site them."

"And the Kensingtons?" The artillery officer seemed to assume he was commanding the heavy weapons. Carter decided not to correct him. He couldn't be everywhere, so delegation was appropriate.

"Either side of the two guns on the side of the hill."

It worried Carter that his flanks were so exposed and he had to hope that the Germans didn't discover the weakness. He looked at his watch and did a quick calculation of how long they might have to hold until relieved. At least forty hours if the Bailey Bridge wasn't completed until the morning of the 5th, but maybe longer than that. The arrival of a Panzer division meant that 78 Div would have to fight their way through to the town and, after Sicily, Carter knew what that might mean for the beleaguered commando brigade.

[1] This was the Universal Carrier, often called a Bren Carrier, because there was space in front to mount a forward firing Bren gun. It was a three and a half ton, lightly armoured tracked vehicle, open to the sky. It's V8 petrol engine gave it a top speed of about thirty mph (50 kph). When used as a towing unit by the Royal Artillery its crew would also crew the gun. A typical crew would be the commander, a driver, a gunner and a rifleman, but a 6 pounder gun had a crew of six, which could be accommodated. When towing artillery two were used, one to tow the gun and the other to tow an ammunition limber. Over 113,000 were built and they remained in use around the world in various countries until the 1960s. The original design was based on one by Vickers Armstrong, but several companies built them under licence for the British army, including Ford and Bedford.

[2] Officers commanding sub formations within a battalion are referred to as the Officer Commanding (OC) or Officer in Charge

(OIC) to avoid confusion with unit's Commanding Officer (CO). There may be several OCs, but there can be only one CO.

* * *

The Germans came at sunset, attacking out of the glare of the sun, making them hard to see. It was a text book approach, with infantry spread out on each side of the road. They advanced from cover to cover, which was mainly stone walls and scrubby bushes. Carter estimated that there was about a company of them.

"Hold your fire until I give the word." Carter said to the nearest men, knowing the order would be repeated along the line. He had dug his own slit trench right next to the road, midway along the line of commandos.

The German infantry would be *Panzer Grenadiers*, he thought. They normally took the advanced role in Panzer divisions as they were mechanised infantry, transported in armoured halftrack vehicles. It meant they could keep up with the tanks they supported.

A company strength was too much for it just to be a reconnaissance patrol, which made Carter think that the enemy at least suspected their presence on the hilltop even though they didn't know it to be a certainty.

How close should he let them get? He wondered. Already each commando would have selected a target and they wouldn't miss at anything at under two hundred yards. How far were they now? One hundred he estimated. From where he was lying, he couldn't see any of the range markers that the NCOs would have positioned along the road and across their front

But his Tommy gun would be effective at fifty yards, he knew that. Fifty yards it would be then.

The Germans continued to close the gap. They didn't hurry, which suggested they were experienced troops. Each one moved quickly from one source of cover to the next, then waited until his comrades straightened out the line before moving again. There were light machine guns on both flanks and one on either side of the road. His Bren gunners would take care of those.

A command was shouted and the line of German soldiers rose as one. They may have been fifty yards away, or it may have been more, but it was time to make sure they didn't get any closer.

As the Germans started to move in for their final rush up the hill, Carter shouted at the top of his voice. "Fire!" was all he had time to say. The crack of rifles seemed to blend together as a single sound before becoming more ragged as each soldier re-cocked his weapon. The Bren guns started their staccato chattering. The light machine gun team directly to his front seemed to disappear in a fountain of blood as they were hit by several rounds at once.

That was the problem in these situations. There was no way of directing fire so that several troopers didn't select the same target. But as each target fell the trooper that fired would shift his aim to the next one that was visible.

The German line broke under the onslaught almost immediately and soldiers scuttled back down the hill, making their way out of range to safety. Carter doubted they'd see them again that evening.

Round one to the good guys, he thought.

"Ernie!" Carter called. "Send a man out to find out what unit they're from."

It wasn't just idle curiosity. Knowing which division they were facing would tell him what sort of armour he was going to have to deal with. If it was an older mark of tank, their 6 pounder guns would be adequate, but if they were the newer Tiger tanks, which they had met up with in Sicily, things would be more serious. The Tiger was far more heavily armoured, which made it much harder to kill, even with anti-tank guns.

The sun was almost down when a German soldier appeared, carrying a white flag. He asked in broken English if they could gather their wounded and Carter gave his permission. They were allowed to use no more than four men and all had to be unarmed.

Ernie Barraclough appeared holding a scrap of cloth embroidered with a symbol. It had been cut off the sleeve of a dead German. The divisional symbol was yellow and Y shaped, with a cross bar on the upright,

"Doesn't mean anything to me." Carter admitted. "We didn't see it in Sicily. I'll radio back to Brigade and ask them to identify it."

As the sun slipped below the horizon, clouds began to sweep in from the north and the rain soon followed. Artillery shells began to fall on the top of the hill as the Germans retaliated for their ignominious treatment, but in the dark the shellfire was undirected and few shells landed close enough to cause concern.

* * *

Apart from the persistent rain and the occasional salvo of artillery shells, the night was uneventful. Commando patrols crept forward as far as the closest German listening posts but didn't interfere with them. In their isolated position, Carter couldn't risk losing men to pointless acts of bravado. One patrol managed to creep through the lines as far as the factory and reported that Hanomag halftracks were parked there, but they hadn't been able see any tanks.

Dawn stand-to brought the daily hate and another attempt to approach the hill along the road, but it was half hearted and Carter's force had no trouble stopping it well short of the low summit. Carter suspected that whoever was in command had done it more because it was expected of him than because it had any chance of success.

No doubt a new plan was being formulated even as they were dealing with that assault. But they would have to see how the day unfolded.

That was the problem with being on the defensive. The initiative was always held by the enemy. It was why the commandos had been formed; to take the fight to the enemy and keep him wrong footed. Defence didn't come naturally to them. But all the officers had been trained as infantrymen first, so they understood the principles of defensive actions, even if they didn't like having to take on that role.

During the night the carriers had been used to ferry ammunition, food and water up the hill from the town, so they wouldn't have to worry about those commodities for a while. Charlie Cousens had hitched a ride on one of them and inspected their positions, pronouncing himself satisfied with the arrangements that Carter had made before returning to the town once more.

News came through from Brigade that the division facing them was the 16th Panzer, which had last been seen near Naples. Their arrival here, across mountainous roads made muddy by the storms, was no mean fete. Their tanks were Panzer IVs, quite a formidable weapon and thought to be almost as good as the Tiger, but they weren't so heavily armoured. So long as the 6 pounders could hit them, they should be able to disable them.

The big problem for Carter was trying to work out the enemy commander's battle plan. What were his orders? If he could solve that riddle, he could work out what his own counter-strategy should be.

On the one hand, the commandos held the town. But the town wasn't worth anything to the Germans by itself.

On the other hand, if 78 Div got across the river they could sweep a single division aside and advance north almost unopposed until a suitable point and then cross the spine of Italy to outflank the Germans in their positions around Naples. The Germans would have to withdraw, possibly as far north as Rome. 78 Div could even advance as far north as Pescara, seventy miles away and then turn west to threaten Rome itself.

Which made the defence of the river the priority for the Germans.

But if they didn't re-take the town, the British could use its port, small as it was, to bring in reinforcements by sea, thereby outflanking the Germans where they held the river.

So the Germans needed to send a strong enough force to at least threaten the town, in the hope that the British would withdraw by sea, while at the same time using most of their resources to prevent the British from crossing the river.

That seemed to be confirmed by the reports from his patrols. There were sufficient Hanomags to transport a battalion strength of *Panzergrenadiers*. A sizeable force and one the lightly armed commandos wouldn't want to have to defend against. There had been no tanks located, but they had been seen the previous day by the Argyll's patrols. They would still be in the area somewhere but were being protected from anti-tank guns until they were needed.

But how many tanks? A squadron would be about right, he thought. A dozen or so tanks were all that was needed against defenders that had none.

Of course, tanks were of little use in the narrow streets of Termoli, but they could sit back and pound the buildings to rubble, making the job of the infantry easier.

But first they had to take the hill on which Carter small force sat. The tanks could move across country through the shallow valley to his front, as could the Hanomags, but the wheeled vehicles needed to use the road which ran over the top of the hill. And those vehicles carried the fuel and the ammunition that the tanks required to keep them operational.

So, there were probably around a dozen tanks and between eight hundred and a thousand infantry for him to deal with. He, on the other hand, had three understrength troops numbering barely one hundred and thirty men and a company of Jock infantry, perhaps a hundred and twenty of them if they were at full strength, three anti-tank guns and a couple of Vickers machine guns.

Battles had been won with worse odds, but not very often.

The Germans started to probe the rear of the hill, where the SRS were patrolling. They played a clever game against the advancing Germans, directing their patrols to converge on each probing force and then attacking them, to make it appear that the rear of the hill was well defended. Everywhere the Germans tried to ascend, they were repulsed by the same small group of men, though they didn't know it.

That was the pattern for the morning across the whole of his front. The Germans would send out a force of a couple of platoons and the British would send them scampering back to their own lines again. But Carter knew what the enemy commander was doing. Every time the British opened fire, he got a better feel for where their strong points were located. And where the weak points were.

Particularly vulnerable was the gap between the hill and the left flank of the Argylls. Carter had it covered by 4 Troop's Bren guns on the hill, but the lack of fire from the gap itself would tell the Germans all they would need to know. But if he moved the Argyll's and his own 5 Troop closer to the hill, it opened up a gap on the northern side between the right hand flank and the stream that flowed eastwards.

He remembered the games of "British Bulldog"[1] that he had played at school, where one child had to defend the whole width of the playground, crabbing from side to side to try and intercept the advancing boys. But in that game the enemy didn't have machines guns which could mow down anyone who climbed out of their slit trench to move to intercept the attacker.

No, it was better to keep the gap on this side, where he could provide cover from the hilltop. It would also bring the German tanks closer to the 6 pounder guns.

"Sir! Jerry's on the move." A shout came from his left, close to the road and dragged him from his reverie

Carter crawled forward to where the sentry sat in his trench. He pointed. Carter raised his binoculars and aimed them along the road. Sure enough, a Panzer tank crawled towards the, hill with German infantry packed in behind it, using its bulk for cover.

"Gunners!" Carter shouted.

"Seen." Came an instant reply. He heard the sound of a shell being rammed into a breach and the breach being slammed shut.

"Wait till he's too close for you to miss." Carter called. The Corporal in charge of the gun gave his back a scornful look, resentful that the commando had felt it necessary to give such an instruction.

But the closer the tank got, the more the gun barrel had to be depressed and there was a limit to the angle of depression. Leave it too late and the shell would scream over the top of the tank to explode harmlessly in the fields beyond.

The tank was allowed to reach the Y junction when the gunner fired. The aim was good and the tanks stopped dead in its tracks. Carter had expected an explosion, but none came. Smoke did trickle out of the diver's viewing slot and from around the hatch of the closed down turret, but that was all.[2]

A ragged cheer went up from the commando positions but quickly died as two more tanks emerged from behind the factory building and started to crawl forward. The German infantry ran towards them to take cover once again, so they could continue their advance and the Bren guns opened up at extreme range, but no casualties seemed to have been inflicted.

The tank turrets swung to aim their guns at the point on the hill from where the 6 pounder had fired. Both of them fired their seven and a half centimetre guns at the same time and the face of the hill erupted in flying earth and rocks.

Something landed on Carter's head and he was glad he had worn his helmet. But he realised that some of his men were still wearing their green berets. No matter how often they were told, they wanted to wear that badge of honour.

"Helmets on." Carter bawled. "Any man found not wearing a helmet will have me to deal with!"

The 6 pounder gun fired again, just as the tank it was aiming at changed course to get off the road. The shell hit the side a glancing blow and exploded, killing or injuring a number of the infantry that were hurrying to keep up.

The tank's turret turned back onto its target and fired again. This time the shell flew high and Carter could hear it scything through the olive trees. He had no idea where it landed, though he did hear the explosion.

"Ernie!" Carter called. "Get one of those Vickers up here." The rapid firing machine gun would deter the infantry far more effectively than the Bren guns and they were serving no purpose where they were currently located. If he could get the infantry to retreat, the tanks would have to retire with them.

The big disadvantage for a tank was that most of its visibility was forward and the view from the turret was equally limited, depending on which way the turret was facing. If infantry could get into a position where they couldn't be seen, they could jam the tracks to stop the tank from moving. After that the tank could be disabled by something as simple as a petrol bomb lobbed into the air intakes causing the crew to suffocate, which is quite feasible at close range.

Which is why, Carter knew, tanks always needed infantry support so that enemy infantry couldn't get close enough to do any damage. The only time tanks fought without it was in tank-on-tank engagements, where it came down to which side had the greater firepower and the best defensive armour – or the most tanks.

But it would take time for the Vickers to be repositioned and that time would allow the enemy to get closer and possibly overrun the commando positions.

The second tank had left the road now, angling to Carter's left, the opposite side to its companion. The 6 pounder couldn't engage both targets. It wouldn't be long before the gunners had to lift the 'trail' of the gun to reposition it, because it could only be traversed forty five degree on either side of its forward axis and at the speed the Panzer was advancing, the infantry trotting behind, that angle would soon be exceeded.

And then the gunners would be exposed to the murderous fire of the Panzer's secondary armament, an MG 34 machinegun, nicknamed the *Spandau* by British troops. Though they tended to call all German machine guns by that name.

The left-hand tank's turret started to turn, but its gun was still canted at a high angle, so it wasn't intending to fire on the hilltop with that. But its machine gun did open up, raking along the line of the commandos' trenches, forcing them to keep their heads down. Bullets cracked and whined around Carter, then passed on along the line.

The angle of the tank's progress started to expose the flanks of the infantry huddled in behind them and some commandos started taking pot-shots at them. That forced them to the far side of the tank.

Which was when an SRS patrol intervened. They must have seen the threat and moved around towards the front of the hill to add some support. A Bren gun opened fire from that side, followed by the crack of Lee Enfield rifles. The infantry were caught between a crossfire formed by the commandos on the hell and the SRS on its southern slopes. The bulk of the tank was doing nothing to protect them. In fact, its continued forward movement was making them even more vulnerable.

They were only human. They faltered, then started to retreat, looking for cover, of which there wasn't much.

The tank commander must have been told that his support was no longer with him, so he brought his vehicle to a halt, making it a sitting target for the 6 pounder. It fired a shot. The front armour deflected it upwards, but the crew got the message. They started to reverse the vehicle back down the hill.

Satisfied that the threat to his left flank was being held at least, Carter turned his attention to his right. A similar problem was now facing the infantry on that side. The Argylls had their Bren guns working, firing at the infantry from the bottom of the valley. They, too sought cover. Carter's own Bren teams on the curve of the hill's slope fired to keep them away from the top of the hill even as the tank turned its turret to bring its machine gun into play. But the turret couldn't face two ways at once. If he engaged the Argyll's it gave the commandos free reign and if he engaged the commandos the Argylls would be unmolested.

The matter was settled by another of the 6 pounders, positioned four hundred yards away, along the top of the hill with 6 Troop. The gunners had turned the gun and were now able to fire across the face of the hill at the tank. The first shell caught it on one of its tracks, bringing it to a juddering halt. The Germans turned the turret to take a shot at the new threat but couldn't be sure where the round had come from. They fired the 75 mm gun, but the shot obviously did no damage. The 6 pounder fired again and this time scored a direct hit on the frontal armour.

Stranded now that their track was broken, the tank crew got the message and decided to abandon the vehicle. The turret hatch flew open and a figure started to climb out. All along the top of the hill, rifle fire cracked, taking shots at the escaping men. Infantry hated tank crews because of their seeming invulnerability and Carter's men weren't going to miss the opportunity to take get some retaliation in.

The first man out, probably the commander, managed to get his feet on the top of the turret before being hit and tumbling over the far side, out of sight. The second man only got half his body out before he was hit and slid back down inside. The third man just stuck his hand through and waved something white, probably a handkerchief.

With their sledgehammer destroyed, the infantry realised they hadn't a hope of taking the hill. They worked their way back down the slope, harried continually by the Bren guns. Carter ordered his men to stop firing on the tank and, one by one, the rifles fell silent as the message was passed from trench to trench. Once the infantry were at a safe distance he would send out a section of men to take the prisoners under guard and search the tank.

That had been close.

The three-man Vickers crew arrived and Carter directed them to a position where they could fire along the road.

"You took your time." Carter heard a commando say as the crew started to dig a gun pit.

"You try carrying a thirty pound gun four hundred yards at the run." The gunner retorted. "Wanker."

"I'll race you any day of the week." The commando replied.

Things were getting out of hand and Carter didn't want his troops arguing amongst themselves, though such banter was common enough. "Quiet, the pair of you, or I'll have you both on latrine duty when we get back to Termoli." If we get back, he didn't say out loud.

The hill shook as an artillery round exploded in the middle of the olive trees. The Germans getting their own retaliation in. Probably using the other tanks for the purpose, Carter thought. He raised his glasses, wondering if they had any observers out, capable of directing the fire more accurately. On a low hill about half a mile away, much lower than the one on which he was currently sitting, Carter made out the shape of a small chapel, surrounded by a graveyard. The graves were all mausoleums built above the ground, which was too stony to dig. It had a squat bell tower. That would make a good OP, he thought. It was too far to target with rifle fire, but he might risk a few bursts with the Vickers when it was set up. He made a note to send a patrol in that direction when it got dark. If there were Germans in it, the least he could do was discourage them.

The afternoon wore on with a similar pattern to the morning, but there was no significant attempt to attack until just before sunset. It was a frontal assault on the Argyll's positions along the track that led to the bridge across the stream. From the top of the hill all Carter could do was provide some covering fire from a Vickers gun, but as the Germans got closer to the Argyll's positions he had to order the gun to cease firing for fear of hitting their own men in the backs. It looked as though the Argylls might be pushed out of their positions, but 5 Troop made a bayonet charge into the German flank. It took them by surprise and sent them back the way they had come.

It had been a foolhardy thing for Jeremy Groves to do. If the Germans had stood and fought, the troop were outnumbered and the Argylls couldn't cover them for fear of hitting their own side. The troop could well have been wiped out. But the Germans weren't used to British troops, or any enemy troops, doing mad things like that. They were used to defenders falling back under their assaults, so the commandos sudden sortie had unnerved them.

Carter shook his head in mock amazement. He should go down and give Groves a rocket up the backside, but he knew that if he did anything at all it would be to give him a pat on the back. Aggression was a commando strength and he had used it to his advantage.

As the sun set the artillery started up again but it was now just part of a general background noise. Guns were firing off to the south, which was where the Biferno river lay and shells were roaring overhead as longer range artillery fired on the town, then there was the more targeted assault on the hill. 4 Troop had discovered that if they moved about twenty feet further down the hill and dug in again, they avoided the worst of the barrage.

As soon as it was dark, Carter put Ernie Barraclough in charge at the top of the hill and made his way down to show his face among 5 Troop. Prof Green insisted on going with him and it was easier and less time consuming to acquiesce than it was to argue. Since he had been wounded at Honfleur, Green never let Carter out of his sight. "Mrs Hamilton would never forgive me if I let anything happen to you, Lucky." He had said one night a few months before.

"Does that worry you?" Carter had chuckled.

"A grieving widow with access to a shotgun? It doesn't just worry me; it terrifies me." Carter could understand his concerns. He and Fiona hadn't been together long enough as a married couple to have had any serious arguments, but from the few brief flashes of her temper he had seen, she had terrified him as well.

The route would take him close to the rear of the Argyll's positions, so he decided to visit Fraser McInnes, their OC. After the pleasantries were over, McInnes' voice took on a serious note.

"I'm afraid we've had orders from Brigade. We're to pull out before dawn tomorrow morning."

That news came as a body blow to Carter. Without the Argyll's his job would become a whole lot harder. "Did they say why?"

"They're concentrating everyone on the defence of the town, so we're needed to fill a gap in the perimeter."

As if his own men weren't defending the town! Carter thought. The only difference was that they were doing it at a greater distance. McInnes could see from Carter's expression how he felt. "I've been told that there have been Jerry tanks seen closer in than we are, so Brigade doesn't want to risk us getting cut off, out here on a limb so to speak."

"No such consideration for him and his men, Carter noted. But he was under the command of Colonel Vernon, who was a commando and thought like a commando. And commandos went where no one else would consider going – or staying for that matter. Carter had no option but to accept the decisions that had been made. "What time are you leaving?"

"Oh three hundred will get us back before dawn and the Jerries are less likely to suspect we're on the move at that time in the morning. I'm to take the carriers with me as well. No one wants them to fall into Jerry hands."

"What happens when we pull back? We won't be able to take the guns."

"You'll have to disable them and leave them behind. The Vickers guns can be broken down and carried."

"What's your plan?"

"One platoon at a time, so the remainder can cover our backs until they have to leave as well."

"OK. I'll move some sections of 5 Troop into the positions you vacate, so if any Jerry patrols see their heads they'll think you're still there."

"Will you pull out as well?"

"From down here I will. I don't have any choice. I can't protect a front this long with one troop and I can't provide enough fire support from the top of the hill either."

"How long will you stay?"

"Until the Jerry's are about to land in the slit trenches up there." Carter nodded his head towards the hill. "Then I'll try to make a fighting retreat back into the lines. If we can hold out all day, I may withdraw during tomorrow night if we get no other orders."

"I don't envy you."

Carter gave a grim smile, invisible in the dark. "It's what we do."

"Bunch of fucking madmen." McInnes chuckled.

"That's been said before." Carter laughed back. "I'll brief Jeremy Groves on your plan. Just keep close communication with him so he can cover your back."

"I'll be the last man out of here, so you need have no concerns on that score. I don't want a company of *Panzergrenadiers* chasing me all the way back to Termoli."

Carter wished him good luck and went to find his own men.

[1] A game adopted by the British when in India, where it is known as kabaddi. In the Indian version it is an adult sport played by two teams of seven. There are differences in the rules of the two versions, but they both have the same roots in Indian culture.

[2] An armoured piercing shell doesn't explode on contact. It drills into the armour and the explosive, in the form of a 'shaped' charge, melts the inside of the armour, sending blast waves and molten fragments of metal flying around the tank's interior. This will start fires, kill the crew and possibly set off the tank's own ammunition. Very little exterior damage may be visible, other than the entry hole. Modern anti-tank missiles may contain a third element, which is another explosive charge which is propelled into the tank's interior to explode.

* * *

"Fancy a cup of tea?" Prof Green asked.
"No fires, no naked flames. You know the rules." Carter replied. He and Green had evicted a couple of troopers from their slit trench in the front line. Carter wasn't there to command 5 Troop, he was there to be seen by them and that wouldn't happen if he skulked around in the rear of the positions. The two men were due out on a patrol anyway. When they returned he would send them to one of the trenches vacated by the Argylls.
"Try telling that to the Jerries." Green nodded towards a farmhouse about fifty yards away, which had a large bonfire lit in front of it. Carter assumed it was to light up any commandos who might be sneaking up on them, but it was just as likely it was to keep the Germans warm on a damp and drizzly night. At this end of the line the two sides were so close that Carter had been able to hear the German's conversations.
"But we're not Jerries." Carter reminded him.

"I wasn't thinking of lighting a fire, or even a Tommy cooker. But they've got a fire going anyway. It would be shame not to make use of it."

"You can't be serious! It's far too risky."

"But it might be worth the risk." Green lowered his voice to a whisper. "Some of the men were sounding a bit glum when I went and chatted with them. They think we've been abandoned out here. Maybe this would boost their morale a bit, getting one over on the Jerries in that way."

Green was right. After three days in the field, the morale of any troops would be bound to flag. But after so much enemy action even the best soldiers would be feeling a bit low. Perhaps a morale boost might be in order.

"It's very risky."

"So is being here, fifty yards from Jerry's front line." Green countered. "The next artillery shell might land right on top of us. Or Jerry might decide he wants a few prisoners, so he mounts a raid."

"But that would be random. What you're talking about is deliberate."

"It's my life Lucky. If I go this way, it's no worse than going any other way and considerably better than some we've seen in the last couple of years."

That was something even Carter couldn't argue with. His mind flashed back to Honfleur and Dickie Bird, 2 Troop's commander. There was pretty much nothing left of him to bury after he had been struck by an enemy shell. And then there had been Arthur Murray, whose life had bled painfully out of him as he lay in a cowshed, a prisoner of the Germans, left behind when carter and his men had escaped.

"OK! But don't do anything stupid. If it looks like you've been spotted, get back here as fast as you can. I'll cover you with my Tommy gun."

In the firelight Carter made out Green's smile as it spread over his face. He shrugged his way out of his webbing, fished around inside his pack for a mess tin, then half filled it with water. Picking up his

Tommy gun, he wriggled over the edge of his slit trench. Kitten crawling his way forward, Carter watched his slow progress.

The Germans were on the far side of the fire, careful not to silhouette themselves against the flames, which would invite death. Which meant that none of the ones directly behind the fire would be able to see Green. But anyone watching from a different angle couldn't fail to spot him when he reached the fire's glow.

But the increasing level of the sound of the voices suggested that a bottle might be being passed around and the soldiers wouldn't want to be too far from it in case they missed their turn. So if they stayed where they were, Green might just get away with it.

If he came back as slowly as he went out, the water would be cold by the time he returned, making it useless for tea making. But, of course, that wasn't the point. Already Carter could hear voices from the neighbouring trenches as commandos spotted Green moving forward.

"Quiet!" Carter hissed. If the Germans heard the voices, they would wonder why the commandos had become so animated. They never made any sound if they didn't have to and, after two days in close proximity, the Germans would know that.

As he watched he saw Green slide the mess tin a few inches further forward, raise his body off the ground a fraction then pivot forward on his elbows and toes before lowering himself to the ground again. It was a slow way of moving, but it was almost undetectable. It made no sound and the motion was so slow it rarely caught the eye the way other movements did.

Carter saw movement behind the flames and raised his Tommy gun, easing off the safety catch and taking aim. A match flared; just a packet of cigarettes being passed around. Good, the Germans were still relaxed.

There was the sound of an artillery shell exploding at the top of the hill, quickly followed by the thump of the gun that fired it, somewhere over behind the factory. Good, the more noise the better as far as Carter was concerned. It was just the Germans keeping the commandos awake, hoping to tire them out. No doubt the troops they we planning to use for their next attack were far enough away to be able to get some sleep. After such a long time at war, the German soldiers would be able to sleep draped across a washing line. His own men had the same skill. Some of the commandos slept well enough to not even notice the artillery anymore; or so they claimed.

More shells exploded and Green took the opportunity to sped up his advance, switching from a kitten crawl to a leopard crawl. The only difference was that the knees were brought into play to give greater thrust and therefore more speed.

At last Green made it to the fire. Even at that distance, Carter could see steam rising from his damp uniform as the heat got to work on him. Green slid the mess tin the last few inches forward, raising a small cloud of sparks as a piece of wood settled under it. But they went unnoticed amongst the flames.

Why the Germans had built the bonfire so large, Carter couldn't quite work out. It must have been the height of a man and equally as broad across the base. It was far bigger than it needed to be to provide either light or heat. But that was to Green's advantage.

A soldier rose from the group behind the flames and Carter swore that he could feel the tension in the commandos rise to a new level. The sound of something rattling across stones came from Carter's left as a soldier pushed his rifle forward to take up an aiming position. Carter was about to warn him against firing but realised he didn't have to. The commando wouldn't want to stir up a hornets' nest. He was just making sure that if the soldier made a move towards Green's side of the fire, it would be a journey he would never complete.

In the cool night air, Carter could see steam start to rise above the mess tin. The agony of waiting would soon be over. The wandering soldier disappeared behind the farm building, then returned a few minutes later, buttoning his fly. Just a call of nature. He took his seat beyond the flames once more.

Something collapsed in the centre of the blaze, sending a cloud of sparks spiralling upwards. It also brought a chorus of laughter from the Germans, though what they were laughing about Carter couldn't fathom.

A voice started to sing, something soft and tuneful. The Jerry could carry a note, that was for sure. Carter had no idea what the song was. Both the Germans and the British sang Lilli Marleen[1], but it wasn't that.

Satisfied that the water was hot enough, Green started the slow journey back to the British lines. He couldn't turn round without making too much noise, so he had to crawl backwards. Fortunately, the sporadic artillery barrage was continuing, which meant that the rattle of small stones that he sometimes dislodged wasn't audible.

Carter's jaw ached with the tension of keeping it clenched as he watched and he had to force himself to relax. Glancing to his left and right, he could make out the dim shapes of the commando's faces, illuminated in the residual glow of the fire even from this distance. Their expressions were as taught as his, willing the Germans to stay put on their side of the fire and for Green to get back to his trench undetected.

He almost made it, as well.

He was within five yards when a German soldier got up and went to the wood pile that had been assembled and drew a plank from it to add to the blaze, not that it really needed it. He was just returning to the fire when something must have caught his eye. It might have been a reflection from the mess tin, although it had been blackened by the fire. It might just have been the fire lighting up Green's prone shape. Whatever it was, it caused the German to turn and take a closer look.

Dropping the plank, he put his hand around his back to find his rifle, only to remember that he must have left it where he had been sitting. He called something to his comrades and it caused an instant reaction, with soldiers diving to the left and right to find cover.

Carter raised his Tommy gun and fired a burst of rounds to his left, away from the line where Green might be hit. Green wasted no time, rising to his feet and making a dash for the trench, his mess tin in one hand and his Tommy gun in the other. Water sloshed over the side of the container as he ran.

Rifles fired from the darkness beyond the bonfire as the Germans tried to hit Green, but they were wild, suggesting that Carter's quick thinking had made them keep their heads down. Shots were fired in retaliation from the British side, but it was unlikely that they hit any Germans.

Green slid into the trench feet first and Carter felt a searing pain as scalding water splashed across his hand.

Carter stopped firing and called on his men to cease fire as well. A cheer went up from the British lines as they realised that Green had made it back safely.

"Why do you cheer, Tommy?" A voice called from the darkness.

"Thanks for the hot water, Fritz." Green shouted back. "I'm going to make some tea now. Do you want some?"

The commandos laughed, the tension flowing out of them. "Make us a cup, Srage." One trooper called.

"Sorry, just enough hot water for me and Lucky." Green called back. "If you want some, you'll have to get your own."

By the time the tea was made there was barely enough for a couple of sips each, so much had been lost in transit. But to the both of them it tasted like the nectar of the Gods.

"One of these days, you're going to get yourself killed." Carter observed.

"So are you." Green grinned back at him.

"But I won't get myself killed for a cup of tea."

"A cup of tea is as good a reason to get yourself killed as any other. Fighting fascism may look great in newspaper headlines, but when you get down to it, all that's happening here is that a bunch of working-class Germans are fighting a bunch of working class Englishmen to decide who rules Europe on behalf of big business."

Carter stifled a groan, keeping it inside himself. It was a familiar refrain from Green. But he couldn't stop himself from answering. "I thought you were ant-fascist to the core. All part of your socialist beliefs."

"I am, but we're not fighting it here. We're just fighting for our lives and that's different. And whichever side wins in the end, it would be nice to think we're going to create a brave new world after it's over. But we know from the last lot that it didn't happen. The same faces sat in Parliament, making laws that favoured the same friends as they always favoured."

"Maybe this time your Labour Party will win and it will all change."

"I'd like to think it will, but let's face it, the Tories will still have Churchill at the top and it's hard to see anyone beating him in an election, especially as he would have led us to victory[2]. So, in the meantime, I'd rather get killed for a cup of tea than to keep the Tory party in Westminster for another term."

"If we win, you could go into politics and change things that way."

"That's my plan. But the end of the war seems to be a long way away still. And even when we've beaten the Jerries, we've still got the Japs to contend with and they're winning everywhere right now. To be honest with you, I can't see the war being over before the end of the decade and I can't see us surviving that long. You just have to look around you. How many of the lads we met up with in forty-one are still here?"

"Not many. But they're not all dead. Some are prisoners of war and they'll go home once the war's ended. Some have been transferred to other commandos, or as trainers at Achnacarry. Some have only been wounded. They'll be back at work in civvie street long before we are."

"But plenty are propping up gravestones as well. How many have we lost, just since we landed in Sicily?"

"Too many." Carter had to admit.

"Yes, too many. And how many more will we lose just waiting for 78 Div to get across that river, eh?"

That gave Carter pause for thought. That was much more of an immediate concern than the end of the war. He felt it in his water that the next day would be decisive. The German divisional commander couldn't allow the commandos to block his advance any longer, because he had a stopwatch running as well and that stopwatch was the same one as Carter was using, measuring the time until 78 Div arrived. If necessary, the German commander would throw everything he had into taking the hill and Carter simply didn't have the resources to stop him. And it would be Carter's timing of his decision on when to withdraw that would determine the casualty rate.

Carter heard a noise behind him and found Capt McInnes in the trench beside him. "Just about to start the withdrawal." He advised. "What was that shooting about a few minutes ago?"

Carter indicated the tea he and Green were just finishing and told him the story. McInnes shook his head in mock disbelief. "You commandos are nutters, you know that?"

"That has been said before." Carter acknowledged.

"Well, do us a favour and don't stir the Jerries up anymore. We can do without a shooting-match going on while we withdraw. Now, I'm pulling my platoons out one by one, starting from this end. Are your men ready to replace them?"

Carter could only put two sections into space occupied by each platoon, less than half the number of defenders for each section of line that the Argylls vacated. "As ready as we'll ever be."

"Right. We'll be on our way. Good luck, Major." He said, as he slithered over the rear of the trench and made a crouching run back the way he had come.

"I hope luck won't have any part to play in things." Carter whispered at his retreating back.

[1] Written in 1915 as a poem, Lilli Marleen was first recorded in German in 1939, by Lale Andersen and she recorded it again in English in 1942, for use in German propaganda broadcasts to British troops. It wasn't a hit, as such, until it began to be broadcast on *Soldatensender* Belgrade (formerly Radio Belgrade) in 1941, the station broadcasting to German troops in Eastern Europe, the Balkans and North Africa. It is from that station that Allied troops

first heard it in the Mediterranean theatre and took a liking to it. The Nazis didn't approve of the song and German propaganda Minister Joseph Goebbels banned it. But the Belgrade station continued to play it on the personal intervention of General Erwin Rommel. As a consequence, Goebbels relented, but insisted that the song should only be played when the station closed down each night at 10 pm. It was then played every night until Belgrade was liberated by the Russians in 1944. It became a habit of both British and German soldiers to tune in each night at 10, just to hear that song. The best-known version of it, sung by German émigré Marlene Dietrich, wasn't recorded until 1944, as a special project for the Office of Strategic Services (OSS), the American special operations organisation, for use in their own propaganda broadcasts. British soldiers in Italy adapted the tune to their own words for the song "We Are The D-Day Dodgers" (see historical notes). The spelling used here is the original German.

[2] Green couldn't know it at the time, but he was wrong. At the General Election held in July 1945, The Conservative Party lost 189 seats, leaving Labour well and truly in power with 393, with 47% of the share of the vote, against only 36% for the Tories. It was a 10% swing toward Labour and a 12% swing away from the Conservatives. A lot of the losses were put down to complacency on the part of both Tory voters and politicians, who were convinced that Churchill was a shoo-in for Prime Minister, for the very reason Green gives. The campaign was almost totally fought on the basis of Churchill's personal appeal, which allowed Labour to campaign on the basis of issues of much broader public concern.

7 – 5th October

Carter would have liked to have been proven wrong, but the sun had barely crept above the horizon when he found out he was right.

Out of the north came a flight of five Ju88 light bombers, heading straight for the hill. "Take cover!" A sentry yelled; a cry taken up across the hilltop as the commandos hunkered down in the bottom of their slit trenches.

The bombs crashed amongst the trees throwing gouts of earth and rocks into the sky and sending deadly splinters of wood to scythe through any soft surface they met. The bombardment felt as though it went on for hours, but in fact it was barely a minute before the aircraft had crossed over the target and turned back the way they had come.

But it wasn't over. Out of the rising sun came the dots of more aircraft, growing larger until they seemed to fill the view of every trooper on the hillside. They swept across the face of the hill, cannon shells and machine gun rounds ripping up furrows of earth. It was an efficient form of attack, taking in in the whole of 5 and 6 troops positions as well as those of the right-hand flank of 4 troop, who were still covering the western approach.

These were a pair of Me 109's, the fighters that had failed to defeat the RAF over southern England. But here they didn't have Spitfires to contend with, just a few Bren gun rounds fired by soldiers brave, or foolish, enough to raise their heads above the level of their trench.

The two aircraft turned in a majestic arc and came in for a second assault, but this time strafing the positions where, until the previous night, the Argylls and 5 Troop had been defending. As the aircraft overshot and started to climb, 4 Troop's positions were also shot up, before the attackers turned away and headed back the way they had come.

NCO's started shouting, trying to identify the wounded, ordering men to check on the slit trenches where no reply was heard.

But the raid hadn't really been intended to devastate the commando. If it had that result, so much the better from the German perspective, but as Carter raised his binoculars, he knew what the real intention had been.

It was to keep the heads of the Argylls down as the Germans advanced on their positions, which, he saw, they had nearly reached.

There must have been a company strength of Germans, certainly more than a hundred, the early morning sun twinkling on the bayonets of their rifles as they sprinted forwards before the dazed soldiers had time to recover their wits.

But there were no dazed soldiers, only empty slit trenches. The Argylls were back in the relative safety of Termoli and 5 Troop were now holding a position sandwiched between 4 and 6 troops. Relative safety, of course, because Carter could hear the thunder of the morning hate as shells fell on the town's defenders.

But the Germans didn't stop running when they reached the Argyll's positions. Most of them ran through to take up defensive positions on the other side of the trenches, no doubt wondering why they were empty. A few, it looked like a single platoon, went from trench to trench to check that they were really vacant.

Carter watched one soldier jump down into a trench before being thrown straight out again by an explosion. His companions dived for cover. Carter shook his head in wonder at the man's stupidity. They must have been told to be on the lookout for booby traps, yet here was a dead, or at least badly wounded, soldier who had ignored the warning.

A brave soul got to his feet and checked the man over before crawling back into cover again, leaving the body where it was; so dead then. A Vickers gun opened up on the cluster of men around the dead man, sending them scuttling backwards to find better cover. The trenches would have been the best place for them, but they daren't risk them now until they had all been checked for traps.

Bren guns opened fire on the soldiers on Carter's side of the trenches, but he shouted orders for them to cease firing. They would need all the ammunition they had for what was to come and the Germans were too difficult to hit at that range.

Carter heard the sound of engines and turned to look along the road, where four Panzers were turning along the track to pass through the position that the Germans had just seized. As they reached there, turrets turned to keep their 75 mm guns trained on the side of the hill, a clear warning to the commandos not to attempt a counter attack. They needn't have worried. Carter had no intention of doing anything so foolhardy.

"Lucky, can you come here." The voice of Sgt Maj Chalk echoed across the hilltop. The man had a voice that could be heard above an artillery bombardment.

What now? Carter climbed out of his trench and trotted in the direction from which the voice had come. This had better be good. The Jerries were forming up for their main assault and Carter needed to make an assessment of their strength so he could plan his defence better.

He found the NCO levelling his Tommy gun at a group of artillery men, a Sergeant and a handful of gunners. Two of the gunners held large objects in their hand, chunks of machined metal.

"What's the matter, Fred?" Carter puffed as he reached them.

"These gentlemen seem intent on leaving us, Lucky. I was trying to explain to them that it wasn't a good idea."

Fixing the artillery sergeant with a glare, Carter challenged him. "Is that correct?"

"The Lieutenant left me in charge, Sir, so I thought it was time for us to withdraw. With the Argylls gone there's nothing much we can do now."

"I would debate that with you Sergeant, but I'm not going to. I have orders to hold this hill for as long as I can, which I intend doing. You may have been placed in charge by your officer, but that doesn't give you the right to decide when or where you can go. Where is your officer anyway?"

"He was called back to Termoli last night, for a briefing I think. But he hasn't come back."

There were a dozen legitimate reasons why the artillery officer hadn't returned and Carter wasn't in a position to find out which of them applied. But without the anti-tank guns his position on the hill was untenable.

"What are those?" He pointed to the chunks of metal being held by the two gunners.

"Breach blocks, Sir. Without them the guns can't be fired. Standing orders are to disable the guns if we have to abandon them."

"Which means that my men would be left here to fend for themselves without the only weapons that would give us any chance of holding off the Germans." Carter injected as much venom as he could into his words. The sergeant had the good sense not to meet his eye.

"We're not commandos, Sir. We don't have to sacrifice ourselves."

"No, but you are soldiers who don't have orders to withdraw. I'm in command here, so I give the orders unless you have a direct line to your Regiment. Do you have orders from them?"

"No, Sir, not as such but …"

"But nothing, Sergeant. Without orders you are deserting your post in the face of the enemy. You know what the penalty for cowardice is?"

"Y … Yes, Sir."

"Good." Carter turned his attention to Fred Chalk. "Now that we've cleared up that little misunderstanding, these men will return to their guns and prepare to carry out their duties. However …" he turned to sweep a threatening gaze over the gunners "… if these men leave their posts without my orders, you have my permission to shoot them as deserters."

"B … but you can't … you can't do that." The sergeant stuttered. "Kings Regulations[1] … say …."

"Quiet!" Carter barked. He raised his hand and pointed to the red and white commando flash that adorned the sleeve of his shirt. "This says I don't give a flying fuck about King's Regulations right now. If we get back to Termoli, then we'll worry about the rules then. In the meantime, …" he turned back to address Fred Chalk again "… you have your orders Sergeant Major, and so do these gunners. Make sure they are carried out."

"Yes, Sir." Fred Chalk seemed to think that a more formal form of address was necessary for the circumstances.

Carter turned on his heel and stalked off back towards the western end of the hill.

He had been on hard on the gunners, he knew. They weren't commandos; this wasn't what they had signed up for. He could see how things looked to them, but he couldn't let them leave the hill. At least, not yet. If the commandos saw them leaving it would harm their morale. They wouldn't run, they were too well trained for that, but they were only human. They might decide that surrender was a better option than dying on the end of a German bayonet.

Fred Chalk wouldn't shoot the gunners, but the gunners had to at least believe that he would and the commands' reputation for ruthlessness meant that he would be believed. At least, Carter didn't think that Chalk would shoot them. He shrugged, the risk of having to face a court martial didn't seem important right now.

Right now, he had a battle to prepare for.

[1] King's Regulations (now Queen's Regulations) are the rules that govern the 'command and administration' of the British armed forces. Each of the three branches, (Royal Navy, Army and RAF) have their own version, but they essentially say the same thing, with the regulations being modified to deal with the different environments within which the three branches have to function. Regulations that apply to all three services have the letter J (for joint) as a prefix to the regulation number and can't be changed without the agreement of all three services. The regulations cover everything from the growing of beards, to criminal offences, the membership of political parties and trades unions (they can't be members of either) and the holding of political meetings within barracks (they can't be

held). Their existence is enshrined by Act of Parliament (The Defence (Transfer of Functions) Act 1964) and they hold the full weight of British law for the personnel who fall under their remit which can, under certain circumstances, include civilians working on military establishments. The copy the author used when in the RAF was almost 2.5 inches (5cm) thick without the cover. They contain more words than the Bible (The King James Authorised Bible has 783,137 words). As a legal point, Carter wouldn't have had the authority to carry out his threat to shoot deserters, but he could have placed them in 'close arrest' in order to have them court martialled later.

* * *

The Germans weren't in any hurry to attack. The Panzergrenadiers moved along the track to the bridge, getting as far as possible from the deadly Vickers guns, before turning along the riverbank to get into position behind the tanks. Then they waited.

It didn't take Carter long to find out what they had been waiting for. More tanks emerged along the road, from behind the factory building; four of them. Two didn't make any attempt to climb the hill, they turned off the side of the road and headed south, the direction that would take them around the base of the hill on the other side. The intention was clear enough. They would come at the hill from three side, maybe four. They knew how many anti-tank guns Carter had available and knew where they were. They could be repositioned, of course, but they couldn't provide a three-sixty degree coverage of the hill. Neither could the Vickers guns.

There were no infantry with those tanks. Perhaps the Germans didn't think they needed them. Or perhaps they were just going to stand at the bottom of the hill and rain seventy five mm shells down on the hilltop while the main force attacked on the other side.

The SRS troop was still on that side of the hill, spread out to provide some sort of defence. Carter had no choice but to leave that problem to them. Their troop commander would act on his own initiative and Carter knew he would do all he could to repel the tanks, not that there was that much he could do.

But the two tanks in front of the hill, still sat squarely on the road, waiting for orders to attack, was something Carter could do something about.

He sent word along the slit trenches to the 6 pounder's position to open fire on the tanks in front. The first round exploded in front of the leading vehicle only seconds after the order reached the gunners. The gun could keep up a rate of fire of 15 rounds per minute, limited only by the energy of the gun's crew and the amount of ammunition that was available.

But the miss had antagonised the tank crew and they fired back, accurately targeting the gun. The crew dived for cover as rocks and dirt rained down around them. It became a race between the two opposing gun crews. The 6 pounder crew dashed back, ejected the heavy brass cartridge from the beach as the loader slid another into the barrel in its place. The gunner pulled the lanyard to fire the weapon and the crash of its discharged echoed across the hilltop as the crew dived for cover again.

But the gun had wheels and every time it discharged the wheels bucked off the ground, alighting again in a slightly different position. Which meant that the gun was no longer trained on the front of the tank. The miss wasn't a few feet this time, it was several yards off to the side.

The *Panzer* crew, inside their armoured protection, didn't have the same problems. After loading they had the chance to adjust their aim. The next round from their gun exploded directly in front of the gun, the blast lifting it off the ground and tipping it over.

Prof Green was the first to react. Jumping out of his slit trench he started bellowing orders. The nearest commandos hurried to obey, grabbing the upturned gun carriage and wrestling it back onto its wheel. At around a ton in weight it wasn't an easy task and Green had to chivvy more men out of their cover to lend a hand.

Machine gun bullets from the tank's secondary armament buzzed around their ears and a trooper dropped with a yelp of pain and blood fountaining from his neck.

As the gun carriage rocked back onto its wheels, Carter ran to the trench where the gunners sat, cowering in the bottom.

"Who's the gun layer?" He called down to them.

"Me S … S … Sir" A man stammered.

"I want that tank stopped. Now get out of there before I come in and get you out."

The man could see that Carter wasn't bluffing. He clambered out of the trench and hurried across to take his position behind the gunsight, pressing his eye against it as he span the brass wheels that controlled azimuth and elevation with practiced ease.

"Loader?" Carter bellowed again. A hand was raised. "The gun's no use without a round up the spout. Get out there now. And the ammunition carriers." Two more men clambered out after the loader.

Carter took up the commander's position behind the gun, lifting the firing lanyard that hung from the rear of the breach assembly. He stood tall, wanting the men to see him.

"Ready" The layer shouted, raising his hand.

The breach block of the gun slammed shut. "Ready!" the loader repeated, raising his hand as well.

"My job, I think, Sir." Carter felt a touch on his hand and turned to see the Bombardier[1] standing next to him. Carter allowed him to take the lanyard and stepped away from the gun.

The Bombardier jerked the length of thin rope and the crash of the gun rang out across the hill as the weapon jumped back on its carriage, lifting the wheels off the ground and raising a cloud of dust.

Carter peered through the haze. The leading tank began to turn off line. If it had been under command the turret would also have been turning, maintaining its aim up the hill towards their position, but the gun remained pointing forward.

The following infantry knew something was wrong. They tried to keep the tank between themselves and the angry rattle of Bren guns and the Vickers but the tank started to move faster, outstripping them as the tank's driver slumped over the controls, his dead foot still on the accelerator.

"Well done, chaps. Reload!" Carter bellowed, though the loader was already taking a fresh round off of one of the ammunition carriers. The barrel of the gun swung a fraction to the left as the layer bent over the sights, seeking out the second tank.

The gun from the second tank was already lining itself up on the top of the hill. The 6 pounder crew eyed it nervously. Worried that they might abandon their weapon once again, Carter stepped in closer. "That's good, men." He encouraged. "Just one round on target is all we need."

"Ready!"

"Ready"

"Fire" Carter shouted, though Bombardier's hand was already moving.

The second round wasn't quite so well aimed, but it blew the track off one side of the tank. It continued to move forward, the broken links trailing in its wake until the tank's weight caused the bogies to dig into the dirt. The tank ground to a halt. But it wasn't dead. Like a wounded predator, it was still dangerous.

Carter didn't hear the explosion. He just felt a blast and some shooting pain, then the world went black.

[1] A corporal in the Royal Artillery is called a Bombardier, a rank that has been in use since at least the 16th century. However, it was only formally adopted by the Royal Artillery in 1920. The Bombardier commands a gun's crew. His second in command will be a Lance Bombardier, not a Lance Corporal. Colloquially a Bombardier is referred to as "Bomb".

* * *

Carter's consciousness swam towards the surface in response to the insistent slaps he was feeling to his face. He forced his eyes open, looking into a vaguely familiar face. Its lips were moving but he couldn't make any sense of the words that were being spoken. For some reason he recalled his childhood, standing next to a field near his house, watching a tractor towing a disc harrow and wondering what it would be like to be run over by such an implement. From the agony coursing through his body he thought he might be starting to get some sort of clue.

"Come … Lucky. Wake …" slaps came again but Carter could still only comprehend a few words. He gasped aloud as a shooting pain ran through is upper arm.

"M'wam" he slurred.

"Sorry, Lucky. Didn't catch that."

"M'wam." He tried again.

"Nope, still not got that."

The trooper's name popped into Carter's mind. Haskell, that was it; one of the medics. "Has'll … m'wam." he tried again, raising his other arm and trying to point.

"Oh, y'r arm. Yes, bit of a flesh wound. Nothing to worry about." He showed Carter a field dressing. "Just going to put this on it."

Looking down at the source of the pain, Carter could see the short sleeve of his desert issue shirt hanging in bloody shreds. Though the pain suggested otherwise, the rest of his arm seemed to still be present.

"Wha .. happ …"

"Gun took a direct hit, or as near as dammit." The trooper replied, concentrating on binding Carter's arm.

"Crew! What' bout … crew?" The trooper ignored the question, which didn't bode well.

"You were lucky again, Lucky. Just this flesh wound. Probably a bit of shrapnel. Though you were unconscious for a few minutes. That was the blast. It creates a vacuum, apparently, and you black out through lack of air. But they got you back here to me quick enough."

The trooper chatted on about inconsequential stuff, trying to distract Carter from his pain. "Now, you just lie there and let someone else run the war for a bit. You need time to recover your wits before you do anything else."

The trooper straightened up, picked up his Red Cross emblazoned rucksack and went to off to find more customers, whistling a song from a show that had been popular in London before they had sailed for the Mediterranean.

Carter struggled to sit up and was about to try standing, when a firm hand pressed down on his shoulder. "Oh no you don't, Lucky."

Carter looked up to see Ernie Barraclough looming over him. "Who's in charge?" he demanded, worried that the defence of the hill was in unreliable hands.

"I've delegated. That's why they give me two lieutenants. Don't worry. Just checking to see how you are, then I'm going back there."

"The tanks?"

"Both out of action. The infantry have withdrawn back towards the factory."

"The gun crew?" If the medic wouldn't tell him, he'd have to get it out of Barraclough.

"The layer and the Bombardier are both dead; the loader and one ammunition carrier both wounded, one of them badly, but the other two are OK. Shaken up a bit, but they'll live to fight another day. The gun's a write-off though."

"Get the wounded back to the far edge of the wood, ready to be evacuated. The two uninjured gunners too. They aren't much use here anymore; no point in keeping them in danger if they don't need to be. Pass them along the hilltop in relays, so that no one is way from his position for longer than he needs to be."

"OK, no problem. What do you want 4 Troop to do?"

Trying to imagine the enemy's dispositions, Carter thought about the best way to use the troop now that the immediate threat from the west had been dealt with. "Keep two sections covering the road and move the rest around to face north, closing up on 5 Troop's flank. Reposition the Vickers as well, so it can fire into Jerry's left flank and discourage any attempt to take this end of the hill."

"OK. What do we do if the Jerry's try another attack from the west?"

"Get ready to withdraw. Without a gun on that end of the hill, there's no hope of holding it. We'll hold for as long as we can, but I'm not going to sacrifice lives just for the sake of it."

"I don't think you'll get any argument from the men on that one." Barraclough let out a sardonic chuckle. He gave a big sigh. "Just think, with a Jeep I could be at my family's villa in a few hours."

"I think the Germans might have something to say about that. Now, my head's hurting, so fuck off and give me some peace."

Waiting until Barraclough had gone far enough for it to be necessary for him to drop to his belly and crawl to the edge of the tree-line, Carter rose unsteadily to his feet. There wasn't a part of him that wasn't hurting. He made his way towards the junction between 5 and 6 troops, where the two 6 pounder guns had been dug in. He had to stop once to throw up what little there was in his stomach, but in the end he made it to where he wanted to be.

The gunners were hunkered down behind the protection of the thick metal shielding at the front of the gun's carriage. Carter crawled forward, wincing at almost every move, until he could take in the view below.

The normal practice for an attack such as this would have been for both forces to advance at the same time, but with the defeat of the two tanks at the western end, that pincer movement could no longer be achieved. But the enemy to the north was now moving, albeit slowly.

The original four *panzers* had been joined by two more and in the distance, Carter could see two more crawling along the distant riverbank, coming to reinforce the attack. It was a big force and Carter was under no illusions about the ability of his much smaller one to withstand the attack. The tanks wouldn't come up as far as the tree-line. They daren't get stranded between the thick trunks of the olive trees, but they didn't need to. They just had to get to a point where they were firing into the trenches at short range, while the infantry rushed past to finally close with the commandos.

They advanced at the same pace as the infantry who were, as usual, huddled in behind, seeking the protection of the tanks' armour. That slowed the whole advance down. If they rushed the hill with the armour moving at a faster pace, they might have overrun the defences by now. But they were being cautious. Carter wondered if the enemy troops were fresh from training. The attrition rates in both Russia and North Africa had stripped the *Wehrmacht* of most of their experienced soldiers. The ones being conscripted were getting younger and younger, barely into their late teens, and that could account for the timid way in which these attacks were being launched.

The tanks fired a ragged volley from their big guns, which seemed to be targeting the 6 pounders. Certainly, several of them exploded in their immediate vicinity, showering Carter in more rubble.

The 6 pounders retaliated with rounds of their own. One tank in the middle of the line came to a halt, clearly hit. The turret hatch flew open and a solider, probably the tank's commander, tried to clamber out. Bren guns and rifles crackled and even at that range Carter could see the spark of bullets striking the armour around the German's head. The figure ducked back inside and pulled the hatch closed behind him. They would have to exit by the other route, the hatch in the floor.

The guns fired again, hitting the same tank again.

An explosion sounded to the right and Carter saw a gout of earth fly up from the right flank of the advancing German armour. Where had it come from? Certainly not from either of the two 6 pounders, which were both aiming directly forward and, currently, still being reloaded.

He scrabbled for his binoculars and raised them, scanning to ground to the east. His heart soared as he picked out the shape of three Sherman tanks, advancing in a V formation around the side of the hill. Smoke wafted backwards from the muzzle of the leading tank. The cavalry had arrived at last.

But three tanks would be no match for six Germans Mk IVs.

Already the two *panzers* on the right flank, as viewed from the top of the hill, were turning out of line to face the new threat, while the other four continued steadfastly forward. The infantry scurried to get behind them, not wishing to become embroiled in the tank-on-tank engagement that seemed about to start. The two tank types were pretty evenly matched for both armament and armour. It would come down to gunnery and bravery to decide the outcome.

The tank furthest from Carter fired and hit the leading Sherman just below the turret. The vehicle slewed to a stop. Two on two now.

Standing up, Carter hurried towards the right hand of the two 6 pounders. He found the sergeant that he had berated earlier. "Target those two." He pointed towards the breakaway pair of *panzers*. Their armour was thinner on the sides and they also presented a larger target. If he could immobilise them, the Germans would have to make a decision; attack the two remaining Shermans, leaving the infantry to advance up the hill unsupported, or concentrate on the hill and risk the Shermans mauling them as they came in from the flank, with a clear line of fire on the German infantry massed behind them.

Or, Carter could only hope, break off the attack entirely and withdraw.

But it wasn't the Germans who blinked first, it was the occupants of the Sherman tanks. They started to reverse away from the two *panzers* facing them. That allowed the one nearest to the hill to turn its turret and engage the 6 pounder that had started to get its rounds a bit too close for comfort. 75 mm shells began to pepper the area around Carter again and he had to seek refuge in a slit trench once more.

But it had still reduced the German advance to three tanks, with the reinforcements still not in no position to provide anything more than long range artillery support. But now the infantry were bunched in a much smaller area and that made an inviting target. There were so many of them that the Vickers guns at each end of the tree-line were able to acquire targets. As the tanks advanced, Carter could see bodies lying in their wake.

"Mortars!" someone shouted, which was soon followed by the cough of the weapons being fired. They were the smaller 2 inch variants, the 3 inch ones having been left with the Heavy Weapons Troop, to defend Termoli.

Bombs began to explode all around the tanks. Soldiers wavered and fell back, but there must have been an NCO made in the Fred Chalk mould, whom the German infantry feared even more than the mortar bombs, because they were rallied and continued forward. But they started to creep into the gaps between the tanks, seeking better protection from the mortars, which meant that the Bren guns and the rifles could start to take a toll as the range reduced.

It was becoming difficult for Carter to get any more than a fleeting impression of the overall picture of the German deployment. He saw two men sprinting out to one flank before diving for cover. An MG 42 crew, undoubtedly, looking for a position where they could provide covering fire for the infantry as they pressed home their final attack. They couldn't be the only ones, though he couldn't see any others. Puffs of smoke erupted in front of the commandos' positions. Smoke shells, perhaps fired by the tanks but maybe from heavy calibre mortars dig in along the line of the small river. The smoke would cover the German advance for the last hundred yards. This was it.

The smoke made it difficult for the 6 pounders to pick out their targets, but they continued firing blindly. Now that their 'wobble' was over, the gunners were performing well.

The commandos were ready though; Carter could see that. In the trenches that he could see the men gripped their rifles and Bren guns, their eyes lowered to the rear sights. Mortars continued to fire, but at a much higher angle as the operators attempted to land their bombs either in, or just behind the smoke. They couldn't know if they were effective, but given the number of Germans advancing up the hill, they had to be causing some casualties and sending others in search of cover, damaging both the enemy moral and the cohesion of the attack.

Carter gripped his Tommy gun in his left hand, his right being too weak from his injury to be able to hold tight enough to the pistol grip.

He had never tried to fire it left-handed before and hoped that by cradling it in the crook of his right elbow he'd be able to hold it steady enough.

Shapes moved in the smoke. The bravest of the enemy were almost through. A final tank shell exploded behind Carter then fell silent, the gunners not wanting to hit their own men. But the MG 42s clattered away on the flanks, firing through the smoke in an attempt to keep the commandos' heads below the tops of their trenches.

A rifle cracked and one of the shadows fell, then more joined in. But the wave of enemy infantry continued forward. One, then another, then an almost solid wall of *feldgrau* uniforms emerged from the smoke. All along the British line the rifles opened fire as each soldier acquired a target. The Vickers guns spat venom along with the rapid clatter of the Bren guns.

"George Section, charge!" a voice rose above the rattle of small arms fire. Carter recognised the voice of Jeremy Groves, 5 Troop's commander. He was hoping to shock the enemy once again, the way he had the previous day.

The man himself appeared, hurdling the trench that Carter was occupying, slightly ahead of the line of eight men that he had ordered to attack. He held a bayonet tipped rifle, no doubt borrowed from one of his men. Well, done Jeremy, Carter thought. He had a section back in reserve for this very purpose. As they said at Achnacarry, the best form of defence was to attack.

The commandos screamed incoherent battle cries into the face of the enemy and battered into them like rugby forwards attacking a maul, their bayonets stabbing. But their flanks were exposed, Carter could see. If just a few of the enemy got behind them they'd be cut off and butchered. He rose out of his trench. "With me!" He yelled at no one in particular. Whoever heard would either follow him or they wouldn't. But he sensed men rising out of the trenches on both sides of him. Carter crabbed to his right to get the attacking commandos out of his firing line, then opened up with his Tommy gun, firing into the smoke. He couldn't aim, but with a Thompson that wasn't necessary. It sprayed death in whatever direction it was pointed and with the Germans running forward, someone was bound to run into the stream of bullets. A Commando stopped, raised his rifle, pulled the trigger, worked the bolt and then ran forward, all in a split second. Others did the same. Then they, too, were in amongst the attackers and stabbing with their bayonets.

Whatever the Germans had been expecting when they reached the top of the hill, it wasn't the aggression being shown by the commandos. First they stopped, then they took a step back. One of you; just one of you! Thought Carter. It only needed the one German to turn and run and it would be the start of a rout.

The two lines, attackers and defenders, broke into pairs of single combatants, with those not engaged seeking to sneak in and slide a bayonet into a vulnerable spot while the enemy was engaged. It was no different to the tactics of Anglo-Saxons who had fought the Danes, or the Normans, a thousand years before. There was no order, no co-ordination, just sheer bloody murder with a pointed weapon.

Carter saw a German get close in beside a trooper, pulling his rifle forwards in preparation for bayoneting the man. He raised his Tommy gun and pulled the trigger. It fired two rounds then the firing pin fell on an empty chamber. One thing Carter knew was that he wouldn't be able to reload the Tommy gun one handed.

The German turned away from his intended target to face the new threat. He saw Carter, realised his predicament and opened his mouth in a wicked leer. In one corner of his mind Carter noted that he was older than some of the others and had no front teeth. At some point he had taken a rifle butt in the face.

Carter tossed his Tommy gun to one side and fumbled for his Webley with his left hand. It was reluctant to leave its holster. The German soldier broke into a trot as he realised that he had to hurry to close the gap before Carter could re-arm himself.

Pulling with all his might, Carter freed his weapon, raised it and pulled the trigger all in one motion. The German's face erupted in a spray of blood. His weapon fell to the ground as he put his hands up in some sort of defensive reflex, then he sank to his knees. Carter fired again, a more deliberate shot aimed at the centre of his chest, the largest target available. The German fell forward, twitched for a few seconds, then lay still.

The nearest Gemans saw the man go down and Carter could tell they were wavering. Perhaps the dead man was an NCO, or maybe just a talisman, but the attacking soldiers' confidence seemed to drain away at the same speed as the man's life had drained away. One stepped backwards, breaking off the duel he had been having with a commando. It was stupid mistake. The Commando stabbed him with his bayonet, kicked him in the crutch, withdrew his weapon and moved on to find another target, all in one smooth movement.

Others withdrew in front of the commandos' onslaught and, finally, one turned and ran. Several others needed no second bidding and followed. Those made of sterner stuff realised they were becoming isolated. They may have wanted to continue to press home the attack, but they had no option but to follow their comrades back down the hill.

The smoke was starting to thin and Carter could make out the shapes of the tanks some fifty yards down the slope of the hill. With holes appearing in the attack they would soon be able to fire their machine guns. And it wouldn't just be them. The MG-42s that had been positioned on the flanks would also have a clear field of fire.

"Withdraw!" Carter yelled at the top of his voice. "Back to your trenches lads."

But he stood his ground himself, looking for another target for his Webley. But there weren't any. Bodies lay strewn around the top of the hill, many dead but some only wounded. The rest were pacing backwards, away from the commandos and back into the cover of the tanks.

The armour didn't wait for them to arrive. The three tanks started to reverse down the hill. Once they were sure that their own men were clear, they would start shelling the British positions again, unless the two Shermans intervened. He had lost sight of them once the smoke bombs had started falling.

Once Carter was sure his men were following his orders, he backed his way up the slope until he almost fell into a slit trench. Looking down he saw it was occupied with two troopers, blood trickling from their bayonets and along the polished wood that encased the barrels of the weapons. Even here the commandos kept their weapons in pristine condition.

"Well done, lads." He said, stepping over their heads.

"We showed 'em, didn't we Lucky?" One of them said, wiping stream of blood from his ear with his hanky.

"We did that, Trotter. Better find the Medic and get that gash tended."

"T'ain't nothing. I'll live."

"Not if you get blood poisoning you won't. Now do as your told. You've got plenty of time to get back here. The Jerries won't be back for a bit."

Carter passed on, looking for his radio operator. He found him in the middle of the olive grove, dug well into the ground. Olives seemed to cover the ground here, where they had been shaken from the trees by the constant battering of the barrage. The harvest should be starting about then, but he suspected it wouldn't be happening for a while yet. But these fruit wouldn't need harvesting, they would only need someone to come along with a shovel and scoop them up.

This was nominally Carter's command post, though he had spent almost no time in it. He had only returned when he needed to send radio messages back to his CO, or when the CO had summoned him to take a message

Dropping into the trench alongside Tpr James, Carter started trying to reload his Tommy gun, retrieved from the ground as he withdrew. James took the weapon from him, slid the fresh magazine into the housing and handed it back. "Have you still got power for that?" Carter nodded at the set. The night after they had arrived Carter had requested additional batteries be sent up in the Bren carriers and a few had arrived, but Carter knew they must be staring to lose power by now.

"Enough for a couple of hours. Less if you have any long conversations."

"I'm not planning on that. There will be two messages. One when I've briefed the troop commanders and one after we've left here. I'll brief you myself, but you'll be heading off before me to find a safe place to send the second message from."

He paused as a trooper hurried past with an ammunition box dangling from each hand. "Akers!" Carter attracted his attention. "When you've delivered those, find all three troop commanders and ask them to join me here. Then find Sgt Maj Chalk and ask him to join me, along with the artillery sergeant."

"No problem, boss." He nodded his head and carried on in the direction he had been travelling, to where 4 and 5 Troops were dug in.

* * *

The Germans came again an hour later.

"Why wait for the Jerries to attack?" Barraclough had asked during the briefing, not unreasonably.

"Because every minute we sit up here is another minute 78 Div have to get across the river in enough force to deal with the Jerries. The arrival of those Shermans tells us that they're getting some units across, but the artillery from over there" Carter jerked his head to the south west, "tells us they're under attack. So, the longer we keep this lot engaged here, the longer 78 Div have to get more men and equipment across the Biferno to defend Termoli. They've got one bridge and ten thousand men, their equipment and their transport to get across it. That isn't going to be a ten minute job."

"Well, when you put it like that …"

"I do. Look, I'm going to start the withdrawal the moment the Jerries start their next attack. We can see they're bringing up fresh troops and more tanks. They'll use different tactics next time, now they know what they're up against and this time they'll get to the top and it will be all over. So we have to leave before they do that.

"The plan's a simple enough one." Carter continued. "Bombardier, when I give the word, I want your guns to give me everything you've got, for either five minutes or until you run out of ammunition. After that, you can disable the guns and head off down the road with my blessing."

"Thank fuck for that." The Bombardier muttered. If Carter heard him, he chose to ignore the insubordination. There are times when an officer has to be selectively deaf. And the Bombardier was only present because his Sergeant had been killed during the last attack. Some resentment for the danger he was being put in had to be expected. Out loud he said "Yes Sir. Understood. Five minutes maximum rate of fire then disable the guns."

"During that five minute period, 4 Troop will withdraw through the back of the olive grove, out of sight of the Jerries. 5 Troop will follow, then 6 Troop. So, Molly, your troop will be the rear-guard." Molly Brown nodded bis head in assent, having already worked that out for himself. He was a steady man, Carter knew, that's why he had picked him.

"What's to stop those tanks chasing us down?" Groves, 5 Troop's commander asked. "We'll be wide open for both the main guns and the machine guns."

"First of all, our withdrawal will take them by surprise and it will take them a bit of time to change their direction of attack. I'm going to organise a bit of a surprise for them that should keep their minds on other things while we get to a safe distance. Providing we're not under direct attack, 4 and 5 troops will withdraw at the double march. 6 Troop will withdraw by half troops. I'll be with one half and you'll take the other, Molly."

With the troop commander and the 2IC in charge of the two halves of the troop, the men would know their leaders were with them. It always stiffened their resolve. No one wanted to let the troop down, or themselves down, in front of the senior most officers. Half the troop would maintain covering fire on the enemy while the other half withdrew, then they would stop and change over. It was a standard manoeuvre and one that the commandos had practised many times. It was always assumed that the enemy would be in pursuit when the commandos left at the end of a raid. The only difference this time was that there would be no landing craft waiting for them, only the defences of Termoli.

"OK, gentlemen, I think we have a plan."

"What do want from me, Lucky?" Fred Chalk asked. Carter had summoned him specifically, but his role in the withdrawal hadn't been mentioned.

"You stay with me and when I give the signal, you fire your Very pistol. One flare, doesn't matter what colour."

The officers were just rising to their feet, getting ready to return to their troops, when a runner puffed his way through the trees.

"Begin' yer pardon, Sir. Lt Jenkins' compliments." The trooper came to attention in front of Carter. Jenkins was one of the troop commanders from the SRS, the unit that had been covering the other side of the hill for the previous 48 hours.

"You'd better stay to hear this." Carter called his officers back. "It may affect the withdrawal. At ease, Trooper. You'd better tell us what's happening on the other side of the hill."

"We've been keeping the Jerry infantry's heads down, but they've two tanks with them. They were looking to get past us to cut the road to Termoli. A Sherman turned up and got one of them before he even knew it was there, but then the other one buggered off back towards the factory. Now the Jerries look to be trying to get up the hill behind us. There aren't enough of us to stop a full-scale assault, so Lt Jenkins asks what he should do now."

"What are they doing right now?"

"Last time I saw, they were waiting. They've spread out in a skirmish line, as you'd expect and they've found some cover, but it's pretty clear they're coming up over the top of the hill, rather than trying to get around like before."

"Sounds like the Jerries are going to co-ordinate their attacks, Lucky." Barraclough commented.

"That would make sense. We can't defend both sides of the hill at the same time without leaving gaps, which is what the Jerries will be counting on." Carter returned his attention to the SRS trooper. "OK, tell Lt Jenkins to move your troop to the east end of the hill. Ask him to take charge of evacuating the wounded back to Termoli, but hold the right flank of the hill until we're ready to withdraw, which will be as soon as the attack starts. We'll be withdrawing through his positions, but he won't be the rear-guard. As soon as you see Lt Groves here ..." Carter pointed out 5 Troops' commander, "Start withdrawing yourselves. Keep the rear-guard in sight and if it looks like they're in trouble, you're to come to its assistance ... my assistance because I'll be with them."

"Very good Sir." The trooper came to attention again but didn't salute. He jogged back the way he had come.

"OK. Let's get ready. Once the 6 pounders start firing, the Vickers can be dismantled and evacuated. I take it you've got enough men to carry them?"

"They're heavy, Lucky." Groves said.

"I know. No need to take the ammo, but if they look like becoming a liability, disable them and ditch them." Carter was reluctant to abandon such useful weapons. In a defensive position they were worth half a troop in firepower alone.

* * *

As soon as the tanks started to move forward, Carter blew his whistle 3 times, the signal to start the barrage with the 6 pounders. The order had been anticipated and the two guns crashed out in unison. The shell from first one hit a *Panzer* head on, stopping it in its tracks, while the second ricocheted off the turret of another tank, but did no actual damage, other than to the paintwork.

The guns lost their rhythm from then on, firing as soon as a round had been slammed into the breach. At maximum rate at which they could fire was fifteen rounds per minute, meaning they would need about seventy five rounds each to keep up the rate for the five minutes Carter had asked for. That was one hundred and fifty rounds in total. He knew they didn't have that much ammunition left. He had ordered the leftover ammunition to be moved across from the gun that had been destroyed on the western end of the hill, but even with that they still wouldn't have enough. But the gunners had done their sums as well and Carter could tell that they were keeping up the best rate of fire they could with the ammunition they had, doing their utmost to give him the full five minutes.

The ammunition was a mix of armour piercing, high explosive, smoke and even flares, which were setting fire to the dried grass over which the tanks were advancing. It didn't matter to Carter. It was the impact he was after and he could see he was getting that. The guns couldn't be fired with any accuracy at that rate. As each one bucked on its wheels its point of aim changed and there was no time to adjust the aim before the next round crashed out. If it hit a tank it was by accident. More easy to hit was the infantry crammed in behind.

The line of German tanks slowed as they sought to return fire, peppering the ridge with their high explosive retaliation. But the Shermans to the east came to life again and started adding their weight to the battle. There were three of them once more, presumably the one on the far side of the hill had come around to join them. Not only were they able to attack the *panzers* from their more vulnerable sides, but they were also able to defilade the following infantry.

Carter turned to watch 4 Troop hurrying along the rear edge of the olive grove. Men appeared between trees then vanished behind others. A man fell, apparently hit. Hardly breaking stride, the man behind him hauled him to his feet and he hobbled on with the support of his comrade.

Barraclough called a section of men across to him and they turned to face this new source of danger, coming from the far side of the hill.

Carter stood and hurried towards them.

"Jeremy!" Carter called over his shoulder, having to almost scream to make himself heard above the crash of the guns and the explosions of the tank shells. "Two sections, on me".

Men from 5 Troop clambered from their trenches and ran to him. "Find cover and pin those Jerries down." Carter pointed across the road and down the slope. The men did as they were told, diving to the ground and crawling forward as quickly as they could to get into firing positions. The trees on that side of the grove were less damaged and provided more hiding places and there was also a tumble-down wall that offered some good firing positions. He went with them to add the weight of his Tommy gun.

"Ernie, keep your 4 troop men moving." He shouted at the men who were still returning fire to the south. "I've got this covered." Barraclough obeyed, going from man to man and signalling for him to leave the area.

Peering past a tree, Carter could see about a company strength of men working their way up the hill, while MG 42s laid down covering fire. But they hadn't worked out yet that there were no defensive positions on that side of the hill and the guns weren't firing in the right direction; the direction they thought might be best defended. They would know now though.

A Bren gun opened up, then rifles crackled, sending the Germans back into cover once more. But they were well trained and well disciplined. They kept creeping forward, returning fire every time a commando showed his head to take a shot.

A man close to Carter cried out in pain and rolled onto his back. "Get him back into cover." Carter called to the man on the far side of him. "The medics are at the far end of the hill." He pointed in the general direction. The man stood, grabbed his wounded comrade by the arm and hoisted him over his shoulder into a fireman's lift, in one fluid movement. Blood soaked one leg of the man's trousers. An unlucky shot for him, a lucky one for the German who had fired it.

"My rifle!" The wounded man protested. "The QM will 'ave my guts for garters if I leave that be'ind."

Carter picked the weapon up and tossed it to the wounded man, the top half of his body suspended upside down over his rescuer's shoulder. He caught it with practised ease. The QM's wrath wasn't what the trooper was worried about. It was a point of honour that no commando ever left his weapon behind.

Behind him Carter knew that 5 Troop would now be on the move, so he had to let these men go too. "I want two magazines from each man." Carter called. "Then you can get out of here." It wouldn't take long. A commando could fire off a magazine in less than thirty seconds, two magazines would take less than a minute and that included the pause to reload. The Brens would do it even faster. But it was a unit of measurement that was easy to relate to for the men.

The rifles clattered so fast that they sounded almost like sub-machine guns. "Ready!" A Corporal shouted. "Withdraw."

Carter, lying at the base of an olive tree, stood up and emptied the magazine of his Tommy gun in an arc from left to right across the face of the hill. The undirected fire would probably not find any targets, but it helped to keep the enemy at bay while the men of 5 Troop withdrew.

A rifle cracked almost in Carter's ear and he turned to see Prof Green standing next to him, taking steady aim down the hill as he fired a second shot.

"You're supposed to be hoofing it down the road with 4 Troop." Carter admonished.

"Got separated." Green replied with a straight face.

"And I suppose O'Driscoll and Glass got separated as well."

"That we did, Sorr." O'Driscoll's voice came from the other side of the olive tree as he, too, took aim. Carter heaved an inward sigh of resignation. If he ordered them to leave, they'd probably just move a few yards along the hilltop and wait for him. To be truthful to himself, Carter wasn't really displeased to see them. It would have been very lonely holding this position by himself. And Danny Glass had a Bren gun, which was worth ten men right now.

Between them they kept up a steady fore on the enemy. It still wasn't enough to keep them at bay, but it was slowing them down, which was what mattered.

Carter became aware that the 6 pounders had stopped firing. They'd either run out of ammunition or the specified five minutes had elapsed. Carter wasn't sure which and he had more important things to do than look at his watch. Time had no real meaning in a battle. You were either dead or you were alive. That was the only measure that could be used.

A whistle blast sound, telling Carter that 6 Troop, the designated rear-guard, were on the move. Time for him to leave as well.

"OK, you Three Stooges[1], let's get out of here.

[1] The Three Stooges were an American comedy troop who performed from 1922 to 1970, made up (in 1943) of Moe Howard, Larry Fine and Jerome "Curly" Howard, Moe's younger brother. They started out in vaudeville and the basis of the act was that one of them would attempt to sing or recite something as part of a performance, while the other two would constantly interrupt on various pretexts. This then descended into both verbal and physical abuse. That particular trio (they had changes of personnel at various times) made over 90 short films for Columbia between 1934 and 1946, when Curly Howard suffered a stroke and had to retire. They were well known in UK as a result of their film work. Examples of their work may be found on the internet.

* * *

Carter and his companions sprinted to the eastern end of the olive grove, aware that the enemy on the southern side of the hill would be advancing to cut them off. Glancing to his left, he could also see that the tanks and accompanying infantry were moving more quickly as well. The silence of the 6 pounder guns and the lack of small arms fire told its own story.

The Shermans were still firing, harrying the Germans as best they could, but they couldn't approach the hilltop for the same reason as the *panzers*. To get trapped amongst the trees meant certain death. It was footrace, plain and simple.

Bursting through the last of the trees they heard machine guns bullets buzzing around their heads like angry bees. About fifty yards away 6 Troop were retreating in good order, half of them firing towards the advancing Germans, while the remainder dashed past them to find fresh cover from which to fire.

The downward sloped helped Carter and the other three. The Germans still hadn't changed direction, so were moving more slowly on the upwards slope. But already the closest tank was turning towards them, trying to bring its forward facing machinegun to bear on the retreating commandos. Others were heading towards the Shermans, forcing them to reverse.

Carter took up a position with the left-hand half of the troop, assured by the solid presence of Fred Chalk as he barked the order to move back. Jefferson, the officer who should have been commanding this group, was nowhere to be seen. He wasn't the type to desert his post, so Carter had to assume he was amongst the wounded, evacuated earlier and hopefully well on the way back to Termoli. It was only two miles away, but it might as well have been a million, given their current situation. To turn their back on the enemy and run was suicidal.

Any experienced soldier knew that retreating troops often panicked. They ran when they should seek out cover and they sought out cover when they should run. Some just stood, frozen to the spot. Back in the days of cavalry, commanders sent their horsemen to hunt down fleeing troops. Most died with sabre slashes across their backs and shoulders. Their modern equivalent, the tanks, were already accelerating ahead of their infantry support, eager to wreak similar carnage on the commandos.

But these weren't just any troops, these were commandos and they didn't retreat, they withdrew. So long as they had weapons to fire they would fight on and the experienced men would make sure the less experienced didn't freeze. And a good commando officer always had a plan, no matter how hastily prepared and flimsy it might appear.

"Got your Very pistol, Fred?" Carter asked as they reached a point about two hundred yards from the top of the hill. He eyed the panzers, judging how quickly they were advancing and estimating their position against the one he had mentally picked out earlier.

The Sergeant Major pulled the thick barrelled weapon from his belt and showed it to Carter.

"I think now would be a good time to fire it." Carter grinned.

Chalk raised his arm, pulled the trigger and the flare shot skywards in burst of bright white light.

The wait would be interminable.

A quarter of a mile away, shielded by a wall around a field, Tpr James saw the light and raised the microphone of his radio to his lips. "Red, this is Red One. Execute, execute, execute. Over."

"Roger Red 1. Execute. Out." The reply came back.

After what seemed an age, James heard the whoosh of an artillery shell pass high above his head.

Back towards the hill, Carter heard the same sound a fraction of a second later.

"Down!" He shouted, as half of 6 Troops men trotted past, seeking out fresh cover. They didn't wait for a second shout. When you heard that sound you made yourself as small as possible and hoped for the best.

Some of the men were still half standing, half lying, when the shell exploded. It wasn't accurate, but it was of a large calibre and threw up an impressive amount of soil and rocks, The blast threw the slower men to the ground.

But it was only the first round. More shells fell, shaking the ground with the thunder of their explosions. The whole hilltop and the slopes on either side seemed to be one vast volcanic eruption as the artillery barrage swept all before it. Bits of tank flew in all direction and Carter could see infantrymen being scythed down by shrapnel. The blast waves battered at any of the commandos rash enough to raise their faces from the dirt.

"Ok, Fred." Carter shouted above the cannon's roar. "Second flare."

As the flare popped above their heads, Tpr James saw it and made a second radio call. "Red this is Red1, cease fire but stand bye. Over."

"Roger Red 1. Standing bye. Out."

Half a minute later the final shell exploded as the message reached the guns of 78 Division, still several miles to the south. The division was still engaged in its own battle and its commanding officer, Maj Gen Evelegh, would only divert his artillery effort for a few minutes. But it looked as though it had been enough.

The Germans, those that were still alive, would understand the message they had been sent. If they attempted to follow again, they would get more of the same. It would take a lot to get the infantry to move in any direction that didn't lead to safety. The tanks, any that could still move, wouldn't follow either. They were better protected, but they weren't invulnerable.

6 Troop stood up and started to move back again, leap frogging past each other as before. The danger may have been reduced, but it wasn't gone completely. Sporadic outbreaks of machine gun fire followed them, but it was opportunistic and as the commandos increased the distance between themselves and the enemy, it finally dwindled into silence.

The troop didn't need him anymore, so Carter rose and turned towards Termoli, breaking into a gentle trot that he could keep up for miles, even when wearing his full kit. "I could do with a cup of tea." Carter commented to his three bodyguards.

"Ach, that would be grand, Sorr." O'Driscoll replied on behalf of all three of them.

8 - Dawn Attack

Charlie Cousens looked at his watch. "I can give your men three hours rest, up until the evening stand-to. Now that the road is open, the Germans will pull out the troops that you mauled and put in fresh units. They'll come down that road like the hounds of hell and they'll be baying for our blood. So, get your men rested, fed, re-equipped and ready for more fighting."

Carter had just finished delivering his verbal report and receiving a pat on the back for the efforts of his men. Cousens would go around the troops and speak to them in person as soon as he had the time. He attempted to speak through a mouthful of hard tack biscuits smeared with sardines. To help them down, he gulped a swallow of tea. "They'll be ready when needed, Sir. They're tired, but so is everyone, I guess. What have things been like here?"

"Mainly artillery barrages and air attacks, as you can see, but we haven't suffered too many casualties. We've also had a few reconnaissance probes. That's the what the firing is about now, that you can hear from the Argyll's positions. The men are well dug in, so most of the injuries are mild. The odd bump on the head from flying bricks, a few blast injuries; that sort of thing. But the Jerries have given us plenty of rubble with which to build defensive positions, which is good. Take a look at the map."

He pointed to a street map of the town laid out on the crude table that had been constructed from an old door and some ammunition boxes. It was the sort of map that could be bought in any petrol station. Cousens laid his finger on the point on the map where the road from Guglionesi entered the town.

"We're here, astride the road, just as you were on the top of the hill. I'll be putting 4 and 5 troops into the line to the left of 3 Troop. There's a bit of a gap between them and the SRS, who are covering the southern approach, so they can fill that. I'll keep 6 Troop back in reserve for now. To our right we have Four-Nine, covering the north west and then the Argylls. We've still got three 6 pounder guns left from the anti-tank battery. They're well dug in, one facing along the road in front of us, thankfully. The other two are further round to the north. We're relying on 78 Div's artillery to cover the southern approach. The County of London Yeomanry[1] are covering the northern most approaches to stop the Jerries reaching the sea on that side. If they get tanks or artillery there, they can prevent reinforcements from landing"

"The Yeomanry? Where did they come from? They're not part of 78 Div."

"They're the chaps with the Sherman tanks that came to your aid. A squadron of them have been attached from 4th Armoured Brigade and managed to get across the river during the night. Not enough of them to stop the German advance, but enough to protect one flank."

"What are the chances of reinforcement?"

"Not before nightfall. 38 (Irish) Brigade are out at sea, waiting for darkness to make their approach to the harbour and disembark. The divisional commander doesn't want them attracting the attention of the Luftwaffe by getting too close inshore during daylight hours. We could do with them right now, but I can understand the General's caution. They're on board merchant ships, so they'd have trouble fighting off an air attack.

Carter grunted an acknowledgement, but disappointed that there wasn't better news.

"There was something that puzzled me while were out on that hill. Why the Germans took so long coming at us. It's hardly *Blitzkrieg*[2] stuff."

"Yes. Brigade has noticed that. Intelligence thinks that in Russia, several unit commanders were taken out and shot for not achieving their objectives; for the encouragement of others so to speak. That may have something to do with it."

"But that's absurd. It just creates a climate of fear."

"Yes and it seems to be benefiting us. They think that nobody at lower level wants to pass on bad news, so they misreport the situation to cover their backs. You were probably described as a battalion strength with a full battery of anti-tank guns. That way they could account for not taking your positions sooner."

"Well, I have to say, the men performed as well as if they had been a full battalion. But the Jerries could have been a lot more aggressive."

"But that thinking means that the Jerry division can't advance on a broad front. It has to focus resources in certain areas while other parts of the battlefield go without. Right now, the main thrust of the 16th *Panzer* Division is towards the river, to try and prevent the whole of 78 Div getting across. That means they could only spare a certain amount of resource to deal with you. On top of that, the division got badly beaten up in Russia. A lot of the middle ranking commanders have come in as replacements from the occupied countries to the north; France, Norway and so on. They got their promotions on the basis of garrison duties, so they haven't got the experience to manoeuvre whole battalions in the field against a well-equipped adversary. They also haven't encountered commandos before, so we've taken them by surprise with our own aggression."

"They'll understand the rule of three[3] though. It's as much part of German military doctrine as it is ours. Do we know what the enemy intentions are?"

"It's only a guess, but Intelligence thinks they want to push us out of the town, so they can concentrate on stopping 78 Div from getting across the Biferno. They are slowing them down with their artillery bombardments, but they need to get infantry into position to hold the ground, which they can't do with us behind them. So, they'll be looking to defeat us first. The good news is that Kesselring is short of troops on this side of the mountains, which is why we have only 16th *Panzer* and the paratroops to contend with. But I'm glad I'm not *Generalmajor* Sieckenius, their commander. If this end of the German line falls, he'll get the blame."

"Not our problem, thankfully." Carter responded with a cheery grin. He had enough problems of his own, without considering the problems the enemy divisional commander might have. "What about the Canadians?"

"They've got the Germans between them and us. At the moment, their priority is keeping German tanks away from the river. If they're allowed to advance along the northern bank, they'll be a real threat to the units trying to cross the bridge. So I don't think we can expect them any time soon."

"OK, back to more immediate matters, what do you want me to do."

"Get that wound of yours properly seen to and find yourself a clean shirt if you can. Then grab yourself a couple of hours sleep. At stand-to, you can take forward command of the defences while I keep an eye on things from here. Not that there's a lot I can do from here, but I need to be able to contact Brigade if it all goes wrong."

[1] Formed as irregular cavalry in 1901, for the Second Boer War, The 3rd County of London Yeomanry were known as the "Sharpshooters". (Yeomanry was a term used to distinguish volunteer units, raised in time of need, from the regular army). After their return from South Africa they became part of the Territorial Army, Britain's reserve forces, but were active during both World Wars. Their lineage still exists as a unit of the Reserve Army, now known as 265 (Kent and County of London Yeomanry) Support Squadron (Sharpshooters).

[2] *Blitzkrieg* (lightning war) was the term used to describe the tactics the Germans used for the invasion of Poland in 1939 and in the Low Countries and France in 1940. It was characterised by rapid advances using tanks and mechanised infantry, supported from the air by dive bombers. In a shortened form the term came to be used for the aerial bombardment of British cities by the *Luftwaffe* – the Blitz. The Germans were only able to adopt this tactic if they could be sure of being able to refuel without having to stop to wait for their logistics tail to catch up with them. In Poland and the western countries, they either refuelled from ordinary petrol stations or from captured Allied fuel stocks.

[3] The military doctrine of the rule of three is that it takes three times as many troops to capture a position than it does to defend it. If the force defending a position is one company strong, it will require three companies to overcome them. It is a rule that has held good, with a few exceptions, since the dawn of warfare. For a smaller attacking force to be victorious, it must have some sort of advantage, such as armour or artillery, or the defending troops must have poorly constructed defences, be poorly trained or demoralised. Such victories have occurred, but are rare, as the defenders usually have the advantage of fighting from behind cover while the attackers have to advance in the open. In medieval times, one of the most common ways of defeating a castle defended by quite a small garrison, was to bribe the defenders to leave. This was a common occurrence – on both sides – during the Hundred Years War and was essentially copied for the World War II film Kelly's Heroes.

* * *

Commanding the front line meant, in effect, finding a suitable defensive position, being seen to be present there and then firing his weapon when it was necessary. The commandos in their slit trenches and fox holes knew what they had to do, their NCOs made sure that they did it and their officers moved them around when gaps appeared. With the commando spread along several hundred yards of the town's perimeter, Carter could only appreciate the situation directly to his front. For everything else he had to rely on the radio reports from the troop commanders.

"Have you replaced the battery in that?" Carter asked Tpr James, his radio operator.

"What with? There's no power in the town, so no way of recharging the batteries. If I could scrounge up enough car or lorry batteries, I could daisy-chain them together to provide enough juice, but that would mean a major scavenger hunt.!"

"Looks like we're going to have to use runners a lot then." Carter grunted.

"I did manage to find a battery in a damaged set." Admitted James. "But I don't know how much power it has left and we don't know how long the rest of the sets are going to last. We've been here four days and these sets were never meant to last that long without a re-charge."

"OK, well, do what you can to conserve battery power." Carter knew the risks involved in using runners to carry messages around a battlefield. During the previous war the highest casualty rates outside of an actual attack were amongst runners who passed through the rifle sights of enemy snipers.

The arrival of the Luftwaffe told Carter that an attack was imminent. Charlie Cousens, or someone higher up the chain, had guessed correctly. It was only a small force, one Ju 88 light bomber escorted by a pair of Me 109s. They approached from the north, avoiding the antiaircraft guns that were now defending the bridge. The bombs fell in a line from north to south, then the JU 88 turned for home, it's job done. The two fighters stayed on to deliver the ritual strafing, while the commandos huddled at the bottom of their trenches, making themselves as small a target as possible.

The bombs fell along the wrong line, creating a series of craters about thirty yards in front of the foremost trenches, suggesting that the aircrew's mind was more on the possibility of RAF fighters finding them. The Me 109's however, stitched cannon shells and machine gun bullets along a trail far closer to the positions, sending stone chips flying in all directions. Carter heard one buzz above his head and he instinctively ducked lower.

"Medic!" a voice shouted from Carter's left, indicating that one man, at least, had been hit. A soldier moved out of cover and sprinted across to the source of the shout, having to dive for cover on the way as the two fighters returned for a second pass. A Bren gun retaliated from one trench, but unless it got a lucky hit it wasn't going to be effective. But it made the men feel better to be able to fight back.

No sooner had the fighters soared skywards again than the artillery started up. The first rounds fell short, but the aim was soon adjusted, suggesting that there was a forward observation post operating, relaying instructions for the adjustment of the guns.

All infantrymen, commandos included, hated artillery bombardments. They might be able to fire on aircraft, but there was nothing they could do against heavy guns, which could be firing from miles away. It was that sort of bombardment that had a caused so much "shell shock" during the previous war. A short barrage was unnerving, while a longer one had the power to drive men mad.

Carter knew roughly how long this one would last. Long enough for tanks to get from their assembly area to within range to take over the barrage using their own main armament. With mechanised infantry riding in Hanomags, that was likely to be less than ten minutes.

The tanks wouldn't enter the town. It was as bad, if not worse, than entering closely packed trees. The tanks would be unable to turn in the narrow streets and would be vulnerable to bombs dropped from the upstairs windows of houses. If a wide enough path could be created through the houses they could advance along that with infantry in close support, but that would require a much heavier barrage and might take days to achieve. And the enemy was starting to run out of time as more and more units from 78 Div made it across the bridge.

So, the tanks would stop short while the infantry dismounted from their armoured half tracks and closed for the final attack. Or what they hoped would be the final attack. The commandos hope was that they would repulse them once again.

There was less than an hour to go before sunset. If they hadn't overcome the defences by then it was unlikely that the Germans would continue to fight. The Germans rarely fought at night and they would know that the commandos spent most of their time training for just such fighting. They would either succeed during daylight and push the commandos out of their positions, or they would withdraw to a safe distance and try again in the morning.

It was very much Carter's intention that it would be the latter.

The commandos held their fire, relying on the anti-tank gun to reduce the enemy's numbers. As always, the primary target was the tanks, but hitting Hanomags would help as well. Even if the infantry inside them survived, they would be forced to leave the armoured protection of the vehicle, where the Vickers and Bren guns could target them.

Carter cursed the lack of artillery. Every tank stopped was a tank that couldn't target the defences and every *Panzergrenadier* killed at long range was one less that could storm into the commandos' positions behind a bayonet.

The Sherman tanks of the Yeomanry to the north of the town tried to engage from longer range, but accuracy was an issue. They daren't leave their own positions in case this attack was just a feint. Carter hoped they would have more effect when the infantry left their vehicles.

A wall crumbled behind Carter as a tank shell exploded, sending rubble flying around his head. He shrank to the bottom of the trench, where James was huddled, the radio's headset clamped over his ears.

"That was close." Was all he said, dusting brick dust off himself.

Some long range artillery joined in from closer to the bridge over the river, no doubt called in by brigade HQ. Anything that helped to keep the Jerries' heads down was to be welcomed. But what they really needed was more infantry of their own. What would stop the final attack wasn't artillery, it would be rifles.

Smoke bombs began to fall along the front of the commandos positions, indicating that the German infantry would be starting to debuss. It would take a few minutes for them to organise themselves, sending machine gunners out onto the flanks, assembling into skirmish lines and so on. But if they were well trained they wouldn't take long. Standing still on a battlefield was a very bad idea. The commando's mortars began to fire, blinded by the smoke but aiming for the places where the Hanomags had last been seen. 2 Troop was the heavy weapons troop. Not wanting to leave them isolated, they would have withdrawn their observation posts before stand-to. But the observers would have placed range markers on the ground and would now be on high vantage points, trying to pick out the vehicles over the top of the smoke and comparing their positions with those of the markers. The fall of the bombs would help them to make adjustments to their aim. As these were 3 inch mortars, they had a longer range and larger bombs, so they engaged earlier and caused more damage.

"I'm going forward." Carter shouted to James. The radio had to stay where it was, protected by its rubble walls, but if he needed to send a radio message he could dispatch a runner. Not that either Commando or Brigade HQs could do anything. There were no reserves, other than 6 Troop.

Carter rolled over the front edge of the trench, keeping his body as low as possible. His ribs and arm still hurt and he got a painful protest to remind him of his earlier wounds. He suppressed the pain as well as he could, but he had to grit his teeth to do it.

He duck walked forward, keeping obstructions in front of him for as long as he could before he had to move into the open. As luck would have it, he found himself on the end of 4 Troops positions, where they joined up with 3 Troop. A puff of cigarette smoke appeared above the top of a trench. He crabbed sideways and rolled himself into it, narrowly avoiding landing on Danny Glass.

"Who gave you permission to smoke." Carter wasn't really chiding Glass, but he was breaking the rules.

"The Jerries, when they started dropping smoke on us. I figured that a bit of fag smoke wasn't going to be noticed."

Carter suppressed a smile. He didn't smoke himself, but he had noticed how tetchy the smokers got if they hadn't had a cigarette in a while. Long night patrols were the worst. Men who normally never said a bad word to each other would start snapping like dogs around a contested bone after a few hours.

Glass removed the cigarette from his lips and passed it across his front to O'Driscoll. After this long in the field, few of the commandos had any cigarettes left, so what they had they shared. The Italians had been starved of tobacco supplies for so long that they none at all, so the commandos couldn't even buy any from their reluctant hosts.

"I'm going to have to ask yez to move, Sorr. I'm needing to get close to Danny's Bren gun so I can do me job."

Strictly speaking it should be the section's Lance Corporal, O'Driscoll, who would be the Bren gunner with a trooper acting as his loader. But Glass loved the weapon and refused to give it up and if he was the gunner, it meant that O'Driscoll was always going to be his loader.

"You know the plan?" Carter asked.

Both O'Driscoll and Glass gave him a look of disdain and didn't answer. Glass raised himself until he could see over the top of the trench. The German artillery bombardment had moved on from the front line and was now focused further into the town, from where reinforcements would arrive. Only there were no reinforcements, though the Jerries didn't seem to know that yet. It also meant that the German infantry must be on their way. Not even the Germans shelled their own troops. Not on purpose, anyway.

"I think it's time." Glass said, propping the Bren gun on its bipod legs and settling his check against the smooth wood of the stock. He reached forward with his left hand a pulled the cocking handle firmly backwards, before pushing it forward again to drive a bullet into the barrel.

O'Driscoll propped his rifle up against the trench wall in front of him and started laying out the curved magazines along the parapet., ready for use. A well drilled Bren crew could replace an empty magazine in less time than it took to count to five. For a time, in France, the Germans had thought that the British were using a belt fed weapon, so rapid were the magazine changes.

What Carter had called 'the plan' was just the tactic they had used before, at Honfleur and on the hill two miles along the road in front of them. They would hold their fire until the Germans appeared through the smoke and then open up with one great salvo of shots. The impact was devastating on troops, seeing men falling on all sides of them and knowing how quickly the Tommies could re-cock their weapons. Even the best trained troops wavered. Badly trained troops, or those with low levels of morale, turned and ran.

Carter propped his own Tommy gun on the lip of the trench and snicked the safety catch off. The rear sight was raised, but he wouldn't use it. If he fired his weapon at all it would be a spray of bullets and you didn't need sights for that.

As the Germans appeared through the smoke in front of each section, the commanders screamed the order to open fire. Carter must have been the first in his section of line to spot one of the Germans. He pulled the trigger on his Tommy gun and rounds spat from the barrel. Along the line to his left and right, rifles cracked and Bren guns hammered a staccato tattoo.

It was as if the Germans had run into an invisible wall. Some fell immediately, but all of them seemed to come to a sudden stop. A voice shouted a command and they stepped forward again, but the momentary delay had allowed the commandos to cock their weapons again and pick out fresh targets. A second volley, more ragged than the first, crashed out and more Germans fell. Carter could see one in front of him roll over so he was facing in the other direction and start to crawl away. A German close by halted his advance and went to help his fallen comrade. Carter let them both go. It took two men out of the fight if he allowed the rescue to go ahead, rather than just the one. The effect on morale was also damaging, to see comrades retreating. Besides, he felt a bit queasy at the thought of killing a wounded man who was offering no threat.

Many of the Germans had dropped to the ground, seeking out whatever cover they could so that they could return fire. The commandos hadn't left them much to hide behind though. They had a pretty clear field of fire for about two hundred yards, barring the smoke and even that was starting to drift away. In places, the two forces were barely twenty yards apart.

A potato masher[2] grenade flew over Carter's head and he heard it clatter on the rubble behind him. Instinctively he ducked his head, waiting for it to explode. The wait seemed to go on forever before the missile finally exploded, though Carter knew it couldn't have lasted more than four seconds. It sent a shower of shrapnel buzzing across the top of Carter's head. There was a clang, causing his head to jerk, as a bit hit his helmet and span off, dropping to the ground a few feet away. Carter made a mental note to collect it as a souvenir later, when it had cooled down.

Carter decided to fight fire with fire and pulled a grenade[3] from his webbing, extracting the pin. Gripping the safety lever, he looked for the German who had thrown the grenade at him. It could have been any one of four, he concluded, but he spotted two lying close together; they'd do.

He hurled the grenade towards them and then ducked his head below the lip of the trench. It's whiplash crack told him when it had exploded. Half standing in the trench, he let another stream of Tommy gun bullets rip towards the place where his targets had been lying. If they weren't dead, they were doing a good job of pretending they were.

But, unlike that morning, the Germans weren't retreating.

The attack had stalled, though, which meant that it would be a war of attrition. The more casualties the commandos inflicted on their exposed enemies, the closer they would get to withdrawing. But on the other hand, the Germans would be inflicting casualties of their own.

An officer must have managed to rally a small force of men, about a dozen, who clambered to their feet and attempted a bayonet charge into 3 Troop's front line, but three men fell before they got halfway and the remainder dived for cover once more. But they were closer. If the officer could rally them again, they might make it next time. And if one group got through, others would be encouraged to follow.

"Grenades!" Carter yelled, pulling another one from the loop on his webbing harness. "On my command." He had no idea if anyone had heard him. The constant crackle of rifles and hammering of Bren guns drowned out so much.

The German officer rose, screaming at his men to follow. A few half rose to obey.

"Release". Carter yelled. Half a dozen missiles arced across the gap between the two sides, thudding and rolling on the ground. A German aimed a kick at one, just as it exploded, and was left with a bloody mess where his foot had been. He keeled over with the shock. The shrapnel from the remainder gouged furrows in other men as they exploded. Those that weren't wounded dived for cover anyway.

But the officer was still on his feet, the sleeve of his uniform hanging in tatters. He was berating his men, gesticulating that they should move forward. He aimed his MP 40[4] machine pistol and fired a stream of bullets towards the head of one of his own men, trying to show him that he was a greater danger to them than the British Tommies.

Carter raised his Tommy gun to his shoulder and peered through the rear sight. Lining up the blade at other end of the gun's barrel with the centre of the German's chest, he squeezed the trigger. The weapon spat fire, pulling to the right as it did so; a characteristic of submachine guns. But enough bullets had struck the German to send him tumbling to the ground. No sooner had he hit the dirt than the men that he had been commanding started to crawl backwards, dragging their weapons along with them. One man tried to pull a wounded comrade as well, but it was too much for him and he let go, leaving injured man lying, whimpering.

The close quarters exchange of small arms fire went on for another few minutes, though it seemed like longer, then the Germans must have started to run out of ammunition; or nerve. First individuals started to crawl away, then small groups, then whole sections of men. Smoke grenades were discharged to provide some localised cover, then the only firing was from the flanking machine guns and the ones on the armoured vehicles as they continued to provide covering fire for their men. After an interval, that too stopped.

When the smoke of battel cleared, it revealed that the undamaged tanks and Hanomags had withdraw, not wanting to be left as easy targets for the anti-tank guns. But the infantry were still there.

digging frantically to construct defensive positions, just in case the Tommies mounted a counterattack.

Carter did consider it, but decided against. The men he had commanded on the hill were tired after two fights in the one day and the ones that had held the town's perimeter were little better. If he ordered it, they would follow; that much he knew. But they would need their energy to mount patrols that night and in the morning …

[1] A WS 18 (Wireless set type 18), the most common type of radio set in use with British infantry and commando units, required a power supply of 162 volts for its valves. The batteries were specially designed for use with the radio, but the limitation on their size and weight was a major factor in constraining the power output of the radio and the duration of its operation, which is why their useable range was so limited (8-10 miles maximum). At that time the electrical systems of most cars worked off a 6 volt battery, meaning twenty seven of them would be needed to power a WS 18 radio set. The batteries for the radio made up nearly half of its weight (approx 10 kg), such was the technology of the day.

[2] The M24 *Stielhandgranate* (literally 'stalk hand grenade') was the standard issue grenade for the *Wehrmacht* during World War II. It consisted of an explosive head on the end of a wooden handle. It was triggered by pulling a chord running through the hollow handle, to activate a fused detonator in the head. It was modelled on the earlier M15 (and inter-war variants), which had first been used during World War I (the number in the designation indicates the year in which a variant was introduced). The grenade had a four and a half second fuse, which is why Carter knew that was the maximum delay possible before it exploded. An image of an M24 grenade is used on the cover of this book.

[3] The standard British hand grenade was often referred to as a Mills Bomb (named after its designer, William Mills) and was the classic 'pineapple' shaped grenade depicted in World War II films.

They entered production during World War I and had been modified a number of times. Contrary to popular belief, the classic grooved segmentation lines in the casing were to make the bomb easier to grip, not to assist in its fragmentation. In fact, the grenade often didn't shatter along the segmentation lines. Films often show the grenade being held for a count of five or even seven, before being thrown. If they had been held for that long they would almost certainly have killed the user as the original delay was only seven seconds and after the Battle of France (1940), where several had been thrown back at the British by brave (or foolhardy) Germans, that was shortened to four seconds. Also incorrect is the image of the user pulling the pin out with their teeth. The safety pin is split, with the ends splayed to prevent it from being pulled out by accident. The user's teeth would be more likely to be pulled out than the pin. The 36M mk 1 variant was the one in use between the 1930s and 1972.

[4] More commonly (and incorrectly) referred to by the British as a *Schmeisser*, after Hugo Schmeisser, who had designed the MP 18, the design from which the MP 40 was descended. It had gone through several changes during the intervening period. The MP 18 was a World War I weapon; the MP 40 didn't enter service until 1940. The most notable difference between the MP 18 and the MP 40 is that on the MP 18 the magazine housing is on the left side of the weapon and on the MP 40 it is on the underside. Schmeisser wasn't actually involved in the design of the MP 40 and the only connection that he had with the weapon was that he held the patent on the design of the magazine. The poor design of the magazine meant the MP 40 was prone to jamming, especially when the magazine was misused as a handhold, which is how it is usually shown in use in films. The correct place to grip the weapon is on the wooden cladding behind the magazine mount, in front of the trigger guard. Versions of the weapon are still in use in some parts of the world and the feed from the magazine is still problematic.

* * *

"Is there any tea on the go?" Carter deposited his weapon and webbing on the makeshift table and lowered himself onto the rickety chair that had been salvaged from a ruined house.

"Just brewing up now, boss." Trooper James replied. Curled up in the corner, Charlie Cousens was making the rafters rattle as he snored.

"If the radio's still working, you can report all quiet on the Western Front." Carter said, rooting through his pack for something to eat. He found the remnants of a chocolate bar and started munching on it. His rounds of the forward positions had revealed nothing of interest. The patrols were reporting back that the Germans had settled in for the night and showed no signs of any aggressive acts. At least, not yet.

"Look who we found, Lucky." A voice said from the doorway of the room. Carter turned to see Danny Glass standing behind a German solider. In his hand he held something white, but Carter couldn't make out what it was. Glass's uncharacteristic grin showed that he found something amusing.

"Where did you find him?" Carter asked, taking the mug of tea that James was offering. The steam that drifted off the top had an aroma that suggested that James had put a bit more than just powdered milk and sugar in it. James winked at him. "The CO's private stock." He whispered.

Glass answered the question. "Wandering around near one of our listening posts. Capt Barraclough sent my section out a on a patrol, just to make sure that the posts were all awake. We heard someone coming towards us, so we lay doggo[1] for a bit and he just fell into our arms. Quite literally, he tripped over Paddy."

"What's that in his hand?" Carter pointed.

Glass laughed, anticipating the punchline to his story. "It's bog paper. The idiot was looking for somewhere to take a shit. He didn't even have his weapon with him."

Carter suppressed a smile. The soldier looked no more than fifteen years old, wearing an ill-fitting helmet and even his uniform looked as though it had been borrowed from someone who carried a lot more weight.

"Does he speak any English?"

"Not that we can make out. But I think he may be about to burst if he doesn't do what he wanted to do before we caught him."

"Well, I don't want him bursting around here. Find him a latrine and then escort him back to the prisoner holding area."

"OK, Lucky." Glass chuckled at the misfortunes of the young soldier again, then prodded him with his Bren gun barrel to get him moving. "Come on Fritz. Let's find you somewhere to take a dump."

Once Glass was gone, Carter allowed himself to laugh. It wasn't the funniest thing he had encountered, but it was the funniest thing he'd heard of for a few days. "Oh dear, James, doesn't that just beat everything?"

"Just goes to prove, when you got to go, you've got to go, boss."

"But he had the whole of central Italy to use as a toilet. He didn't have to come in our direction." Carter shook his head in disbelief. "Ah, well. Worse things happen at sea. At least he wasn't shot by one of the sentries." Commandos weren't known for challenging figures appearing out of the darkness. They preferred to shoot first and ask questions later. If a sentry expected a patrol to return that way, that would be different, but any figure appearing out of the dark without warning was dealt with by the most expedient method, not by polite inquires as to their identity.

Brigade HQ had a couple of German speakers attached to them from X Troop of 10 (Inter-Allied) Commando, the unit made up of nationalities from across Europe who had managed toe scape from their native land ahead of the Nazis. They'd interrogate the prisoner to find out what the Germans were planning. It was unlikely they'd learn anything of value form the lad, but he might have overheard something of use. The Germans had proved to be quite chatty once they'd been given a mug of coffee and a cigarette.

Carter checked the luminous dial of his watch. Thirty minutes until the CO had asked to be woken. He wished he could light a lantern, or even a torch. Now would be a good time to start writing his formal report, while the events on the hill were still fresh in his mind. If he died in the morning, the story might never be told. He scolded himself internally for being such a pessimist. But they all knew the Germans would come again in the morning. They had no choice but to take the town or lose the battle.

"Bugger!" A voice hissed from the darkness outside the tumbledown house. Another visitor, by the sounds of it. He was right, through the doorway ducked a bulky shape.

"Steven! Good to see you. Heard you'd made it back safe and sound." Carter was knocked sideways by the hearty slap on the back given to him by Alex Trent. They had first met in Troon, when Carter joined the commando and Trent was still a Major; 15 Cdo's quartermaster. Now he was a Lieutenant Colonel and attached to Colonel Vernon's Brigade HQ staff.

Carter rose to his feet. "What brings you slumming it on the front line, Sir?" Carter hoped Trent could see the glint of his teeth to show that he was smiling and he was joking, not criticising.

"I like to get out an about from time to time, you know. I'm not sat in Brigade HQ sipping champers and eating canapes all the time. Now, is that Charlie Cousens down there, keeping the whole of Italy awake with his snoring."

"It is, Sir. Shall I wake him?"

"Please do. I've got good news."

"Oh?"

"All in good time, Steven. Protocol insists that your CO is the first to know."

"Can you rustle up some tea for Colonel[2] Trent, James? And I'm guessing the CO will want a cup when he regains consciousness."

"No problem, Sir." Carter noted the use of a more formal address in the presence of a senior officer from Brigade.

Carter bent over Cousens and gave his shoulder a firm shake.

"Wh… oog … wh …" Cousens shook himself out of his deep sleep.

"Col Trent here to see you, Sir." Carter gave him another firm shake, just to make sure he didn't drift off again before the message reached his brain.

Cousens sat up so suddenly his head nearly collided with Carter's. "Alex, good grief, wasn't expecting to see you tonight." He rubbed at his eyes and clambered to his feet.

"Seems nobody was expecting me, but no matter. Good news for your commando."

"Hang on, let me gather my thoughts before I have to start doing things. Wouldn't want any misunderstandings." It wouldn't be the first time that orders had been misunderstood because the recipient had still been half asleep when he was given them.

"No rush, you take your time."

Cousens straightened out his uniform, not that it made much difference to his appearance even if there had been enough light to see it. They were all looking a bit careworn after almost five days without clean uniforms or bathing facilities. Cousens had managed to keep himself shaved, but that was all. All the officers shaved every day, just to set a good example to the men. They usually used the last remnants of their morning tea for the purpose if water was in short supply, as it often was in the field. Fortunately, Termoli's water supply was still functioning.

"Right, Alex. What can we do for you?" Cousens asked, satisfied that he was awake enough to listen to orders.

"38 Brigade have arrived at last and are disembarking as we speak. So we're pulling back into the town and they're taking over the front line. I've got men laying white tape[3] right now, marking a route for you to follow. You'll never find your way through the rubble without it; not in the dark, anyway. It took me long enough to find my way here. Can't have a whole commando brigade stumbling about in the dark."

"When will we leave?"

"As soon as the senior officers from the lead battalions arrive. You'll have to brief them on the layout of your defences, what they have in front of them, that sort of thing. Fortunately, they've brought more anti-tank guns with them, if they can get them forward quickly enough. It will be two-way traffic most of the time, your men going back in single file as the Irish come forward."

"Where are we going? Back to the harbour?" Carter asked, relief flooding through him that reinforcements had finally arrived.

"No, you're only being withdrawn into the town. You'll be a reserve unit. We've earmarked the railway station for your base. Hopefully you won't be needed, but you never know."

Well, it was better than nothing.

"Be ready to move by oh two hundred."

[1] To lie doggo: an archaic expression meaning to lie motionless to escape detection. First recorded in the 1880s. Used quite often in books and comics with stories set in private schools, such as the Billy Bunter cartoon strip.

[2] Officers with Lieutenant or Major in front of their rank, such as Lieutenant Colonel or Major General, are routinely referred to as Colonel or General as a short form of spoken address. In written correspondence their full rank would be used.

[3] Remarkably, no one had considered marking routes in this way before. White cotton or linen tape was used only to mark safe routes cleared through minefields. From Termoli onwards the commandos used the method whenever they moved at night, with the leading sections marking the way for those following behind. Now it is standard practice throughout the British army and plastic tape is more commonly used because it is lighter and cheaper, though not so environmentally friendly.

* * *

"No rest for the wicked." a trooper muttered just loud enough for Carter to hear as he walked past carrying a crate of 3 inch mortar bombs, but not loud enough for it to be obvious that he wanted it heard. Carter pretended he hadn't heard at all and concentrated on digging himself a slit trench. As all officers knew, it wasn't the grumbling of men that you had to worry about, it was when they stopped grumbling, because it probably meant they were plotting something.

They may no longer be in the front line, but the commandos weren't being allowed to become complacent. The nearest enemy troops were less than a mile away, so the CO ordered defensive positions to be set up around the railway station. The numerous craters scattered around the area also showed that it was a convenient aiming point for bombers and artillery so everyone, Carter included, needed a place of shelter, regardless of how crude it might be.

Carter chose to enlarge one of the bomb craters by digging downwards but made it more defensible at the same time by piling the spoil around the crater's rim. If they were going to be there much longer than a few hours, he might dig out the base to make it flatter and easier to stand in, rather than the deep dish shape it currently was.

The withdrawal had gone smoothly enough. A battalion of Royal Irish Fusiliers moved forward to occupy the commandos' recently vacated positions. Carter had managed to exchange a few words with one of the platoon officers as he chivvied his men forward.

"You've got a fight on your hands defending here." He had said. In the darkness he saw the glint of teeth as the young subaltern smiled. "Oh, we're not defending, Sir. We're attacking. Getting our boots into Jerry before he even knows what's hit him. I've been given an objective about half a mile in front of your old positions." The officer had a smooth brogue which spoke of green hills and picturesque valleys. Carter had no idea if that was what Northern Ireland looked like, but that was how he had imagined it. That and shipyards, of course.

"Well, good luck then. You'll need it."

"Here, before y' go, have wee drop o' this." He handed Carter a hip flask.

Carter took a sip and appreciated the warm glow of the spirit. "That's good whisky." He commented.

"The very finest. From my own hometown of Bushmills. I'll send you a bottle when the fighting's over." Carter hoped he the man would still be alive to keep his promise and hoped that he'd still be alive himself, to appreciate the gift. In the darkness they parted company, knowing it was unlikely they'd ever meet again. The army was a big place and they normally moved in different parts of it.

As they made their way back towards the town, following the strip of white tape that had been secured to the ground by chunks of rubble or tied around bits of projecting wood and metal, Carter had heard the Irishmen coming the other way as they said "Dead on, commandos. Well done." And "Yez did grand lads" and more, as the two forces moved past each other. The story of their defence of the town must have been reached the troop ship before it docked.

O'Driscoll told him later that not all the Irishmen were from the north. "I heard Donegal, Galway, Sligo and other accents. I'm sure I even heard a Kerryman. Wouldn't be at all surprised if there weren't men from my own sweet Mayo with them." While having no love for the English, the Irish felt threatened by Hitler's ambitions. It was a strong motivator for them to fight and there were plenty of Irish exiles spread across the various commandos.[1]

Carter thought back to the night of their arrival, when the town had seemed so peaceful. The only bomb craters at that time had been inflicted by the Allies and the town wasn't badly damaged. Now it was more rubble than buildings, from what he could see. It would take a major clean-up operation for trains to use the station again, that was sure. Hardly any of the buildings remained upright, at least as far as Carter could make out. He wondered where the population had gone and if they were still as supportive of the German war effort as they had been before the *Luftwaffe's* bombs started falling.

Brigade HQ was established in what had been the station's ticket hall, one of the few surviving structures. Cousens set up the commando's HQ in the left luggage store, which still had part of its roof; enough to keep out the steady drizzle that had set in shortly after their arrival.

Carter's new home in the crater was a few yards away along the platform, handy if Cousens needed him, but without making the space too crowded. There was still a bit of an overhang from the platform roof and that kept him dry enough, along with his poncho, which he spread out across a crudely constructed frame.

He checked his watch; six fifteen. Dawn would be with them soon. He couldn't see eastwards, but he guessed that the sky would already be getting paler, despite the thick cloud.

On that side of the town were 49 Cdo, protecting the stretch of coast that lay to the north of the harbour. There was no threat of a seaborn landing by the Germans, but if they managed to circle around the north side of the town undetected, they might use that as an approach to enter Termoli and cut the British troops off from the sea. It was unlikely, but a wise precaution to cover the area, nonetheless. The SRS were doing a similar job on the south side of the harbour. The merchant ships had transported the Irish brigade had already been withdrawn so they would be out of sight of land before the sun rose.

Dawn stand-to was called early, in response to the sound of artillery fire starting up in the distance. Whose it was, British or German, it wasn't possible to identify. There was no crash of explosions in the town and no answering fire from any of the guns that had arrived with the Irish and were now mounted close by. That suggested it was either the Germans renewing their assault on the river crossing or the British attempting to break out of their bridgehead. But the commando took no chances. Someone somewhere was fighting and the commando had to be ready, just in case.

Above the rumble of artillery Carter made out a new sound. Faint at first but getting louder. A monotonous drone. It couldn't be anything other than aircraft engines.

"Take cover!" Someone with sharper ears than his had already identified the danger. The cry was taken up across the station and in the positions that surrounded it.

This was it, the start of the final German attempt to take the town. Carter had no doubt that today would be the decisive day. Today the battle would be won – or lost.

He dropped into the bottom of his slit trench and made himself as small as he could. He was at no risk from blast, but when bombs threw debris into the air there was no way of telling where it might land. He pulled on the chinstrap of his helmet to make sure it was in no danger of slipping off. He might survive a bit of rubble hitting him elsewhere on his body, but a strike to the head might well fracture his skull. He had been very close to dying from such an injury once before, he reminded himself.

The bombs started falling a few moments later. He heard the growing crump, crump, crump of detonations getting closer. Probably the lead aircraft of the formation using the railway lines to navigate by. The steel tracks might not be visible from the air, but the scar they made across the countryside could probably be identified.

Other bombs joined the cacophony, dropping to either side of the railway station and then behind it as the aircraft flew over, invisible high above their heads. A second series of explosions started in front again as the following wave of bombers started their run. How many were there? Carter wondered. He'd seen the newsreel footage of the attacks that had happened during the Battle of Britain, formation after formation of enemy bombers darkening the sky as they headed towards London. Surely the Germans didn't have that many aircraft left in Italy?

He heard the thump of masonry falling around him and smaller bits pattered down to clatter against his helmet and pepper his body, but none of it was large enough to cause an injury. Without standing up, he dusted himself off.

At last the sound of aero engines faded into the distance, the *Luftwaffe's* part in the battle concluded.

But there was to be no respite. No sooner had the smoke and dust started to drift away than he heard the explosions of artillery shells, some near, but others further away, targeting the front lines. If the Irish were going to attack with the dawn, they would probably be out of the trenches already, creeping forward in the darkness to get closer to the enemy lines before they had to stand up and charge. Carter hoped they were, because the artillery barrage sounded murderous.

But the traffic wasn't one way. Close by, a battery of 25 pounders erupted like the crack of doom as the order was given to fire their first salvo. They continued to fire, though the rate became more and more ragged as each gun was re-loaded at a slightly different speed. There was no pause to re-align them after each shot, so they must have been laying down a barrage to cover the Irish advance.

"Capt Groves compliments, Lucky. Better come and take a look at this!" Carter's attention was attracted by the arrival of a commando.

"What is it, Harris?"

"Tanks. Coming straight down the tracks."

Carter wasted no more time with questions. He leapt from his cover and hurried in the man's wake as he led the way out of the station and along the railway line. 5 Troop were out there. That made sense, Harris was from 5 Troop. An old hand, he'd been with the commando since before Carter's arrival. Which was why he had been chosen as runner, probably. You didn't choose a raw recruit for a responsible job like that. But the man had never held any rank. Carter wondered why and filed away a mental note to find out, when he had less on his mind.

"The skipper's over there." Harris pointed the way to a mound of rubble, before moving to the other side of the track, presumably to re-take his position.

Carter ran forward at a crouch and nearly stood on Jeremy Groves. "Mind how you go, Lucky."

"Sorry, can't see much in the dark. Harris mentioned tanks."

"Yes, see along there?"

Carter followed the line of his outstretched arm. About half a mile away, along the railway line and about the place where it passed the first buildings of the town, there was fire burning. It provided some illumination around it, but Carter couldn't see any tanks. He told Groves as much.

"The first ones are already passed, heading towards us. Hold on a mo, there may be more.

He was right, a few seconds later the squat shape of a Panzer was lit up for a few seconds, before disappearing again as it moved away from the flames.

"How many, do you reckon?"

"That's at least the fourth, maybe the fifth."

"Have you told the CO?"

"I sent a runner to him at the same time as I sent Harris to find you. No way of knowing if he made it though. He might have been hit by a bomb blast."

"Let's assume that he didn't make it. Send another runner." It was the communications system of the previous war, but none of the troops had working radios anymore. They had hoped to scrounge some fresh batteries from the Irish, but no one had yet encountered a radio operator. Besides, if it had been him, Carter wouldn't have been handing out batteries to other units. There was no way of knowing when they might be needed. To the best of his knowledge, Cousens had the last working radio in the commando, which he needed to communicate with brigade HQ and 78 Div.

Carter raised his binoculars to his eyes as Groves scurried off to find another runner. With the help of their magnification he could just about make out the tank's silhouettes as the flames flickered behind them. Three of them, he thought, in line abreast, coming directly towards them along the railway lines.

In tactical terms it made sense. As the infantry attacked the defenders on the edge of the town, the tanks would use what they thought was an undefended route in behind the commandos, so they could turn right in the centre of the town and bulldoze their way into the rubble to attack the rear of the positions. Carter wondered if the

Germans had been tipped off about the possible access route from someone inside the town. Too much of a coincidence for them not have been.

If they had, it was before the commandos had been withdrawn from the front line and replaced by the Irish. The Germans probably didn't even know they were there. If they did, they would be blasting at their positions with their 75 mm gins and raking them with machine gun fire by now.

But what could the commandos do about tanks? It was the same dilemma as they had faced before, only now they didn't have the 6 pounder guns to help out. They'd also exhausted their supply of PIAT ammunition.

But the tanks wouldn't be by themselves. They'd have some infantry support and that was something Carter could do something about.

"Runner." He called. It was a general call, but someone should respond. Sure enough, a figure slid into the cover of the mound of rubble a few seconds later.

"Yes, Sir." The commando didn't know who he was talking to, yet. For all he knew it might be the CO. Better to be on the safe side.

"Do you know where the mortar section is?" Carter asked.

"I should do. I delivered their ammunition to them." The man grinned. Carter realised it must be the trooper who had passed him earlier, burdened down by the crate of mortar bombs.

"OK. Go and find them and tell them to fire a ranging bomb, directly along the line of the railway tracks, range 500 yards." Carter was guessing that the tanks were still a quarter mile away and added a few extra yards to account for the position of the mortars to his rear. "Send me a couple more men to act as runners before you go."

Once the ranging bomb had been fired, he'd need to send orders for adjusting both direction and range.

The man sprinted away and Carter was joined shortly afterwards by two more men. These were new boys and Carter didn't know their names yet.

"Names?" He returned his eyes to his binoculars.

"Charteris, Sir." The nearest one replied.

"Peebles, Sir. Not from there though." The second had a broad Scottish accent.

"OK, I'm going to need you two to run relays, carrying fire orders to the mortars. Have you done it before?"

"Not since training, Sir."

"Me neither."

"OK, just remember what I say to you and repeat it to whoever is in charge back at the mortar positions. Do you know where they are?

At that moment the crump of a 3 inch mortar sounded behind them. "I do now, Sir." One of them chuckled.

"Stop calling me Sir." Carter said, but mildly. "We're not on the parade ground."

The bomb crashed to earth and lit up the area with a flash, before leaving it in darkness once again. The light had lasted long enough for him to see that it had landed short. He needed better visibility. "OK, fire order. I want one illuminating bomb, followed by one HE. Same direction, but down two degrees." It should be enough, but he would soon find out.

Peebles scuttled off towards the station. Carter could see that dawn was fast approaching, but it still wasn't possible to make out what was in front of them. The illuminating, or star burst, would help. He cursed himself for his stupidity. He should have asked for that first, before firing the ranging shot.

But he had alerted the tanks to their presence and there was the flare of a gun being fired, followed by the whoosh of a shell passing above his head and the crash of its explosion somewhere behind him. Most of the commandos were out on the perimeter of the station, it was unlikely to have injured anyone. He half turned to see where it had struck. Just about where the station's buffet had once stood. That had been a ruin, so probably no one there.

The sky lit up as the illuminating bomb reached its zenith above the tanks. Yes, he had been right. Three tanks in line abreast, with two … no, three more behind. But he couldn't see any infantry. Had they taken the risk of coming without? It would have allowed them to travel faster.

Of course, they would have circled around to the north, staying as far as possible from the British lines to avoid the sound of their engines being detected then, when the bombers arrived and their attack drowned them out, they had dashed along the railway lines to enter the town. Their need for speed meant that the infantry had to be left behind, though Carter had no doubt they would now be following at the best pace they could manage.

The station had four platforms, which meant that the railway lines started to diverge as they got closer to the station. The increase in width also gave the tanks more room to manoeuvre. They started to spread apart, making them a harder target to hit if there was any artillery in the area. Sadly for 15 Cdo, there wasn't.

It was going to be a numbers game. The tanks would continue to advance, their crews safe inside their armoured shell, while the commandos retaliated with the only weapons that might make a dent, which was the three inch mortars. They'd had PIATs, an effective anti-tank weapon, when they had arrived in the town but all the bombs for those had already been used up and no fresh supplies had reached them. But, while mortars might dent the tanks, they were unlikely to stop them. A lucky strike on a track might be the only thing to do so.

It was only a matter of time before the commando would have to withdraw.

A figure slumped into the rubble beside him. "I've sent Jeremy to ask the gunners if they can move a 25 pounder in here to even things up a bit." Charlie Cousens shouted as another tank shell crashed into the station.

"That will take time."

"It's our only hope."

"Unless we send someone forward to try and stop them with grenades." A grenade exploding inside an air intake had been known to do enough damage to stop a tank. But the person who placed it had to be right on top of the rear of the tank, where he would be a sitting target for the machine guns of the following tanks.

"Anyone would have to be mad to try something like that, Steven. I couldn't possibly order it."

"No, but I could volunteer. I just need a couple of men mad enough to go with me and I think I know where I can find them."

"Are you sure, Steven?"

"If those tanks get through, the chances are the town will fall. We've been here too long and lost too many men for me to let that happen."

"Mad bugger. OK. But only if you can find men to go with you. No solo heroics."

"Understood, Sir. Oh, I was acting as forward mortar observer. You'll need to take over that duty, Sir." Carter didn't wait for a reply so he didn't hear the CO mutter "I'm starting to wonder who's in command her." He just levered his way to his feet and trotted to the left, towards 4 Troop's positions. A tank's machine gunner spotted him and chanced a burst of fire, but Carter was already behind a crumbling wall before the bullets passed harmlessly by.

"Ernie!" Carter shouted.

"Over here." An arm waved at him from a trench. Carter realised that he could see it without too much difficulty; a measure of how much light there now was.

Carter jumped down into the Captain's trench. "I've got a special job and need to borrow three of your men."

"No need to ask who. What are their chances of coming back in one piece?"

"Almost zero."

"They'll probably accept those odds. You'll find them over there." Barraclough pointed the way resignedly.

Green was lying in the bottom of the trench staring upwards and at first Carter thought he might be dead, but he was just resting. Above him Glass and O'Driscoll manned the Bren gun, ready to fire if a target presented itself.

"Welcome to you, Sorr. "O'Driscoll greeted him. "'Tis a fine morning."

"I'm never sure how much of that accent you're putting on, Paddy. I've heard you speak as though you attended Trinity.?"

"Oh, you mean like that gobshite George Bernard Shaw."

"Nothing wrong with Shaw." Green butted in. "A fine socialist. And he didn't go to Trinity."

Carter could feel an argument developing and he had no time for that.

"If I could bring your attention back to the war, I'd like to offer you the opportunity, once more, to die for King and Country."

"It's not my fecking country."

"If you feel like that, Paddy, you can take off that uniform that His Majesty so generously provided you with." Glass retorted.

"Gentlemen, the war is waiting. Are you coming with me or not?"

"Would it have anything to do with those tanks?" Green asked, the noise of their engines now clearly audible.

"Yes. Someone has to try and stop them."

"Well, why didn't ye just say that." O'Driscoll started packing Bren gun magazines back into a canvass satchel as Glass lifted up the gun and folded its bipod out of the way.

"Have you all got grenades?"

"You'll be asking us next if we've got our teeth." Green replied. Carter would never have accepted such insubordination form anyone other than these three. They had earned the right to be rude to him when he asked what, in their opinion, were stupid questions.

Given that the total amount of teeth the men had between them wouldn't add up to the number in his own mouth, Carter was tempted to respond to that, but decided he didn't have time and it risked starting another round of banter. Instead, he climbed out of the trench and angled right, towards the railway tracks.

The tanks had slowed their advance. Knowing that they had troops in front of them, possibly commandos, they were taking more care. They picked their way around craters and heaps of rubble, rather than climbing through them. German tank crews had learnt all about PIATs in Sicily and knew that to expose the underside of the tank by climbing a slope, even briefly, increased their vulnerability. The armour on a tank's belly was much thinner than that on its sides or top.

Ducking down, the four men scuttled from cover to cover. The narrow slits and ports through which the tank crews viewed the outside world limited their field of vision, so by keeping to one side of the tracks they reduced the chance of their being seen. But while the centre tank kept firing forward, the two flanking tanks were now turning their turrets too and fro, seeking out just such a threat. The distance was down to less than a hundred and fifty yards now, before they reached the first line of commando trenches. Carter didn't have much time left.

He unhooked a grenade from his webbing and held it in his left hand, while his right arm cradled his Tommy gun. His upper arm still ached from his wound, but it was strong enough. He didn't really have a plan. It made sense for three of them to tackle one tank each, seeking out a weak spot. The fourth would lie in wait for one of the tanks behind and maybe fire at the viewing slits in the hope of hitting someone inside.

Damaging a track would help, but the main armament would still be able to fire. They would need a killing blow. It would be too much to hope that any of the crew would be foolish enough to open any of the hatches. They'd have to climb on the beast's back behind the turret and try to jamb a grenade into an air intake, then pull the pin and jump off again.

They moved forward a little further, closing the distance. None of them really wanted to do this. Their reluctance could be felt, crackling between them like static electricity. But if they didn't do it, who would?

A single shot cracked past Carter's head, making him flinch. That wasn't from a tank. They would fire a burst from a machine gun, not single shots.

It meant that there was a German sniper within range, which also meant that the rest of the infantry couldn't be far behind. They were running out of time. The sniper would know what they were up to and no doubt was already thinking about the shots that would stop them.

"Sniper." Carter shouted to his companions. The sound of the bullet's discharge had been drowned out by the squeal of tank tracks and growl of engines, so the others wouldn't have heard it.

"Dat's all we need. One of dem fuckers." O'Driscoll grumbled.

"Do you want me and Paddy to see if we can locate him?" Glass shouted. They could play a game of cat and mouse, with one man offering a target while the other looked for the puff of smoke that showed where the shot had come from. Once identified he'd be inundated by fire from the Bren gun.

"No time. Just keep your heads down."

Fifty yards, no more. The centre tank fired again and followed the large calibre round with a stream of machine gun bullets. Rifle shots pinged off the armour as commandos retaliated. They might as well try to stop a charging rhino with a feather duster.

A crashing sound came from Carter's left and he had to throw himself to the ground to avoid being crushed under the tracks of another tank. He saw his men scattering to get out of the way. It had appeared through a gap in a wall and Carter doubted the crew even knew he and his men were there. They were lucky they weren't already dead, crushed beneath its tracks.

But the crew of the centre tank didn't have as much luck. The turret on the new arrival swung towards it and fired in one smooth movement. At that range there was no possibility that it could miss.

As the centre tank exploded, the Sherman's turret continued to traverse until it was aiming at the left-hand tank. That too went the way of its brother in the centre. A second Sherman appeared, following behind the first. It was already lined up on the third tank and the tank was dead long before the crew realised the danger and started to turn their own turret to face the new threat. Already the following line of tanks had stopped. The one on the left fired, hitting the second Sherman square in the side[3]. Smoke billowed out of the turret and hull hatches as fires started inside. Carter knew the crews had complained that they seemed to catch fire very easily. No hatches opened for the crew to start evacuating, so there was no doubt as to their fate.

But a third Sherman was coming in from the side, with a fourth almost on its tail. The Panzers decided that discretion was the better part of valour and started to withdraw. The Shermans helped them on their way with more shots and another of the *Panzers* ground to a halt.

As Carter clambered back to his feet and dusted himself down again, he saw the large red maple leaf painted on the side of the tank's turret.

"About time you bloody Canuks[4] arrived." Carter muttered.

[1] Approximately 70,000 Irish people, predominantly men, volunteered to serve in the British armed forces during World War II. The dual nationality clause that was part of the peace agreement of 1922 allowed them to do so on the same basis as if they were British citizens. A number deserted from the Irish Army so they could fight the Germans and were treated appallingly badly when they returned home after the war, being barred from government jobs, welfare schemes, social housing and pensions. Around 5,000 Irishmen from the Republic died fighting for Britain with many more wounded. In addition, about 200,000 Irish people travelled to Britain to do civilian war work. At Eamon de Valera's insistence (he was Taoiseach (Prime Minister) of the Republic) there was no conscription in Northern Ireland. Approximately 50,000 men from there volunteered for service.

[2] Trinity College Dublin is Ireland's oldest University, founded in 1592. It is Ireland's equivalent to Oxford or Cambridge but regards itself as superior to both. Students attending Trinity during this timeframe would have had a very mild Irish accent, if any at all. They might well have lost it while attending an English boarding school.

[3] Although well armoured at the front, the M4 Sherman tank had much thinner protection on the sides and so were vulnerable to being hit there. They also had a reputation for fires starting inside the crew compartments, which sometimes caused ammunition to explode. The reason the Sherman was so successful during World War II wasn't because it was superior to German tanks, because it wasn't. It was because they were mass produced in such numbers that they were always able to defeat the smaller numbers of their enemies. Over 49,000 Sherman tanks were built, compared to a combined total of about 15,000 Panzer IVs, Panthers, Tiger I's and IIs, their German contemporaries on the battlefield. Even taking into account those Shermans deployed to the Pacific theatre, they still outnumbered their enemy about two or even three to one because half the German tanks were on the Eastern Front fighting the Russians..

[4] Although not formally identified in any of the author's sources, this was probably the 12th Canadian Armoured Regiment, also called the Three Rivers Regiment, which was from Quebec. Termoli is listed as one of their battle honours. Because of the French speaking preponderance in Quebec, the regiment has been retitled using its French translation, the 12e Régiment blindé du Canada and is still part of the Canadian Armed Forces.

9 – Homeward Bound

Looking out over the aft railing of the troop ship, Carter took in the sight of Bari harbour, as they slipped through the breakwaters and out into the open sea. So much shipping, all in one place. He turned his gaze skyward, looking for any hint that there might be Allied aircraft up there to protect the vital supplies that these ships carried, but could see nothing but puffs of winter cloud. What a target this would make for the *Luftwaffe*[1].

He felt the arrival of someone along side him and wasn't surprised to find it was Prof Green.

"So, homeward bound then?" Prof Green fished.

"That's what the rumours are saying. All I know is that this ship is only going as far as Catania. I have a feeling we'll be seeing a lot of transit camps before we get to sleep under our own roofs again.

"The war here is far from over. Why do you think they're sending us home now?"

It was true that after the capture of Termoli, the British advance along the east coast of Italy had stalled. With the Americans still slugging it out with the Germans along the Volturno river on the other side of the Apennine Mountains, it was decided they had to take priority for supplies, especially fuel. Winter also played its part, turning mountain roads to quagmires keeping river levels high and dangerous.

After two more days of fighting the battle for Termoli was declared over and the commandos were sent down to Bari with instructions from Montgomery himself to "have a damn good party." It was an order that the commandos had no trouble obeying. After a month in the city, Carter was sure that it would be difficult to find a bottle of beer or wine that had remained undrunk.

"Rumour has it that Monty himself asked for us, which suggests that he has some plan or other to get us killed again. But it's more likely that we're so under-strength now that we aren't any use out here. Better to send us home, rebuild us and then put us to good use with whatever's coming.

"The Second Front?

"Probably."

"Why do they call it that? Surely this is the second front."

"You'd think so, wouldn't you. I think it's because we aren't going to get to Berlin by this route. If we land in northern France, say Calais, we'll only be about two hundred miles from the German border. Hitler will have to pull troops out of Russia to defend the Fatherland. The eastern front will be weakned, and the Russians will advance. The Yanks can't allow the Russians to be in Berlin before them, so it will be a bit of a footrace for the glory hunters like Patton and Monty.

"You think Monty's a glory hunter, Lucky?" Green sounded genuinely scandalised.

"I do. He might not have started that way, but his face is all over the newsreels these days, speaking to the troops, pointing at maps and such like. That sort of thing can go to a man's head."

They went quiet for a few moments, contemplating the receding view of Italy.

"Do you ever feel afraid, Lucky? Green asked after a while.

"Hmm, can't say I've thought about it that much. I know I get very tense before we go into action, butterflies in the stomach, that sort of thing. Is that fear?"

Green didn't answer the question, so Carter continued. "Why, do you feel afraid?"

"Every time. I think 'will this be the day I cop a bullet?' I sometimes look around me and wonder if the others are feeling the same."

"I'm sure they are. Has anything in particular made you feel this way?"

"Not really. Well, maybe. That attack on the tanks at Termoli station. It was total madness. My brain kept screaming at me to get back in my trench. Let some other bugger do it this time."

"And you think I didn't feel exactly the same? Or the other men, when they go into action? Of course they feel fear."

"Do you really think so? They don't show any signs of it."

"No, because it's been trained out of them. Not the fear, but the showing of fear. You know the way things are done at Achnacarry. First sign of weakness and you're on the train back to your unit. So, the men become very good at hiding weaknesses and fear is the biggest weakness of all."

"But they still go over the top. We haven't had a single man fail in his duty."

"I sometimes wonder if the only real difference between a hero and a coward is that the hero buries his fear and the coward lets it control him. But they both feel equally afraid. Let's face it, you'd have to be insane not to be afraid, wouldn't you?"

"I suppose so."

Green's face said he was still worried about his admission.

"Do you know how I deal with it, Prof? I keep myself busy. That's why I'm forever going round the slit trenches, talking to the men, making sure they have everything they need, if it's in my power to get it for them. I plan everything I do so many times I spend more time planning it than actually doing it sometimes. Having a good plan saves lives and one of the lives it might save is my own. As long as my brain is working, I can keep the fear at bay.

I'm an officer. We're trained to put on a stiff upper lip at all times. Any officer who didn't, would soon find himself posted off to some military backwater where he can't do any harm. In the commando's it's even more important not to show doubt or fear. So, I keep my stiff upper lip despite how I feel inside. And when the time comes to attack, I make sure I'm at the very front. Not because I'm brave, but because I'm scared stiff and I know the men are as well. And if they think I'm being brave, it makes them try to overcome their own fear, so as to not let me down.

Look how many men we've had KIA[2] since we joined Fifteen. Must be over a hundred. Then there are the wounded and the MIAs[3] that's what, another hundred and fifty maybe. The men know those numbers just as well as we do, but they go over the top anyway. That isn't because they're brave, it's because they're in control of their fear. And you're one of the bravest I know. Who was it came back and rescued me when I got that bang on the head at Honfluer? It was you. Were you afraid then?"

"Of course. I thought I was just about to get away and found out I had to go back and try to help you."

"But you came back despite your fear. See what I mean."

Green fell silent.

"Thanks, Lucky. This has helped."

Carter let out a short chuckle. "Good. Now all I need to do is find someone who can give me the same pep talk."

"Well, I better get back below. Danny Glass managed to smuggle a bottle of wine aboard and he and Paddy will have drunk it all if I'm not there. Care to join us?"

"No. I've got paperwork to do. Since we became part of a brigade it seems to have multiplied."

As Green turned towards the entrance to the men's sleeping quarters, the converted freight holds of the ship, Carter knew there was another reason for not going with him to drink wine. Two reasons in fact. The first was that the mail had caught up with them again and there were several letters from Fiona for him to read and the second was that, just before they had left the transit camp outside of Bari, a bottle of Black Bush single malt Irish whiskey had been delivered to him.

[1] Carter was not the only one to think that. On 2nd December 1943 Air Marshall Sir Arthur Coningham, Commander in Chief of The North West Africa Allied Tactical Air Force, declared that the air war against the *Luftwaffe* in the Mediterranean theatre had been won. At 7 pm on the same day the *Luftwaffe* launched a raid on Bari made up of 100 Ju 88 bombers. The raid destroyed 28 Allied ships in the harbour and seriously damaged several more. The loss of supplies seriously impacted on the Allied advance through Italy, resulting in Rome not being liberated until June 1944. About 1,000 Allied sailors

and military personnel and another 1,000 Italian civilians were killed. An inquiry into the lack of air defences over Bari concluded that Air Marshall Coningham was not responsible for the lack of air cover (so who was?) but noted that complacency had set in because there had been no previous such raids on harbours.

[2] KIA – Killed in action.

[3] MIA – Missing in action. It is presumed that the missing have been taken prisoner unless there is evidence to suggest they have died. Their status isn't changed until the Red Cross notifies the soldier's government that the man has been taken prisoner, or confirmation is received, again via the Red Cross usually, that the missing soldier has died. In some cases, soldiers remained listed as missing even after the end of the war because it wasn't possible to establish what happened to them. They may have been buried in unmarked graves. They may have been buried but not identified and some may even have been buried under the wrong name. A legacy from World War I is that thousands of men lie under gravestones that say only "Known Unto God" and thousands more still lie on the battlefields with no grave at all. In total there are over 212,000 such gravestones marking British and Coomonwealth dead around the world. Technically, those men are still missing. The Grave of the Unknown Soldier, in Westminster Abbey, represents all of those men.

This ends the sixth story in the "Carter's Commandos" series.

Historical Notes

This book takes up the story of the fictitious 15 Cdo following the invasion of Sicily in 1943 and moves it forward four months. A lot happened during that period and I apologise to those who think I have missed significant events from that campaign. This is because I am following the trail taken by 3 Cdo, my father's unit, and their involvement wasn't always in the centre of the action, where the history books record the major operations. It was the nature of commando operations that their involvement was often peripheral to the main events, though not insignificant in itself.

There was a significant hiatus between 3 Cdo's operation at Malati Bridge and their next call to action. The commando had lost a lot of men, replacements were slow to arrive and had to be bedded into the unit. For this reason, I have taken a few liberties and invented one operation and some of the events described as part of a second, genuine operation.

Operation Manchester is fictitious. To the best of my knowledge the commandos, or the Special Raiding Squadron, never undertook such an operation. 12 Cdo had been used to cover the extraction of paratroops in France (Operation Biting, 27th/28th February 1942), so it is consistent with history to give 15 Cdo a similar task. I'm sure that it would have whetted the appetite of Mgr 'Paddy' Mayne for his SRS to have been offered such a job, which is why I have involved them. I have taken poetic license and attributed the SRS's leadership to David Stirling, their founder, because his is a more famous name. Stirling had actually been taken prisoner in North Africa in January 1943. After numerous escape attempts, he was eventually sent to Colditz Castle, where he sat out the rest of the war. The SRS were genuinely brigaded with 3 Cdo and 40 (RM) Cdo while in Sicily and Italy so that part, at least, is true, as is their involvement in the fighting at Termoli.

The operation in the area around Bova Marina, which I have called Operation Tablet (to the best of my knowledge it didn't have a formal operational name), was real. Major Peter Young, as 2IC, led the recovery operation that I have attributed to Carter and his LC(I) was forced aground due firstly to an error by its crew, which was then aggravated by the power of the sea. Young did make contact with Italian partisans and mounted ambushes against Italian and German forces sent to search for the commandos, but the attack on the warehouses and workshops that is described in this book is the product of my own imagination.

"Walter" is my own invention. I wanted to include some reference to the SOE and the men of that organisation who risked their lives, mainly unrecognised by the world at large. They deserve far more recognition than they have ever had for the bravery and the sacrifices they made. The majority of SOE's agents never saw the end of the war. Much of that lack of recognition can be attributed to the Official Secrets Act, which kept many of their operations under wraps until well after the war ended, by which time interest in World War II had started to dwindle in the media.

The commandos did take signallers of 156th Field Regiment, Royal Artillery, with them to Bova Marina to operate more powerful radios and the records showed that they adapted well to the task.

The operation around Bova Marina didn't have much value in terms of intelligence gathering. In fact, it seemed to serve no purpose at all, even at the time. More than one 3 Cdo veteran has since surmised that the patrols might have been a carrot dangled in front of the German and Italian armies, trying to lure them away from Reggio Calabria in the belief that the invasion of Italy was to take place on the southern coast of Italy' toe. If that was the intention, it failed. However, the commandos revelled in their freedom to operate behind the lines in that way and they did cause some disruption.

The rescue of the commandos was pretty much as I described, and they did have to leave several Italian prisoners behind, much to the disgust of the Italians themselves. By and large the Italian citizens received the commandos warmly at Bova Marina (if not elsewhere). Snr Manfreddi and his wife were real people and did provide the commandos with much needed food. Peter Young made a point of visiting them after 3 Cdo landed on the mainland, to thank them for what they had done.

The commandos were rather side-lined for the invasion of the Italian mainland. That was a three-pronged assault conducted by the British first, followed by the Americans. On 3rd September 1943 the British launched Operation Baytown, landing to the north and south of the town of Reggio Calabria, on the eastern side of the Straits of Messina. Their landing was intended to draw German and Italian forces down into the toe of Italy to counter them, while the Americans landed further north, behind them. Montgomery wasn't in favour of the plan, as intelligence and aerial reconnaissance showed the Axis armies were already heading northwards. In the end he was right, leaving his 8th Army three hundred miles away from the main action at Salerno.

XIII Corps spearheaded the landings, just as they had several weeks earlier in Sicily. There was no significant commando involvement. 2 Cdo were involved later in the Salerno landings.

On the first day of operations, XIII Corps faced significant opposition from the *15th Panzergrenadier* Regiment, who had been left as a rear guard. That force and the 129th Reconnaissance Battalion fought delaying actions for several days, holding XIII Corps in the toe of Italy. The Germans then destroyed bridges on the roads northward, which slowed Montgomery's progress as military engineers had to construct replacements while still under fire from the German rear-guard. It was an effective delaying tactic.

The Italian government surrendered the same day as the British landed, having sent Giuseppe Castellano, a senior member of the fascist government, to Cassibile (Sicily) to sign an act of surrender. An armistice was agreed for 7th September and that short interval proved to be critical. Unfortunately, news of the impending armistice had leaked ahead of time, which allowed the Germans to disarm their former allies, preventing them from re-joining the war on the side of the Allies, though they did formally declare war on Germany on 14th October.

A government in exile was established in Brindisi under Pietro Badoglio, who had replaced Mussolini after he had resigned. At the same time, the Germans set up Mussolini, who they had rescued from his prison, as their puppet dictator. It was loyalty to Mussolini that made some Italians hostile to the Allies.

On 9th September the British mounted Operation Slapstick, which was a landing by paratroops around the port city of Taranto, which is located in on the eastern side of Italy's "instep", to the west of the Adriatic city of Brindisi. This had been intended as an airborne invasion, but with all of the available transport aircraft needed by the Americans, the paratroops and their follow-on forces were transported from North Africa by sea. 3 Cdo joined up with this force and followed them along the Italian coast to Bari.

As the landing force approached Taranto, the Italian fleet based there set out to sea and headed for the British colony of Malta, where they surrendered in accordance with the peace treaty. The invading force reached the cities of Brindisi and Bari within forty-eight hours, but then had to halt in order to allow 78th Division, the follow-on force, to catch up with them and to mop up the garrisons that had been by-passed on the way. 3 Cdo carried out a number of landings behind the German lines, forcing the Germans to either retreat or surrender.

The main landings for the invasion (Operation Avalanche) were carried out on 9th September at Salerno, just south of Naples. American forces (along with British commandos) were transported from Tunisia, Algeria and Sicily to participate.

Because Montgomery's diversionary landings at Reggio Calabria had failed to distract the Germans, they faced much heavier fighting than anticipated. The Germans had established their main defensive line on the Volturno river between Naples, on the west coast and Termoli on the Adriatic coast. The bulk of the Italian mountains that form a "spine" along the peninsula, prevented the Allies from moving inland in strength on either side, which made the defence a lot easier than it might have been. This was to be the consistent story of the Italian campaign which resulted in fighting in Italy not being concluded until a few days before the end of the war in Europe, in May 1945.

The 8th Army earned the undeserved nickname of the D-Day Dodgers as the public assumed they were having an easy time in Sunny Italy, while the main thrust of the war had moved to Normandy. Nothing could be further from the truth. The war in Italy was every bit as intense as it was a thousand miles further north, as any veteran of the campaign could attest. The Battle of Monte Cassino (a mountaintop monastery occupied by the Germans, 17th Jan – 18th May 1944) resulted in 55,000 Allied casualties. It delayed the liberation of Rome until 5th June, an event that went almost unnoticed because of D-Day taking place the following day in Normandy and grabbing all the headlines.

But the main story for this book, the operation I gave the name Terminus (it is the English translation of Termoli), was genuine. This was Operation Devon (1st to 8th Oct 1943), or the Battle of Biferno as you will find it called in history books. The operation unfolded and concluded pretty much as I have described it, though I have fictionalised some of it for dramatic effect. For truthful accounts, please refer to the books by John Durnford-Slater and Peter Young, detailed under "Further Reading". I have also borrowed from the recollections of Tpr Jack Cox of 6 Troop, 3 Cdo. You may read his full account here.

The bridge across the Biferno had been destroyed by the Germans in the face of 78 Div's advance and the first replacement, a pontoon bridge, was washed away by the flooding of the river due to storms in the mountains. Italian rivers were (and probably still are) notorious for the speed at which they could rise following storms.

The second replacement was a 100 ft span Bailey Bridge erected on the piers of the original stone structure. But the badly damaged piers first had to be reinforced to take the weight, which required the laying of 5,000 bricks. It was a feat completed by just four engineers in nine hours while under constant German artillery fire. A skilled bricklayer would normally expect to lay 240 bricks per hour, but wouldn't be under artillery fire, nor would they work non-stop for 9 hours.

The story of the defence of the hill alongside the Guglionesi road is part truth and part fiction. The commandos did occupy that position and there was some fearsome fighting there against a much larger force, which included tanks, but I have fictionalised the version given here because I don't have any first-hand account of the actual combat on which to hang an accurate depiction. My father was quite reticent about his part in Operation Devon, apart from confirming he was at Termoli, Tpr Cox saw the fighting from the narrow viewpoint of his own slit trench, John Durnford-Slater was back in Termoli in his Brigade HQ and Peter Young was there some of the time but not all the time. The manoeuvring I have described for the German tanks, however, is reasonably accurate.

The story of the German troops being taken prisoner while sleeping on a train is true. Captured German paratroops really did cook breakfast for the commandos and did so willingly. There was a considerable amount of respect shown between the two sets of combatants, just as there had been on their previous encounter at Malati Bridge. Even the story of Paddy O'Driscoll being reproved by a German paratrooper for the state of his slit trench is taken from real life and the trooper involved was Jack Cox. He doesn't relate what he said to the German paratrooper who criticised his efforts.

The tea loving Sergeant Major King really did sneak up on a German bonfire to boil up a mess tin of water, the action I attributed to Prof Green. However, Sgt Maj King made it back without being detected and the British didn't antagonise the Germans by celebrating his little victory. A German prisoner was captured when he bumped into a British patrol while looking for somewhere to relieve himself.

Italian civilians sniping on the commandos was a problem. John Durnford-Slater, in command of the Brigade, did round up some civilians and threaten to execute them if the sniping didn't stop, using the rationale that I have attributed to Vernon. The level of sniping was reduced and when the commandos left the town the detainees were released unharmed.

Operation Devon was another of those that was ordered in haste and repented at leisure. Montgomery had received notification that he was to return to the UK to start the planning for D-Day and his staff wanted to give him a farewell present. It was considered that the speedy capture of the strategically important port of Termoli would be a suitable gift.

Nobody could anticipate the weather cutting the commandos off but, just like at Malati Bridge, no contingency had been prepared for any delay to the relief force. The dispatch of 38th (Irish) Brigade was hastily put together after the event, which was why they were slow to arrive. They first had to be moved back down to Bari to board a troop ship. That ship then ran aground as it approached Termoli.

This was the second attempt that 8th Army HQ had made to get my father killed. It's a wonder he didn't start to take it personally. For the Brigade as a whole it was costly, with three officers and 29 other ranks (ORs) killed, 7 officers and 78 ORs wounded and one officer and 22 ORs missing. This doesn't include casualties suffered by 38th (Irish) Brigade or the rest of 78th Infantry Division. Considering the intensity of the fighting, 3 Cdo regarded that level of casualties as getting off lightly.

In this instance, knowledge of the presence of a German armoured division wasn't an intelligence failure, as it had been in Sicily. At the commencement of the operation there had been no large formations of German armour on the east coast. Field Marshal Kesselring, the Commander-in-Chief of German forces in Italy, realised the danger presented by the British advance quite belatedly and ordered the re-deployment of the 16th *Panzer* Division from the Volturno river, on the west coast of Italy, to Termoli. The re-deployment took two days to complete, which was why no large concentrations of German armour were seen near Termoli until 4th October. The telephoned reports of armour, received in Termoli on 3rd October, were of the advance units arriving at the assembly point at Guglionesi. The arrival of the tanks of the 1st Canadian Division at the same time as the attack on the town by the 16th *Panzer* Division was a convenient and lifesaving coincidence for the commandos. The *Panzers* did advance towards the centre of the town along the railway line, threatening 3 Cdo who were dug in around the railways station.

Major General Rudolf Sieckenius, commander of 16th *Panzer* Division and once considered to be a national hero for his performance in Russia, was relieved of his command in November 1943 as a consequence of his failure to stop the Allies capturing Termoli. His rank was frozen permanently and he was forced to undergo National Socialist Leadership Training to "rehabilitate" him, then to undertake a variety of mundane training and administration roles in Berlin. He wasn't given command of another operational unit until the closing months of the war. He was killed in April 1945 in action in Berlin. leading an attack with a handful of men on foot, against Russian positions, though some reports state that he committed suicide. Given the nature of his attack and the strength of the enemy, his death could be interpreted that way.

Having crossed the Biferno river and established a safe bridgehead, 78 Div then sat and waited out the winter. Having breached one end of the Volturno-Biferno defence line, it didn't cause the Germans to withdraw from the other end. Winter made campaigning difficult and a major air raid on the port of Bari on 2nd December (mentioned in the footnotes in Ch 9) deprived the Allies of huge quantities of supplies they needed to fight. By the time the Allies were ready to advance again, 3 Cdo were already back in Britain.

The use of commandos in brigade strength in Italy had signalled a shift in Montgomery's thinking about how they might be used in the future. While small scale raiding would continue until D-Day (and later than that in Italy and the Balkans), the emphasis would change and they would become the 'shock troops' of the British Army, the units chosen to crack the hardest nuts under the most difficult conditions. It wasn't a role that 3 Cdo would appreciate, but one they carried out with distinction – as always.

At the end of October, my fictitious 15 Cdo started a very tortuous two month return journey to the UK via Catania, Bone (now known as Annaba in Algeria) and Algiers. On the way a parade will be held to award them their first campaign medal, the Africa Star (the medal depicted on the cover of the 4th book of the series, Operation Carthage), just as they were awarded to the troopers of 3 Cdo. In due course they will also receive the Italy Star. They will disembark in Liverpool on New Year's Day, 1944 and we know for what that year is most famous.

* * *

The Army commandos were established in June 1940 on the direct orders of Winston Churchill. The original concept, a force that could raid across the channel into occupied France, was the brainchild of Col (later Brigadier) Dudley Clarke, a Royal Artillery officer who was a genius at devising deception operations. His suggestion found its way to Churchill's ear and he was taken by it.

It was Churchill who recognised that to maintain the war effort until victory could be achieved, he needed to maintain the morale of the British people following the disaster that had been the evacuation from Dunkirk. The skilful use of propaganda had turned that defeat into a sort of victory, the 'miracle of Dunkirk, but genuine victories, however small, would be needed if he was to convince the British people that the war could be won.

It would be the commandos that would provide those small victories. Often the targets of their raids were insignificant in military terms but, on occasions, they had a far greater impact than could ever have been imagined. For example, following successive raids on Norway, Adolf Hitler became convinced that they were the prelude to an invasion of that country as a steppingstone for invading Denmark and then Germany itself. No such plan existed, but Hitler ordered 300,000 additional troops to be sent to Norway, where they remained for the rest of the war, along with additional Luftwaffe and naval units. The fact that the invasion of Norway never came about was proof to Hitler that his counterstrategy had worked. Had those troops been available at Stalingrad, El Alamein or in Normandy in 1944, who knows how the outcomes of those battles might have been affected.

15 Commando is a fictitious unit. The Army commandos were numbered 1 to 14 (excluding 13). 50, 51 and 52 commandos were formed in North Africa.

The Parachute Regiment were formed from No 2 Commando, who had originally been set up to take on the role of paratroops. Even after the establishment of the Parachute Regiment in 1942, the commandos still trained some of their troops in parachuting, though there is no record of them ever having undertaken that role. A new 2 Cdo was formed in 1941.

No 10 (Inter Allied) Commando was made up of members of the armed forces from occupied countries in Europe who had escaped. There were two French troops, one Norwegian, one Dutch, one Belgian, one Polish, one Yugoslavian and a troop of German speakers, many of whom were Jewish. They often accompanied other commandos on raids to act as guides and interpreters, as well as carrying out raids of their own.

Achnacarry House is the ancestral home of Clan Cameron and it was taken over by the War Office to become the Commando Training Centre. The original occupants of the house moved into cottages in the grounds. During the course of World War II over 25,000 commandos were trained there, plus some of their American counterparts, the Rangers, who were modelled on the commandos. Originally each commando was responsible for providing their own training, before the first training centres were set up at Inveraray and Lochailort, in late 1940, before moving to Achnacarry.

The first Royal Marine commandos didn't come into being until 19th February 1942. 40 (RM) Cdo was, like the army commandos, made up of volunteers, but subsequent units (41- 48) were RM battalions who were ordered to convert. For this reason the army commandos tended to look down on their RM counterparts. However, the RM commandos fought bravely and in all theatres of the war. They carried the commando legacy onwards at the end of the war and continue to do so to this day.

If you wish to find out more about the Army commandos there are a number of books on the subject, including my own, which details my father's wartime service; it's called "A Commando's Story". I have provided the titles of some of these books at the end of these notes. These also provided the sources for much of my research for this book and the others in the series.

Operations in Sicily and Italy saw the commandos start to operate more in brigades and less as independent raiders and this was the trend that would continue to be followed during 1944. While commando raids continued, they were much smaller in scale and aimed at keeping the Axis guessing about Britain's true intentions, especially in North West Europe.

In the fictional world, Major Carter and Sgt Green, Cpl Glass and LCpl O'Driscoll are travelling home to the UK with 15 Commando, but they are destined, like my father, to have many more adventures before the war comes to an end.

Further Reading.

For first hand accounts of Commando operations and training at Achnacarry, try the following:

Cubitt, Robert; A Commando's Story; Selfishgenie Publishing; 2018.
Durnford-Slater, John, Brigadier: Commando: Memoirs of a Fighting Commando in World War II; Greenhill Books; new edition 2002.
Gilchrist, Donald; Castle Commando; The Highland Council; 3rd revised edition, 1993.
Scott, Stan and Barber, Neil; Fighting With The Commandos; Pen and Sword Military; 2008.
Young, Peter, Brigadier; Storm from the Sea; Greenhill Books; new edition 2002.

For a more general overview of the commandos and their operations:

Saunders, Hilary St George; The Green Beret; YBS The Book Service Ltd; new edition 1972.

A wealth of information, photographs and personal accounts can be found on the Commando Veterans Archive website: **http://www.commandoveterans.org/**

PREVIEW

CARTER'S COMMANDOS BOOK 7

OPERATION PEGASUS

1 – Back in Training

A flurry of snow greeted Carter as he left the shelter of the station's main entrance. Not serious snow; not the sort of snow he had seen recently in the Scottish Highlands, but enough to let the good citizens of Worthing know that winter was here.

The front of the town's station was busy with troops as they exited the station. NCO's shouted at soldiers, soldiers shouted to friends and lorries tooted to try and clear a path through the milling crowds of men that had just arrived off of trains. Soldiers clambered onto the backs of trucks while others were chivvied into ranks in readiness to march to closer destinations.

To one side Carter could see a Sergeant with a 15 Cdo flash on his shoulder, organising men into three ranks. They looked different from the other troops; were they more upright, more confident, more ready? Whatever it was, they were noticeable. Or was that just his imagination?

Carter wasn't going to interrupt the NCO's activities. He didn't need an officer interfering. Instead he hefted his kitbag onto his shoulder and followed two other officers along the station's frontage to where a single taxi stood.

He had seen them on the train, so young they looked like they had borrowed their big brother's uniforms. But officer candidates for the commandos were harder to come by these days, as were volunteers from the other ranks. It wasn't as if there was a shortage on men adventurous enough to apply, it was commanding officers discouraging them. It was easier to go into the recruit depots, the Young Soldiers battalions and officer training units and recruit them there, before the doors were slammed shut.

But it carried a penalty in a lack of experience. It was always better for a commando to have heard the sound of weapons fired in anger before he joined, so everyone would know he wouldn't funk[1] it the next time he heard the sound.

Carter's rail journey from Scotland was the one that most commandos would take when they left the training depot at Achnacarry to join their new units, at least until they got to the southern part of the country and had to diverge towards the various towns where the commandos were located. He had spotted these two at Glasgow Central Station and managed to avoid getting into the same carriage. If he wanted a peaceful journey and a couple of hours of sleep, it was best not to travel with hero worshipping subalterns who wanted to know how it felt to be in combat, or to hear the stories of how he had won his medals.

So Carter had slunk off to another carriage. He hadn't had a peaceful journey, however. The neighbouring compartment had been occupied by American officers who had just discovered the joys of Scotch whisky and had brought plenty of the product along with them for the journey.

But now, with only one taxi available, he would need to introduce himself.

"Joining 15Cdo?" he called at their backs. He knew they were, they couldn't be joining any other commando, not in Worthing. But it was a conversation starter.

They stopped and turned, spotted the crowns on his epaulettes and snapped to attention. Their hands were occupied by their luggage, as were Carter's, so they were unable to salute.

"Yes Sir!" One said crisply.

"Perhaps we should share this cab." He made it sound like a suggestion rather than an order.

"Of course, Sir." The other replied. "Our Pleasure." It probably was. As a Major, Carter was more likely to pay the fare.

Carter dropped his luggage and offered his hand. The two officers also dropped their luggage, but threw up salutes before accepting the courtesy.

"Carter, 2IC."

"Holdsworth." The first replied."

"Marchant, Sir." The second added.

"Ah, yes. I was up at Achnacarry a couple of weeks ago and Col Vaughan[2] mentioned your names."

"Did he Sir?" Holdsworth blushed pink at the honour of being singled out. In fact, it had been Carter's mission, given to him by his CO Charlie Cousens, to interrupt his leave and travel to Achnacarry to identify likely candidates for the commando. He could have left the job to the Combined Operations staff officer responsible for personnel, but Cousens didn't like to leave things to chance. If he could give the man a list of names of men he wanted, there was a much better chance that he'd get the pick of the men that were available. Although it wasn't an approved practice, it had worked in the past and Carter could see that it had worked again on this occasion.

"Oh yes. Colonel Vaughan was most complementary about you. That's a big reputation to have to live up to though, so don't let the Colonel down by proving him wrong." Carter chuckled.

"We won't Sir."

"Good. Now, let's grab this taxi before another train arrives and some bloody Yank nicks it." Americans were always more popular passengers for taxi drivers because they could be persuaded to pay in dollars, which were more easily exchangeable for black market goods which had originated on American bases. The dollars would find their way back there and into the pockets of GI[3]s who would send them around the circuit again by buying things in their PX[4] to sell to the black marketeers.

The journey to the barracks took only a few minutes. It was late in the evening and there were few people around. At the main gate a commando sentry threw up a brisk salute after checking their identity documents, then directed them to the Officers' Mess. A civilian employee was roused from his doze behind the reception desk and handed them the keys to their rooms. Carter persuaded him to seek out some tea and sandwiches from the kitchens. A hubbub of noise came from the bar, but Carter wasn't yet ready to face his colleagues. After a journey that had lasted over twelve hours, but had felt like it was three times as long, he needed some sleep before he was ready to socialise. He would face his friends and colleagues best over breakfast, before he located his new office and set about getting the commando organised.

His leave hadn't been a great success. The tension between himself and his wife that had been present before his departure for Gibraltar, fifteen months earlier, was back. The freshly healed scar on his upper arm, a souvenir from the fighting at Termoli, hadn't helped to ease the tension.

While Carter had dismissed the scar as a mere scratch, Fiona had used the span of her hands to measure the distance to his heart. She had said nothing, but the fearful expression she had tried to hide spoke volumes.

"But it, missed. That's the important thing." He had tried to make light of it.

"It missed this time." She replied, turning over in bed so that her back was towards him. Later, in the darkness, he felt her body vibrating as she sobbed.

He had enjoyed seeing his twins, a boy and a girl, bouncing them on his knees until they got sick and then taking delight at changing their clothes. He even volunteered to change their nappies, a task that seemed to increase in frequency every day.

Seeing Carter so clearly enjoying being a father had been one of the few things that had brought a smile to Fiona's face. Cousens' request that he travel to Achnacarry and make forays into the

Scottish garrisons to try to find new recruits, had caused an argument between them.

"You're supposed to be on leave!" Fiona had snapped. "Why can't they leave you alone for just a few weeks?"

"It goes with the territory, Darling. I'm not a junior officer anymore. I have responsibilities." Carter had tried to placate her. "We lost a lot of men in the Med and they have to be replaced. The CO just wants to make sure we get the best men available." On the morning he had left to take the train north, she had turned her back in a silence frostier than the ground beneath his feet.

At the garrisons and barracks his reception had been even colder than at home. Commanding officers were fed up losing their best men to the commandos. The only place he was made welcome was at the recruit training depots. They were sausage machines, taking in civilians and churning out soldiers with the basic skills necessary to keep themselves alive while fighting the enemy. Where their charges went after they left the depots was of little interest to the commandants, so it might as well be to the commandos as anyone.

At Achnacarry it had been different. Vaughan had welcomed him home like a long-lost son and had wined and dined him, while pumping him for news about his experiences and the welfare of other former students. He was also keen to find out what alterations to the training might be made to help improve the commandos' performance.

"To tell you the truth," Carter had replied, "most of what you teach is good. What is sometimes the problem is whether a soldier really has what it takes to be a commando in the first place. Up here you can weed out the weaklings and those without the drive and determination that is needed. But until they've heard bullets fired, we can't know if they're going to fight or flee. Nowadays so few of the volunteers have experienced real combat."

"Is it much of a problem?" Vaughan had asked.

"Not a major one. At least, not so far. But we had an officer recently who let us down a bit. It was when we were cut off behind enemy lines …."

263

"The River Gabriel operation." Vaughan had interrupted.

"You've heard the story?"

"Some of it. I'd like to hear more if you have the time to tell it. You had to disperse and make your own way back to the Allied lines, if what we've heard is correct."

"It is. Well, the CO … he was still the 2IC then … rounded up a few of the men and was set on ambushing German traffic on the road from the bridge. One of the junior officers, I won't name him as he's not here to defend himself, wasn't keen on the idea at all. He just wanted to get back to the Allied lines as quickly as possible.[5] The CO wasn't best pleased with the example he was setting. He didn't think he was being aggressive enough."

"I can imagine that. Charlie Cousens always was a bit of a fire brand if I recall correctly. So, what do you think we should be doing here at Achnacarry?"

"I'm not sure what can be done. I don't think there is a way to test a man's bravery in battle. Up here you make things as real as they can be, but at the back of the mind we always knew that you weren't really trying to kill us. Unlike the enemy, who are always trying to kill us. It is that final step that is the one some men can't make."

"Perhaps there is a way of helping. I was at a meeting at the War Office recently and over lunch there was some discussion about selection procedures for officers. It seems that some of the boffins, psychiatrists or whatever, think that they can devise tests that will assess genuine leadership potential. As you know, at present if a man comes from the right family or went to the right school, he can pretty much walk in as an officer. But, as we know, some of them aren't that great and some of the men who get promoted from the ranks do just as well, if not better."

Carter knew that Vaughan had risen from the ranks, whereas he himself had just come from the right family and done well at school. But the point was valid. There was good and bad in both systems of selection.

"Well, anything that can be done to weed out any weak links before they get to the commando would be welcomed."

"I'll look into that a bit more. There may be something we can do.[6] What happened to the officer that earned Charlie Cousens' disapproval."

"Charlie, sorry, the CO, made sure he was posted out. I think he's counting paperclips at a supply depot in Cairo now. He's still nominally a commando, but those in the know will make sure he never gets into the front line in a commando unit again." Carter knew it was probably worse than that for the man. Once he'd been given the mark of Cain from a commando unit, it was unlikely he'd ever be promoted again.

As before, Fiona had thawed a little by the time Carter's leave came to an end, but she would never be happy while he was a commando and he would never be happy being anything else. At least, not while the war was still going on. He hoped, for the sake of his marriage, that it would be over soon.

[1] In 1944 the word 'funk', as in 'to be in a funk' meant to be frightened. To be extremely frightened would be 'to be in a blue funk'. It started out in the 14th century as a German word, *fonke*, meaning spark, migrated somehow to mean ill-humour or depression and from that it appeared in Scotland and Northern Ireland in the 1740a as a term meaning fear. How the term became associated with music isn't known, but that started in the USA, as a racial slur referring to body odour. This probably evolved from a French word meaning smoke, as applied to smoked cheese. Some American refer to food with a suspicious taste as being funky. Its musical links started to appear during the Jazz age, meaning a song that was earthy or deeply felt.

[2] When Achnacarry was established as the primary training establishment for the commandos, in March 1942, Lt Colonel Charles Vaughan was appointed as its commandant, having served in both 4 and 7 Cdos. He had risen from the enlisted ranks of the Buffs (East Kent) Regiment to reach this senior position and was

something of a legend amongst the commandos. He appears in cameo form in Book 1 of this series, Operation Absolom.

[3] GI – General Issue. The description given to items of military uniform and equipment that were standard issue to all new recruits and conscripts into the US army. The term became attached to the soldiers themselves, replacing "Dough Boys", a term that went all the way back to the Continental Army of the American Revolution. That had become a nickname because pipeclay had been used to keep the white piping on soldier's uniforms pristine and when it got wet it turned into a doughy blob. The replacement of pipe clay with specialist products (Blanco (meaning white) in the British army) made the term obsolete, to be replaced by GI.

[4] PX – Post exchange, a shop providing American soldiers with everything from chocolate bars to hi-fi equipment. They were established on most American bases and still exist today. They accept only dollars in payment and the goods are cheap because they are sold at American prices and, outside of the USA, are free of both American and local taxes. The ability of American GIs to offer British girls presents of nylon stockings, perfume and cigarettes was one of the reasons their presence was resented by British men, spawning the slur "overpaid, oversexed and over here." It was forbidden to sell products bought in the PX to the British, but the prohibition was hard to enforce, which led to a healthy black market.

[5] This a conflation of a couple of true stories. Peter Young was the 2IC at the time and his accounts can be read in his book (see "Further Reading").

[6] Selection and training procedures for both officer candidates and for special forces now contain a high level of psychological testing for suitability. It is no longer possible to become an officer just because you went to the "right" school or just because a relative had once been an officer (though it probably still helps). The author of

this book came from a humble (though military) background and worked his way through the ranks to pass the selection process and become an officer.

* * *

As Carter came out of the dining room after breakfast, he bumped into the CO in full marching order.

"I didn't know there was an exercise planned for this morning." Carter said. He had planned on getting to grips with compiling a training programme for the commando.

"No one knows yet. My little surprise for the men." It was the first day that everyone from the commando was back from leave and they were usually quite relaxed affairs, as everyone sought to settle into new accommodation and establish some sort of order in the barracks.

"I'd better go and get ready then." Carter turned to leave.

"No, that's OK, Steven. I want you to concentrate on compiling the training programme. We have no idea what's in store for us yet, so concentrate on the three Fs."

If you didn't know what your mission was to be, the three Fs provided a basis for any training plan: fitness, fieldcraft and fighting skills. They were the three things the commandos always needed.

"What we do know," The CO continued, "is that whatever we are asked to do, we'll have to travel by water to do it, so set up contacts with Combined Ops for the use of landing craft. When we go ashore, I want the men to be able to do it in their sleep. We can refine the training once we know more. I'm going to a briefing later in the week which might tell us something."

Carter doubted it. It was still only January. The invasion wouldn't take place in winter or even early Spring. Carter thought May at the earliest, with June more likely. Late enough for the weather to have improved but early enough to get a solid campaign in before the next winter set in.

That being the case, only the high-level objectives would have been settled so far. Probably the location of the landing beaches and the major objectives to be captured on the first day. The allocation of units to tasks wouldn't happen until they had all been put under the microscope to see which divisions were best prepared and ready to do whatever was needed. Competition to be part of the first wave ashore would be high. Not from the men, obviously, but from the senior officers, who would see participation as an opportunity to stake their claim for promotion.

Making sure 15 Cdo was ready for anything was Carter's job and he was determined they wouldn't be found wanting.

To hell with promotion, thought Carter, the better prepared the men are, the more likely it is that they'll survive.

* * *

The Military Police corporal handed Carter his identity documents back and pointed him in the direction he needed to go. "Through the double doors, Sir. The Brigadier is at the far end, beneath the big map."

Vernon was now formally a brigadier and in command of 5th Special Service Brigade. The commandos didn't like the name, the initials having unpleasant connotations considering their use by the Germans. Representation had been made to Combined Operations to have it changed to 'Commando Brigade', but so far without any success.

The brigadier rose to his feet and stretched out a hand to be shaken. Carter stamped to a halt, saluted and took the proffered hand. "Take a seat, make yourself comfortable." The brigadier told him. "I've ordered coffee. We get it from the Americans, so it's good quality."

Carter wondered why Vernon was rolling out the red carpet. Normally on a visit to Brigade HQ, Carter was given over sweetened tea and, if he was lucky, a couple of biscuits. He recalled Paddy

O'Driscoll's observation that when the Army start being nice to you, it's time to start worrying.

"How are things going down in Worthing?" The Brigadier asked.

Small talk, Carter noted. The Brigadier knew exactly how things were going. He had visited the commando only the previous week and observed them making a beach landing followed by an assault on Arundel Castle, several miles inland. He had been quite complimentary about the exercise.

"Pretty well, Sir. We're rather hoping to undertake some opposed landings, if we can find a unit willing to act as enemy for us."

Vernon let out a laugh. "Good luck with that. They don't like your men beating them up when they come ashore."

"We'll promise to play nice." Carter grinned, still wondering what the summons to HQ was about. He knew that Charlie Cousens had already been there that day, but there was no sign of him in the Operations Room.

Around and behind him there was the muted buzz of men going about their duties. A million things needed to be done before the invasion could take place and the men in this room were just a handful of the ones that were responsible for making sure that they were completed on time. He knew many of the faces; experienced commandos who knew just what was needed to mount a successful operation. They would be cutting no corners and fighting for every scrap of equipment that the units needed to achieve their objectives, whatever they were.

On which note ... "Any news on what our role is to be yet, Sir?"

"All in good time, Steven. It's still months away. The daffs have hardly started blooming yet. Ah, you're wondering why I've called you in."

"If it's not for ...." Even in this room he felt unsure if he should use the word 'invasion' No one seemed to use it, just in case it was overheard. "... whatever is to come, then it must be for something else. Have you got an op for us? A raid perhaps?"

"No. We're not risking units such as yours for pin pinpricks in the enemy's skin. We've got other units for that, who won't be going ashore on the big day. No, I've got some other news for you. Good and bad, I'm afraid. Which do you want first?"

This wasn't the first time that Vernon had said those words to him. The last time was to hand him his Major's crowns. Was that what this was all about. Was he going to get posted and the bad news was that someone else would be getting his place in 15 Cdo?

"Bad news first, if you don't mind, Sir. Get it out of the way." He pasted an expectant smile on his face, but behind his lips his teeth were gritted.

"Charlie Cousens is being posted to my staff. In fact, he's already upstairs being briefed on his duties."

In the great scheme of things that wasn't really bad news, in Carter's opinion. He liked Charlie Cousens and so did the men. He was a good CO and to lose him would be a shame. But the worse news was probably who would replace him. A new boy coming in from outside the commando wouldn't know their style, the way they operated, the way they did things. It could be disruptive and they didn't need that right now. But Carter was expected to say something; he could see that from the expectant look on Vernon's face.

"We're going to miss him, Sir." Carter admitted, truthfully. "He's been a good CO. We thought it was hard enough when you went, but he'll be just as hard to replace. Do we know who will take over the commando?"

"We do, Steven. I had it confirmed this morning." A small smile played around Vernon's lips. Carter realised that he was playing some sort of game. Teasing him. "Come on, Steven. Haven't you guessed yet? I haven't called you up here just to tell you something that Charlie Cousens could tell you when he got back to Worthing tonight."

Carter was still at a loss. He was missing something, he knew. No, maybe not missing something. His brain was trying to avoid something. That was different.

"It's you, Steven. You're taking over command of Fifteen."

* * *

There was something not … Carter struggled to put his finger on the right word. 'Not quite right' made it sound like he was visibly at odds with the world. 'Unlikeable' suggested a snap judgment. Apart from saying 'Good morning, Sir.' The man hadn't even spoken yet.

But there was definitely something that was setting Carter's teeth on edge.

It wasn't the fact that the man was wearing his Number 2 Dress uniform, complete with Sam Brown belt and shiny leather holster for his revolver. He had come from an environment where such attire was normal. It wasn't the fact that his peaked cap still bore the red band of a staff officer, matched by the tabs on the collar of his jacket. His cap badge, for a regiment that had been founded during the British Civil War and had fought in every war since, was shining brass, as were the miniature versions on his jacket lapels, but that wasn't it either. The commandos blackened all their brass work so that it didn't shine in the dark, but again for a staff officer, shiny brass was nothing unusual. Then it hit Carter.

The left breast of his uniform jacket was devoid of medal ribbons. The man was a Major in the commandos, but Carter couldn't think of a single officer of Captain rank or higher that didn't sport a medal ribbon of some sort. The commandos attracted Military Crosses and Distinguish Service Orders the way a magnet attracted iron filings. And there were no campaign medals either. OK, he had only just received his Africa and Italy Stars, but this officer didn't even have those.

In physical appearance, the man was unremarkable: medium height, medium build, a face that was neither handsome nor ugly, but sporting the sort of thin, matinee idol moustache that Carter had always disliked. Perhaps that was what was setting his teeth on edge.

"Take a seat, Howard." Carter said, pointing to a chair in the corner of the office that his new officer could fetch for himself.

Things had moved quickly since Carter's meeting with the Brigadier the previous day. Cousens had returned from HQ in time to be the guest of honour at his own farewell party. His and that of Andrew Fraser. The Scotsman was going to HQ as well, as one of Vernon's new staff officers. Molly Brown was taking over as 15 Cdo's QM, with a promotion to go with it. Carter had just seen Cousens out of the gate, with most of the commando cheering him along, when the new man had arrived.

Opening up the posting notice, Carter read the name again. Major Howard Ramsey; posted to 15 Cdo as Second in Command with effect from that day's date.

"So, tell me about yourself. When did you join up?"

The man's face broke into a smile of pride. "The day after war was declared. My father contacted his old CO, who now commands the old man's regiment and asked if he could give me a place. He agreed, so that was that."

It would be wrong to condemn Ramsey for using that bit of influence. It would make Carter a hypocrite. His own father had done the same for him when he had volunteered for service. Not that it had done him any favours. He and his CO had never got on and the need to escape was one of the things that had prompted Carter to volunteer for the commandos.

"By the time I'd finished OCTU[1,] the 1st Battalion was already in France with the expeditionary force, so I was posted to the 3rd Battalion, who were TA. When it looked like Italy was going to enter the war we were sent to Egypt. I'm afraid I was getting a bit bored out there, so when a signal came around asking for volunteers for special duties, unspecified, I threw my hat into the ring. Next thing I know I'm back in Blighty as a junior officer in 1 Cdo."

Carter did some quick mental arithmetic. Italy had entered the war on the Axis side[2] at around the same time as the Dunkirk evacuation and fighting started in Libya and Egypt only days later. But the commandos hadn't started to form until later in the month. Which meant … What precisely? Had Ramsey volunteered in order to avoid the fighting in Libya or Abyssinia[3], which was a worrying thought, or had he heard that there was more adventure to be had by volunteering? 1 Cdo had formed on 13th June by merging two existing units, so the recruiting signals must have gone out after that. Something to think about, at least.

"As you know," Ramsey continued, unaware of the thoughts racing through Carter's brain. "No 1 was disbanded[4] a few weeks later so I found myself on the train to Manchester to join No 2 instead, to be told I was going to train to be a parachutist. That was fine, but before I got to do my first jump, I was sent up to Inveraray. They'd just started to undertake formalised commando training there. That was before Achnacarry opened, of course. So I stayed there for a while, then I was posted to Northern Ireland as a Troop Commander with 19 Cdo. I stayed with them for a bit, then went o Combined Ops as a junior staff officer, then to the War Office as a specialist advisor on commando operations. That's where I was when I was told I was being promoted and posted here."

Forcing his jaw to stay shut when all it wanted to do was drop open, Carter realised that although Ramsey had been a commando for almost four years, he had probably never actually seen combat.

"Just out of curiosity, what did you do before the war?" Carter kept his tone light, trying not to betray his suspicions.

"I was an accountant, studying for my Charter examinations."

The penny dropped. Probably a good administrator, so when those skills were needed he was the right man for the job. Being a good administrator would help him as Carter's 2IC, that was for sure. But when they went ashore in France, assuming it wasn't Belgium instead as some rumours suggested, Carter would need fighting men and leaders, not pen pushers.

"What raids did you go on?" Carter suspected he knew the answer but had to give the man the benefit of the doubt.

"None actually, Sir." His face fell into a frown, realising this exposed his lack of combat experience. "When I was in Northern Ireland we were supposed to go on a raid into Norway. We got as far as the Shetland Isles when our landing ship developed engine trouble, so the Op was cancelled. Then when I was in London, at the War Office, I was supposed to go on a raid to France with 18 Cdo. I came down to the coast and did all the training and everything. On the day before the Op I popped back to London for the afternoon and on the way back my train got held up by an unexploded Jerry bomb next to the railway line. By the time I got back to the docks the landing ship had set off. It was the damnedest bad luck."

But he shouldn't have been in London the afternoon before an Op anyway. Carter knew that and Ramsey should have as well. "What did you go to London for?" Again, the tone was light.

A smile, almost a leer, spread across Ramsey's face. "I went to see a girl. A right corker. The ladies love a commando and, for a change, I was wearing a green beret. She practically fell into my arms."

So, Ramsey had put his sex life before his duty, had he? Carter started to appreciate that his instincts had been warning him about this man since the moment he had stepped into his office. But don't judge too soon, he warned himself. He'd done some pretty stupid things himself in his time. But then again, he was now a Lieutenant Colonel at the age of twenty five, whereas Ramsey was at least five years his senior, had been in both the army and the commandos for longer and had only just managed to clamber up to the rank of Major and even that seemed to be based on time served, not on merit.

Never judge a book by its cover, he reminded himself. There might be more to Ramsey than what met the eye. Carter could only hope.

"OK, well, thank you for that. Most informative. First of all, I'd better tell you a bit about how we work in Fifteen. Every commando unit has its own personality and we pride ourselves on being reasonably relaxed. The only time we have parades is to hand out medals or to honour visiting dignitaries, for a start.

We treat the men with respect. We rely on each other and the man you berate today for not calling you 'Sir' may be the man who saves your life tomorrow, so think on that when you are dealing with disciplinary issues. We're part of the Army and we never forget it, but we trust our men and a sign of that trust is to let them think for themselves. If the men don't live up to expectations we get rid of them back to whence they came and that is sufficient deterrent for most of them. I'll do as much with an officer that doesn't step up to the mark as well." Carter let the threat hang in the air for a moment before continuing.

"In terms of dress, you are a bit out of step with us ..." He put up his hand to forestall the protest that Ramsey was about to make "... That isn't a criticism, but what is good for Horse Guards isn't necessarily good for here. We wear battledress all the time, even when we visit Brigade. If anyone wants to you to dress more formally, they'll let you know. We never wear peaked caps, even with our No 2 Dress. Only the green beret. That is a hard and fast rule. If the King himself were to pay us a call, we'd parade wearing our berets. It's a badge of honour, not just something to attract the ladies." Ramsey at least had the decency to blush. "We also blacken all our brass work; badges, buckles, webbing, rifle slings, the lot. We don't want Jerry seeing anything glinting in the sunlight when we're trying to sneak up on him.

Your main responsibilities will be the training programme and everything related to it: finding the training areas, organising transport, landing craft etc. It's a pretty basic plan at the moment, because we don't know what our objectives will be. As we find out more, I will expect you to refine the programme to tailor it to the mission. Think you can manage that?"

"I'm sure that won't challenge me too much, Sir."

Carter didn't like the way he was so dismissive of his role. Carter knew just how complicated the delivery of the training plan could get at times. But he let it pass.

"As well as delivering the training plan, you will also have to participate in it. You will have a role to play when we go ashore and you will have to be ready to fulfil it. If it comes to a choice between doing the training or doing the admin, there is no choice. You do the training. Understood?"

"Understood, Sir."

"Now, I'm a little concerned that you haven't seen any action yet, so I'm going to make arrangements for that to change. I'll contact Combined Ops and arrange for you to go along on a couple of raids as an observer." Carter knew there was no such thing during a raid. You were either a fighting commando or you were left behind in barracks. But it provided an excuse for Ramsey to be on the raid, without disclosing that he needed the experience.

"Speaking of which, there will be no trips to London unless you are on leave or you've been summoned there. I'm not passing judgement on the way you run your social life, but the way travel is disrupted by the Jerry bombers I can't risk you being stuck on a train when you're needed here or you're supposed to be participating on a raid. Do I make myself clear?"

"That seems rather harsh, Sir. I mean, a trip to the big city cheers a chap up …"

"When I start sloping off having fun, you can do the same." Carter made sure his voice carried the appropriate degree of threat. "If you don't like my rules, you are free to ask for a transfer to another unit."

"N … No, of course, Sir. Understood."

Carter smiled inwardly. To apply for a transfer would not give out the right messages. Carter was pretty sure Ramsey's new rank was only temporary, to be confirmed after a period of probation and a satisfactory report from his CO; from himself. Ramsey wouldn't want to lose that nice shiny new crown on his shoulder. He probably thought it impressed the ladies.

"Finally, we pride ourselves on being the fittest soldiers in the British army. That means all the way from me down to the newest recruit. No officer in this unit is ever the last man to finish an exercise. The only acceptable excuse for doing so is death and I do mean the officer's death, not someone else's. What is your fitness like after sitting around Whitehall for the last few months?"

"Not bad, Sir. I do regular exercise. I play a lot of squash and tennis as well. Got to maintain standards and all that."

Carter doubted the statement. There was more than a hint of a paunch on the man and Carter was sure that he could see paler cloth along the side seams of the man's jacket, where it had been let out an inch. There were also signs of strain on the buttons. "Well, we'll find out tomorrow morning. 6 Troop are doing a ten-mile speed march and you can join them." He was sure he saw Ramsey go several shades paler at this news. Carter stifled a smile. "Oh six hundred start, from the main gate. I suggest you take the opportunity to meet the men today. If you collapse halfway, they're the ones that will have to get you back here.

[1] OCTU - Officer Cadet Training Unit. Officers recruits spent several weeks learning military and leadership skills before transferring to a specialist unit for further training in the specific role for the job they would do (artillery, engineering, signals etc). Course lengths varied as training needs were re-evaluated as the war progressed. In 1939 the duration was as little as 8 weeks for an infantry officer but by 1943 had gone up to 15 weeks as specialist infantry training was added to the basic course. Different from the Royal Military College Sandhurst, which trained officers for a career in the Army and whose courses were too long to meet the wartime demands for new officers. Its peacetime training role was suspended and Sandhurst first of all became an OCTU, then a specialist training establishment for officers of the Royal Armoured Corps.

[2] Italy declared war on Britain on 10th June 1940. The British evacuation of Dunkirk had been completed on 4th June.

[3] Abyssinia is now called by its older Ancient Greek name of Ethiopia, however, it is still sometimes referred to by its other name. Ethiopia is more used by the Coptic Christian communities, while Abyssinia is more Muslim in nature.

[4] It is unclear why 1 Cdo was disbanded, but it probably amounted to political wrangling over who should have operational command over them. They became No 1 Special Service Battalion and weren't under the control of Combined Operations (established in June 1940 under Admiral of the Fleet Sir Roger Keyes, succeeded

in March 1942 by Commodore Lord Louis Mountbatten). They were soon disbanded. 1 Cdo was re-established in March 1941.

* * *

There weren't Many rules for the speed marches. The troop had to stick to the prescribed route, they had to be in full fighting order, including carrying one hundred rounds of ammunition, they had to finish together, even if it meant carrying a man and the clock didn't stop until the last man crossed the finish line. The target pace was ten-minute miles, but a troop that didn't improve on that could expect some degree of censure from their Troop Commander. Course lengths varied from a relatively unchallenging five miles to the seventeen-mile torture of the final march at Achnacarry. Commando units rarely felt it necessary to repeat that distance, but fifteen-mile marches weren't unheard of.

All the commandos hated them, but the only way to avoid doing more of them was to beat the target time.

The march was conducted at a cross between a fast march and a run. Generally the running was downhill or on the flat, while the men lent forward, put their backs into it and made the best pace they could up the slopes of the Sussex Downs.

Carter leant over the shoulder of the Sergeant that was the designated timekeeper for this particular march. It wasn't that no-one trusted the commandos to report their correct time, it was just easier for someone from a different troop to take on the task. It also helped to engender competition if everyone knew the times achieved by the other troops. Already Carter had promised cases of beer for the troop with the fastest average time over a set series of marches.

In the distance he could make out the troop struggling up the final hill towards the barracks. Local children ran alongside, cheering the men on or shouting casual insults, whichever took their fancy. Each section took turns to lead for a set distance, then dropped to the rear to allow the next section to set the pace for the next leg.

The troop appeared to be in good order, no sign of them straggling along the road. That was always a good sign. In front, as he should be, was Stefan Podborsky, who had taken over from Molly Brown as the troop commander. Marchant, one of the new officers, had replaced him as the subaltern[1] in charge of one half of the troop. Carter couldn't make out Ramsey. He was probably towards the back. There was no problem with that, at least for this march. When the commando as a whole did a speed march, which they did from time to time, Carter would expect him to be up at the front, running right on his own heels.

About a hundred yards from the gates, Podborsky brought the men to a halt and harried them into three ranks. He must have seen Carter hovering and decided to put on a show. It would cost him time, but he had a minute or so to play with so Carter permitted him the small vanity. All the troop commanders liked to show off from time to time.

Even from that distance Carter could hear the orders being shouted. "By the left, quick march!" The men stepped out smartly. After six paces another order was shouted. "Into double time, double …. march!" The men broke into the trot of one hundred and eighty paces per minute that fit soldiers could maintain for quite some distance. Making the final hundred yards to the gate would be no problem for the commandos, tired as they undoubtedly were.

The troop doubled through the gate and Podborsky brought them to a smart parade ground halt, turned them into line abreast, marched to the centre of the front rank and a threw up a parade ground salute for Carter's benefit.

"Very good, Captain Podborsky." Carter made sure his voice could be heard above the panting of the men. "That was an impressive time. Something for 3 Troop to think about." They were current leaders in the speed marching contest. "You may dismiss your …" Carter stopped speaking as he caught sight of Ramsey, hovering near what had been the rear of the column of troops and was now the right hand end of the front rank.

"Major Ramsey. A word, if you please."

Ransey made a half turn to the right to break ranks and marched stiffly across to stand in front of Carter. His salute was a little sloppy, but Carter could forgive that considering what he had been through during the previous couple of hours. His chest was heaving still, though most of the troops had caught their breath. He was also coated in sweat, despite the chill of the early March day. But that wasn't what had attracted Carter's attention.

As Ramsey saluted, Carter lowered his voice so no one but the 2IC would hear. "Would you care to describe what the men of 6 Troop are wearing, Major." Ramsey should have noted the use of his rank. Its formality should have warned him that his CO wasn't pleased about something.

"They're in battledress, Sir. The normal ...."

"I'm aware of what is normal attire for a speed march, thank you Major. Which is why I am asking the question. What else are they wearing?"

"Fighting order, Sir." It was the name used for the assembly of webbing and kit that the men would carry if they were conducting a patrol or advancing to make contact with the enemy.

"And what are they carrying?"

By this point Ramsey must have been starting to get suspicious about the questions. He turned around to look at the troops still standing at attention in their ranks, as though he needed to check before he gave his answer.. Each man had a Short Magazine Lee Enfield (SMLE) rifle held in his right hand, the butt resting on the ground, snuggly against the toe of his right boot. Even the officers.

"Er ... Erm."

"Spit it out man!" Carter barked, loud enough for the soldiers at the far end of the troop to hear.

"They're carrying rifles, Sir."

"And ammunition?"

"I don't know about ...."

"Captain Podborsky." Carter addressed the troop commander directly. "Are your men carrying ammunition."

"Yes, Sir!" The Polish exile barked back. "The ammunition was issued when the troop paraded this morning, Sir."

"Thank you, Captain." Carter retuned his baleful stare to Ramsey, lowering his voice again.

"Would you mind explaining to me, Major, why you are not carrying your webbing, neither are you carrying a rifle. You aren't even wearing a side arm."

"I didn't think …"

"What didn't you think?" Carter growled at his subordinate.

Ramsey gaze darted back and forth as though he was looking for an escape route. Perhaps he was. "I didn't think that a senior officer would have to carry so much, Sir."

"So, when we invade France and you go ashore, tell me: who is going to be carrying your kit?"

"I don't know, Sir. My batman I guess."

"The only person in this commando who has a batman is me, Major." In fact, Carter hadn't yet selected a man to undertake that duty, nor was he in any hurry to do so. "And I can assure you that on the day we land in France, he will not be carrying my kit. What about your weapon? Don't you intend killing any Jerries?"

"Surely, I'll be with our HQ troop, Sir. I probably won't need to get involved in the fighting. I'll have my pistol …"

"Ramsey. Stop talking." Carter growled.

Carter surveyed the front rank of soldiers, looking for a familiar face. "Tpr Pengelly." Most of the men were struggling to keep a straight face by now; none more so than Pengelly.

Pengelly took two smart steps forward. "Sir!"

"Tpr Pengelly, when the commando went ashore in Italy, at Termoli, where was the HQ troop?"

"There weren't one Sir. They'd been split up into the rifle troops."

"And where was I when we went ashore?" Carter asked.

"You were with our troop, Sir."

"Thank you. And when we went ashore to capture the bridge over the river Gabriel. Where was the HQ troop then?"

"Same, Sir. In the rifle troops."

"And where was the 2IC then, Maj Cousens?"

"He was leading the second wave ashore Sir. He was right in front of me when we left the landing craft."

"Thank you, Pengelly. Return to your place.

"Are you starting to get the message now, Major?" Carter was standing so close to the man that their noses were practically touching. Carter could smell his sweat and, by now, not all of it was being caused by his physical exertions.

"I think so, Sir."

"Good. Now, tomorrow morning at 0600 hrs, 1 Troop are scheduled to do this same speed march. I have just decided that I will join them. I have also decided that you will also join them."

Two speed marches in two days was a significant challenge for any commando. It would be more so for the less fit Ramsey.

"Yes, Sir." He said the words though gritted teeth.

"And may I assure you, Maj Ramsey, that if you don't finish ahead of me, you will be on the next train out of here. And you won't go back to a cushy billet[2] in the War Office. You will go to Burma, where I understand it is hot and they have diseases that soldiers can't even imagine. I believe that is where your old battalion is currently serving, is it not?"

"Yes, it is Sir."

"I thought so. The last news I read from there suggested things aren't going too well for the 14th Army. Maybe your old battalion needs the assistance of a fully trained commando Major."

Before the man had time to answer, Carter turned away. Grins of delight vanished off the faces of the sixty men of 6 Troop, to be replaced by the commandos' normal look of steely eyed determination.

"Thank you, Captain Podborsky. Your men did well. It is a shame that they were set such a bad example. You may dismiss."

[1] Subaltern – an officer of Second Lieutenant or Lieutenant rank. In use in the British army from as far back as 1680. From the Latin

sub, meaning under and alternus, meaning everyone. A subaltern is literally under, or inferior, to everyone else.

[2] Cushy billet – a soft posting or easy assignment. From the Hindi word *Khush*, meaning healthy or happy and the French *bilet*. Cushy could also descend from late 19th century Scottish and Northumbrian slang for a soft or useless person. A billet was a short length of flat wood which the quartermaster would hang on the doorway of a house which he had commandeered for the accommodation of soldiers. The billet was annotated in chalk with the number of soldiers that were to live there. The practice dates all the way back to medieval times. If the house's occupants were lucky, they would get paid for the privilege but usually only if the army was in friendly territory. In modern usage a billet is any accommodation assigned to a soldier.

* * *

Back in his office Carter was surprised to find Prof Green laying a buff folder in the middle of his desk. As he wasn't wearing his beret the sergeant had obviously not been sent on some errand.

"What are you doing here, Sgt Green." Out of the line, Carter always made sure to behave more formerly with his subordinates, even one like Green who had shared so many adventures with him.

"The RSM thought that HQ Troop needed an NCO to keep things organised, now that it's expanded so much." Carter couldn't argue that the headquarters was bigger these days. When he had joined the commando in 1941 it had been the CO, his clerk, the 2IC, the QM, the Padre, the Medical Officer, the QM's assistant, a couple of RP[1]s and the RSM[2].

Now the HQ Troop had over thirty men in it, from clerks to signallers, to mechanics. But, as the point had been so forcefully made to Ramsey, when they went ashore, they did so as fighting commandos.

"I wonder where the RSM got such an idea." Carter said dryly. "I hope you aren't angling for a promotion to Staff Sergeant." Such a post would normally be held by the more senior rank.

"Never crossed my mind, Sir." Green grinned.

"And I suppose O'Driscoll is my new company clerk."

"Heaven forbid, Sir. O'Driscoll is a man of many talents but being company clerk is probably not one of them. No, he's your new driver."

Carter shook his head in wonder at the amount of manipulation that must have gone in to secure such a job. Driving the CO was prestigious post. "And Glass?" Carter knew that Glass wouldn't be far away, though as a corporal it would be harder to find him a job in the headquarters.

"He's looking after the Registry."

"Since when have we had a Registry?" Carter's mouth opened wide with shock.

"Since this morning. Sir."

"Do we have enough files that need looking after to warrant such a post?"

"As the NCO in charge of the commando's HQ, I am anticipating future demands upon the unit, Sir." Green was struggling to keep a straight face. "We're doing far more paperwork these days and someone has to make sure it doesn't all get lost. And some of it is classified as well, so we have to be doubly careful it doesn't go astray."

That was true enough, Carter had to concede. When they started to get information in on their objectives it would have to be kept under lock and key.

"Well, you can tell the corporal in charge of the Registry that I'm in need of a cup of tea."

"Right here, Sir." Glass appeared in the doorway suspiciously quickly, a steaming china mug in one hand a and a plate of biscuits in the other. He marched across the room, placed both objects on the desk in front of Carter, one on each side of the buff folder, then stepped back, standing to attention.

"Since when have we had biscuits?" Carter asked. He had never seen such luxury on the desks of any of his predecessors. The best he had ever seen was a couple of hard tack biscuits taken from a field ration pack.

"Since the same time as we got a Registry, Sir". Glass said with a grin.

Perhaps the manoeuvring of the three of his oldest comrades wasn't so terrible, after all, Carter conceded.

"Make sure Major Ramsey doesn't find out about them." Carter said through a mouthful of custard cream.

[1] RP – Regimental police. Nothing to do with the Royal Military Police. They are drawn from the within the unit and maintain discipline on behalf of the RSM. They could be thought of as a type of Special Constable. Often chosen for their size rather than their intellect.

[2] RSM – Regimental Sergeant Major. The senior most NCO in a unit, responsible for organising duty rosters, maintaining discipline and the organisation of ceremonial occasions. It is considered to be the pinnacle of a soldier's career to be appointed to the post. Even being selected to become an officer can't compare to becoming the RSM.

* * *

A cold wind whipped in from the English Channel, but Carter didn't feel it. His mind was distracted as he gazed through the dawn light towards the mouth of the estuary.

This nervousness wasn't a feeling Carter was used to. It was usually someone else standing on a cold quayside waiting for news. But the Brigadier had been quite explicit in his instructions. "Under no circumstances are you to go on this raid, Steven." He had said, stabbing his finger into the map that showed where it would take place. "If I know you, you wouldn't stop until you got to Paris.

Besides, it would be unfair on the officer leading it to have to babysit a Lieutenant Colonel."

"But Ramsey's going." Carter objected.

"Yes and I'm far from happy about that. But I take your point about his operational experience, so I'm allowing it. But only because of that. You don't have that excuse."

So Carter paced up and down the quay at Seaford, waiting for the raid to return. Ramsey had appeared to be nervous, but that was hardly surprising. Carter had been nervous on his first raid, just over three years earlier. That had been a full-scale operation, the whole commando with additional troops attached from other units, the RAF above, a Royal Navy cruiser offshore and four destroyers offering close support.

This was very different. Just ten men under the command of a Lieutenant, travelling on board a Motor Torpedo Boat. It was supposed to plant in the enemy's mind the idea that the invasion, when it came, would be across the Pas de Calais. By sending what appeared to be a reconnaissance team ashore to grab a couple of prisoners, the Germans might be persuaded. On the other hand, they had been fooled before and might not be so easily duped this time. It was just one a series of raids that had been planned with the same purpose in mind. Ramsey was scheduled to go on another one the following month.

He could see Brigadier Vernon's point. Already he knew enough about the invasion to be of use to the Germans if he were to be captured. None of the commandos who were due to go ashore on the day of the landings was allowed out onto the sea for any reason other than practice landings on friendly beaches and there was always a warship loitering off the coast, ready to fend off any E-Boats rash enough to approach the shore. They just couldn't take the risk of soldiers, even commandos, revealing information by accident if they were captured.

The Germans didn't have to beat information out of prisoners. Sometimes all they had to do was chat to them and offer them a cup of something hot to drink. He had seen it done with captured

Germans who had started out by insisting that all they would provide was their service number, rank and name, in accordance with the Geneva Convention.

The technique was simple enough. Examine the prisoner's possessions to see what information could be gleaned from them and use it to gain the prisoner's trust, or at least dilute their distrust. There were usually letters or photos, which always provided a starting point for a conversation. Offer the prisoner a cigarette, make a few jokes, let the prisoner talk about home and hearth. Then ask about how things were on the other side of the Channel. What was the food like, did they get to meet any pretty French girls, how were they treated by their officers? Very often the prisoner answered questions that he hadn't even been asked, just because he was being treated well.

It helped to have two prisoners, who could be kept in different rooms and interrogated separately. That way the interrogator could pretend to know more than he did, using titbits gleaned from one prisoner to feed into the conversation with the other. If the prisoner thought that the other man was giving away things, he had no reason to keep his own mouth shut and the information began to flow more freely

Over a period of a few hours a picture could be built up, a bit like doing a jigsaw puzzle. Over days the missing bits could be discovered and inserted. A casual word about an ammunition depot might well result in a high flying Spitfire being sent across the channel to take photographs, to confirm what was said and that would provide further leverage for use against the prisoner.

It was remarkable how subtle the technique was and it never once required the interrogator to threaten violence or raise his voice. All it required was patience, a supply of decent coffee (the Germans loved coffee, which was almost totally unavailable to them) and some cigarettes.

But patience wasn't something that Carter had a lot of, particularly when he was waiting for news of a raid. Had they made it ashore? Had they succeeded in their mission? Were they on their way back? There was no way of knowing. All he could do was pace

He had heard a pair of fighters cross the coast just before first light. That was the aerial escort sent to rendezvous with them and protect them against vengeful enemy fighters. Not that there were many of those these days. The RAF and the American Air Corps dominated the skies over both France and the English Channel. The only aircraft the Germans sent up now were night fighters and bombers and even the bombers only flew at night.

But raids had been attacked on their homeward journey before; Carter knew that from bitter personal experience. So the pair of fighters had been sent to cover the MTB on its homeward journey. Carter wondered what they might be. Spitfires seemed the most likely choice, but the RAF were flying American P-51 Mustangs[1] now, as well. Carter had never seen one, but he might this morning.

O'Driscoll arrived at his elbow and offered him a mug of tea. It looked strong enough to stand a spoon up in it.

"Where did you get that at this time of day?" Carter asked, blowing across the top of the cup before attempting a sip.

"Early morning caff over that way." O'Driscoll nodded his head towards a point further along the quayside. "I can get you a sandwich if you want. I think I smelt bacon frying."

Carter's mouth watered, but at the same time his stomach rebelled. His nervousness wouldn't allow him to eat right now.

"Not for me thanks. But don't let me stop you."

"I already have, Sorr." O'Driscoll grinned. "Be careful with that mug. The owner made me leave a two bob[2] deposit for it. Bloody cheek."

Carter wasn't interested in any usury being practised by local café owners but he appreciated the tea.

Ramsey's performance had improved in the weeks running up to the raid. The second speed march had seen the two of them arriving at the armoury to draw rifles from a sleepy armourer, before moving to the magazine, some distance away, to draw the requisite hundred rounds of ammunition, carefully counting each clip of five rounds, checking to make sure each clip was complete and stowing them in their pouches.

Despite the amount of ammunition that a commando expended in daily practice, each round had to be fully accounted for and it wasn't unknown for an armourer to cover losses, or even his own theft, by issuing a soldier with fewer rounds than he had asked for, getting a signature for the full amount, then blaming the soldier for the loss when he returned the rounds later in the day. It was unlikely that the man would try the trick on him, but Carter wasn't taking any chances.

Unsurprisingly, Ramsey had been even more exhausted, so the pace was slower this time, but Carter could see that the man was making an effort to keep up. As they approached the barrack gates Carter dropped back to run alongside him, then, as they passed through, Carter made sure that he was one pace behind him so that he didn't have to carry out his threat to dismiss Ramsey from the commando. The lesson had been learnt, that was the important thing.

The time was a slow one, barely achieving the maximum allowed, but Carter took the blame for that on himself and promised the troop it wouldn't count for the contest. None of them believed for a second that he was to blame for the slow time, but they appreciated the gesture. On the other hand, it meant that the troop would now have to do an additional march to provide a qualifying time. Carter told Ramsey to substitute a ten-mile run for one of the longer ones they'd have to do later, so that they wouldn't suffer just because he'd had to teach his subordinate a lesson in leadership.

"You did well enough, but you need to be fitter to keep up on operations. Go and see the PTI[3] and do an hour of instruction with him each day. If he doesn't think you're fit enough, you won't go on any raids and if you don't go on raids, you won't go with us on the big day. We can't afford to carry passengers." 'The big day' was now the euphemism being used for the invasion of France.

Ramsey had dutifully obeyed and Carter noted, from the reports submitted by the PTI, that his fitness levels had improved steadily.

His paunch soon disappeared and he took part in more speed marches without having to be prompted by Carter.

When Carter received approval from Brigade for Ramsey to go on this raid, he allowed him to join 21 Cdo, who were mounting the Op, to train with the men who would go ashore. Their CO gave the final nod of approval for Ramsey to go with the raiding party.

Which was why Carter was now standing on the quayside, shivering and wondering if his 2IC had survived.

"Is that the escort?" O'Driscoll peered into the growing dawn light, pointing out towards the horizon. Carter fumbled for his binoculars, his haste making him clumsy. Into view sprang a pair of Spitfires, flying lazy circles above something beneath them on the surface. The MTB, assuming it was what they were escorting, was still invisible, below the horizon.

Carter could have calculated how far away they were if he'd had his slide rule, but he didn't. The aircraft were just beneath the cloud base, which was at about two thousand feet. All he needed was the approximate angle of elevation of the aircraft above the horizon and it was simple trigonometry after that. He wished he'd gone up to stand on the cliffs on the far side of the town, where the extra height would have given him a better view, but it was too late now. By the time he got up there, even in the Jeep with O'Drsicoll driving in his customary mad fashion, the MTB would be in sight from the quayside anyway.

"No sign of enemy fighters." Carter declared. "That's something, anyway."

"They're too short of dem to go slamming stable doors after the horse has bolted, Sorr. They daren't risk getting fighters shot down just because they got banjaxed[4] again."

Carter wished that had been the case back in 1942, when his friend Huelen had been killed commanding the MTB that they'd been coming home in after just such a raid. If they'd been that short of aircraft back then, Huelen might still be alive. Carter pushed the thought from his head. No point in worrying about what might have been. Huelen was dead, that was all there was too it.

Carter's arms were starting to tire from holding the binoculars to his eyes, but he was loathe to lower them. Not that seeing the MTB would answer any of his questions. The boat might be fine, but it could be carrying a cargo of dead men, or even no commandos at all if they had been captured.

One of the Spitfires broke off from the pair and dived towards the sea, disappearing over the horizon. What was that about? Carter wondered. Unlikely to be a fighter plane, it would be flying too low. An E-Boat perhaps. Maybe sent from Boulogne to try to intercept the MTB. E-Boats were a bit faster, so even though the MTB had a head start it would eventually be overhauled.

A minute dragged by, then another. Finally, the Spitfire reappeared above the horizon again, soaring skywards to disappear into the clouds before reappearing behind its partner and taking station once more. Whatever the threat had been, it was passed and there was still something down on the surface that needed an escort.

A dot appeared at the distant edge of the sea, then disappeared and emerged again several times as it dipped and rose on the waves. At last, it resolved itself into the front view a boat, a white bone of foam in its mouth as it drove through the water at maximum speed.

"I can see it, Paddy." Carter commented.

"They're expected that's for sure." Came a reply. Carter looked around to see what he meant. Driving down the sloping road that led to the quayside was a small convoy of vehicles. In the lead were two military ambulances, followed by a Military Police Jeep. Were the ambulances just precautionary, or did someone know something? None of the occupants got out of the vehicles after they drew to a stop. Was that because of the cold? Or were they just reluctant to make small talk with a Lieutenant Colonel. There were no Royal Navy vehicles present, Carter could see. If the MTB's crew had suffered casualties, a senior officer from its flotilla would surely have come to greet them and take a report before the details of the incident were forgotten. A 3 Ton truck rumbled down the road and drew up at the rear of the group of vehicles. That would be to take the commandos back to their barracks. Behind that was a Jeep.

Carter could see the face of Lt Col Morgan, the CO of 21 Cdo, come to welcome his men back.

He wasn't reluctant to climb out of his vehicle. He strode across to greet Carter, his hand extended to be shaken.

"Couldn't stay away, eh Steven?" Morgan grinned.

"No …. Malcolm." Carter had almost called him Sir, forgetting that they were now of equal rank. It was the hardest thing he had found about getting promoted, the change in status between him and other officers. Majors now called him Sir and he called Lieutenant Colonels by their first names.[5] "You got here quickly."

"Watching from up there." Morgan pointed to the cliffs. "I must have picked the boat out about ten minutes before you."

"Were this lot with you?" Carter nodded towards the other vehicle.

"Not the lorry. He was parked up the road a bit and saw me coming down the hill. But the others must have got a message from somewhere. Maybe the Coastguard, or maybe from whoever runs the Navy in this part of the world. The MTB will have radioed ahead."

The Navy used a lot of VHF radio to communicate between ships and also, when they were close enough inshore, between them and the shore. It could only communicate on 'line of sight', but if the receivers were on top of the cliffs, they would be able to pick up signals from much further out at sea. But when they left Hardelot, their target, they would have been much further east along the Channel, where the gap between England and France was much narrower. On a clear day you could see the opposite shore from the cliffs above Folkstone. From Dover you see France from the harbour wall.

Although the German High Command thought they had built an impregnable defensive wall from Denmark to the Atlantic Ocean, in places it was still no more than a tangle of barbed wire. The beach at Hardelot was one of those places. There were hardened strong points, pill boxes and artillery emplacements, but in between there were plenty of places where the defences were less than adequate. To make matters worse, many of the strong points weren't routinely manned. Troops would occupy them only if an alarm was raised from one of the positions that was manned. It was like trying to prevent water running through a colander by putting your finger over the holes. It wasn't the first time the commandos had raided in that area and, Carter was sure, it wouldn't be the last.

Anxiety finally got the better of Carter. He crossed over to the leading ambulance and tapped on the passenger side window. An Army medic wound it down and a cloud of cigarette smoke emerged, causing Carter to cough and pull his face away.

"Have you heard anything about casualties?" Carter asked, wafting the smoke away with his hand.

"No, Sir. We were at the local TA barracks, waiting to be told what to do when we got a call to come here for the RV. We've been there on standby for this all night."

"Is it normal for you to be here, even if there are no casualties?"

"We've never had a time when there weren't casualties, Sir. After Dieppe we were back and forth between here and Brighton all day, there were so many injured."

Being one of those casualties himself, Carter hadn't known about that until he woke up, but the stories had emerged over time. The raids on Dieppe and Honfluer had been a bloodbath, mainly for the Canadians, who had made up the largest part of the raiding forces, but also for the commandos.

"OK, thank you." Carter went back to stand with Morgan as the window was wound up again to keep the heat in the ambulance's cab. Carter noticed that O'Driscoll had disappeared, along with the mug that had held Carter's tea. Gone to reclaim his deposit, Carter assumed.

The MTB was much larger now, clearly identifiable for what it was. It looked like a fighting vessel, the torpedo tubes in the bow making black holes like a predator's eyes. Above and behind those sat a 6 pounder gun. Behind that was the squat superstructure, giving the craft the lowest possible profile, so it might not be seen until it was too late for its prey to evade it.

Another mile, Carter guessed, before the power to the engines was reduced and it started to slow down to make a more sedate approach into the harbour.

Behind them people started to gather along the wall that separated the harbour from the seafront. Idle curiosity mixed with a ghoulish desire to see if there were any dead bodies, Carter guessed. It was a small town and not much happened here. The only reason that the MTB was here was because it was easier to bring it to 21 Cdo than it was to take 21 Cdo to the boat. Seaford had its own naval residents, steam gun boats, but they weren't present, presumably away carrying out coastal patrols or escorting merchant shipping.

The boat entered the river through the pair of breakwaters, headed upstream for a few yards past the quayside, then turned back to have its bows pointed towards the sea once more. Huelen had explained that they tried to moor that way whenever possible so they could make a quicker exit if it was necessary.

There was no sign of any damage to the MTB, which was a positive. If they had been targeted by shore based artillery there might be some sign, even if it was only a broken bridge window. The protective cover was still on the mouth of the barrel 6 pounder and the Oerlikons behind the superstructure were also covered, suggesting the boat hadn't had to deal with any attacks.

The bad news came when the boat was securely tied up and the gangway had been run ashore to bridge the gap between the quay and the boats main deck.

The first casualty to be led out had his head bandaged so much that it was difficult to make out his face at all. His battledress was shredded, but Carter could just about make out corporal's stripes. So, not Ramsey. He was helped ashore by naval ratings, who returned below decks. When they came back they were carrying a Robinson stretcher between them. The soldier had one hand free of the stretcher's tight embrace and was holding a cigarette. Between the sections of the stretcher Carter could make out bandages on both legs.

The two casualties were loaded carefully into the ambulances, which sped off, the clattering of their bells sending the gulls skywards, shrieking in protest. Next ashore were two German prisoners. They were in shirt sleeves, probably how they were dressed when they were caught. They cast morose looks around them but there was no fighting spirit. Two commandos followed them, their bayoneted rifles at the ready. At the top of the gangway the two military policemen placed handcuffs on their wrists and prodded them towards their Jeep, where the handcuffs were removed from one wrist before being attached to the frame that supported the canvass tilt of the vehicle.

Only then did the rest of the commandos appear from below decks and head towards the gangway. At the rear was Lt Freeman, who had led the raid, and Howard Ramsey.

Carter searched the faces of the men as they stepped off the gangway, looking for one in particular. There he was, second man from the rear of the file.

"LCpl Garraway. Good to see you again." Carter made a show of greeting the man who, until a few weeks earlier, had been in 15 Cdo. He led him along the quay a few yards, out of earshot of the others.

"How did he do?"

"Pretty well, actually Sir. When we stumbled into the mine field … that was when we got the casualties, it was Maj Ramsey that led us out again. Lt Freeman was at the front, right behind the injured men, so he couldn't do anything. Then, when we were out, he helped the Lieutenant to get the causalities clear so we could patch them up.

A minefield. So that was how the casualties had been caused. They weren't always marked on the seaward side. "Didn't the mine going off raise the alarm?

"You'd have thought it would, but it didn't. Maybe they go off a lot. There were signs the dunes have been used for sheep pasture. If they tread on a mine it's just the same as a person doing it. Anyway, we took the casualties back to the beach and the Navy took care of them, while we carried on with the raid. Found the two prisoners sitting in a wooden hut, playing cards. Came along like lambs, so they did. So, we planted a few booby traps, cut some telephone cables and went back to the beach."

"And Maj Ramsey played a full part in the riad?"

"Lt Freeman gave all the orders, but Maj Ramsey seemed to be enjoying the whole thing. Kept asking where the Jerries were so he could take a few pots at them." Ramsey had taken a Tommy gun with him and seemed keen to use it.

"Well, thank you, Garraway. I'll let you get back to your mates. I'm sure you're tired."

"I am that, thank you Sir."

Ramsey was waiting at the foot of the gangway for him. "Checking up on me, Sir?" Ramsey said, a slight sneer in his voice.

"Yes, as it happens, Major. Just wanted a trooper's take on how you did. You'll be pleased to know he was quite impressed."

Ramsey seemed taken aback by the honest answer.

"I'll get a copy of Lt Freeman's report, of course, but if the men think you did well, it speaks volumes. Now, can I offer you a lift back to Worthing?"

"Actually, Lt Freeman has invited me to breakfast with him and his men. I think it may involve a little bit more than bacon and eggs."

"I think it probably will. That's OK, I don't expect you to undertake any duties after a night like you've had. I'll send my Jeep to pick you up in a couple of hours."

Carter watched as the man strolled towards the truck and climbed into the back. He could have pulled rank to take the favoured seat up next to the driver, but he left that to Freeman as one of the privileges of being the raid's leader.

After a faltering start, Carter wasn't too proud to concede that Ramsey was coming along nicely.

[1] The North American Aviation P-51 Mustang first entered RAF service in 1942. Although American manufactured, the aircraft was designed to meet a British specification. The early marks were fitted with an Allison engine which had a severe power drop off above

15,000 ft, making it unsuitable for use as a fighter. Instead they were used as an army co-operation aircraft, carrying out ground attack sorties. Later marks were fitted with a Packard built Merlin engine (manufactured under licence from Rolls-Royce), making it suitable for high altitude operations so it could be used as a fighter. They carried out hundreds of sweeps across France ahead of D-Day. They also proved quite effective against V-1 flying bombs, shooting down 232 of them (the record of 638 was set by the Hawker Tempest).

[2] Two Bob – two shillings, ten pence in today's coinage but worth a lot more back then. Two bob would have been enough for an evening at the cinema with a fish supper on the way home.

[3] PTI = Physical training instructor. Formed in 1860, the Army Physical Training Corps (it wasn't granted the title 'Royal' until 13th November 2010) provided instructors for units in the British army to raise the standard of fitness amongst soldiers. Although PTIs are still found in gymnasiums on garrisons and recruit training depots, nowadays their focus is mainly on physiotherapy, rehabilitation and remedial fitness training. At unit level, ordinary soldiers are provided with specialist training to allow them to run day-to-day fitness training sessions.

[4] Banjaxed = Irish slang for being beaten up, broken or injured.

[5] By tradition, junior officers up to and including Captain are permitted to address each other by their first names, even if they are of unequal rank. Above that rank, all officers address their superiors as "Sir". Also by tradition, a junior officer entering a colleague's office will salute him, even if he is of a more junior or of equal rank. It is a mark of respect for his authority within his own area of command.

END OF EXTRACT

Operation Pegasus will be released in December 2021.

And Now

Both the author Robert Cubitt and Selfishgenie Publishing hope that you have enjoyed reading this story.

Please tell people about this eBook, write a review on Amazon or mention it on your favourite social networking site. Word of mouth is an author's best friend and is much appreciated. Thank you.

Find Robert Cubitt on Facebook at https://www.facebook.com/robertocubitt and 'like' his page; follow him on Twitter **@Robert_Cubitt**

For further titles that may be of interest to you please visit our website at **selfishgenie.com** where you can optionally join our information list.

Printed in Great Britain
by Amazon